VACANT GRAVE

Marnie Reilly Mysteries Book 4

SHARI T. MITCHELL

Also by Shari T. Mitchell
Marnie Reilly Mysteries Series

Divine Guidance, Book 1
Torn Veil, Book 2
Fatal Vow, Book 3
Vacant Grave, Book 4

Marnie Reilly Mysteries Novellas and Short Stories

The Island
Christmas Eve in Creekwood
Friday the 13th

Praise for Fatal Vow

Danger is at every turn when an ugly part of Creekwood's past, once buried, rises to haunt Marnie and a host of characters. The realistic dialogue is a treat, making readers feel like they are sitting at the local coffee shop listening to town gossip, or walking, even running frantically, through Marnie's country property. The tension throughout is tightly woven, often using humor or everyday activities like cooking to settle the nerves. The introduction of a few new characters is a treat and hopefully we will see more of them. Mitchell has woven a complicated plot full of angst, interesting characters, and humor.

-Chronicles of Crime, Victoria, BC, Canada

Praise for the Series

Author Shari T. Mitchell has me hooked! If you love thrillers, this series belongs on your bookshelf.

-TL Brown, Door to Door Paranormal Mysteries

Dedication

For Nik. Look what you started.

Table of Contents

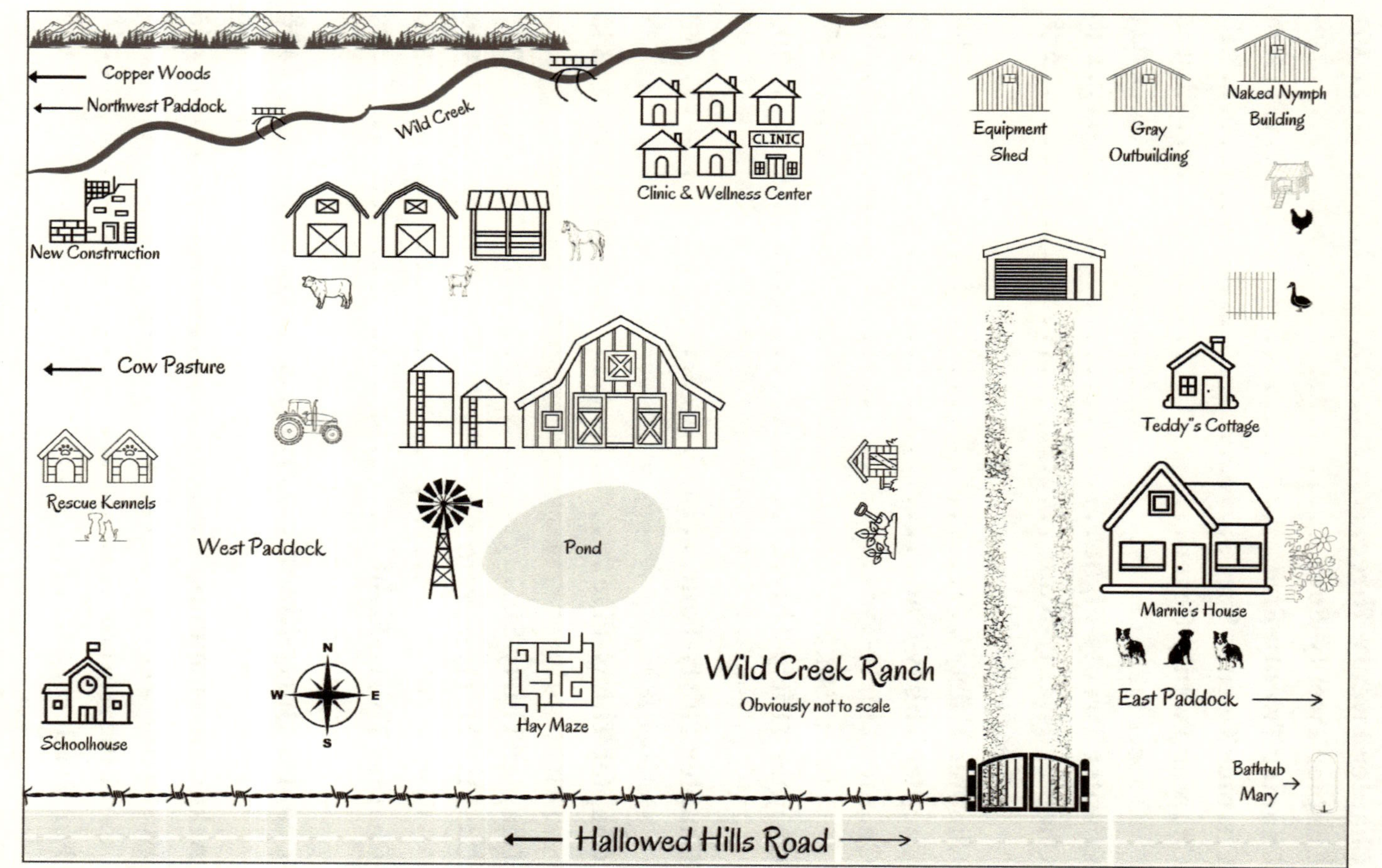

Copper Woods
Northwest Paddock
Wild Creek
Equipment Shed
Gray Outbuilding
Naked Nymph Building
Clinic & Wellness Center
CLINIC
New Construction
Cow Pasture
Teddy's Cottage
Rescue Kennels
West Paddock
Pond
Marnie's House
Wild Creek Ranch
Obviously not to scale
East Paddock
Schoolhouse
N
E
W
S
Hay Maze
Bathtub Mary
Hallowed Hills Road

Introduction

It's shocking I'm still alive. That explosion on July fourth was ... well ... earth-shattering, heartbreaking, and it changed my life forever.

I'm Marnie Reilly. We've met before in Divine Guidance, Torn Veil, Fatal Vow and a few short stories. I thought it would be helpful to give you the rundown on the last eleven months. It's October 9th here in Creekwood.

After the accident, time stood still for a while. Between operations, physical therapy, and many sessions with my psychiatrist, Carl Parkins, I guess today is the day I buck up and get back to living. Anyway. I shouldn't complain. I'm still drawing breath and it's my favorite season.

What's the weather outlook? Fall in the Adirondack Mountains gives crispness to the air and big blue skies that go on forever. Look to the heavens at night and you'll see a canvas of navy-blue velvet dotted with a gazillion brilliant diamonds. If you've never been, I recommend it. Any time of the year is lovely, but the last bit of September and all of October are spectacular.

Mingling scents of fall fill the air with dried leaves, pinecones, magic, and water. If you're thinking magic and water don't have odors, you're mistaken. The former is a mix of cookies, spices, pot roast, and pies cooking in the oven. And the latter? That depends on the season, but in the mountains, you get hints of musk, fish, algae, soil, and rain. It's heavenly.

Here's a quick refresher on me. I'm a psychologist and a clairvoyant, which comes in handy when spirits make themselves available for consultation. My "divine guidance" has helped solve a murder or two. I did the math a few days ago and I hate to say the body count here in Creekwood has spiked to ten or eleven. That's insane!

I've lived here on the Hudson River most of my life. After college, I lived in Washington, DC, but then my mother was murdered, so I moved home to be with Dad. Carl Parkins says I did it because I'm a rescuer. He's not wrong.

Let me give you some family history. My mother and father have both passed and my brother Sam was a federal agent until a few years ago when he entered a building during a drug raid and the whole place exploded. More on that later.

Detective Danny Gregg is my boyfriend, and we've been together for almost a year. He's tall and handsome and has the cutest dimples, and he's gifted like me. He doesn't hear spirits, but he sees them, and he's intuitive. The guy knows everything! A lot of people think he's grumpy. He can be, but only if his buttons are pushed, or he's interviewing a criminal.

My best friend, Tom Keller, was a detective with Creekwood PD and Danny's partner. There have been some changes since July and you'll meet the new partner soon enough. Allow me to prepare you for Randolph Stuyvesant. The guy is a dick!

I have two beautiful Border Collies named Tater and Dickens. They are loyal and smart, and if they had thumbs, they would be dangerous. Tom's black Labrador, Gus, is living with us now. He's a lovely boy.

Anyway, I'm here to fill you in on the unsavory things happening here. A year ago, I would have said that Creekwood is a peaceful, sleepy place—like those towns you read about in a cozy mystery. I should warn you; cozy is not a word I would use. Hellish, treacherous, and tempestuous may be apt. Hmm ... It's not *all* bad, but at times it sure feels like evil crept into town and rained hellfire.

Like just before Thanksgiving last year, a crazed killer murdered my abusive ex, Ken Wilder, and dumped his corpse in my shed, setting me up to take the fall. Fortunately for me, the murderer didn't succeed, even though I was a suspect for a while. Danny Gregg was the lead detective, and let me tell you, he and I argued about everything. In the end, when he finally listened to me, the police caught the killers, and I was off the hook. Thank goodness!

Then, a week after Thanksgiving, a man turned up dead on the railroad tracks in a dodgy part of town. Tom and Danny were called to the scene, and they found one of my old business cards in the victim's pocket. Long story short, the decedent was a childhood friend who discovered some things about the ugly underbelly of our little town. I couldn't believe it! Who would have thought that Creekwood had one? With the help of Carl Parkins, two DEA agents and, of course, the detectives, the case was closed in time for a quiet Christmas Eve.

The calm didn't last long, though. On Christmas Day, I received a nasty threat, and I worried for the people I love, so I disappeared with my Border Collies to keep everyone safe. I was in the doghouse for a while, but that didn't last once trouble started in the summer.

Then we come to June and July. Gawd! Tom and I lost two childhood friends. And when I say lost, I mean they were murdered. My brother broke out of prison and returned to Creekwood with law enforcement officers in hot pursuit—but hold your judgment. There is more to that story. There was an electrical fire in my barn and one at Tom's house. Three people got electrocuted, and a prominent psychiatrist got found out. Talk about a mad scientist! Wow!

Anyway, the whole mess came to a head on Independence Day when I had a housewarming party to celebrate my new home, Wild Creek Ranch. What can I say? The party bombed—miserably.

Oh! Before I go. Let me be the first to welcome you back to Creekwood, where the holidays are murder.

Warmest,
Marnie

Chapter One

October 9th

Creekwood, New York—Copper Woods, 7:43 AM

Jess Eloise Alder crouched at the base of a sugar maple, its brilliant fall leaves blanketing the ground. She held her breath—listening for footsteps, tears streaking the dirt on her pretty freckled face.

"No!" she screamed, as her kidnapper grabbed her by the scruff of her neck and scooped her over his shoulder. "Let me go! I have class! I'm gonna be late!"

"In more ways than one," growled her abductor.

Creekwood, New York—Hudson Pass, AKA The Ridge, 10:06 AM

A cyclone of dead leaves swirled, riding the wave of a crisp north breeze. Vibrant orange, yellow, and crimson foliage mingled mid-air before settling on the mossy forest floor.

Ranger Abel Jackson grasped for the feathery branch of a Tamarack to steady himself but dropped to his knees, blood dripping from his broken nose.

"Get back here!" he shouted.

With an extended middle finger, the ranger's attacker walked away, mumbling to himself, shoulders hunched, hands in his pockets.

October 10th

Wild Creek Ranch, 10:03 AM

A cerulean October sky welcomed mid-morning—the temperatures promising to soar into the fifties. The distant roar of moose followed by a single gunshot caught Detective Danny Gregg's attention. He turned to the woods beyond the big red barn, scanning the tree line. Rut season had ended, and hunting season had begun. While moose were off limits in the Adirondack region, that didn't mean poachers weren't seeking a trophy kill. Shaking his head, he called the game warden as he strolled across the pasture, searching for Marnie Reilly.

He stopped at the entry of an impressive hay maze she and Wild Creek Ranch's farmhands had been building for the past two weeks. At six bales high, even he couldn't see over the top edge.

"Marnie, I have to get to the station! Do you have Tater, Gus, and Dickens in there with you?"

"They took Carl for a walk. Hang on a minute! I'm coming out. I got twisted around in the sections Elk and Arnie built last night."

"Looks like they accomplished a lot! How big are you planning to go?" he asked.

"It's taken on a life of its own, but I think we need to stop now. I can't find my way outta here!" she said with a giggle.

"Want me to come find you? Or better yet, I'll send in the knuckleheads. They're herding Carl this way!"

On catching sight of the detective, the two Border Collies and Labrador barked and raced across the open field. With their tongues hanging out, they kicked up dried grass in their eagerness to be the first one to Danny. Carl Parkins, Marnie's business partner, trudged behind them, hands in the air.

"They got into the burdock down by the creek. I tried to stop them, but as you can see, they found the burrs."

Danny laughed. "We know the routine." He bent to welcome the dogs into his arms. "Tater Reilly, your mother won't be happy."

Inspecting the prickles in the canine's ears, he eased a few out but gave up. "We'll have to get those later. I'm late for work."

Chin nodding to the maze, Carl said, "Is she still exploring?"

"Yeah. She lost her way."

"Hey, Danny! Can you come here?" Marnie yelled; her tone marked with urgency.

He snorted. "You can't find your way out, so how the heck am I going to find you?"

"Umm ..."

An eerie moment of silence passed, sending chills up the men's backs.

"Well, a cadaver dog would help. There's a dead guy in here."

Wild Creek Ranch, The Kitchen 11:08 AM

Detective Randolph Stuyvesant counted the ticks of the wall clock as he waited for Danny in the kitchen at Marnie's farmhouse. She didn't offer him a seat at the trestle table, nor a cup of coffee. His presence irked her. Not only was he Danny's new partner, but to add salt to her gaping emotional wounds, he had been a friend of Ken Wilder, Marnie's abusive ex-boyfriend.

Stuyvesant broke the awkward silence. "You recognized the man?"

Giving a stiff nod, she slunk deeper into her seat at the kitchen table, where she skimmed through an agricultural textbook.

"Are you going to share his name?" he pushed.

With a toss of the book to the center of the table, she slid out of the bench and walked to the counter, ignoring his question.

"Marnie? Who is he?"

Leaning her hip against the counter, she shrugged. "Can't help you with that, but I've seen him at the four-way on McDougal Road, heading out to Hudson Hollow."

"What type of vehicle does he drive? We might find it at the side of the road."

Not one to hide her feelings, she rolled her eyes and offered Stuyvesant a lopsided sneer. "Not everyone has a vehicle, *Randy*. The guy was homeless. He's been camping out in the old schoolhouse."

"You didn't report to authorities that there was a vagrant in the area?" His face reddened, and he grasped at his tie, pulling the knot tighter.

Marnie smirked. In her mind, she compared him to the coffee klatch gals at Drake's lunch counter, who clutched at their pearls when shocked by her irreverence.

"The situation is not funny." His hands moved to his waist, and he tugged at his belt, straightening his trousers around his paunch. "May I remind you that there is yet another corpse on *your* property?"

"No, *Randy*, you don't need to remind me. The forensics team and Detective Gregg have already mentioned it. Like I didn't realize it myself. Why don't you go wait for Danny on the porch? Better yet, do your job and go over to the crime scene, or are you worried about getting your Italian loafers muddy?" She waved a dismissive hand before pouring herself another coffee.

"Where is Detective Gregg?" Stuyvesant asked, ending his sentence with a haughty harrumph.

"In the living room, speaking with Captain Sterling. Something about Abel Jackson getting attacked up at Hudson Pass."

"Who is Abel Jackson?"

Marnie screwed up her face. "A bit of unsolicited advice ... get to know local law enforcement. Abel is a park ranger. Really nice man."

Creekwood's head of forensics, Rick Price, tapped on the window, and pushed open the back door, forcing Stuyvesant to step further into the room. Rick and Doctor Giles Markson entered the kitchen and both assessed the detective with a distasteful glance.

Rick Price was Creekwood's forensics doctor extraordinaire. He had connections throughout the intelligence agencies in the US and abroad. If he couldn't find information, there was likely nothing to find. Doctor Giles Markson was Creekwood's medical examiner and Marnie's godfather. Since the passing of her parents, Giles doted on his goddaughter, providing fatherly advice when needed—or not.

"Got hot coffee for two working stiffs? Highly inappropriate pun intended." Rick's smile and playful wink lightened the tension, and his joke drew a chuckle from Giles and a giggle from Marnie, but it flew over Randolph's head. Or could it be worse? He didn't like puns.

The doctors knew Marnie didn't like the man. No one did, to be honest. His connection to Ken Wilder had the least to do with it. Randy was lazy, entitled, and ... Danny's new partner. It felt wrong and disloyal to accept him into the fold. He could never replace Detective Tom Keller. After all, he had only been gone a few months. They were still reeling from the tragedy of July fourth. Marnie's shoulder and knee ached most days. Her thoughts were fuzzy, but hearing had returned to her left ear and she was thankful to be standing in her kitchen having a cup of coffee on this bright October day. Her best friend hadn't been as lucky.

The dogs stirred under the table, each grumbling to the other about the people standing in their kitchen. Marnie had placed an old sweatshirt and blanket of Tom's on the floor for them. It seemed to calm the canines, but for how long?

Pouring two strong coffees, Marnie handed the doctors steaming mugs. "I hope you're okay with black. I'm out of milk and the sugar bowl is empty."

She noticed a flash of concern on her godfather's face. "Don't worry, Uncle Giles. I have a grocery delivery arriving later. I used up the last of the sugar making peanut butter cookies last night."

"Well, that's fine, then. I was afraid you weren't taking care of yourself." He blew on the coffee, then sipped. "Ah! Cinnamon!" he said, and his face lit up with the first sip.

Rick pulled off his toque and slid onto a bench at the table, releasing a pained grunt as he sat. "Too many hours bent over a microscope yesterday. How's your knee doing, Marnie? Are you driving yet?"

"Uh-huh. Danny bought his Jeep from the station so that we could swap vehicles, and I don't have to shift gears. It's been a lifesaver."

"Seems you have a way of getting people to do that," said Stuyvesant, stepping toward the table. "How do you persuade your friends to accommodate so easily? Black magic, perhaps?"

"Voodoo," remarked Danny as he walked into the kitchen and dropped a kiss on top of Marnie's head, garnering an eye roll. Peering at Randy, he said, "You go check out the schoolhouse, then meet me at the station. I'll get the paperwork started. Cap wants a report on his desk, A.S.A.P."

She grabbed her detective's hand, giving it a squeeze. "I'll see you tonight then?"

Brushing a thumb across the back of hers, he nodded.

"Yeah. Where's Carl?" he asked, glancing around, searching for the psychiatrist.

"He's in the study dealing with paperwork. Don't worry. He'll stick around. We have miles of work to do."

"Good." He directed his attention to the doctors. "How soon on your reports?"

Giles cleared his throat and set down his coffee mug. "I can do the autopsy right away. There's another waiting, but we know cause so it can wait."

Rick added, "I'll go to the morgue with Giles and get what I need. You'll have a report earliest tomorrow morning. Tests take time, but I'll get prints over to you early afternoon."

Danny nodded. "Any initial thoughts?"

Giles scratched his forehead and took a handkerchief from his breast pocket. Considering the question, he removed his glasses and polished the lenses. "Don't hold me to it, but blunt force trauma most likely played a part, but I won't rule out exposure, malnutrition, or natural causes."

"I prefer the latter to the rest," Marnie chimed in. "Anything other than murder."

Chapter Two

Pine Ridge Sanitarium, 11:28 AM

A long pout turned down the corners of Kate Parish's mouth, her pretty face flushed as she launched a couch cushion across the room, narrowly missing a well-groomed man in his late fifties. He thought nothing of it and picked it up, tossing it into the closest chair.

"I hate it here! Did you think being moved to a private suite would make me happy? I want to go home!"

Preston Belmont ran a finger across his tidy hunting season mustache and quirked up the side of his mouth in disgust. "I may be your blood, but I will not put up with your tantrums. Do you have any idea how many strings I had to pull to get you out of prison? For once in your life, be thankful!"

"Ha! Thankful? I'm still locked up, Uncle dear! I want to be out there!" Kate pointed out the barred window at a meadow of grass and Whorled Wood Asters.

"That will never happen." Dropping his head and giving it a shake, he took a deep breath and sighed. "Pine Ridge is your home, Kate. You may as well face facts. What you did ... Jesus! How could you ever believe freedom was an option?"

"What I did?" Mouth hanging open, she flopped into the nearest overstuffed chair. "What about what Marnie Reilly did? She goaded me and manipulated facts!"

"No, she didn't." Belmont stooped to smooth the crease in his tailored chinos and snickered before heading to the door. "Get out of that jumpsuit. I brought you some clothes. Check the bureau. Not the type of high fashion you're used to, but them's the breaks, kid."

"Don't rush back!" she growled.

"See you in a couple of days." He didn't look back, holding up a hand before closing the door.

Waiting for a beat in case he returned, Kate pushed herself to her feet with a childish huff when she was sure he was gone. Yanking open the middle drawer of the dresser, her face fell. Navy and gray sweatpants, matching sweatshirts, two pairs of no-name jeans, long and short-sleeved T-shirts—two navy, two white—stared back at her. The bottom drawer wasn't much better: cable-knit sweaters of black, forest green, and peacock blue and seven pairs of wool socks.

"He wouldn't have!" Face reddened with anger, she snatched open the top drawer and cried. Seven pairs of freshly laundered cotton briefs, a sports bra for each day of the week, and plain tank tops—all in white.

Hopeful her uncle wasn't a complete fashion idiot, she threw open the closet door and dropped to her knees with a screech.

"No! Bobo sneakers!"

Leaning against the wall outside Kate's room, Preston Belmont chuckled. He threw a knowing glance at Sheila Winthrop, Pine Ridge

Sanitarium's chief security officer, and said, "She's only going to get worse in the days to come. Wait until she sees that her room is devoid of creature comforts."

Sheila shrugged. "We'll handle her. She should thank her lucky stars that Bobo sneakers are the least of her worries. The new shrink insists she take all meals in the cafeteria like everyone else. I can tell you, folks in here don't like your niece, Mr. Belmont. Most of them know Marnie Reilly and Tom Keller. Marnie has treated many of them and Tom, well, he was in school with some. All people here talk about is what the Parish family did."

Preston clutched his bearded jaw with worry. "Is Kate at risk?"

With a shake of her head, Sheila said no. "We'll keep a close eye on the situation and keep you apprised. She'll be jeered and scolded and even threatened, but we won't allow violence. Although it might be good if she's afraid to act up."

"Kate will never be afraid. She has an inflated sense of entitlement and believes she is invincible."

A soothing voice came over the intercom, announcing lunch service was now available to all patients and staff.

Sheila cocked her head. "Stay for lunch, Mr. Belmont?"

"Uh ... No. I'm heading to the diner for a Reuben. Thanks anyway."

Chapter Three

Wild Creek Ranch, The Living Room, 12:10 PM

With a stack of unopened envelopes in her lap, Marnie sat in her favorite chair next to a crackling fire. The knuckleheads gathered around her and settled on the rug at her feet. She took a sip of English breakfast tea with a splash of half and half and smiled, thankful for the grocery delivery. Setting the teacup in its saucer, she eyed a tuna and celery sandwich on oatmeal bread that sat on the coffee table untouched. Ever since the explosion, she had little appetite. Her balance was wonky, and her stomach would lurch if she stood too fast or bent over for more than a minute or two. Carl and her doctor kept telling her the dizzy spells would ease and that her appetite would return to its usual gusto, but neither had. She crossed her fingers, picked up a wedge and took a bite, and then another and another until the offending lunch was gone.

"Okay. That wasn't so bad. Let's see what happens when I stand up."

Moving the envelopes aside, she stood, waiting for the nausea to push her to retreat to the safety of her chair, but no wave of sickness came.

"Huh! That's interesting," she said, tucking her leg beneath her backside and taking a seat.

"What is?" asked Carl, who entered the room from the hallway.

"I ate a whole sandwich and didn't feel ill when I stood up."

"Hmm … I wonder how much of that dizziness was your blood sugar telling you to eat?"

Marnie grinned, knowing he was probably right.

"Shut up, smarty pants."

"Seriously, I've never seen you so thin."

"I'm not thin! Gawd, Carl. I've lost a bit of weight."

"A bit? You have no ass!" Theodora "Teddy" Jones poked her head around the doorway and giggled.

Marnie rolled her eyes. "When did you arrive?"

"Early. I snuck into the study through the French doors when the cops arrived this morning."

Carl waggled an empty coffee mug and headed off to the kitchen. Over his shoulder, he said, "I'll leave you gals to it. I need fuel."

Teddy nodded to the stack of mail. "Slowly, but surely, you're getting through the backlog, huh?"

Marnie nodded and reached for the pile. "Yeah. I feel like I've lost so much time. Thanks for keeping on top of things. I couldn't have gotten through the last many months without you, Danny, Carl … everybody."

"Eh … that's what friends are for." She took a seat on the sofa and bent to scratch Tater's exposed tummy. "Is Randolph Stuyvesant going to be a problem?"

Resting her head against the back of her seat, Marnie considered the question. "Hmm … I think he could be. We'll leave him to Danny, Mac, and Captain Sterling, though. We have more than enough to keep us busy without strategizing how to foil Randy's evil plans. He doesn't like me—that's for sure."

"I saw him cozying up to Carrie Sutherland at Town Square last week. They had their heads together and kept looking around to see who was watching them."

At the mention of the reporter's name, Marnie dropped her feet to the floor. "Carrie Sutherland? Are you sure?"

"Yeah. She's back in town to revive the newspaper."

"I knew Mr. Heslop was planning to retire, but I hadn't a clue she was coming back or that she had the requisite qualifications to be an editor."

"Uh-huh. Carter Belmont bought the paper, and he's hiring all new staff."

"Belmont? As in Kitty Belmont Parish? That Belmont?"

"I guess, but I'm not sure. Shall I do some snooping?"

Marnie shook her head. "No. We should stay out of it. Unless ..."

"I can do it quietly?"

With a knee slap, the psychologist grinned unashamedly. "Call it a coincidence, but I need a few things at Drake's. Let's take a field trip."

"You sit tight. They'll tell me more if I'm alone. Got any gossip to trade?"

"The corpse in the hay maze should be all you need."

"Good point. What should I say?"

"Make up shit that will curl their lashes."

"On it!"

Creekwood Police Station, 12:10 PM

Danny entered Captain Sterling's office in the middle of a conversation between his boss and his partner.

"No, sir, but I think Marnie Reilly knows more than she's telling us. She knew the victim was camping in the old schoolhouse." Detective Randolph Stuyvesant stood facing Captain Sterling's desk, notebook in hand.

"Gregg? Is Marnie impeding our investigation?" The captain cocked his head, trying to hide his irritation.

"Why ask him? The accused is his girlfriend!" Stuyvesant's pasty complexion reddened.

Danny's tightened jaw muscles and blank stare pushed his partner to move a step away.

"No, Cap. If she had helpful information, she would tell us. We have both seen the victim around the four-corners and over by the schoolhouse. I can assure you, had either of us believed he was a threat or in danger, we would have addressed the matter. I know Marnie dropped off food and blankets when the temps fell a few weeks ago, but as far as I am aware, she has not spoken with him."

Stuyvesant bounced his pencil eraser on the cover of his notebook, eyes squinting with contempt. "Why didn't she admit to that? She should have told us about the food and blankets."

Danny snatched the pencil and notebook out of his partner's hands and put them on the desk.

"She told me. I had that knowledge and if you had bothered to look, it's in the report."

Randolph cleared his throat. "I was busy looking for a whiteboard."

"For what?" asked the captain.

"Standard procedure. Don't we always plot out a murder on a whiteboard?"

"Who says this is a murder? We don't even have reports from Doctors Markson or Price."

Danny shook his head, but Stuyvesant couldn't help himself.

"The body *was* found at Wild Creek Ranch—Marnie Reilly's property. If past events tell us anything, we should assume foul play."

"You're an idiot!" said Danny, before storming out of the office.

Drake's Drugstore, Town Square, Creekwood, NY, 12:28 PM

Teddy pulled her car to a stop outside Drake's Drugstore, took her keys out of the ignition, and unsnapped her seatbelt. Scanning the street, she couldn't help but wonder if the dead man in the hay maze was a harbinger of doom, bad luck, or a stroke. She pulled on her hoodie to ease the chill running up her spine and opened the door. With a skip in her step, she was off to do what she did best. Gossip!

Pushing open the door, she made sure her voice reached the lunch counter where Creekwood's coffee klatch gathered each day.

"Hi, Mrs. Drake. I'm here to pick up Marnie's order. Is everything ready to go?"

Heads turned at the mention of the psychic psychologist, and it could have been Teddy's imagination, but she was certain they all leaned back on their stools in unison.

Susanne Connors, Corrine Hooper, Irene Hazelton, and Carol Chadwick had a reputation for babbling about everyone in town. Telling tall tales with a hint of truth gave them half an ounce of credibility. Via their network, they could spread news from one side of town to the other in less than a minute. Whether anyone believed them was another story.

"Oh, yes, dear. Doctor Peck has everything you need at the pharmacy desk." Scooting away from her register, Mrs. Drake led the way to the back of the store.

As they passed by the women, Corrine Hooper called out, "Theodora! How is Marnie feeling? We haven't seen her in ages."

Teddy cringed at the use of her full name, plastered on a smile, and waved. "Back in a snap!"

Susanne Connor, elbows propped on the counter, leaned forward. "I heard the police were out at the ranch this morning. Something about a body in that hay maze they've been constructing. I can't believe it! After everything that happened in July. Some might think Marnie Reilly is cursed!'

"I hear that Grace Wilmot put a hex on her from her prison cell. They caught her with strands of Marnie's hair and a voodoo doll made from the mattress ticking." Corrine clutched her cup and glanced sideways to see who else might be listening.

Alice Wells giggled and stepped to the counter with a coffeepot to refill the gossipers' white ceramic mugs. "Don't believe a word of that, Corinne. Grace Wilmot doesn't have that kind of power. She never did. Especially over Marnie."

Irene Hazelton perked up, cocking her head like a spaniel. "What's that mean? *Especially over Marnie?*"

Eyes twinkling, Alice shrugged and turned away. "You know what they say about that one."

"Oh, Alice. Stop it! You're winding us up." Carol Chadwick brushed a napkin across her frowning lips.

Their heads snapped right when Teddy dropped a small carton on the counter. "Alice, could I please get two chocolate malts to go? Would you please charge them to the house account?"

"Does that mean her appetite's back?" asked Alice, hope in her eyes.

"No. Not really, but I thought a milkshake might tempt her."

"It's all that guilt affecting her appetite." Carol nudged Irene, who shared a knowing glance.

Forgetting the reason she was there, Teddy picked up the box, ready to storm out—but remembering the original mission, she stayed to defend her friend.

"Guilt? What does that have to do with appetite? Marnie isn't guilty of anything."

"Of course!" Carol slapped the countertop to make her point, and coffee spluttered from her full cup. "What happened to poor Tom Keller..."

"Don't you dare blame that on Marnie! The Parishes and Dalton Hooley did that, and you know it!"

Irene chimed in. "Tom really should have known better. After all, the company we keep..."

Alice scowled as she wiped up the spill. "What's that supposed to mean? Marnie and Tom were friends long before the Parishes' plotting and scheming began."

"From the time they were five years old, they were almost inseparable. You people are sick!"

Mrs. Drake patted Teddy's arm. "Come now. What about that incident on the island? Everyone here remembers Marnie's tales of old Mr. Barnes' ghost pushing her and Tom down the stairs. Nonsense, I say! The Reilly family has had their fair share of scandal. Sophia's murder. Colin's disappearance." She stopped, covered her mouth, then whispered, "Sam."

Nearing a fit of rage, Teddy spun around, standing nose to nose with the proprietor. "Scandal? You've got nerve! Your husband was in cahoots with that murderous witch, Grace Wilmot! How dare you point a finger! How can we be so sure you weren't in on it, too?"

The bell over the pharmacy door rang, announcing a visitor. They all turned to see Carrie Sutherland—perfectly coiffed and dressed to kill.

Feigning ignorance, Teddy asked, "What's she doing back in Creekwood? I thought she had some fancy network job in the city."

With a hand half covering her mouth, Irene stretched back and leaned closer to Teddy. "She was let go. The network made cuts and word is, Carrie was beginning to show her age. Botox can only do so much, you know."

Teddy stared dead into Irene's eyes. "I can see that."

Mouth slack and red-faced, Irene turned away with a huff.

Teddy watched the reporter search the shelves and pick up a few essentials. While she wasn't a fan, she did admire Carrie's gumption and her thousand-dollar cashmere suit.

Mrs. Drake left them to help. "Ms. Sutherland? Can I help you with anything?"

Carrie looked the older woman up and down. Flashing a saccharine smile, she spotted the other gals leaning back on their stools to hear—and not-so-nonchalantly.

"Well then. Shall we get this over with, ladies? We wouldn't want any of you missing out on the latest scoop. I'm back in Creekwood to help Mr. Heslop breathe life back into The Creekwood Times. He and his team have dropped the ball on serious reporting. It's shocking how many stories haven't been covered in the last twelve months."

"I heard Mr. Heslop sold the paper. Is that truth or fiction?" asked Teddy.

"Carter Belmont bought the paper. He and his brother Preston have invested heavily." She took a breath, chewing over what more she should share. "Everett Channing will assume the role of Editor-in-chief when Mr. Heslop retires, and I will be the lead reporter. Oh! Not that it's any of your business, the network did not fire me nor did my age have anything to do with me leaving. A new opportunity presented itself and I snapped it up. End of report!"

Carol Chadwick stood and pulled on her cardigan and picked up her handbag, readying to depart. "Are you excited to be back?"

Carrie considered the question, looking up at the ceiling while she pondered.

"Excited? No. Happy to be living in a house instead of a tiny apartment. Yes."

"Well, I hope your return is a success," said Teddy, as she set the milkshakes in the carton and turned, leaving the group.

"Who is she?" Carrie asked with a frown.

"Theodora Jones," said Mrs. Drake. "Strange girl. The town gossip, you know! She grew up here and lives out at Marnie Reilly's ranch."

"Really?" The reporter eyed the door. "Marnie has a ranch? Is she still counseling the demented and unfortunate?"

Irene Hazelton shook her head. "Not since the accident. We haven't seen her in town in months."

Carrie nodded. "Hmm ... I heard about that. The newspaper should have been all over it, but they never did do an in-depth story. All that business with Sam Reilly, too. I left the local station because they wouldn't allow me to dig into it."

Mrs. Drake agreed. "I think Mr. Heslop's friendship and his enduring loyalty to Colin Reilly kept that *mostly* out of the papers. He would have convinced Marv over at the television station to steer clear, too."

"What about Tom Keller's parents? Are they still in town?" Carrie asked.

"They come and go. After clearing out Tom's house, they traveled downstate. I haven't seen them in a few months." She turned to the other ladies. "Have you seen them?"

Susanne shook her head. "Not recently. After the electrical fire last July, I think they wanted to make necessary repairs to the house and unload it before something else happened. It's very old, you know. Hardly worth the bother."

The gossipers nodded in agreement as Alice pretended not to listen.

"What about that grouchy detective? The one with the odd face and dimples. Is he still around?"

Carol pulled a face. "Detective Gregg? He doesn't have an odd face! But never mind him. He's smitten with Marnie."

Pointing at Alice, Carrie said, "You back there! Why are you smirking? You look like a fool."

Alice held up her hands, keeping the grin in place. "If your intent is to go after Marnie Reilly, it's you who is the fool but give it your best shot. It will be fun to watch."

Carrie pretended to inspect the items in her basket—not meeting Alice's eyes. "I believe the public has a right to know why people associated with the *psychic psychologist* end up dead. Friends, relatives, cops! Don't you think the people of Creekwood should arm themselves with facts?"

"While you convince yourself that you're doing the right thing, I'll phone Detective Gregg. He should know about the target you're putting on his girlfriend's back." Alice reached for the old pay phone that hung on the wall behind the counter, then turned back. "The Parish family should be your focus. Or are you afraid to investigate your boss' family? Kate and Kitty are at Pine Ridge. That's your story, Madame Reporter. Kate is the cop killer—not Marnie or Sam Reilly."

With an exasperated sigh, Carrie kicked out her hip, resting her basket. "It's my understanding Lawrence Parish was responsible, and that Kitty and Kate got caught in the crossfire."

"Ha! Ask anyone here." Scanning the faces of the coffee klatch, Alice knew they would never give an honest answer. "Better yet. Talk to Chief Gregg and Captain Sterling. They will give you the truth."

"They'll give me their version of it, but perhaps not all the facts. I'll do my own digging." Carrie turned to Mrs. Drake. "I'm ready to pay for this," she said, holding up her shopping.

"I would be careful, Miss Sutherland. If you put your shovel in the wrong patch of grass, you might dig your own grave." Alice said this to herself, of course. She wasn't stupid. The rumor mill would gladly turn her statement into a threat if they were short on news.

Once Carrie was gone, Alice phoned Teddy to tell her what the women said after she'd departed. It's not really gossiping if you're protecting a friend.

Chapter Four

Creekwood Police Station, Forensics Lab, 12:42 PM

"Does the name Bob Humboldt mean anything to you?" Rick Price took a sip of the takeout coffee Danny delivered moments before.

The detective screwed up his face in thought. "Nope. Can't say it does. Why?"

Rick tossed three stapled pages across his desk. "He's your hay maze corpse."

"That was fast! He's in the system?"

"Yes, sir! He's a Creekwood native. Volunteer at the fire station and he was a reporter at the Times."

"I'm surprised Marnie didn't recognize him," said Danny.

"She may not have known him."

"Tchah! She knows everyone in town."

"She didn't seem to this morning. Unless she hasn't seen him in a long time. Give her a call."

"I'm heading out to the ranch soon. Elk and Arnie asked if they could talk to me after their morning chores and I don't want to get there too late, or it will be milking time again. Got anything else?"

"Everything is in that report. Any word from Giles?"

"Not yet. He caught a case from Hudson, but he promises his prelim notes by six."

Rick leaned back in his chair and took a deep breath. "I hope Bob Humboldt isn't someone Marnie knows. The poor kid doesn't need more bad news."

"Like a dead man in her hay maze wasn't enough, right?"

"Keep me posted."

"Catch ya!" said Danny as he left the forensic lab.

North Main Street, Creekwood, NY, 12:52 PM

Pulling his jacket collar up against a brisk wind that funneled leaves and discarded papers into the air, Danny shivered and jammed his hands into his coat pockets.

"Please, Mr. Humboldt, don't be a friend of the Reilly family. I don't think Marnie will cope with more shitty news," he said to himself as he walked to his vehicle.

Frowning, he recalled at last count the cycle of three was at one remaining, but then the blast occurred. *Marnie completed one cycle of three, and Tom began a new one. Why do bad things happen in threes? Why can't it be tens, and this might be over? Perhaps I should stop counting? Does the death in the hay maze count? If so, there's only one left.*

"You're deep in thought, Detective. Anything you'd like to share?"

Danny glanced to his left and recognized Carrie Sutherland instantly.

"Ah! No!"

With a giddy laugh, the reporter wrapped a hand through his arm.

"I'm trying to find out what happened at the old Billingsly ranch this morning. Can you give me a clue?"

"You can cozy up to me all you like, Miss Sutherland, but I am not sharing squat."

"Oh! C'mon, Detective!" She squeezed his arm with her own and leaned against him. "We both know the police department should work with the media. We can help each other."

Danny pulled his hands from his pockets, plucked hers from his arm, and dropped it to her side. Stopping on the sidewalk, he turned and looked down at her. At six-foot-five, everyone seemed short, but the reporter did her best to stretch her five-foot-six-inch frame.

"You'll get information as soon as Captain Sterling and Chief Gregg are ready to send a release. Until then, no scoop for you. Have a good day!"

"Fine. I have other ways of getting what I want," she said to his back.

"I'm not stupid. But your mole is," he countered and continued on his way.

Wild Creek Ranch, The Living Room, 1:45 PM

Feet propped on the coffee table and with a fresh cup of tea in hand, Marnie gathered a new stack of envelopes into her lap. As she opened get-well cards and letters, she kept a running list of the thank-you notes she should write. Carl traipsed in with a mug of coffee and sat on the couch.

"How goes it?" he asked.

"Nearly done. I shouldn't have let these pile up."

"Don't should on yourself. You were out of action and rehabbing most of July and August. You deserve time off to heal."

"What about September?" Rolling her eyes, she pulled a card from an envelope and teared up when she read the inscription.

Carl noticed the tears but didn't comment. "As I recall, you spent the first half of September beating up on yourself and the last half feeling sorry for yourself. Is that right?"

She poked out her tongue and reached out to hand him the card. "This is lovely. It's from Tom's folks. They've been so kind." She took a long, shaky breath and brushed a tear from her eye. "Why do they put up with me?"

"Because you did nothing wrong. You, Dorie, Tom, Paige, Lanie ... you're all the victims in this. Dalton Hooley and Jonas Billingsly took lives. Not you."

"Yes, but Dalton is a victim, too. Lawrence and Kitty Parish ... Argh! I get so angry when I think about how they manipulated people."

"Don't worry about Dalton. He's my patient now. He'll be fine in time."

"What about Kate? Did you get her too?"

Carl smirked. "Indeed, I did! There was minimal concern about a conflict of interest. I'm the only game in town when it comes to psychopaths. It's rare to meet one, you know."

"Hmm ... only two percent of the population based on current criteria. Although, I have my doubts. I think there's more than that."

"I won't disagree with you, but the criteria are what they are."

Grumbling from under the coffee table made them turn toward the windows overlooking the back porch, where Teddy stood punching in a code and with her key in the lock. The canine greeting committee scrambled to their feet and raced to the door.

Carl stood and drank the last of his coffee. "Now that Teddy has returned, I'll take my leave."

"You didn't have to stay with me. I'm fine on my own."

"Until you walk across a room without a dizzy spell or nausea, we're not leaving you alone."

Teddy cooed greetings at the canines and dropped the box on the kitchen table and burst into the room.

"Carrie Sutherland is here to dig up dirt on you and your family," she said, eyes wide.

Wild Creek Ranch, The Living Room, 2:22 PM

"This looks like trouble. Who are you two conspiring against? You didn't even hear me come in?" Danny stood at the doorway of the study, grinning—the dogs flanking him side, back, and side.

Marnie and Teddy eyed one another before the former responded.

"Carrie Sutherland is back in town and plans to do a tell-all about my family."

With a slow nod, the detective entered the room.

"Why don't you tell me about it over dinner? I have to speak with Elk and Arnie before their evening chores. Okay?"

Marnie slapped her forehead. "Geez! I haven't given dinner a thought!"

"Don't worry about it. I saw Gram earlier. She'll be here at six with chicken soup and pastrami sandwiches."

"She's too good to us."

Teddy shoved her playfully. "Speak for yourself. She can feed me anytime. Uh … If I'm invited. Sorry."

Danny stretched his lips and scratched the side of his head as Teddy's cheeks flushed.

"I'm intruding, aren't I?"

The detective cracked a smile. "Ha-ha! No! You're welcome to stay. I'm guessing you're the one who gathered the gossip on Carrie Sutherland."

"Yeah. She's a piece of work!"

Sticking his jaw out in thought, he agreed. "That she is. I'll tell you about my encounter with the reporter later. I'll be back soon. Can I take the knuckleheads for a walk?"

"Please." Marnie hopped up from her seat on the couch and wrapped her arms around her boyfriend. "You're a wonderful man, you know that?"

"I do," he said, giving her a squeeze as he leaned down and kissed her. "Back shortly."

After he was out of earshot, Teddy sidled up to Marnie and pushed her with her shoulder.

"So … Do you think you and Danny will ever get married?"

Marnie shrugged, glancing at her friend out of the corner of her eye. "I have no idea, but I plan to stick around to find out."

Wild Creek Ranch, Western Paddock, 2:41 PM

"Hey, Detective!" said Elk, leaning his back against a post and holding a beat-up tin coffee mug.

"How ya doin'?"

"Yeah. Good. I'm waitin' on Arnie. He had to run into town to drop off a load of hay. There's a square dance at the Moose Lodge tonight. Somebody on the decorating committee forgot that loose hay strewn around the floor is aesthetically pleasing to rednecks. Ha!"

"We are not in short supply of rednecks around Creekwood."

"Present company included. I got no problem bein' lumped in with most of 'em."

Danny grinned. "I wouldn't have it any other way. We're outdoorsmen. We can take care of our womenfolk when times are hard. Hehe! I better not say that too loud. Marnie might deck me."

"I reckon she could. That girl is tough as nails and ornerier than Buford."

"Buford?"

"Yeah. That's what she called the new bull. Hey, she can call 'em whatever she likes, but she can't make pets of 'em."

"Good luck with that!" Danny chuckled and shifted the topic. "Elk, what time did you and Arnie finish in the maze last night?"

"I'm not sure. I don't wear a watch and the light on my microwave hasn't been reset since the last power outage a month ago. We'll have to ask Arnie. His phone and smartwatch know everything."

"Don't you have a phone?"

Elk pulled a two-way radio off his belt. "Nah! If the lady of the manor needs anything, she calls me on this." He waggled the radio before returning it to his belt. "I come fully equipped with her safety in mind. Radio on one hip. A nine-millimeter on the other."

Danny frowned. "Licensed, of course."

"I'm not an idiot, Detective. I have a concealed carry permit."

"Just checking."

"Here comes Arnie. We better call Dickens over. He's got a new thing for chasing tires. We'll have to break him of that."

"Dickens! Come!" Danny kneeled and held out his arms. The dogs all turned and galloped across the field to the detective, who snagged Dickens' collar and held tight. "How long has he been doin' that?"

"A few days. The poor guy needs sheep to round up or somethin' else to chase besides the geese. He's bored."

"I'll talk to Marnie. She might have an idea."

Arnie pulled the truck to a halt and waved. Sticking his head out the window, he said, "Thanks for grabbin' that little tire biter. We gotta teach him he can't herd the truck. I've seen good farm dogs put down for that."

Danny patted the pup and whispered in his ear. "I won't let that happen, buddy. We'll find you a job." He got to his feet and brushed dirt from his knee. "I'll take care of it."

The farmhand got out of the truck and nodded. "Elk and I will do what we can to watch out for him." Slamming the door, he added, "I'd hate to see him get run over."

"Thanks, I appreciate it. Can we talk about what time you guys finished at the maze last night before you get back to chores?" He pulled a notepad and pen from his pocket, opening the cover, ready to write.

Elk tapped the watch on Arnie's wrist. "I told the detective you'd have a better idea seein' I don't wear one or have a phone."

Arnie laughed. "Ha-ha! You don't need 'em. The livestock and birds tell you the time. But I'd say we left the maze around ten-fifteen or so. It was ten-thirty by the time I got home and that's a ten-minute drive. Took us five to walk to my truck."

"You didn't see or hear anything suspicious?" Danny asked.

"Nah! Just the normal rustling of leaves and wildlife noises out in the trees, but we had music on. We might have missed something."

"Have you seen anyone hanging around? Someone who shouldn't be here?"

Elk snapped his fingers. "I did see that old tramp who lives in the schoolhouse talkin' to a guy out on the road a few days ago."

"Yeah? What did he look like?"

"Big fella. Dark hoodie. Jeans. Boots. Couldn't see his face, but the old guy looked pissed about somethin'. He was wagging his finger around and his face was red hot."

"You said big. Do you mean fat? Tall?"

"Very tall. Like you, but I'd say bigger." Elk did his best impression of The Hulk, before he added, "I don't reckon I'd wrangle with him."

Arnie chimed in. "I saw that guy. Thought he was one of Carl's patients."

"Where'd you see him?"

"The construction site down at the creek. Big dude like that— could be he's one of their crew."

Running a hand through his hair, Danny scanned the horizon and wondered if the security cameras had captured the man in question. Back in mid-July, he broached the topic of full-time security personnel to Marnie, but she had bristled at the thought of constant surveillance. She felt the security staff at the veteran's mental health and wellness clinic she and Carl managed was intrusive enough. An argument had escalated, and she had marched him to the door, telling him he could come back only when he stopped being a control freak.

An image of Dalton Hooley entered Danny's mind, and he wondered if the Parish family had influenced another victim they hadn't come across. Shivering away the horrific thought, he reached out a hand to Elk and then Arnie, each shaking with a firm, calloused grip.

"Thanks for the info. If you or your guys think of anything else, call me. I'm headin' down to the creek to see if the foreman is still around. Could one of you take the knuckleheads up to the house for me? I don't want Dickens to chase a backhoe."

Arnie opened the door of his truck and patted the front seat. The dogs dove in, panting and happy.

Chapter Five

Wild Creek Ranch, Riding Trail, 3:03 PM

Silage is a scent you either love or hate, and like other distinctive odors, it can touch a nerve as our olfactory sense takes over. Detective Danny Gregg breathed in a lungful of the sweet and vinegary scent. as he passed by the silos on his way to the creek. A sad smile tugged at the corners of his mouth as he remembered why he became a cop, but also of summers of his youth when he worked on a farm, mucking out barns and other odd jobs. The smell of silage always conjured images of the owner's daughter, Cissy Miller. She was two years his senior, but he was quite smitten with her long-tanned arms and legs, sparkling hazel eyes, luxurious auburn curls that fell to the middle of her back. He smiled at the thought of her teeny-tiny cut-offs. She never paid him much attention until he returned the summer of his sixteenth year.

Danny had grown a good six inches and had broadened through the chest and shoulders thanks to playing football through the fall and hockey through the winter months. His part-time job as a Zamboni driver had kept him away from home and his mother's and grandmother's homemade pastries. Gone was the chubby farmhand,

and Cissy noticed. While they didn't date, the two enjoyed long conversations on hot summer days when Danny would take a break and join her on an old wooden raft floating in the farm pond, where Cissy sunned herself every afternoon.

One unbearably hot and humid day, Cissy made Danny's summer, suggesting she would meet him that evening after his baseball game, but she never showed. When he arrived at work the next day, her parents were frantic and his father, Detective Mac Gregg, was there with his partner, Detective Gavin Anderson. Standing under an old-growth oak tree, the detectives asked the Millers when they had last seen their daughter and if she'd had plans for the previous night. They explained she'd gone to her room right after dinner and she was in bed, asleep, when they retired to their bedroom at eight o'clock.

Knowing Cissy often snuck out, Danny wondered if he should rat out his friend, but didn't want to snitch. After mulling it over, he approached the adults and told them what he knew.

"Uh ... Mr. and Mrs. Miller. Cissy was supposed to meet me after my ball game last night. I waited for her for about an hour. When she didn't show, I figured she had better things to do, so I went home."

Mrs. Miller guffawed. "Well, that's nonsense. She wouldn't have a way into town. Why would she say that she would meet you?"

He stared down at his feet and shifted them through the clover and chickweed carpet where they stood. His father planted a huge hand on his shoulder and gave it a reassuring squeeze.

"Daniel, if you have information, you better tell us."

Lifting his eyes to his father's, he nodded. "Cissy sneaks out sometimes and ..." He glanced away, stalling for time—hoping she would magically appear from the other side of the house. Turning back, he continued, "... and borrows the car."

"Why would you say that?" gasped the girl's mother.

Mr. Miller put a protective arm around his wife's shoulders and shook his head in disbelief. "Look, Detective, our daughter gets up to mischief, but she doesn't take the car. She would never do that. She knows I'd tan her hide."

Detective Anderson asked, "Daniel, how do you know Cissy sneaks out? Did she tell you, or have you seen her take the car?"

The teenager offered an awkward shrug and ran a hand through his unruly mop of sun-bleached waves,. He tightened his lips, unhappy with being a snitch, but if they could find her, it would be worth it.

"Both," he said. "I've seen her in town with her friends and she's mentioned that she climbs down the maple tree outside her window."

"I don't believe it!" Mrs. Miller twisted the front of her apron, angry eyes on Danny. "My Cissy would not ..."

Mr. Miller grasped her shoulder. "Jean. Our Cissy ain't an angel, as we like to pretend. I believe the boy. He's got no reason to lie."

"Daniel, does Cissy have a place she hangs out? A place she goes when she sneaks out?" asked Anderson.

"Not sure. We really don't hang out except out on the raft when I'm on a break. I was kind of surprised when she said she'd meet me after my game. I've never even seen her at the ballpark."

Mrs. Miller choked on her words, but asked, "Were the two of you dating?"

Danny's face reddened. "Gosh! No! She's older than me and we're just friends."

Detective Gregg rubbed his big hands together and squinted into the sun, scoping out the property.

"Well, I suggest we get a team of officers over here and we search every acre, nook, cranny, and hidey-hole. The pickup is here and as is Mrs. Miller's station wagon, so she didn't take a vehicle. She's here, or a friend picked her up. Or ... Does she have a bike? May she have ridden a bicycle into town?"

Mr. Miller pulled a face. "Detective, that's five miles. She wouldn't ride her bike that far. Besides, it's at the side of the house. I saw it this morning when I checked for her in the garden shed. She and her girlfriends hide peach schnapps in there. It's the first place I looked."

"What? She's been drinking, and you didn't tell me?" Mouth agape, Mrs. Miller threw her hands to her face and sobbed. "My god, Andrew, why wouldn't you tell me?"

"Jean, kids gotta have a place where they misbehave. Better here than somewhere else." Andrew Miller closed his eyes and sighed. "You woulda grounded her and that wouldn't a done no good. She'd rebel and we don't need that."

Detective Gregg stepped to his car and made a call on his radio. Returning, he said, "Officers are on their way. We'll search the property and let you know when we find Cissy. I've got officers checking teen haunts in town and I gave them a list of her girlfriends to visit. Even though you already called them, police have a way of getting teenagers to spill the beans on their friends."

Jean Miller grabbed the detective's arm. "Will you find her?"

He patted her hand. "Yes, ma'am."

"Thank you." The distraught woman turned to leave, saying she would make a fresh pot of coffee and lemonade.

"What can I do to help?" Mr. Miller asked the detectives.

"You can get on with your day, sir. We'll have a look around and find you when we have something to report." Anderson clapped a reassuring hand on the farmer's back and stepped toward his unmarked vehicle.

Once Mr. Miller had left the detectives and Danny alone, the teen asked his father if he could help.

"How'd you get to work, son?"

"I rode my dirt bike down along Crow Creek. Fastest way here from our house."

"Okay. How about you go to every spot on the property you think Cissy might be? If you find her, you know the rules, right?"

"Yeah. Don't touch anything and come and get you or Detective Anderson."

"That's right."

"She's dead, isn't she, Dad?" Danny blurted out his question, then grimaced and wondered why he had said it.

Mac Gregg grimly looked down at his son and nodded. "That's what my gut's telling me."

"Mine, too," said Anderson.

"Mine, three," said Danny, walking off to get his dirt bike.

One hour into the search for Cissy Miller, the detectives walked out of the vast cornfield as Danny roared up an access road in a cloud of dust, skidding to a halt beside them. Sunburnt and weary, his eyes shined with tears.

"Dad! I found her! I found Cissy! She's in the east field! There's a utility shed, and she's ... she's ... Ah! Geez! Dad! She's sittin' there on the step! I called her name, and she stared at me!"

"Did you get close?"

Shaking his head, he said, "No, sir! I told you I wouldn't and came right back to get you."

The detective climbed onto his son's dirt bike, sitting awkwardly behind him. "Show me."

"Your birthday is next week. We should look at getting you a bigger bike." Mac Gregg unfolded himself from the back of Danny's ride and brushed dust from his jeans.

"There she is, Dad. Over there!"

The detective cocked his head to one side, considering the girl's placement on the step and the slackness of the skin on her face. Without turning around, he gave his instructions.

"Son. I need you to go back and tell Anderson to get the forensics team out here. Do it discreetly. Let's not upset the Millers."

"Our guts were right?"

"Yeah."

As Danny made his way to the construction site, he realized that August day, right before his sixteenth birthday, held a lot of firsts for him. It was the one and only time he ratted on a friend.

The corpse of Cissy Miller was his introduction to murder and the first inkling he wanted to be a cop. He and his dad had never had a close relationship until that day. Their desire to find the person responsible was the glue that bonded father and son. Even though he was too young to be involved in a homicide investigation, Mac Gregg kept him in the loop until the trail went dead.

More importantly, it was the first time a woman he loved died tragically, and while his broken heart healed, a part of him always wondered what happened. Cissy's murder was still unsolved and open. Spontaneously, he called the precinct and asked Cheryl Garcia to pull the file and drop it on his desk.

"Thanks for helping me out, Garcia. And hey," he said before hanging up, "Have a look at the file and tell me what you think. A different perspective and a fresh set of eyes might find something. Besides, you've got your sergeant's test coming up soon. You help me with this, and you might learn something—especially if you want to be a detective. Ha-ha."

Keen to work with the detective, Garcia agreed quickly to reviewing the files. She also suggested Danny may learn a few things from her—most importantly, a woman's attention to finer details men might miss.

"Is that right?" he said, chuckling. "Go get 'em, Garcia. Can't wait to hear your thoughts."

They clicked off, and he made his way across the yard to investigate the sighting of the big dude.

Wild Creek Ranch, Construction Site, 3:16 PM

Construction manager Hugh Barber packed tools into the bed of his pickup truck, one eye squinted and a cigarette dangling from his lips. Covered in cement dust, his carpenter pants hung low on his waist and his soiled T-shirt had seen better days. He pulled it over his head and tossed it onto the tailgate, grabbing a clean one from a duffle.

"Mr. Barber?"

Hugh turned to see Danny Gregg striding up the grassy incline to the site. He waved and quickly put on the clean shirt.

"Evening, Detective. Apologies for the quick change. My wife gets angry when I wear work clothes into the house."

"Ha-ha! No worries. But aren't you getting clean clothes dirty by changing here?"

"Nah! I have a system. Our laundry room is off the back door, so when I get home, I drop the dirty clothes into the washer, take these off, fold 'em for the next day, then take a nudie run through to the shower. No kids in the house, so I get away with it unless the wife has company—then I'm in trouble. Ha! It's only happened once, and it couldn't have been worse. My mother-in-law. Was sittin' right there at the kitchen table and she choked on her wine."

Danny winced at the thought. "Crap! Mothers-in-law, eh?"

"You can say that again." Hugh furrowed his brow. "You been married? I mean, Marnie's mom hasn't been around for a long time."

"Uh ... My wife died."

"Sorry to hear. But back to what you came here for. What can I do for ya?"

"Have you seen anyone hanging around? A big guy wearing a dark-colored hoodie?"

"Detective, you described half my crew."

"Yeah. How about a guy who isn't in your crew? Someone suspicious?"

Hugh thought for a moment, scratching his five o'clock shadow, and gave his head a negative jerk.

"No, but I can ask my guys tomorrow. Most of 'em are gone now."

"What time do they arrive?"

"We gather for coffee and a production meeting around six. Wanna come back and talk to them yourself?"

"Yeah. I'm staying at the ranch tonight. I'll drop by if it isn't inconvenient."

"It's fine. Even better if Marnie has homemade cookies to donate to the cause."

"I think she may have baked a batch today. I'll see what I can do. Catch ya. I've gotta check in with the clinic. I doubt a building full of veterans would miss someone like that wandering around."

As Danny turned to leave, he glimpsed movement in the trees and jerked around.

"You see something?" asked Hugh.

"Nah. Probably a deer."

Chapter Six

Wild Creek Ranch, The Kitchen, 5:30 PM

"Should I open a bottle of wine?" Eyebrows raised, Marnie wagged a Pinot Noir at Teddy.

"Uh. No. I'm fine. Besides, I want to have cider and Fireball later. What's that old saying? Wine and liquor never sicker."

"Beer and wine, you'll be fine," continued Marnie, putting the bottle back in the rack. "Your idea sounds better. The guys brought me a jug of fresh-pressed from my trees this morning."

"Oo! Perfect? How are the new clients settling in?" Teddy opened a cupboard and pulled out five soup bowls and sandwich plates, setting them on the trestle table.

"They love working on the ranch, so that's a plus. Carl is doing most of the work right now. I can't really comment."

"I met the new nurse. She seems *nice*."

Teddy's snotty tone, sideways glance, and pursed lips told Marnie her friend wasn't a fan of the new RN.

"What's your problem with Millicent?"

"She's up herself."

"Is she?" Marnie lifted one eyebrow and pulled a face.

"Mm-hm. She's a control freak, too."

"Well, I haven't noticed, but I haven't spent much time at the clinic."

Teddy opened a drawer and counted out spoons. "She told me she's my boss. Is she?"

"Really? I wonder why she said that. It doesn't matter. You answer to me and Carl. What were you doing when she said it?" said Marnie, setting paper napkins and quilted placemats down, preparing to lay the table.

Teddy shrugged. "I fixed Carl a coffee and was taking it to him. She told me to make her one, and I told her to make it herself."

The psychic laughed. "Ha-ha! That wouldn't win points."

"I don't care. You didn't hear her tone. All bossy and bitchy."

Nodding, Marnie said, "I'll talk to Carl. In the meantime, tie her up in a tea towel and chuck her in the freezer."

"And please tell her I'm not calling her Nurse Stroud unless the clients are present. Geez! You'd think she was a god or something."

"She told you to call her that?"

"Yeah! It was only us, and I called her Millicent. She 'Tsk. Tsked' me and said, it's Nurse Stroud."

Marnie giggled. "Well, she will not like my penchant for nicknames. I've been calling her Millie when speaking with Carl."

Teddy joined in the laughter and pivoted toward the windows. "Hey. Did a car pull up?"

Hearing the word *car*, the dogs scrambled from under the table, knocking one of the heavy oak benches over onto Marnie's foot in their excitement to be the first at the door.

Flinching in pain, she shouted, "Settle down! Tater! Dickens! Gus! Sit."

The Border Collies and Labrador dropped their backsides to the floor and whimpered with excitement at the prospect of guests.

"Marn, are you okay?" Teddy rushed over and bent to examine her friend's toes.

Caught off guard by the use of Tom's nickname for her, Marnie broke down in tears and limped from the room. The dogs trailed behind her, ready to offer sympathetic licks.

Slapping her forehead, Teddy scolded herself on her way to answer the door. "Damnit! That was stupid."

Wild Creek Ranch, The Kitchen, 5:40 PM

Danny's grandmother and sister Hannah unpacked dinner while Teddy searched for Marnie, who she found curled up on the couch in the study—eyes puffy, cheeks blotchy and with a balled-up tissue to her red nose. The dogs had taken up positions around her, offering nose nudges in the way of kindness. Tater sat closest, his paw resting on her knee.

With a soft rap on the door, she asked, "Can I come in?"

"I'm sorry I reacted like that. No one has called me 'Marn' in months. God, I miss him. I have a horrible knot in my throat from the time I wake up until I go to bed at night."

Teddy glanced around the room and up at the ceiling, trying to find the right words. "I wasn't thinking. It slipped out."

Marnie waved her off and got to her feet. "I'm being a big baby. C'mon. Let's join the others. I'll be fine."

"How's your foot?"

With a shrug, she pulled off her woolen sock. "It's gonna have a bruise tomorrow, but I'll survive."

She hopped on one foot and put on her sock as they headed to greet her guests. When they returned to the kitchen, Danny was there, too. He wrapped an arm around her and kissed her forehead.

"Oh, yummy! I smell chicken soup. Thank you, Gram." Marnie made her way to the stove and lifted the lid, inhaling Gram's cooking. Spinning around with a smile, she said, "Hey! I ate a whole sandwich today and didn't feel like vomiting. That's a positive sign, huh?"

Hannah wove her way to Marnie's side and nudged her with her shoulder. "That's great! I was beginning to worry you'd lose too much weight. Your backside is nearly gone."

Jaw dropped in faux shock, Marnie laughed. "Ha-ha! Says the gal who hasn't an ounce of fat."

Hannah shrugged. "Nervous energy is my secret."

Teddy frowned. "You don't seem like a nervous Nelly."

"Mm ... With the shenanigans we've seen the last year, I'm hypersensitive, waiting for the other shoe to drop."

Hannah pressed her back against the counter and looked up at Marnie. At five-foot-five, she was five inches shorter, but she was fierce and protective of the woman she hoped would be her sister-in-law someday. And while she and Danny were twins, they looked nothing alike. Her thin frame, messy shoulder-length mahogany hair and icy gray eyes shielded by rimless glasses were a glaring contrast to her brother.

With a muss of sandy brown hair and a dimpled smile on his oddly handsome and rugged face, the detective was built to intimidate. His tall and well-toned frame filled an interview room doorway in all the right ways. Armed with a sharp wit, an astute sixth sense, and a piercing blue gaze, he was a criminal's worst nightmare.

As a DEA Special Agent, Hannah Patterson was no slouch. She shared her brother's sense of humor, if often disguised, and his gift of reading people. She tended toward an introvert, while Danny was outgoing.

"Marnie, dear, do you have a platter for the sandwiches?" asked Gram in her lilted Irish brogue.

Margaret "Gram" Ryan was Danny and Hannah's maternal grandmother. Amply built and fit, she wore her thick, wavy white hair short. Like Marnie, she had the gift of second sight and while she couldn't see spirits, she could hear and sense them. There was something magical about Gram. Perhaps that was her Druid ancestors shining through her silver-sparked blue eyes. Creekwood locals have told tales of her practicing the fine art of white magic. No one can prove it, but those in her tight circle suspect she has dabbled when circumstances are dire.

Marnie bent and pulled a large serving board from the cupboard and placed it at the center of the table.

"How about this?"

"Perfect," replied the older woman. "I hope everyone is hungry. There is enough for a small army."

As if on cue, Carl rapped on the back door and came in. "Hope I'm not interrupting."

"Not at all. Want dinner?" asked the psychic.

"Thanks, but I can't stay. I'm catching up with a friend at the pub."

Marnie smirked. "Oh, really? Who might this friend be?" she teased.

With the shake of his head, Carl disappointed her. "No. Nothing like that. It's a guy I roomed with at university. He's driving through on his way to Florida. But I will gladly eat leftovers tomorrow."

Danny snickered. "Good luck with that. Pastrami sandwiches and chicken soup won't last that long."

"Fair enough. Anyway ... Marnie, did you sign those checks Teddy gave you this morning? I want to drop them in the night deposit on my way through town."

"Teddy took care of them earlier. You go. Have fun. I'll see you in the morning. I'm ready to get back to work."

A grin slipped across Carl's lips, and he nodded with enthusiasm. "Best news I've heard all year. Night."

As he walked out the door, Marnie yelled, "Come for breakfast! Bacon and eggs at seven-thirty."

"I'll be here," he replied, as the screen door slammed.

Wild Creek Ranch, The Living Room, 6:50 PM

Dinner dishes cleared and coffee and tea poured, Danny settled on the couch next to the fire, scratching at his beard. The topic of Bob Humboldt had to be handled gingerly, but he decided to dive in rather than wade in the weeds of small talk.

"Thank you all for not bringing up this morning's case at the dinner table. Our new rule of no work talk makes mealtime more enjoyable."

Gram glanced up from the back cover of the book she was reading and set it down next to her teacup on the end table. She straightened the blanket over her knees and leaned back in the club chair opposite him. A telltale tingle hung in the air as she waited for her grandson to continue.

Marnie shivered and ran a hand over the top of her head. She sat beside him and gently nudged him with her elbow.

"Spill it, Detective. I've got goosebumps and that antsy feeling again."

Hannah and Teddy shot one another a knowing glance of *Here we go again.*

With a deep breath, he dove into the murky green depths.

"The dead man is a Creekwood native named Bob Humboldt. Any of you know him?"

Hand over her mouth, Marnie said, "Oh, no. I can't believe I didn't recognize him."

Gram nodded, as did Teddy, and Hannah said she didn't.

Marnie stood, tucked a leg beneath her, and sat again.

"Bob was a dear friend of my father's. He was a reporter at the Times, and he insisted Dad's boating accident wasn't what it appeared to be. It got so bad, I stopped taking his calls. To be honest, I was a mess. Things with Ken were escalating, and I was doing my best to survive. Bob's theories were scaring the hell out of me."

Teddy added, "He was a lovely man. As I recall, your father was on that fishing trip with a group of friends. Why wasn't Bob with them?"

"He'd had his appendix out and couldn't go. It wasn't an average appendectomy. I think it burst. I can't remember all the details. But he should have been there. It was an annual trip."

Danny rearranged himself on the sofa and put an arm across the back behind Marnie.

"Is it possible he was bunking down at the schoolhouse so he could speak with you again?"

"He could have come to the door. It seems absurd that he would pretend to be homeless to get my attention. That seems extreme. Could be wrong, though," she said.

"We couldn't find a record of family. Do you know if he had any?"

"He never married, as far as I am aware. Dad always called him the consummate bachelor, and I never heard mention of siblings or anything else. Bob was a history buff and if he wasn't talking about what role the area played in a war, he was discussing current events. Anything worth knowing, he knew. I'd recommend you chat with Marion Doyle over at the paper. She's in classifieds and has been as long as I can remember. I like her. She has the dirt on everyone, but never says a thing," she said.

"Unless pressed or prodded with a glass of port," added Gram with a twinkle in her eyes.

O-faced, Marnie giggled. "Okay. I didn't realize. Not the teetotaler I thought her to be, then?"

Teddy's amber eyes danced with the prospect of helping and gathering gossip.

"Marion is a close friend of my mother's. I can grill her if you'd like."

"No. Thank. You." The detective's grumbly baritone told Teddy to keep her nose out of police business.

"Meh. Have it your way," she said with a toss of cappuccino waves.

Hannah snapped her fingers. "Hang on a minute. Marnie? Can I use your computer for a sec?"

"Yeah. Go ahead. You know my password?"

"Ha! Like not knowing would stop me." Hannah chuckled to herself as she popped into the study to check her facts.

Danny brushed a strand of strawberry-blonde hair from Marnie's face and examined the pinkish scar that followed her hairline. "When's the last time you saw him?"

"You mean before recently at the schoolhouse? Would have to be a few years. Bob moved to Albany about a year after Dad died. He worked at a paper there, but I'm uncertain which one or for how long he's been back in Creekwood."

"I believe I saw him at the last Christmas parade. He was helpin' us get the little tikes off the flamin' float," said Gram.

Covering her face with both hands, Marnie muttered, "Geez! That day is a blur. My brain has blocked it out."

"How did he look, Gram? Homeless?" asked the detective lieutenant.

"Gracious. I dunno. Sooty."

"He still owns a house on Reddick Lane" Teddy held up her phone, showing them the town hall records.

"How did you get that?" asked Danny with a frown.

"It's public record, duh!"

The detective's steely gaze didn't phase Teddy. She smirked and kept searching.

"Public records dot com, baby!"

Danny's clenched jaw did the trick. Teddy handed over her phone so he could see what she was referencing.

He poked at the screen and growled. "So much for privacy."

Hannah returned a moment later, a piece of paper in hand.

"I knew his name sounded familiar." She handed the page to Danny and sank onto the couch next to him.

"Am I allowed to see this?" he asked, eyes glued to the document.

"Yeah. You're law enforcement. I wouldn't share it with Randy, though. I don't trust him."

"Can I keep it?" he asked.

"Of course. I wouldn't have given it to you if you couldn't. I hope it helps."

"Thanks."

He folded the page and tucked it in his pocket. Feeling three sets of eyes staring at him, he looked up. Marnie, Gram, and Teddy all sat on the edge of their seats, waiting for him to share.

Wagging a finger, he said, "Na-Na-Na! This isn't for public consumption. You'll know when it's public and not until."

Marnie threw herself into the back of the couch with a huff.

"For that, my ice-cold feet will find the middle of your back as you fall asleep."

Chapter Seven

Wild Creek Ranch, Marnie's Bedroom, 11:21 PM

"You okay?" asked Danny, running his thumb across Marnie's goose-fleshed arm.

"A thousand eyes staring at me. Waiting." She shivered and snuggled closer.

The bedroom buzzed with energy, and while the detective and psychic psychologist were very much alive, the swirling vibe disturbing the psychic was from the dead encircling the bed.

"I never get used to them—the way they stand around a room, waiting for me to look at them. Acknowledge their presence. But sometimes I can't."

"Would a night mask help?"

With a shake of her head, she sighed. "Nah! They'll tap my foot, shake the bed, pull on the quilt, or wait for me to fall asleep and speak to me in my dreams. I opened myself up to this. It's my fault. I was hoping to speak ... with ... oh, never mind. I'll have Gram help me shut the door tomorrow."

"Don't lock it, though, huh?"

"I won't."

"Marnie?"

"Hmm?"

"Who is that by the closet door?"

"Lawrence Parish. He never leaves. He lurks and waits."

"Tchah! That's rich! Him coming to you for help."

"Help? Ha! He wants to kill me, and I think he's blocking others from coming to me."

Danny jerked to his elbow, eyes on the door.

"Shh. Did you hear that?"

Sitting up, Marnie reached for her flannel robe draped across the foot of the bed.

"There's someone downstairs."

Tater sprang off the bed and planted himself between his mistress and the entry. Dickens and Gus joined him—their mumbles and grumbles growing in volume.

Pulling back the quilt, the detective swung his feet to the cold floorboards and pulled on his sweatpants.

"I set the alarm," he said, retrieving his sidearm from the nightstand drawer.

"Yeah. Well, from experience, alarms only keep out the good guys, and even that's questionable."

The detective and psychologist locked the protesting knuckleheads in the bedroom and crept down the nightlight lit hallway, floorboards creaking and their hearts pumping. From the top step, they watched the darkness of the front room in silence, and Marnie's breath caught as a light switched on in the kitchen. A dull shadow skulked into the front room, retreating a moment later.

Danny motioned with his hand for her to stay behind him, then proceeded to the first step. He skipped the next because the boards popped with the slightest weight. Marnie held onto the band of his sweatpants and repeated his steps, but both stopped dead, rolling their eyes at one another. A familiar tenor, singing, *I Ain't Got Nobody,* drifted up the staircase.

"Samuel Reilly! What's the big idea? Traipsing in here in the middle of the night!" Marnie skulked into the room and stopped dead, fists on her hips—green eyes blazing.

Sam was Marnie's older brother. He'd lived an interesting life. As an FBI agent, he'd dealt with the worst of the worst and his special skill was one not known to many. He was an assassin. A few years back, he was accused of going rogue when two other agents were caught up in a drug ring. They set Sam and Ransom up to take the fall for them and the former was presumed dead after entering a building that exploded. A few years older than Marnie, the two had shared a difficult relationship for years. Then last June they had learned he had been brainwashed and drugged by Lawrence Parish, Kate Parish's father, in an effort to conceal his daughter's murderous ways.

Danny moved past her, set his gun down, and held out a hand. "It's good to see you, but you could have called."

Sam gave the detective's hand a quick pump and winked at his sister. "I didn't want to wake you. I figured you'd both be sound asleep by now."

Without offering her brother a hug, Marnie whirled around and stomped up the stairs to release the hounds from their confined quarters. When she opened the door, all three made a slip-sliding mad dash for the stairs—the Border Collies trilling with excitement.

Entering the kitchen, her anger disappeared at the sight of her brother kneeling with them, each giving him a tongue wash.

"Sorry, Squirt. I've had enough of this healing nonsense."

"How are you feeling?" she asked, crossing the room and hugging him tight.

He gave his little sister a tight squeeze and examined the scar on the side of her face. "Better. The headaches are gone for now. Let's hope it stays that way, huh? How about you? Is the nausea easing?"

With a nod, she said, "I ate lunch and didn't puke, so that's something."

Turning to Danny, he said, "We saw a guy walking up the road when we drove up. He darted off into the trees when we slowed to take a look."

Danny's face dropped. "Big dude? Wearing a hoodie?"

"Yeah. Ransom hopped out to investigate. I'm heading out to help him, but my pistol is in my bag, and I wanted to take extra fire power along."

"Let me get some shoes and I'll come too."

"Good deal."

Neither left the farmhouse, though, because Ransom knocked on the door before the detective could get his shoes.

US Federal Marshal Ransom Elliott was Marnie's ex-boyfriend and had been an agent in a selection of federal law enforcement agencies. At five-foot-eleven, his sinewy frame, spiked blonde hair, and killer smile gave him a cheeky bad-boy vibe.

Marnie's lip lifted in a distasteful sneer. "Why'd you have to bring him?"

"Ha-ha! You'll live. I'm helping him with a case. A person of interest was seen in the area and the US Marshal's service decided it was high time they put my exemplary outlaw skills to use."

"Exemplary? You got caught!" said Marnie.

He didn't disagree, but countered, "Only because I wanted to be."

Wild Creek Ranch, The Kitchen, 11:31 PM

"Look! Local law enforcement needs to stay out of it. We'll get him." Ransom pushed his cup toward Sam, who was refilling mugs with cinnamon-laced coffee.

"And I'm saying you have to report your activity to the chief and captain. Let them know who you're chasing and give them a description so that we can keep an eye out. Why is that a problem?" Danny crumpled up a paper napkin and threw it down as he stood to rummage through the fridge. "You guys are so fucking annoying with your secrecy. If we locals are meant to keep the community safe, you have to share intel like grown-ups."

"Okay, big guy. If we need help, we'll let you know," replied Ransom with a smirk. "Hey, Kid. You got any cookies?"

"Not for you," retorted Marnie. "How can you be such a jerk?"

The marshal shrugged, offering a wink. "Practice."

Chapter Eight

October 11th

Wild Creek Ranch, The Kitchen, 5:30 AM

Fresh brewed coffee hit her nostrils as Marnie made her way into the kitchen at five-thirty. Danny handed her a cup and settled at the table with his notebook as she kissed him good morning. The knuckleheads were in their usual spot—under the table, snoozing on Tom's blanket and sweatshirt.

"Eggs and bacon?" she asked.

"Hmm ... how about peanut butter toast? I anger-snacked last night and I'm not very hungry."

"He's infuriating, isn't he?" she said, placing two thick slices of sourdough bread into the toaster.

"Dangerous is the word I would use. Irresponsible and arrogant, too."

"I heard arrogant. They must be speaking about you?" said Ransom, as he and Sam came around the corner and into the kitchen.

"Irresponsible, maybe, but not arrogant. That's all you, pal." Sam playfully pinched Marnie as he squeezed by her on his way to the coffeepot.

"Peas in a pod," she said, glowering at her brother and the marshal.

The toast popped, and Ransom reached out to grab a slice, but Marnie slapped him away and snatched the toast, placing it on a plate before handing it to Danny.

"Not for you! Make your own dang breakfast. Or better yet, go away and leave us to have ours in peace."

Sam frowned at her stinging words. "Wow! That is not how Mom taught you to speak to guests."

"Ha! Guests are invited. They don't skulk into my house late at night."

Face red, Ransom slung his jacket over his shoulder and crossed to the door. "C'mon, Sam. Let's grab breakfast down the road."

Sam lifted his chin. "I'll be out in a minute."

After the marshal was out of earshot, he said, "What was that about? I can stay in a hotel?"

Marnie scowled. "No. You are always welcome. He irks me and the way he speaks to Danny ... Why doesn't he want to cooperate with the Creekwood police? The secrecy is ridiculous and unbelievably ignorant."

Sam agreed. "Yes. I spoke to him about that after you had gone to bed. We are going to the station this morning to meet with Captain Sterling."

"Thanks for taking care of that, Sam," said Danny between bites of toast. "I couldn't understand his rationale. It's not as if we're a bunch of bumpkins."

"I told him that, but I didn't need to. He knows but has worked on his own a long time."

"He's letting you help him. Why not the locals?"

He took a gulp of coffee and said, "I have special skills the locals don't, and I am not bragging."

"We know you're not. How about I give him the keys to my cabin? That will keep Ransom out of Marnie's hair. Besides, my father is staying there this week and getting better acquainted with him could put the marshal's mind at ease." Danny pulled a ring of keys from his pocket and handed one to Sam.

"Thanks. That works for me. I want to spend quality time with my little sister, and Carl wants to see if any of Lawrence's nasty work lingers in my subconscious. A break from Ransom will be good—he wants to discuss the case ad nauseam."

"That would suit my father to a tee. He rarely gets sick of repeating himself," added Danny with a chuckle.

"By the way; we are here looking for Jed Rawlins. Eyewitness reports place him in the area. We were at Bayside together. It is hard to believe he is still roaming free. It has been four months."

Marnie glanced up from her coffee. "Can I throw in my two cents?"

"Sure," said Sam.

"There's a voice telling me he has changed." She closed her eyes, and when she opened them, she added. "He has three faces."

"Is he wearing a mask or something? What is that supposed to mean?"

With a shoulder jog, she said, "I deliver the messages I'm fed. You figure it out."

Danny nudged her hand with his own. "Who are you talking to?"

"No idea. There's a voice, but no physical manifestation. It's been there for a while now."

"Huh," said Danny, glancing at Sam.

Creekwood Police Station, Interview Room A, 9:25 AM

Ranger Abel Jackson sat across from Danny on a metal chair whose padding had disintegrated ages ago. The gray metal table between them had seen better days, too. Its chipped legs and pocked top held tales that would shock the average citizen. The drab yellow walls of the interview room and the fluorescent ceiling light gave their complexions a jaundiced glow. Both men sipped from paper cups filled from the Creekwood PD drip coffee maker that brewed something the equivalent of mud.

"You'd think the town could buy you fellas a new Mr. Coffee. This is terrible!" said Jackson, his blackened eyes watering above his plastered nose.

"Yeah. I've thought of replacing it myself, but I rarely drink it. Takeout from the diner is easier."

"It's nice to have family in the food industry. Your grandmother is the best."

"Yes, she is, and her coffee beats every establishment in town."

Pad ready and pen raised, the detective said, "You said your assailant was tall, right?"

The ranger nodded. "Yes, sir. He was bigger than you, Detective."

"What was he wearing?"

Abel glanced at the ceiling and pulled on his bottom lip as if it would help his memory.

"A dark hooded sweatshirt with a big tear in the pocket, jeans, and boots."

"Did you see his face?"

With a shudder, he said, "Yeah. I saw it. Wish I hadn't. Ugly guy. Looks like someone took a wire brush to his face. Red, raw and oozing."

Danny wrinkled his nose. "Oozing?"

"That gooey liquid when you skin your knee and it starts to heal? What is that stuff? Umm ... Blood serum."

Danny thought back to Marnie's earlier comment. *Three faces.*

"What time did it happen? Was he carrying anything?"

"Might have been, but I didn't notice. Uh ... It was around ten or so. I wrote ten-oh-five in my report."

"Why were you trying to speak with him?"

"I got a call from Bernice Hedge. Said there was a guy disrupting their Zonta meeting."

"What were they doing on the ridge? Don't they usually meet at the Town Hall?"

"Leaf peeping."

Danny nodded. "Ah! I never get why people who live here do that. Walk out your front door and there are tons of trees with changing leaves."

"You live in the woods and your girlfriend has the ranch. Folks who live in town like to get above it and look out."

"Fair enough. How many had to be carted down by the paramedics this year?"

"Two. Mrs. Atkins sprained her ankle pretty bad when that big dude rushed them from behind a stand of pines. Uh ... and that teacher. What's her name?" He tapped his fingers on the edge of the table and snapped his fingers. "Miss Fitzgerald. Phoebe is her name."

Danny jotted the names, underlining the teacher.

"You reckon he's camped out in a cave up there? I mean, it's a bad time of year to be living in a cave, but some do."

"I haven't been game to check on that without backup." He cradled his broken nose between his thumb and index finger.

"Yeah. I was surprised when the emergency room nurse told me you probably wouldn't be able to speak with me until today. Did they have to do surgery?"

Jackson nodded. "Whether they had to or not, they did. Rhinoplasty. My nose was pretty bad. That son of a bitch broke the bridge, and my septum was damaged, too. They called in Doc Carver from Albany. That's a hell of a name for a surgeon, huh?"

"Yeah. Anyway, let's discuss the man at the ridge. Who else was up there? Mrs. Hedge. Mrs. Atkins. Miss Fitzgerald. Who else?"

The ranger pursed his lips in thought. "I guess all the Zonta gals. Reach out to Bernice. She'll tell you."

"I'll do that, thanks. Tell me about the altercation. Why did he hit you?"

Jackson held up his hands. "I informed him he couldn't go around harassing women and then I asked him what he was doing up on the ridge. Next thing I knew, he plowed me in the face and walked away. I hollered for him to come back, but he offered a New York salute and kept going."

"Tchah! He flipped you off?"

"Yep."

"Any idea what color hair or eyes?"

Twisting his lips to the right, Jackson thought about the question. "I'm pretty sure brown and brown, but I can't swear to it."

"Anything else?"

"Yeah. The guy reeked to high heaven. No way he's seen soap and water in months. The smell would knock over a bear."

"Okay. Give me ten minutes to get this typed up and you can sign it. Can I get you another cup of coffee?"

"Uh ... no, thanks. I've suffered enough."

Wild Creek Ranch, The Kitchen, 9:38 AM

"This is a fair division of clients. You take the people who need medication. I'll take back my longstanding clients and some of the easier cases here at the ranch. You take the PTSD cases, and I'll focus on domestic violence." Taking a breath, Marnie jotted a note on her planner. "I've been thinking. We should hire a specialist. Neither of us is particularly suited to kids," she said, reaching for a pitcher of maple syrup.

She and Carl discussed clients over bacon, French toast, and coffee, while Teddy busied herself in the study with a supply order.

"Sounds like a plan. I'm terrible with children. I've tried, but they break my heart." He wiped a napkin across his lips and took a sip from his mug. "I've missed your big breakfasts. This is a treat. Thanks."

"Couldn't agree more. About the kids and the other thing. It's time for us to add a child psychologist and for me to pull my head out of my backside. Early morning feasts are back on the agenda."

Sam emerged from a guestroom, sweatpants and a sweatshirt, and carrying running shoes. Tater, Dickens, and Gus trotted behind him with the Border Collies herding him toward the door.

"Can I take the knuckleheads on a run? I'll stick to the property. I thought we'd go up to the construction site and the hay maze to see how they are progressing. Do you still want that arbor built for the Halloween carnival?"

"Yes, please! The maze is complete, but the guys are working hard to get that old millstone turning. Please and thank you to the arbor. Danny and I picked up the lumber weeks ago, but he hasn't had time to work on it."

"That's okay. You've got all of Dad's tools in the red barn, right?"

"No. I mean, yes. I have his tools, but Danny turned one of the old outbuildings into a workshop. It's the bluey-gray granite one with the naked nymph weathervane on the cupola."

Sam raised an eyebrow. "Naked nymph?"

"Yeah. Apparently, a Hudson River boat captain lived here for a time. The building is ancient, but it's made of stone, and it's cool in summer. It has a fireplace in it too. It might not be in working order, but there's a space heater in the garage you can take if you get cold."

"I'll be fine." He sat and put on his sneakers, tying them in double knots. "Carl, what's a good day and time for us?"

"I can meet you at the naked nymph building when Marnie and I finish. Forty minutes?"

"Sounds perfect."

A mobile phone rang, and they all checked to see if it was theirs. Marnie won. It was Danny calling to tell her that Randolph Stuyvesant should be out to check the old schoolhouse for evidence. She scowled and said she would report back when he showed up. When she hung up, she made a face and dropped her forehead on the kitchen table with all the drama of a three-year-old feigning starvation.

"Randy's on his way to investigate the schoolhouse." She lifted her head and stuck a finger down her throat and pretended to gag.

Sam laughed. "Is he that bad?" he asked, looking at Carl.

"Yeah. The guy is a dick. If he was overcompensating because of the shoes he was hired to fill, it would be different, but he's not. I don't trust him," said the psychiatrist. "I mean, he doesn't nauseate me like he does your sister, but there's something energetically off."

"Yikes! That's unfortunate." Sam turned to his sibling. "Does Danny like him?"

Marnie snickered. "Ha! No! He doesn't say much, but the way he says his name is enough for me."

"Well, I shall keep my eyes peeled for the vomit monster while out on my morning constitutional," said Sam, getting up from the bench and heading to the door. "C'mon, knuckleheads. Let's get this run on the road."

After her brother was gone, Marnie nudged Carl's foot with her toe under the table.

"Why don't you go have that chat with Nurse Stroud? We don't want her belittling Teddy again."

He nodded and gathered his papers. "Sure. I'm certain I never gave her the impression she was running the show. Or any inkling she was a supervisor."

Marnie shrugged. "Some people take control. It's not necessarily a bad thing—but we don't need her bossing Teddy around. We're a small team and we have to get along."

"We all have our strong points."

"Exactly! Besides, there isn't room for two bossy women in the business. That's *my* job."

"Ha-ha! Yes. Yes, it is. It's good to have you back."

The Study, 10:23 AM

When Randolph hadn't arrived by ten o'clock, Marnie called Danny to inform him that Randy was a no-show.

"Detective Dipshit hasn't shown up," she said.

"*What?*"

"Randy. He hasn't been here."

"Are you sure?"

"Yeah. I've been checking the cameras."

She heard a loud thud in the background and was sure Danny had thrown something.

"Okay. I'll track him down. Let me know if he makes an appearance."

"Ten-four," she responded in a robotic tone.

"Smartass," he said with a chuckle.

"It is rather smart, isn't it?"

"Gotta go. Keep me posted."

"See you tonight."

The Kitchen, 11:03 AM

The back door of the farmhouse swung open, and Sam stood in the doorway with a guilty grin and three wet dogs.

"I tried to stop them. Gus saw the creek, and that was it. All three of them dove in and I could not get them out."

Marnie opened the pantry door and reached for a stack of towels. She tossed two to Sam and carried one to the door.

"Gus can't help himself. I'm surprised you got past the pond."

"I remembered the pond and took them around the outbuildings and the clinic. Once we got to the new construction, Gus took off," he said, toweling dry the Labrador.

"He's a sneaky boy," said Marnie, fluffing Tater's fur with an old beach towel.

Dickens shook and sprayed water everywhere.

"Geez! Sam, forget about Gus. Dry that little rascal before he drenches the whole house."

Teddy walked into the kitchen, keys in hand. Her eyes widened when she saw the wet canines.

"What the heck?"

Marnie glanced up and tossed her a towel.

"Can you give us a hand?"

Sam stepped back toward the door.

"I left Carl to bring home the dogs. We were walking and talking when they jumped in the water. Okay?"

Narrowing her eyes, Marnie nodded.

"Yeah. Teddy and I can manage it."

With that, Sam opened the door and left.

Hands on her hips, Teddy frowned and asked, "Why'd you volunteer me? I was going out."

"I needed to get rid of him. C'mon! We've got somewhere to be."

Chapter Nine

Wild Creek Ranch, 11:23 AM

"Why did you bring a flashlight, that old wagon, and a gun?" Teddy tramped behind her, glancing up at dark clouds rolling over the mountains. "Where are we going?"

Marnie grabbed her friend's arm, pulling her along the grassy path.

"The schoolhouse."

"Why?" said Teddy, stopping and digging in her heels.

The psychic spun around and said, "What if Bob left me a clue? He *always* carried a notepad, but they didn't find anything on him."

"How do you know?"

"Call it a gut feeling."

"What do you mean? Left you a clue? Why would he do that?"

"Because when I was a little girl, he would leave scraps of paper with notes on them for me to find. The notes always led me to a treat, like chocolate or licorice jellybeans."

"Licorice? Yuck! You think he left you jellybeans?"

Sighing with frustration, Marnie clenched her hand around Teddy's forearm and dragged her forward.

"No! But I believe his notebook is in the schoolhouse and I will find it."

"What do you need me for?"

She patted her arm. "You're my lookout."

Creekwood Police Station, 11:30 AM

Holding back his anger, Danny sat on the edge of his desk, waiting for Randolph Stuyvesant to come through the door. From the station window, he had watched Randy exit Carrie Sutherland's blue fastback and walked up the stone steps to Creekwood PD. He glanced at his watch. Eleven-thirty.

When his partner walked through the door, Danny growled, "Where have you been?"

Insulted by the detective's gruffness, Randy sneered.

"I went to the schoolhouse and found nothing."

"You didn't go to the ranch, and I know that because the security system didn't ping on my phone. Had you been there, I would know it."

"Don't know what to tell you. I did go, but I didn't go up the driveway. I stopped at the side of the road and climbed over the fence."

"Is that right?" Danny drew himself up to his full six-foot-five and puffed out his chest.

The liar shrunk back a step. "Yes."

"Uh-huh. How did you manage that? The fence is electrified. If you had climbed over it, you would have been knocked on your ass."

Sputtering, Randy waved off Danny's comment.

"The fence mustn't have been on."

"The fence was and is on and I know that because I checked it before leaving this morning, and to be sure, I called and asked Elk and Arnie to confirm."

"I can't help you or *Elk and Arnie*—whoever the hell they are. I drove out there and didn't find a thing."

Captain Sterling stuck his head out of his office.

"What's goin' on out here?"

"Randy is a liar. That's what's goin' on. See if you can find out where he's been all morning because he wasn't at the ranch going over the schoolhouse with a fine-tooth comb. He was out with Carrie Sutherland. She dropped him off in her shiny blue Tesla."

Danny grabbed his jacket off the back of his chair and stormed out.

Wild Creek Ranch, 11:40 AM

"Okay. You stand over there by the oil drum while I go inside and search," said Marnie, pointing at an old, rusted cylinder.

"You mean trespass and snoop," said Teddy, taking up her position.

"I am not trespassing. This is my property. I'm looking for anything Bob may have left behind to help Danny," she said, crossing her arms.

"Yeah. Yeah. Justify it however you like, but I'm not going to get scolded by your boyfriend when he finds out what you've been up to. I'm only here because you pay my salary, and I can't afford to be unemployed."

"Bullshit! You want to know what's in here as badly as I do."

Teddy threw back her head. "Get it over with before Danny gets home."

"Back in a sec."

Marnie turned on her flashlight and opened the door. The knob made a grinding sound but gave way with a little effort. Shining the light around the room, she drew in a breath and stepped onto the old plank flooring. She thought back to July when she and Tom had explored Mr. Barnes' house on the island when he got caught up in the spider web. Closing her eyes, the image of him dancing about, long arms and legs flailing, trying to remove the silky and sticky strands, made her smile. When reality sank in again, she ran a hand across her forehead and choked back tears. He should be with her now, looking for clues and scolding her for going where they shouldn't be. Letting the memory fade, she shone the light on the ceiling, down the back wall and across the dusty floor.

A sleeping bag lay rolled up in one corner with a pillow resting against it and a woolen red plaid jacket hung on a hook near the door. A lone school desk with a rickety-looking stool sat under a paned window with wavy glass on the right. Remarkably, none of the panes were broken. Moving a few steps closer to the middle of the room, she inspected the space for a suitcase or knapsack and found both beside the old potbelly woodstove.

The suitcase was a green trolley-style and appeared to be the largest of a set. She rolled it to the window and hefted it on top of the desk. Hesitating for a moment, she wondered if she should invade the man's privacy.

"Sorry, Bob. You're gone and I'm trying to help. Please excuse my intrusion."

She unzipped the bag and threw it open. Inside, she found clothes, a few toiletries, notebooks, and pens. His laptop computer was at the bottom, together with his phone, chargers, and an emergency radio. The pockets held the usual array of socks, underwear, and a pair of reading glasses.

The knapsack was a different story. It was stuffed with fiction books, a digital recorder, and camera, and a yellowed envelope addressed to him in familiar handwriting.

"It can't be!"

Before Marnie could open the letter, Teddy called out.

"Oh, shit! I see your Jeep coming up the road! Dust is flying! I think Danny is pissed off!"

"Damnit! Okay! Give me a sec."

She pulled the wagon inside and loaded the suitcase and knapsack. As she wheeled the wagon toward the door, she heard a *thunk*. Backing up the wagon, she heard it again. Kneeling, she inspected the floorboards, finding one wobbly and loose.

"Hey, Teddy! Do you have anything I can use to pry up a board?"

"Ha! Yeah! Sure! I carry a crowbar with me everywhere."

Marnie rolled her eyes.

"Not helping! How about your keys?"

"No way! It could break!"

Throwing up her hands, Marnie opened the knapsack and searched for a knife and was rewarded with a pocket-size set of tools neatly zipped into a black leather case.

"Never mind!"

Back on her knees, she pushed a flathead screwdriver between the boards and lifted, revealing a black notebook with a loose SD card inside, which she pocketed. Getting to her feet, she dusted off the knees of her jeans, slipped the items into the knapsack, and met her friend outside.

"Wow! You struck the mother lode!" said Teddy, bending to inspect the contents of the wagon.

"Yeah." She pursed her lips together and held up a finger. "I'll be right back. I have to check one more thing."

Clicking on the flashlight, Marnie entered the schoolhouse again and walked straight to the desk. She examined it, searching for a place to put books, pencils, and paper. These weren't like the ones she had in her classroom, so she tugged on the top and it opened on a hinge. She smiled and gathered up a note and a bag of black jellybeans.

"I knew you were up to something, Bob. Thanks for not disappointing me."

Stuffing the items in the pouch of her hoodie, she joined Teddy outside once again.

Wild Creek Ranch, The Driveway. 12:40 PM

Forehead raised, Danny greeted Marnie and Teddy with a lopsided grin.

"What on earth are you dragging behind you?" he asked, his feet crunching on the gravel driveway as he positioned himself to see behind them.

Marnie dropped the handle of the wagon and crossed the short distance, stood on her toes, and planted a kiss on the detective's lips.

"That's my childhood wagon. It's seen better days, but that old Radio Flyer is still solid as the Christmas morning Santa brought it to me."

"I can see that," he said.

Teddy side-eyed Marnie and saw her chance to escape before the shit hit the fan.

"Okay. I'm off to Town Square. I have shopping to do," she said, scurrying around Danny to her hatchback parked a few yards away.

He hooked her arm as she tried to slide past.

"Not so fast. I know a guilty face when I see one. What have you two been up to?"

Teddy shouted, "It wasn't my idea!"

The detective released his grip and said, "Oh! This can't be good."

Chapter Ten

Hallowed Hills Road, 12:43 PM

Eighteen-year-old Krista Hansen flipped an auburn braid over her shoulder, kicked the front tire of her beaten up Chevy pickup and dropped the hood with a bang. She was on her way to a job interview at Ryan's Diner when her truck's radiator overheated and blew its gasket.

Throwing up her hands, she cried, "Now, what am I gonna do?"

Big drops of rain sizzled on the hood as she climbed back into her vehicle and searched for her phone in her handbag. Krista signed into her bank's app, checked her balance, and tears welled in her eyes. Fifty-two dollars and eleven cents would never get her a tow, and a taxi wouldn't come get her out here in the boonies. So, she did what she swore she wouldn't do. She called her father.

"Dad? My truck broke down near the four ways. I know we aren't speaking, but could you come get me?"

"You're not talking to me, Krista. I never stopped talking to you."

"Yeah. Okay. You're right."

"Where are you exactly?"

"Can't you track me with your GPS?"

"No. I disabled it when you accused me of spying on you."

"Oh." Wiping tears from her eyes, she continued, "I'm on the other side of the Billingsly ranch. Near the culvert."

"I'll be there soon."

"Thanks, Dad."

The Driveway, 12:46 PM

A big drop of rain splattered Danny's nose. He brushed it away and moved around Marnie to look at the contents of the wagon.

"Where'd you get that stuff?"

Marnie picked up the wagon's handle and headed for the steps.

"Help me get it inside, and I'll tell you what you need to know."

"Need to know? How about you tell me everything?"

Not meeting his eyes, she shrugged and said, "Yeah. That's what I meant."

"Uh-huh," he said, picking up the wagon and its contents, walking up the steps, and placing it on the deck of the back porch.

Teddy's eyes popped, and she nudged Marnie in the side.

"I can't believe he carried that!"

"Ha! He carried me up and down the stairs for a month before I could manage the steps. That's nothing."

"Wow! That's love."

Marnie cast a long glare Teddy's way.

"I'm not *that* heavy."

"That's not what I meant. Anyway, before these drops turn into an all-out downpour, I'm going to run into town. I'll be back in an hour or two."

"Chicken."

"Damn straight. You deal with the grumpy detective."

"I heard that!" yelled Danny from the porch. "And I am not grumpy."

Teddy hightailed it to her car and zipped out of the driveway.

"Is it my imagination or does she not like me?" he asked.

"She likes you, but I think you scare her. Her father is a little guy who wouldn't say boo. You speak your mind, and you are kind of gruff," she said.

He grinned and shook his head.

"There you go! Those dimples show up and you're not so scary."

"Yeah. Yeah. Yeah." His face reddened, and he picked up the suitcase in one hand and the knapsack in the other. "C'mon. Let's get inside before the rain hits."

She made her way up the steps carefully, not wanting to slip on the slick decking.

"Is your knee giving you trouble?" he asked, setting down the knapsack and offering her his hand.

"Nah. Just being careful."

The Kitchen. 12:55 PM

Marnie filled the kettle and set it on the stove, lighting a fire beneath it. The dogs pranced around the table, getting pats from the detective before settling.

"Let me make a cup of tea and then I'll tell you everything."

"I don't have a lot of time," Danny said. "I have to go meet with the Zonta gals. They saw the guy who assaulted Abel Jackson. He said it was a big dude—bigger than me, and it sounds like the same guy who was arguing with Bob Humboldt."

She poured Danny a cup of coffee, set it in front of him, and turned back to make her tea.

"I can try talking to Bob?"

"Will Lawrence allow that? I mean, if he's blocking you from others, what makes you think he'll let Bob talk?"

She wagged her head and sighed.

"Wishful thinking. At least I can give it a try."

"Okay. Be careful, though. I don't want the mad scientist getting into your head."

"I'll protect myself. Besides, if I can get through to Bob, it might help me get through to others."

A crash from the living room saw humans and canines jump and dash out of the room. Marnie gasped at the sight of a cracked mirror hanging on the wall as a crow swooped her head and landed on the window ledge.

"How did you get in here?" she said, crossing the room with slow, even steps.

"There must be a window open. I'll check the study. The French doors may be ajar." Danny disappeared, but returned a moment later, shaking his head.

The dogs paced in circles, keeping their distance from the bird.

He returned, saying, "Nah. Everything in there is closed, but I'll check upstairs."

Sam and Carl knocked on the back door, drawing barks from the fur balls. They found Marnie in the living room, kneeling before the crow. She glanced back and agreed with what her brother was thinking.

"He does look like Dad's bird, Osiris, doesn't he?" she said.

"Does he talk?" asked Sam.

She shrugged. "Dad was the only one who could get him to speak."

He held out his arm like a perch.

"Come, Osiris," he said.

The bird appraised him, then took flight, flying over them, relieving itself on Sam's head.

Marnie busted into laughter. Danny tried not to laugh, but couldn't help himself, and Carl, with a goofy grin, watched bird poop drip onto Sam's shoulder.

"That's not Osiris!" she said between fits of giggles. "But I hear that having a bird shit on you is good luck."

Sitting aloft on a curtain rod, the crow cawed before taking flight and soaring up the stairs.

"Isn't a bird in your home supposed to be a good omen? I think Gram may have told me that," said Danny.

Sam pulled his sweatshirt over his head, wiped the offending residue from his hair, and crumpled the shirt in a ball.

"I have never heard that one, but I'll take all the luck birds or anyone else wants to throw at me," he said.

Tater bounded to the window on the driveway side of the room and announced a visitor with a quick, shrill bark. Gus raced to the front door and Dickens to the back. Marnie joined Tater and saw a man with rust-colored hair and of average height getting out of a late model black F250. She estimated his age at late forties or early fifties. A moment later, the front doorbell rang, and Danny left to answer it.

Opening the door, he found the same person Marnie had seen, but being a cop, his observations were quite different. The man he saw was in the same age bracket, but the detective also saw a hardworking man, probably an architect or engineer, with a drinking problem, a failed marriage, and a habit of chain smoking.

"Can I help you?" he asked.

"Uh ... yeah. I'm Chris Hansen. My daughter called me a while ago from up the road. Her truck broke down and she wanted a lift to a job interview. I was hoping she walked to a nearby home rather than wait by her vehicle. Her name is Krista. Have you seen her?"

"No, sir, but I only arrived thirty minutes ago. Let me check with Marnie."

Danny stepped back, allowing the man to enter.

"Hey, Marnie! Carl! Has Krista Hansen been by today?"

Marnie replied, "Not that I'm aware. I was only out for a while, but I haven't seen anyone."

Carl said that he had seen no one either.

The man's shoulders dropped, and he rubbed a hand across his forehead.

"Why would she leave her truck? I told her I would be right there."

"Well, let me get my raincoat and I'll come with you and take a look around. There are a number of outbuildings on the property. She may have ducked inside one to get out of ..."

A crack of lightning and a drumroll of thunder shook the house, cutting off the end of Danny's sentence.

"Ah! Geez! I hope that didn't hit the windmill!" shouted Marnie from the other room.

The Kitchen, 2:40 PM

"Look, Mr. Hansen, we've exhausted a search of the property, and Sam and Carl have been up and down every road for miles. Perhaps Krista called a friend," said Danny, stripping off his soppy raincoat and hanging it on a peg beside the back door.

Chris Hansen shook his head. "I don't see her doing that. She'd already called me."

"While we were searching, you mentioned that you and your daughter hadn't been getting along. Could she have called your wife?"

"Ex-wife, and no. Her mother is visiting family in Nova Scotia and won't be back until next week."

"Do you have a list of friends you can call?"

With a quick jerk of his head, Hansen replied, "Yeah. I can do that." He glanced out the window and hesitated. "Look. I need a cigarette. Do you mind if I go out on the porch and smoke?"

"Uh ... no. Go ahead. There's a coffee can out there where you drop your butts."

"Thanks. I'll call a few of her friends while I'm out there."

When he'd left the kitchen, Marnie, Carl, and Sam came in from the living room where they had been eavesdropping.

"Danny, we even investigated the Founder's Cemetery and checked inside the mausoleums and the caretaker's cottage," said Sam.

"If she was nearby, we would have found her. Were you able to ping her phone?" asked Carl.

Danny pursed his lips and ran a hand through his hair. "The guys tried, but it must be off or the battery is dead. We got nothin'."

They all turned to Marnie, who was pulling coffee mugs from the cupboard and setting them on the counter to fill. She felt their eyes on her back and turned to face them.

"Why are you looking at me?" she asked, brow furrowed.

The detective reached out a hand and squeezed her shoulder.

"We're hoping Madame Séance might have an idea where we should look?"

She curled her lip and scrunched her eyebrows together, cranky at being called a nickname she loathed.

"I don't have a clue, and if you keep calling me that, I won't tell you if I do."

"C'mon, Marnie. We could use your help. Any guidance would be useful."

"Where's her truck now?" she asked.

"Twenty yards beyond the four ways," said the detective.

"Take me there. I'll see what I can pick up."

Chapter Eleven

Hallowed Hills Road, 3:05 PM

Marnie Reilly stood in the pouring rain beside Krista Hansen's blue pickup. Water dripped from the hood of her yellow slicker and onto the toes of her bright red Wellingtons. She amused herself momentarily by thinking about how much her outfit looked like fried egg yolks with ketchup, one of her father's favorite combos.

"I've got the keys if you want to sit in the truck," said Danny, dangling them before her.

She grasped them, frowning at the rabbit's foot attached to the chain. Where in the world was Krista Hansen? Out there without her good luck charm. A flash of a moment skipped across her mind. A man wearing a green hunting coat and red scarf, fiddling with marbles. Not any marbles, though. What did her grandfather call them? Shooters, Boulders, Bowlers, and Ducks? The little marbles were ducks, but the bigger ones were for hitting the little ones in proper games. Papa Jack had an old blue tobacco can with a bugler on it, filled with all sorts.

Knuckle down slingshot, she thought. *Why did that pop into my head? Papa Jack? Are you there?*

When her dearly departed granddad didn't reply, she unlocked the truck, climbed into the seat and wrapped her fingers around the steering wheel and closed her eyes. Danny leaped forward when she visibly jolted backward, but she held up her hand to shoo him away. Covering her nose, she gagged and opened her eyes—a look of distaste marring her attractive features.

"She's been taken," she said, as she let go of the wheel and turned her head to the detective. "This is awful, Danny. A very bad man abducted her."

He placed a hand under her elbow and guided her out of the truck. Looking at her face, he saw clarity in the most beautiful aquamarine eyes he had seen in his life.

"You're sure, aren't you?" he said, pulling her into a hug.

Her tense frame relaxed and leaned against him.

"I can tell you what I saw, but I'm not sure it will do much good. The image was old. From ages ago. Like I was … in another time."

"It's a place to start. That's all we need."

Hallowed Hills Road, 3:20 PM

Danny rested a hand on Marnie's knee as they drove to the farmhouse. He only moved it when he had to shift gears.

"Listen. I have to go to that Zonta meeting by four o'clock. How 'bout I pick up a pizza on my way home and we can talk after we eat?"

"Pepperoni, mushrooms, and Italian sausage? Extra crispy?" she replied.

"Is there any other kind?" he said.

She put a hand on his and weaved her slender fingers through the detective's.

"That works for me. It gives me time to process what I saw and felt. And smelled. Yuck!" She cringed, pinching her nose with a thumb and index finger. "What are you going to tell Mr. Hansen?"

"The usual BS."

"Well, he has plenty to do. Talking to her friends and calling her mother will take some time. At least it will keep him busy, and he won't call you too soon."

"Well, I can honestly say that I don't have any information for him. We've got a photo of her, and I can ask everyone to be on the lookout, but that's about it. She hasn't been gone long enough for me to file a missing person's report."

"You do know that sounds lame, right?" she said, squeezing his hand.

"I do," he said.

Wild Creek Ranch, The Kitchen and Study, 3:28 PM

The house was quiet when the detective and Marnie returned. Sam, Carl, and the knuckleheads were nowhere in sight. As they took off their shoes and hung up their coats, Danny called out to them with no response.

"Huh. They must have taken the kids out for a walk," he said.

"In this weather?"

"Yeah. Probably not. Let's check the dungeon before I leave. I don't like you being here alone."

"I'm a big girl, Detective Gregg. It'll be fine. I'll lock up and turn on the security."

"Well, Ms. Reilly, I like it better when someone is around. We don't know what happened to Krista, and I am not taking a chance that the big dude everyone is talking about isn't lurking outside."

"Fair enough, but can you please stop calling it a dungeon? That makes it sound like I have bodies buried down there."

He laughed. "There could be."

"Ha-ha! Not funny."

Wrapping an arm around her shoulders, Danny set off to the study with Marnie, his willing hostage, in lockstep. The trapdoor to the tunnels lay open, and he called out once again. In response, Tater and Dickens raced up the steps and sat for pats. Gus emerged a few moments later with a beaten up tennis ball in his gob. He dropped it at Marnie's feet, who picked it up and squirmed.

"Gawd! This dog has more saliva. Eww!"

She tossed it down the steps, narrowly missing Sam, who caught it and dropped the slimy orb.

"We thought we heard someone upstairs," he said. "We were picking locks on the doors leading to town. Who knows what we might find?"

"Any luck?" asked his sister.

"I was coming back for my lockpicks when you came in."

The detective raised his eyebrows. "Lockpicks?"

Sam's crooked grin was his only reply as he pushed past them.

Carl appeared at the bottom step.

"Hey! You coming down to help?"

Marnie wrinkled her nose.

"No, thanks. The detective is off to a Zonta meeting, and I shall take full advantage of quiet time by soaking in a bubble bath."

But of course, she didn't. She waited for Danny to leave before gathering supplies in a sweetgrass basket, which she would use to shoo away the annoying spirits in her bedroom.

Cleansing The Homestead, 3:50 PM

Upstairs, Marnie changed into navy-blue sweatpants, Danny's XXL gray Tupper Lake hoodie, and a pair of slippers.

"Now, I'm going to deal with you, Lawrence Parish! I made this candle especially for you."

She gave an evil snicker and lit a white sage, lavender, rosemary, cedar, and Frankincense candle with a birch wick. The scent was not only wonderful; it was also divine—well, sort of. One of her spirit guides told her what concoction would push unwanted spirits out of her home, and the other had suggested a wooden wick for good measure.

With the candle sitting on the windowsill next to the closet door, she retrieved a large shaker of Morton's sea salt from the basket. After dropping a pinch in each corner of the room, she took a handful and threw it in the air.

"It won't hurt," she said, shrugging as she walked to the basket and took out a pint-sized canning jar filled with blessed tar water. Danny had helped her make it from scratch using fallen pine trees on her property, and Gram had it blessed by Father Charlebois after mass last Sunday at St. Patrick's. She poured the tar water into a spritzer bottle and got to work.

The dogs ambled in one by one and watched the ritual in comfort from the bed. They mumbled only once when she spritzed them for luck.

"Okay, Universe, do your trick. Bless my home and all who enter, and please kick to the curb anyone ..." She paused and looked warily around the room, then continued. "... or anything that means my loved ones or me harm. So be it!"

With that being said, she spritzed all around the doorways and window casings of her bedroom. Then repeated the same downstairs in each room's entry and exit points, including the French doors and the hatch in her study.

"I thought you were taking a bubble bath?"

She twirled around to find Sam sitting behind her desk.

Grasping a hand to her pounding chest, she shouted, "Jesus! What are you doing there? You were supposed to be in the tunnels with Carl."

"Taking the Lord's name in vain is dangerous, considering the last few years," he said, swinging his legs off her desk. "Carl had an appointment and I am writing a report."

He swiveled his laptop screen toward her and swung it back around before she could read it.

"So, what were you doing?"

She sighed, dropping her chin to her chest. "I'm de-spooking my house."

"Have you got one giving you trouble?"

Eyes filled with tears, she nodded.

"Hey! I didn't mean to upset you," he said, standing and going to her.

He held out his arms, and she fell into them, hugging him tight.

"Lawrence Parish won't go away!"

"Where is he?"

"In my room! He stands by the closet, staring at me."

Sam held her at arm's length and looked into her tear-streaked face.

"Can he hurt you?"

"I doubt it, but why take the chance?"

"Shall I yell at him?"

Her childish nod and trembling bottom lip told him yes, so he took her by the hand and led the way.

"Come on! Let's give him a piece of our minds."

The Kitchen and Marnie's Bedroom, 6:03 PM

Three happy dogs with wagging tails and drool-drenched jowls greeted Danny when he came through the back door. He carried one large and one small pizza box and a white paper bag filled with cannoli.

"Where's your mom?" he asked.

Tater turned and ran out of the room and galloped up the stairs. Dickens and Gus waited for the detective to take off his coat and shoes, then charged ahead of him. When he reached the bedroom doorway, he heard Marnie and Sam yelling. He pushed open the door to see them shouting at the spot where he had seen Lawrence Parish the night before.

"Get out of here, Lawrence! You are not welcome!" they said in unison—each shaking a fist at the ghost.

"Stop blocking people I want to speak with!" said Marnie. "You have no power over me or the spirits who want to communicate with me!"

To his amazement, Danny watched the evil psychiatrist shrink back and dissipate.

Marnie jumped up and down and clapped her hands.

"We did it, Sammy! He's gone!"

The siblings jumped and spun around at the sound of applause behind them.

Seeing the detective, Marnie limp-walked to him and draped her arms over his shoulders.

"We got him, Danny! He's gone!"

He chuckled and lifted her off her feet. "I see that! I saw him disappear before my very own eyes. There's nothing better than teamwork."

Sam held up his hands. "Hey! I did as I was told. She has all the spooky charm."

"And then some," said the detective, giving her a kiss. "Who wants pizza?"

Chapter Twelve

The Kitchen, 6:18 PM

Pizza boxes sat at the center of the kitchen table in Marnie's spacious country kitchen. The trio opted for paper plates and paper towels instead of china and napkins for their feast. The detective, psychic, and, uh ... assassin munched on large slices of pie and drank cold beers while discussing the day. An occasional grumble from beneath the table reminded them to save the top crust for the knuckleheads.

Holding up his notebook, Danny said, "Okay, Marnie. I'm not gonna tell you what the Zonta ladies said until you tell me what you have to say. I don't want to poison your recall."

Mouth full, she nodded in agreement. Once the pizza was chewed, she took a long drink from her beer bottle.

"Well, I wrote it down so I wouldn't forget," she said, pulling a slip of paper from her sweatpants pocket. "Ready?"

"Yes, ma'am."

"Okay. I saw a man rolling marbles in his hand. Not the little ducks, but the big ones for shooting a proper game. He was wearing tan pants, a green jacket, and a red scarf. I couldn't see his face, but he had gray hair. The words family tree kept coming to me, so I'm not sure if he's a relative or what. Anyway, after I saw him, I felt someone put a hand over my mouth and the stench was nauseating. That's what I believe happened to Krista. Someone grabbed her out on the road."

Danny twirled his pen over his knuckles—his steely blue eyes focused above Marnie's head. Without looking at her, he said, "Stench? What sort of smell are we talking about? Skunk? Or worse?"

"Umm ... nothing is worse than skunk, but this was like the worst body odor you've ever smelled in your life. I've worked with a lot of people over the years whose basic hygiene was questionable, so body odor is something you get used to. But this? It was like he hadn't bathed or brushed his teeth in months."

Sam sent her a knowing glance.

"There was a guy at Bayview who smelled of coyote scat. We often wondered if he used toilet paper or cleaned himself when he showered. It was running commentary that the guy smelled like ass."

"Oh, my god! That's it! And chloroform or ether. Is there a difference?" said the psychic.

The corner of the Detective's mouth curled in disgust.

"That's not great dinner conversation. That's enough until we finish eating."

"I don't have anything else disgusting to add. Sam nailed it and that's all I've got," she said.

"Have you tried speaking with Bob?" asked Danny.

"Not yet. But now that Lawrence has amscrayed, I can try."

"Good," he said, finishing his beer.

Marnie got up to fetch them all a fresh drink when her home phone rang.

"Well, that's weird. No one ever calls that line," she said, reaching to answer it.

"Hello?" she said, then rolled her eyes and nearly slammed down the phone. "What do you want?"

She covered the receiver and said, "It's Kate."

"Can you believe the nerve of her? Why would she call me?" said Marnie, plopping down onto the bench next to her brother.

"Kate shouldn't have access to a phone. How the hell did she pull that off?" asked Danny.

"She picked her uncle's pocket. That's what she told me before I hung up."

Sam ran his hands down his face and moaned.

Turning to Danny, he said, "She is a menace. How do we stop her from contacting us?"

With a deep breath through his nose, the detective lifted his shoulders.

"No idea."

Marnie rested her chin on her hand.

"I should go see her and get it over with. I've not told her off in a long time."

"No!" yelled the men in unison.

Her brother rolled his eyes, and he sighed.

"Do not go near her. Geez! That is the worst idea you have had since you wanted to keep that rattlesnake you found when you were four."

She poked out her tongue then lolled back her head. "In my defense, I didn't know it was venomous."

"Well, you know Kate is. Stay away from her."

The detective agreed.

"You don't need her getting inside your head. There's enough going on up there."

"Okay. Then you call Pine Ridge and tell them to take that phone away from her."

Danny pulled out his phone and said, "Done!"

A growl from under the table drew their attention beneath and away from the detective's briefing of his meetup with the Zonta ladies. Marnie, Danny, and Sam peeked at the dogs, who had been less chatty and attention-mongering than usual. Tater's ears were perked and his eyes intense. He stared at the windows looking over the back porch, and he let out a howling bark. The slam of a car door and an eardrum-shattering scream sent them all scrambling for the back door.

Sam pulled a pistol from his waistband and Danny grabbed one from his jacket, which hung on a peg. They glanced at one another before Sam unlocked and yanked open the door. Through the screen, they saw Teddy screeching, one hand in the air, and the other pointing to a figure lying face down on the decking.

"What the fuck?" said Sam, staring at the body.

Danny stepped out, careful not to disturb anything, and scanned left, then right. With an impressive leap, Tater shot past him and raced outside, flying off the top step as if the Devil himself were on his tail. Marnie grabbed Dickens' scruff and Gus' collar before they could launch after him.

"I'll get him," said Sam, vaulting over the victim.

"Get her inside!" said the psychic, voice uneven and high-pitched.

The detective skirted around the figure sprawled on the porch and took all four steps in one. He placed an arm around Teddy's shoulder and shielded her eyes with a big hand.

Looking back, he said, "Marnie, unlock the front door. I'll bring her around, so we don't mess up the scene."

She jogged to the front of the house and slid back the slide latch, twisted the deadbolt and unlocked the knob, before swinging the door open. When she flipped on the porch light, Danny and Teddy hadn't arrived, so she ventured outside to look for them. As she let the storm door close behind her, a thunderous blow to her head hit from her right. She stumbled sideways, sank to her knees, and passed out.

"Where did she go?" asked Sam, standing on the front veranda and searching over the railings.

"She must be off looking for Tater," said Danny as he helped Teddy up the steps and into the house.

Sam turned to go inside, but pivoted on the threshold and stepped back out.

"I don't hear her calling to him." He stood there listening, and then a bark drew his attention to the woods.

"What is it?" asked Danny.

"Tater. He's barking. Marnie's in trouble. We gotta go!"

The detective checked Teddy, told her to lock up, and sprung off the front steps with Sam.

Chapter Thirteen

Wild Creek Ranch, East Paddock Bridal Trail, 7:48 PM

Head throbbing and stomach churning, Marnie felt herself being lifted over someone's shoulder. Dazed but aware, she tried to scream, but the gag in her mouth prevented her.

Oh! Don't throw up! Nausea crept in as her stomach bounced on the shoulder of her captor, and the man who now ran through the woods to the east of her home. Tater barked in the distance, and she prayed he would find her and bring Danny and Sam with him.

Realizing her hands and feet were not bound, she made the brave decision to punch, kick, and twist.

Start with a twist, Reilly. It will throw him off balance and he'll drop you.

She took in a big breath through her nose and gagged.

Oh! Shit! It's the same horrid smell from Krista's truck. Is this the same guy who abducted her? If I clench my hands together and pound on him, I won't hit his back. I'm too tall. What will I hit?

Judging the distance, she knew full well that slugging him in the ass wouldn't do any good, unless she could get his tailbone, which was doubtful. So, she threw her weight sideways and hoped for the best.

Marnie hit the ground harder than she imagined—the wind knocked out of her. She tugged at the gag, pulled it over her head, gasping for breath. As she opened her mouth to scream, she was yanked into the air by her left foot, and she screeched out in pain. But before she could fight back, Tater leaped out of the trees and wrapped his jaws around the man's calf and shook. His mistress was released and fell to the forest floor with an *oof*. The dog released the leg and back-walked in a low crouch, growling and baring his teeth. When the man kicked out at him, Tater darted sideways, jumped and tore into his left buttock.

Marnie got to her knees, steadied herself on a boulder and pushed herself up. With no visible weapons in sight, she called out to Tater and ran toward her house, her dog at her side. Tater nosed her to run faster, but she stopped short as her hair was grabbed and she fell backward into the trees—only this time she didn't screech. She screamed, yelled, kicked and punched until he let her go.

"Get off of me, you animal!"

She clenched her left hand into a fist and struck the man in the nose. He yowled, slapped her across the face, and shoved her to the ground.

Danny and Sam crashed through a thick grouping of pines and trained their weapons on the behemoth standing over Marnie. Neither fired their weapons for fear they wouldn't hit the big dude but put a slug in his quarry.

"Step away from her," roared Sam.

"Do not touch her again!" growled the detective.

The man looked up and laughed, grabbed Marnie's foot again and began dragging her away. Tater dove and clamped onto his forearm, tearing through the black hoodie and skin. He swatted at the dog with his free hand, but he was such a big man his range of motion was stifled by his bulk. The Border Collie let go and darted to Danny, who had given the command, "Come!"

Sam fired off a round, catching the kidnapper between the shoulder blades. He didn't drop as expected, but hunched forward, as if catching his breath. Before Sam could get off another shot, he released Marnie's foot and disappeared into the woods.

"Don't go after him!" shouted Marnie. "It's too dark."

She looked up at the starless sky, and the low, thick clouds rolling west. Tater trotted over to her, nudging her under the chin with his nose. The detective and her brother helped her stand and checked her for injuries.

"Are you okay?"

"Where are you hurt?"

Their questions ran together, and she leaned into Danny, wrapping her arms around his waist.

"I'm okay. Please take me home. Teddy's probably having a cow."

The Living Room, 8:23 PM

The "cow" came in the form of a whiskey and ice filled rocks glass that rattled in Teddy's shaky hand.

"Oh my god, Marnie! Are you okay? What happened? Aw! Geez! Your head is bleeding and so's your lip!"

Covering her mouth, Teddy ran toward the downstairs powder room.

"She going to puke. Why does she do that? It's *my* blood."

The men settled Marnie on the couch next to the fireplace, and Danny built a fire while Sam covered his sister with a quilt. The dogs milled around the room, sensing the tension.

"Can I get you a drink? Tea? Cocoa?" asked her brother.

"No. I'm okay. Really. Uh ... An ice pack for my head. It's pounding!"

Danny sat on the edge of the couch and assessed her wounds.

"I think we should get you to the hospital. You might have a concussion."

"I don't."

"How do you know? You're not a doctor."

"I've had my fair share of them. I am not concussed."

Sam returned with an ice pack, a glass of water, and extra strength Tylenol.

"I called Carl. He'll be here in a minute."

Marnie rolled her eyes. "You guys are making too big a deal of this. I'm fine."

"You're not fine. That guy tried to kidnap you."

"Yeah. That's the guy who grabbed Krista. I'm sure of it."

"Why do you say that?"

"He reeked to high heaven."

Danny nodded.

"Okay. Once Carl gets here, Sam and I are going back out there. See if we can find anything. Tater bit him, so maybe he ripped his clothing, or maybe he dropped something."

"Guys?" said Marnie. "Aren't you forgetting about the corpse on the back porch?"

"Damnit! I'll call Rick." Danny ran fingers through his thick, unruly hair. "When did it get so hard?"

"July fourth," she replied—her expression stoic.

"Yeah."

He squeezed her shoulder before wandering into the study. That's where everyone retreated to lick their wounds.

The Kitchen, 10:35 PM

The clock on the microwave read ten-thirty-five when Marnie, Danny, Sam, and Carl gathered for a stiff drink. Tater sat between the detective and the psychic on a bench at the table, with the psychiatrist and assassin opposite. Teddy was asleep on the couch—snuggled with Dickens and Gus as blankets. Pinecones sprinkled with lavender oil had been added to the fire to help ease her stress.

"It was clear he was wearing body armor. His movements were stiff. When he tried to hit Tater, he couldn't reach him," said Sam.

His sister nodded in agreement as she took a sip of her apple cider laced with generous shots of cinnamon whiskey.

"That's what I thought when he had me over his shoulder. He didn't feel natural, if that makes any sense."

"Ransom's vehicle was ransacked a few nights ago and the only thing missing were a couple of Kevlar vests. I would lay odds he has them."

Carl watched her eyes and held up his index digit across the table.

"Follow my finger," he said.

"Stop it! I'm fine."

"Humor me," he replied more curtly than normal.

She sighed with annoyance, but followed along.

"Okay. You'll be okay, but your face is bruising and will be worse tomorrow."

She tossed her head.

"What else is new? Ever since Ken, I've become an expert at applying makeup to cover up purple and yellow blotches."

The men didn't speak. How could they respond? What she said was true, and each carried a modicum of guilt for her injuries—even if it wasn't their fault.

"C'mon, guys. You couldn't have done anything to stop what happened—tonight or any other time. Bad luck and trouble happen for no reason at all. And remember—I have a knack for being in the wrong place at the worst possible moment."

"Are you claiming that as your superpower?" teased Sam.

She giggled and said, "No. That's saying the wrong thing most of the time.

Levity accomplished; Marnie turned the subject to the reason they gathered.

"So, Danny. What did you find out at your meeting about the goon?"

Savoring a sip of the hot buttered rum he'd opted for, he considered his interviews. The ladies had been more than willing to spill details of what they experienced the day Abel Jackson was attacked, but they all remembered different bits of information.

"I'm gonna summarize what they said because each had a different idea, description, and feeling about it. To the point: the guy smelled terrible—but skunky seems to be where they all landed; he had a dark-colored hoodie, but none could agree if it was black, charcoal gray, or blue; he was big, mammoth, and my favorite—ginormous. They all said he was bigger than me."

"But not as handsome, right?" added Marnie.

He grinned and shook his head.

"Nah! No one said that, but they did say they couldn't see his face. And Abel told me his face looked like someone had taken a wire brush to it."

"Road rash, maybe?" asked Sam.

"Your guess is as good as mine. Once we find him, we'll know, but right now, we have to find Krista Hansen. I can file a report first thing after what happened tonight."

He turned to Marnie.

"Are you sure it's the same guy? Or could what happened earlier have been a premonition? You know—did you see what he was planning to do to you?"

She scrunched her face in thought. "Hmm ... That's never happened before. I get stuff that has or will happen to others, but never me."

A knowing glance passed between the men. None of them wanted to bring up the feeling of doom she had hours before the explosion on July fourth. She'd told them she thought someone was going to die. She said she felt it and was nearing hysteria when her best friend stepped in to reason with her. It was Tom who calmed her down, gave her cotton candy, and convinced her everything was okay.

As if reading their minds, which she did occasionally, she said, "Then again, I had a feeling before the explosion. Perhaps ... No. That was Krista's experience. He didn't chloroform me. He did her."

"Are you sure?" asked the detective.

"Positive. I smelled the chloroform *and* the guy. I am one-hundred percent positive."

Tater's ears perked up, and he woofed as Rick Price knocked on the back door. Danny got up to let him in.

"Whatcha got?"

Rick threw him a shocked and disappointed expression, holding out his hands—palms up.

"What? Doesn't a guy get offered a coffee? You call me out in the middle of a pennant game, and you don't even offer me a drink. Geez! It's like you don't even know me."

Danny laughed and apologized.

"Sorry, pal. Want a coffee?"

"Yes, please," he said, sitting down next to Tater. "Hey, Tater Tot. How are you?"

The Border Collie answered him by sniffing his ear and licking the side of his face.

The forensics doctor nodded to Sam and Carl and offered Marnie's hand a friendly squeeze.

"How are all of you?"

"We'll be better once you tell us who that is or was out on the porch?" said Marnie.

"Ah. That's someone's idea of a sick joke, but it might come in handy here on the ranch."

Her puzzled expression, followed by a scowl, told the doctor she found his response obtuse.

"It's a scarecrow."

"What?"

"If it were any house but yours, I would say it was a Halloween prank."

Danny took over the questioning.

"What makes you think it isn't?"

"Because you sent Giles and me a message earlier, asking us to be on the lookout for a young woman with red hair. You said she was wearing a denim jacket, black jeans, a bright pink, long-sleeved Henley, and black boots."

"That's right. Mr. Hansen spoke to her housemate, and she told him what Krista was wearing when she left the house. He texted me, and I forwarded his text to you. So what?"

"The scarecrow either shops at the same boutique as Miss Hansen or is wearing her clothes."

Marnie and Danny double-checked the locks and security system before turning off the lights and going upstairs. Tater followed them through the house, in tune with their actions whenever the proverbial shit hit the fan. Dickens and Gus sat, waiting to be tucked in for the night.

Marnie hesitated at the bottom step.

"We should leave a light on over the stove. If Teddy wakes up, she might freak out to find the house in darkness."

Danny agreed. "I'll get it. Should we grab her another blanket, too?"

"No. She should be fine. That quilt is magic. It's the one Gram gave me."

"Ah. She'll be toasty. I can't believe she's still asleep."

"Shock does that."

"Then why are you still standing?"

"I'm weird." She screwed up her bruised face and winced when her bottom lip split again. "Dang it!"

"At least it didn't freeze that way," said Danny with a chuckle.

"No. It cracked. Ow!" She touched her lip, checking for blood.

"Right back," said Danny, disappearing into the darkness.

A moment passed and Marnie saw the glow of a light, and Danny returned to her on tip-toes.

"Let's get some sleep," he uttered, gently resting a hand in the middle of her back, coaxing her up the stairs.

"As if!" she said.

Chapter Fourteen

October 12th

Wild Creek Ranch, 3:45 AM

Marnie bolted upright in bed. Tater sat between her and Danny, facing away and looking outside. Gus and Dickens wandered the room anxiously, ears flat and tails tucked. The digital clock radio on her nightstand was black. No red numbers were there to tell her the time. She got up, walked to the window, and looked out. With a shiver, she blinked—not believing her eyes, and returning to the bed, she roused Danny with a gentle shake.

"It's snowing and the power's out. I don't remember snow this early, do you?"

"What? What?" he growled.

"It's snowing!"

"It's not cold enough," he said.

"Well, apparently it is."

Danny pulled on his sweatpants and a T-shirt and crossed the room to see if Marnie was dreaming. He scratched the side of his head and yawned.

"Huh. That is snow and come check this out. We've got company."

"He's back?" she squawked.

"No, but Ms. Sutherland and Detective Dickwad are."

"Let's hope the cameras catch them."

"Doubtful. The Wi-Fi will be out if the power is. Why didn't a generator kick on?" he asked, turning around.

She sunk to the bed and smacked herself in the forehead.

"Shit! I must have forgotten to reattach the batteries."

"Forget about it. I'm not gonna miss a chance to jam him up. I'll be back shortly," he said, pulling on a pair of socks.

"You're going out there?"

"Yeah," he said, tying the laces of a running shoe.

"Take Sam with you."

"No need to wake him. I'll be okay."

Tater hopped off the bed and pranced to the door as someone knocked.

Marnie turned the knob, opened it a crack, and peeked out. Her brother was there, dressed and ready to go.

Wild Creek Ranch, The Kitchen, 4:20 AM

Marnie glanced up from her cup of tea when the back door swung open and Danny and Sam stomped in, brushing snow from their hair. They kicked off their shoes and hung their coats as they griped about Randy Stuyvesant and Carrie Sutherland fleeing when the motion-sensor lights switched on.

"Did you turn on the generator?" asked Danny, more gruffly than intended.

"Nope. The lights came back on before I could get to the cellar."

Sam flipped through pictures on his phone, his face getting redder with each one.

"It was too dark. I doubt any of these can be lightened enough to get enough detail."

Marnie unlocked her phone and handed it to her brother.

"I snapped these from the side window in the front room. See if they're any better."

He slid through the images and shook his head.

"You were too far away. These are grainy."

Danny said, "Send them to me. I'll see if my guy can fix them."

Marnie's eyebrows shot up.

"You've got a guy?"

He laughed. "No. She's actually a gal who works in forensics. She fiddles around with pictures sometimes and cleans them up."

The siblings sent their files and were rewarded with two pings from the detective's phone.

Marnie pointed behind her. "I've made coffee."

Danny looked at his watch and sighed.

"It's four-thirty. No point going back to bed," he said, getting a mug from the cupboard. "Sam? You want a coffee?"

"Yes, thanks. A caffeine buzz will help me think."

Marnie nudged the sugar bowl toward her brother.

"What could they have been looking for at this ungodly hour?"

The detective took a sip of coffee before answering.

"Their steps led to the schoolhouse. I'm guessing Randy brought her out here to help him search it."

"So, you think he delayed his search until she was free to join him?"

"Yeah, I do. I think he's dumb enough to compromise the integrity of the scene to give her the scoop."

A cheeky smile broke across her face. "Ha! Silly him. I beat him to it."

Sam hid a grin behind his mug and Danny pursed his lips, then blew out an annoyed breath.

"You wore gloves, right?"

"Yes, sir, and I left everything but the evidence exactly as I found it. I'm not stupid. I know how to snoop without leaving a trail."

"Let's keep that our little secret, huh? I want him to think that I gathered the evidence. Where is it, by the way?"

"It's in the study locked in the safe."

Danny glanced past her into the living room.

"Is Teddy still asleep?"

Marnie nodded. "Yeah. She was snoring when I took the pictures. I even lit a fire without waking her."

"Is she okay?" asked Sam.

"I'm fine," said Teddy, rubbing her eyes. "Tater and Dickens woke me up."

"Ha-ha! Were they staring at you?" asked the detective.

"Yeah," she said, groggy with sleep.

"Coffee?" asked the psychic.

"Please. A whole pot!"

Wild Creek Ranch, The Kitchen, 5:20 AM

Left alone while everyone got ready for the day, Marnie sat at her kitchen table, twirling her teacup in its saucer. The reality of last night's events had sunk in. *I was almost kidnapped,* she thought. In a state of melancholy and physical pain, she gave herself permission to wallow in sadness and exhaustion, but before it could consume her, she took a series of deep breaths and counted her blessings. Some days she missed her best friend Tom Keller more than others—and her aching heart told her a tough day was ahead.

Unimpressed with the chilly and wet morning, Tater, Dickens, and Gus mumbled and grumbled beneath the table. Their heads poked out when the squeaky third step of the oak staircase alerted them that their secondary treat dealer was on his way. Tails thumped against Marnie's legs when Danny walked in—boots and socks in hand.

"What are your plans for the day?" the detective asked, sitting on a bench to put on his footwear.

"Carl suggested I wait a few days before seeing clients, and he's right. Anyway ... Teddy found a stack of packages I need to open. They were in the credenza. She stored them there when I was in the hospital and forgot about them."

She turned away, hiding the tears welling up in her eyes.

"Want to meet at the diner for lunch?"

"No, thank you." She gave a tight shake of her head and picked up her cup, taking a sip, to end the conversation.

"Okay. I'm catching up with my father at the cabin tonight for dinner. Do you want to come?"

"Uh-uh. I'll have dinner here with Sam."

He gave his bootlace one last tug, then got to his feet and held up his briefcase.

"I have Bob Humboldt's laptop, phone, and that SD card. I'll have Garcia drop them over to Rick to see if his guys can unlock them. The other stuff can stay here and I'll review it in private. I'd prefer Randy not have access."

With his hands in his pockets, he searched her face for the optimism that usually shone through. She'd dealt with so much darkness over the last eleven months, and he was thankful she was still alive. Some days, you would never guess she had a traumatic past. Other moments were like right now, where she would drift away and the light behind her eyes would dim. But he saw her fight for her life last night. The spitfire he fell in love with was still in there. She looked up at him and he saw a tiny flicker of her hiding behind the sorrow. The spark needed air to burst to the surface and ignite, and he knew where to find it. It would take him a few days—maybe weeks, but he'd make it happen as soon as he could.

"Okay," he said, crossing the room and dropping a kiss on her head. "I'll call you a bit later."

"Have a good day," she said, twirling the cup again, staring at the tea leaves in the bottom of the dainty vessel, looking for answers.

Wild Creek Ranch, The Kitchen, 7:10 AM

Teddy rapped on the back door and entered the kitchen to find Marnie peering into a cupboard.

"Mornin'! I've been down at the clinic and I've got a stack of papers for you to sign. Do you have time, or should I come back?"

"Yeah. I've got time before I tackle those packages. What have you got?"

Dropping the paperwork on the counter, a frown creased Teddy's forehead as she assessed her boss' mood.

"Have you eaten breakfast?" she asked.

The psychic shook her head. "I'm not hungry."

Teddy placed her bag on a bench and made her way to the fridge, searching for eggs and breakfast sausage. "Well, I am, and you've got to eat something."

"Okay. Back in a sec. I'm going to grab those packages and start opening them while you cook."

Marnie returned a few minutes later with a wicker laundry basket overflowing with packages.

"I'm embarrassed that I haven't opened these and sent thank-you cards."

"People understand. You've been recuperating. Besides, who sends a gift to someone who has almost died and expects a thanks right away? No one, that's who."

A petite gift wrapped in peridot green paper with a gold ribbon sat atop the pile. Marnie picked it up, untied the bow, and carefully unwrapped the present. The box was from a local jewelry store named Harrington's and was confirmed by the gold script on the lid. Opening it, she smiled at the sterling silver charm necklace with two Border Collies dangling from the chain, and immediately took it out and put it around her neck.

"Look at this, Teddy! Isn't it gorgeous?"

"Is that from Danny?" she asked, leaning to look.

"Could be. There isn't a card."

"You can ask him when he calls. Otherwise, you can call Harrington's and ask them."

"I love it!" she said, looking down at Tater and Dickens, who were snuggled up with Gus by the back door. "I must get a Labrador charm, too. We wouldn't want to leave out Gustifer."

Teddy agreed as she set down two glasses of orange juice.

"I'm sure they could get one."

Marnie turned over the brown paper package, searching for the sender's name. *Where did this come from?* Eyes brimming with tears, she remembered Tom coming into the house and handing it to her. Ransom was there and Sam was hiding out in the tunnel.

"You okay?"

"Yeah. I was remembering the day this package arrived. Tom found it on the porch."

"You'd better open it then."

She tore the paper, revealing the back of a book. When she turned it over to see the cover, she threw it across the table, spilling orange juice.

"Gawd! Three Billy Goats Gruff!"

Taken aback by her reaction, Teddy scowled, grabbed a tea towel and sopped up the juice.

"What the heck? Why'd you throw that? Is there a spider on it?" she asked, jumping away from the table.

"I hate that story. It scared the bejesus out of me as a child."

"Is it inscribed?" asked her friend, picking it up and opening the cover.

The flyleaf had a simple message hand-printed in uppercase letters: I HAVE FOUND YOU.

Teddy snapped closed the cover and set it on the counter, out of Marnie's reach.

The psychologist glanced up from another parcel and asked, "Anything?"

"No. But I'll take the book if it bothers you. There's a little library for kids near the park."

"That's a good idea. I would hate to traumatize another child, though."

"It won't. Remember, not all kids have your gifts. You see stuff most of us believe isn't real."

"Valid point. But a lot of children see spirits."

"We'll leave it up to their parents to censor their reading."

"Fair enough. I'll get a notebook and pen to write down who sent me what."

Marnie got up and headed to her office.

"Food is almost ready. Don't be long!"

As soon as the psychic was gone, Teddy shoved the book into her bag and zipped it up, thinking about how to get it to Danny without her boss knowing.

Chapter Fifteen

The Morgue, 10:10 AM

Danny opened the heavy metal door leading into the morgue. Medical Examiner Doctor Giles Markson heard the squawk of the hinges and glanced up from the report he was writing.

"Detective. I thought I would see you this morning. There's no news. We have seen no one matching Krista Hansen's description."

"Actually, Doc, I was checking in on Bob Humboldt's autopsy."

"Ah! That I do have," he said, removing an envelope from his out basket and handing it to the detective. "How's my goddaughter?"

"Thanks. Uh … she's been better. There was an incident last night."

Danny filled Giles in on the events of last evening, including the kidnap attempt and the creepy effigy.

"So, the scarecrow was wearing Krista Hansen's clothes? That's dreadful. It's only a matter of time before I meet her then."

"We hope not, but I'd say the chances of that are … uh … high. Rick is running DNA tests from a hairbrush and gym clothes he found in her truck. He'll keep you apprised."

"Thank you. Now, about my goddaughter. It might be best for her to have a full-time security team at the ranch. It's utter nonsense that she fights you and everyone else on matters of this nature. There have been far too many incidents."

"Yes, sir. I agree wholeheartedly."

"Should I come out and speak with her? Perhaps her Aunt Janet could talk some sense into her."

"She'll dig in her heels if we tell her what she should do. It has to be her decision."

Giles removed his readers and pinched the bridge of his nose.

"That girl is as stubborn as a goat. Just like her father."

Danny laughed. "I wish I'd met him."

Giles put his glasses in his pocket and patted the detective's arm.

"He would have liked you."

"Well, thank you. I hope so."

"What he wouldn't appreciate is how often she's put herself in danger."

Danny took a step back and his face lost all expression. "Uh ... Wait a minute. You believe that's my fault?"

"Marnie has always been inquisitive and up to mischief of one sort or another. But she seems to find herself in peril more often these days."

The detective held up his hands.

"Now, hang on. I do what I can to keep her safe and the security issue is not entirely up to me. If she doesn't want coverage full time, I can't force her. She doesn't like being controlled. You agreed to that point a few seconds ago."

"We need to do something. Where's Sam in all this?"

"He's with me and thinks the ranch could be tighter."

"You're both clever men. Convince her."

"Easier said than done, Doc."

Wild Creek Ranch, The Kitchen, 10:22 AM

With five packages left to open, Marnie took a sip of tea and sat back on the bench.

"Thanks for helping me, Teddy. I'm overwhelmed by the kindness of friends and strangers."

"You don't know everyone who sent you presents?"

"No. There are few people here I've never heard of."

"Well, isn't it nice that they know you?"

"Does that make me infamous?" she asked with a laugh.

"Your reputation proceeds you? People in town know who you are because of the charity work you do. You shouldn't be surprised."

"Yeah, but I try to keep a low profile."

Teddy smirked at her over her coffee mug.

"Well, clearly you don't."

"I'd like to get the thank-you notes out before Friday."

"Do you have enough stationery?"

"Good question. And no, I do not," said the psychic.

"Field trip?" asked Teddy.

"We could catch up with Danny for lunch, too. Let me open the rest, then we'll go."

Marnie plucked another package from the basket and checked for a return address. There was none. Tearing open the brown paper, she found another book, and it thudded to the table.

"Geez! Another dreadful fairy tale! Gawd! Hansel and Gretel. I hated that one too!"

Teddy snatched it up and looked at the flyleaf.

"No name on this one, either." She tucked it into her bag that sat next to her. "Another one for the kiddy library. I'll take it."

"Please do! I had nightmares about Sam and me getting gobbled up by old Mrs. Mix over there on Montgomery Road. Do you remember her?"

"Yeah. Every kid in town was terrified of her house."

"I truly believed she was a witch the way she used to sweep her front porch and caw at children. She was scary as all get out!"

"She's still alive, you know. Last I heard, she was living at Maple Valley Home."

Sadness spread across Marnie's face.

"Oh! I didn't know. We should take her a care package or something."

Teddy threw out her hands. "And there, ladies and gentlemen, is why everyone in town knows you."

Marnie giggled and shrugged.

"C'mon. Let's go get cards and call Danny on the way."

Teddy wrinkled her nose and drew a circle around her own face with her finger.

"You might want to cover up those bruises before we hit the town. We don't want anyone thinking Danny did that."

Marnie rolled her eyes. "I don't care what others think, but for the good detective's sake, you're right. Give me thirty minutes. I'll get out of these pajamas, and into jeans and a sweater, and put a layer of spackle on my face."

Creekwood Police Station, 10:30 AM

Danny arrived at the station as Officer Cheryl Garcia was leaving, and before she could step down from the entry, he asked her to wait.

"Can you give me a minute?" he asked, standing at the bottom of the granite steps.

"Sure, Lieu."

"Did you dig out that file for me?"

"Yes, sir. It's locked in your top drawer."

"Did you have a look?"

"Of course! My notes are attached."

"Anything helpful?"

She flipped her shoulder-length ebony bob and said, "Uh. Yeah! It's an old case, but there's always something new to discover. I think you'll be pleased with my detecting skills."

"Good stuff! Thanks, Garcia. Want to go through it with me?"

"Any other time, but not right now. I have a coffee date with a handsome public defender."

"A lawyer, Garcia? Geesh!"

"The female to male ratio in Creekwood swings heavy in your favor. Cut me some slack."

"Ha-ha! You've got me there. But hang on a sec. Can you drop these over to Rick before you go? Sorry to ask, but I'm swamped." He opened his briefcase on his knee and removed a large, padded envelope, handing it to her. "Have fun!"

"Thanks! I'll come back with the gory details."

As he ascended the steps, Randolph Stuyvesant walked out the front door, umbrella in hand. He averted his eyes as if it would stop the detective from seeing him.

"You know, when Marnie's dogs hide their eyes, thinking I can't see them, it's funny. When you do it, you look like an idiot. I saw you last night too. What'd you think? We wouldn't know you were on the property. Three dogs, a cop, and an ex-fed. Did you and your girlfriend find anything interesting?"

"Girlfriend? I'm not seeing anyone." Randolph stopped halfway down and stuck out his bottom lip. "Not that it matters. I was home last night watching a game."

"Which one?"

"What?"

"Which game? And at what time?"

With a smarmy grin, Stuyvesant pushed past Danny on the stairs, shoving a shoulder into his chest along the way.

The detective spun around and grabbed the other man's arm, and pulled him back up a step before releasing him.

"Don't fuck with me, Randy."

Stuyvesant stumbled, but regained his balance, and his slimy smile returned.

"You know, Gregg. I'm going to enjoy replacing you at this precinct. You are unprofessional, entitled, and Marnie Reilly has made a horse's ass out of you repeatedly. She's doing it again. The only reason you're angry is because you know if I dig deep enough, I will find something on her and her family."

"Is that right? You and Carrie Sutherland couldn't solve a game of Clue, let alone Bob Humboldt's murder."

"Not with you withholding evidence—I can't."

Danny's eyebrows shot up, and he glared down at his partner.

"What evidence might that be?"

"The autopsy report in your hand, and I know you took something from the schoolhouse."

The detective shook his head and waved the envelope.

"Nah. I picked it up a few minutes ago. And I haven't been in the schoolhouse. You were supposed to secure the crime scene and catalog the contents. Did you ask forensics to do a sweep?"

"I saw no point. There was nothing to find. He must have had another hidey-hole out there and I'm going to find it."

Randy turned his back and started down the stairs again.

"Yeah. Good luck with that, asshole," said Danny to himself.

Then he called Rick, telling him Garcia was on the way with evidence, and asked if one of his guys would go to the schoolhouse and do their thing. Doctor Price was happy to oblige.

Creekwood Town Square, 11:33 AM

The square resembled a ghost town as Marnie and Teddy drove up and parked on a side street. Lunchtime usually found shoppers and office workers buzzing around cafes and food vendors, drinking lattes and munching hot dogs, tacos, or pretzels. But the gloom of the day had people eating at their desks, cafes sparse with diners, and vendors shuttered.

Marnie pulled her jean jacket collar up and shivered.

"That wind is wicked. I bet we see more snow today."

Teddy stuck out her tongue in disgust.

"No! It's too early!"

The psychologist leaned her head back and pointed a finger in the air.

"Those are snow clouds. Ready or not, here comes the first storm of the season."

"Gawd! You almost sound giddy."

"I love the first real snowfall. And if it does snow tonight, I'll be out on the veranda to welcome it."

Teddy gave her a long, wary glance.

"Not on your own, you won't."

Marnie tossed her a grin, crooked an arm through her friend's, and dragged her toward Mrs. Backus' bookstore.

"Thank-you cards and what else do we need?" she asked, her nose pressed to the window that was decorated with pumpkins, ghosts, and witches.

"No idea, but if we're going in there, you better take away my credit card."

Creekwood Police Station, 12:30 PM

At his desk, Danny leafed through Cissy Miller's murder book and frowned when he saw Garcia had found connections to seventeen other cold cases. Within the span of seventy-five years, women in Creekwood, Hudson Hollow, and the tiny hamlet of Oswegatchie Mills had been abducted, gruesomely murdered, and dumped on their own property within a day or two of their disappearance. The detective's blood ran cold when he read Garcia's final note. The women's eyes had been plucked out and replaced with marbles of varying sizes. *Bowlers, boulders, shooters?* thought Danny. *What were the little ones? Ducks?*

He drew in an unsteady breath and flipped through the pages to find Cissy's autopsy and the air burst from his lungs as he read, "two black glass marbles measuring twenty-five millimeters in diameter inserted in ocular sockets." The next line of text made him queasy: "Contents of stomach: apple pie, cornbread, ham, sweet potato, and victim's eyeballs."

The most recent event was last November, when he first met Marnie. While most of the incidents were long before he was born, seven were within the past twenty years. He scratched his beard and wondered if Paige Reynolds was on the killer's list. She had auburn hair. Had Marnie and Tom interrupted him? But Dalton Hooley had confessed to her murder. Danny closed the murder book, locked it in his desk, and pushed back his chair as Marnie and Teddy came through the door.

"Got time for lunch, Detective?" asked Marnie, a grin on her bruised face.

"Uh ... Yeah ... Sure. Gram's diner?" he said.

His visit to Pine Ridge would have to wait.

Chapter Sixteen

Hallowed Hills Road, The Four Ways, 12:37 PM

Sleet fell from the sky but before it could land with grace to earth, a wicked north wind flung it sideways into the stop signs at the four ways where it froze on impact. Carrie Sutherland's bright blue Tesla was pulled off the road, tucked behind a ramshackle gray weathered shed. She watched her rearview for Randolph Stuyvesant's unmarked car to drive up behind her. When she saw him approaching in the mirror, she grabbed her fuchsia umbrella and got out of her vehicle, pulling her scarf tight against the biting air.

"Don't worry, Randolph. I saw Marnie Reilly in town twenty minutes ago."

She held out a hand, feeling for precipitation.

"Do not open that!" Stuyvesant said, pointing at the umbrella and stepping out of his unmarked car. He straightened his shoulders and buttoned his trench coat. "Of all colors for an investigative reporter to carry. Purple?"

"It's not purple. It's fuchsia. There is a difference."

With a dismissive wave of his hand, he said, "Pull your scarf over your hair if you're worried about a little rain. That thing will draw attention we don't need. Danny Gregg is all over my ass about you."

"You're not allowed to have friends in the media?"

"Not really, no," he said as he assessed her choice of wardrobe. "Carrie, that suit and those shoes weren't designed for walking through a field. Did you bring other clothes? A coat at least?"

Cheeks flaming, she shot back. "I did not. Look! I've done fine all these years. A lecture from you about fashion ... Really?" Her eyes looked him up and down with disgust. "Only Sam Spade can pull off a trench coat. Even Columbo looked ridiculous, but I'm sure he was a damn sight better than you at sniffing out the truth. You've got nothing, Randy."

"My coat is practical. Chanel is not."

"Chanel? Ha! It's Ralph Lauren. And that's not the point. You were supposed to help me get information on Mr. Humboldt. Where is the autopsy report?"

"Gregg has it. The medical examiner said it wasn't ready when I visited him, but I know he gave it to Danny. He mocked me with it."

"Mocked you? Are you for real? Jesus, Randolph! Be adult about it. And while you're at it, hold up your end of our little bargain, and I'll make sure Detective Gregg loses his job. Even his father won't be able to protect him. But you must deliver the dirt on Marnie Reilly and her family. What have you found?"

"I know what you know. There are whispers all over town about her, but I am not close enough to anyone for them to confirm it. I've tried looking through files to see if reports have been manipulated to protect her. There's nothing. What's your beef with her, anyway?"

"Never mind about that. I have my reasons. What about Sam Reilly? Isn't he..."

Stuyvesant let out a haughty laugh.

"A hero? Is that what you were going to say? Geez! He helped put away two corrupt feds. His name has been cleared."

Carrie glanced down at the icy ground—her forehead lined with thought.

"I thought he killed those cops at the Reilly house last November."

Randy shook his head.

"No. That was Kate Parish. Now there's a story for you. The Parish family is twisted."

She huffed out a breath and rolled her eyes.

"Hmm … That's what I heard. Besides, that's old news. Everett Channing did a story on it in August. It wasn't anything earth-shattering or brilliant, but it's not worth another look."

"He didn't interview Marnie or her brother, though. There's your angle. Could be an in?"

Closing her eyes, she rubbed three fingers across her forehead. The longer she massaged, the broader her satisfied grin grew.

"You know. It's been a while since I have played nice with a woman to get a story. Hmm … I do like a challenge."

"Weren't you flirty with Gregg yesterday?"

"It's easy with men. You're all so stupid."

Randy bit his lip, allowing the insult to fly by.

"But he didn't tell you anything."

"I didn't try terribly hard. Now! How do I make friends with Marnie?"

"You need therapy."

"Excuse me?"

"She's a psychologist. Don't you want help with your daddy issues?"

"I do not have daddy issues! My father was a wonderful man."

"Have you ever been abused? Domestic violence is her specialty."

Her face dropped, but the smug grin returned.

"You know. I did two years of drama in college. Perhaps it's time to use it."

"I don't get it. How is that going to get you the story?"

"Trust me. It will. But then again, I doubt she'll fall for a ruse."

She reached up and straightened Stuyvesant's tie, pulling it a bit too tight, causing his eyes to bulge.

"You worry about making nice with the detective.," she said.

"Ha! How am I supposed to do that? I threatened him an hour ago."

"Eat crow, Randy. I hear it tastes better with a glass of twelve-year-old scotch—served neat."

Ryan's Diner (and Pub), 12:40 PM

Gram set a plate of meatloaf with mashed potatoes, gravy, and peas before her grandson, who sat on a bench alone—the gals giving him elbow room and sharing the seat opposite. Dorie followed with a basket of rolls, a steaming bowl of Irish stew for Marnie, and a crock of clam chowder with a side of oyster crackers for Teddy. She offered the diners a smile before retreating to tend to other customers.

Danny's grandmother patted Marnie's shoulder.

"It's lovely to see your appetite has returned, lass."

"Well, I can't guarantee I'll finish this, but I will do my best."

"Would you like me to box up somethin' for your dinner tonight?"

"Thanks, but no. Sam and I can fend for ourselves. After we leave here, I'm off to the grocery store to buy fixings for a big pot of chili. We both love it and the leftovers."

"That's perfect for a cold day like this," said Teddy.

"You're welcome to join us."

Spoon in her mouth, Teddy shook her head.

"No, thanks. I'm meeting Casey Lange at Oscars for dinner and drinks."

With a look of surprise and joy, Marnie nudged her friend, who sat next to her at their booth table.

"Oh, really? How long has this been going on?" she teased.

Amused by his girlfriend's mood change, Danny asked, "Who's Casey Lange?"

Eyes lit with mischief, Marnie said, "Oh! Only the second cutest boy in our high school?"

"Who was the cutest?" he asked.

The mood dropped, and both women replied, "Tom."

"Holy crap! Marnie? Teddy?" cried a woman from the front of the diner.

The gals' heads popped up, and both grinned.

Marnie hopped to her feet, stepped into the main aisle of the busy diner, and held out her arms. Danny stood and turned around to see who his girlfriend was fussing about, and standing near the front register was a small woman with an open face, mischievous light blue eyes, and hair the color of the first run of maple syrup in spring.

"Poppy Chomsky! Give me a hug, you ratbag! How long have you been back in town?"

While many would have been embarrassed by Marnie's loud invitation for a hug, and the name-calling, this woman wasn't. She was used to it and trotted headlong into her friend's waiting arms.

"It's so wonderful to see you! Where have you been keeping yourself?" The psychic slid into the booth next to Danny as Teddy handed across her bowl of stew and slid closer to the wall, making space for their chum.

The old friend sat and looked up at the detective, who remained standing.

With a little wave, she said, "Hi ya!"

"Hi. You were classmates of these hooligans?" he said with a teasing smile before taking his seat, clearing his throat, and shoulder nudging Marnie.

Slapping herself on the forehead, she apologized. "Sorry! That was rude of me. Poppy, this is my boyfriend—Danny Gregg."

"Marnie and I were in the same circle, but Teddy was a bit stuck up. Ha-ha!"

"I was not!" cried Teddy.

The psychic psychologist gave an exaggerated snort. "Uh ... Yeah. You were."

Poppy leaned across the table and tapped the end of Marnie's nose. "So glad to see you haven't had your freckles removed."

"Why would I do that?" she asked, scrunching her face.

"I saw Mandy Hodges this morning and she's had hers lasered or something. I don't understand. Who would you or I be without our freckles?"

"Hmm ... My mother always told me mine were angel kisses, so I'm not messing with them," Marnie replied.

Gram approached them and asked the newcomer if she wanted lunch.

"Yes, thanks. Could I have a cup of chowder, please?"

The older woman frowned. "Only a cup? That's not right. You need more fuel than that on this cold day."

"I'm a gal on a budget. I moved back recently and I'm job hunting."

"Bring her a crock, Gram. I've got lunch," said Marnie.

"Well, ya won't. You're all guests of my grandson. I won't take a cent from any of ya."

Gram scuttled off before they could argue.

"What kind of work are you looking for?" asked Danny.

Poppy helped herself to a warm roll and set it on the napkin Teddy slid across the table to her.

"Well, I was going to drop by the school to see if they need help, but Mandy told me they aren't hiring."

Teddy said, "No. They're not. They let me go a few years ago and they had more cuts in August."

"Are you a teacher, Teddy?"

"Ha! No. I worked in admin. Teaching was never on the cards. My lack of patience and all."

Marnie scoffed. "You're patient. Gawd! You put up with me."

"You two work together?" asked Poppy.

Both, with their mouths full, nodded.

Danny took advantage of the brief lull to excuse himself.

"Ladies, I am going to leave you to visit. Work calls."

Poppy studied his face, then burst into laughter.

"Oh. My. God! You're the grumpy detective I've been hearing about."

With an awkward grin, he nodded.

"Yeah. That's what some folks call me around here. But I'm really not. It's just my face."

Marnie grabbed his hand, wrapping her fingers through his.

"Until he smiles, and those dimples make an appearance. Then they see he's a very handsome man."

"Yeah. Yeah. Yeah. Scoot over and let me out. I've got bad guys to catch and a girl to find," he growled playfully, cheeks tinged with red.

Marnie got up from the bench, and the detective stood, giving her a hug.

"I'll call you when I'm on my way to the cabin. Make sure you lock up when you get home," he said.

"Will you be home tonight, or will you stay over?"

"Uh … That depends on how late it gets. But I'll do my best."

"Okay. Well, Sam's at the house, so I think I'm safe."

"He won't let anyone get in. Neither will the knuckleheads."

"Oh! Kiss her goodbye already and go so we can talk about you," said Teddy.

Danny looked down at her and sneered.

"You know. You are as annoying as my sister."

He kissed Marnie, then grabbed his plate of food. Stopping at the counter, he got a to-go box and slid in his meatloaf, dropped money in the tip jar, and collected two takeaway coffees.

"Shit! Did I piss him off?" asked Teddy.

"No. He's got a lead to follow. He grabbed coffees on his way out, which means he's going to see Rick Price."

Marnie sat down and turned her attention back to Poppy.

"Now. What kind of job do you want?"

"I'm a child psychologist. Pine Ridge could be the place to start."

The psychic psychologist threw her hands in the air.

"Hallelujah! Ask and ye shall receive!"

The two women sitting across from her frowned and said, "What?"

Chapter Seventeen

Wild Creek Ranch, The Schoolhouse, 12:42 PM

Red Harwick picked his way through the rubble at the rear of the tiny school, searching for clues. Doctor Price had asked him to come to the farm to dust for fingerprints and gather any forensic evidence he could find. Rick's exact words were, "Give it a good going over and don't leave any stone unturned. That fucking jackass Stuyvesant needs a lesson in Police Detecting 101. Secure the damn scene!"

He had been here before—last July fourth following the explosion. Having arrived as emergency services were pulling Marnie Reilly and Tom Keller from the rubble, Rick sent him to the hill above the tunnel entrance to collect debris. There were two bloodied officers sitting in the grass, refusing help until Ms. Reilly and Detective Keller were on their way to the hospital. *What were their names? Tartetto and Connors, I think.*

Lost in the memory, he didn't hear the footsteps coming up behind, but when he turned, he recognized the detective walking toward him. He had a woman with him who looked familiar.

"What are you doing here?" Stuyvesant asked, hands in his pockets, rocking on his soles.

"Doctor Price sent me out to process the scene. I'm nearly done."

"Why wasn't this done two days ago?"

Red dropped his head, scratched the copper stubble on his chin and played dumb while delivering a well-placed jab.

"Doc told me the jackass who was supposed to notify us didn't. That's all I know. I'm following orders and cleaning up a mess before it becomes an issue for forensics."

Randy pursed his lips, then blustered, "Rick Price is working with bad information. He shouldn't make flippant comments about his co-workers. Creekwood PD is short-staffed. We cannot be everywhere."

The tech shrugged and snapped off his gloves.

"Look. I gotta finish up here. Don't touch anything until I'm done."

"What have you found?" demanded the detective.

"Nothing ominous. I'll check the prints and fibers when I'm back at the lab."

"Personal belongings? A notebook? A sleeping bag? Anything?

Harwick clenched his jaw, wishing he could drop Stuyvesant on his ass.

"Well, yeah. A guy was sleeping here. But I have to process those items."

"I want a full report. Don't give it to anyone but me."

Randy pulled a card from his pocket and thrust it at Harwick, who took it but disagreed.

"Can't do that, Detective. It goes to Doctor Price and then he'll pass it along to whomever asked for the scene to be processed."

"It was Gregg, wasn't it?"

Harwick held up his hands.

"No idea. But at a guess, probably."

Carrie, who had been hiding behind Randy, stepped out from behind the detective.

"C'mon, Randolph. There's no point arguing with a *subordinate*. Take this up with Doctor Price and Detective Gregg. He's only following orders."

"Hey! You're Carrie Sutherland!" said Red. "I've seen you on the news."

"No, she's not," sniped Randy.

"Who are you trying to kid? I'm not blind. I'd know a Ralph Lauren suit anywhere. It's all she wears. My fiancée is in design school. She's talked about it a million times."

Carrie ducked behind the detective. Not so much worried that she'd been seen, but to hide the beam in her proud face and sideways air punch. *Someone knows my brand. Yes!*

"Look! Keep this between us, huh? Don't go tattling to your boss," said Stuyvesant.

"You should mention it to Doctor Price yourself." Red glanced at his cases before locking eyes with Randy.

The detective sensed an edge of aggression in the tech's voice and decided not to push his luck.

"Okay. I look forward to reading your report."

"As I said, that's not up to me."

Red turned his back, pretending to get a pair of fresh gloves out of his bag. Of course, he wasn't. He was sending a text to Rick.

Creekwood Police Station, Forensics Lab, 1:20 PM

At the doorway of Rick Price's office, Danny Gregg held out an offering of hot coffee.

Peering over his glasses, the doctor said, "Excellent timing. I got a call from Red. He's on his way back and asked me for your number."

"Why's that?"

Ding! The detective looked down at his phone and handed Rick a coffee before opening a message.

"Son of a bitch! Randy was over at the school with Carrie Sutherland again. They were lurking around the property last night, too, but the security lights scared them off."

"Why would he do that? He could have gone in daylight. Why sneak around?"

The detective lifted a shoulder.

"Who the hell knows? But I don't trust him. The reporter is looking into Marnie's family. She thinks there's something sinister about the Reillys. My guess is the good witch put her in her place at some point."

"Ha-ha! That girlfriend of yours has a way of doing that."

Danny smirked. "All those times, she accused Tom of not having a filter. Do you reckon she knows she's lacking, too?"

"Peas in a pod."

"Yeah," said the detective, looking out the window, thinking of his old partner.

"Anyway!" Rick pulled him back. "I'll have the report from the schoolhouse when you bring me my morning coffee, but I'm still waiting on Krista Hansen's results. Oh! Garcia dropped off your package this morning. We haven't been able to get into the laptop, phone, or the SD card."

"I figured it would take a while. But, here's a tidbit I forgot to share. My sister was at the house the other night when I asked if anyone knew Bob Humboldt. The name was familiar to her because she took a report from him about a guy dealing drugs at the Ridge."

"No kidding! Maybe he got whacked for squealing. Look. Don't mean to rush you, but my team and I are needed in Hudson Hollow."

"What's goin' on there?"

"A college student has gone missing. Disappeared from the campus library two nights ago."

"Boyfriend?"

"I don't have all the details yet. Detective Beck called and asked if I could come over and dust for prints. Her books, backpack, and Thermos were still there yesterday morning, but she wasn't. It's a bit weird for them to call me, but I think they're grasping at straws. She's Dean Alder's daughter."

"Yikes! Did you say *Detective* Beck?"

"Yeah. Why?"

Danny laughed. "I think that's the guy Marnie punched in the face for kicking Tater."

"Why the hell would anyone kick the Tot?"

"Beck and Hall were keeping an eye on the house last November. I honestly can't remember what happened, but they were stirring shit and Tater growled or nipped at them."

"Well, they must've deserved it. Anyway. I have to get over there before the dean implodes. He's on the warpath, and it sounds like I'm the only one who can calm him down."

"Send him my best, huh?"

"You know him?"

"Yeah. He and Sarah were friends."

"Ah. Sorry."

"No need to apologize. My past isn't taboo. I've come to realize that there wasn't anything more I could have done. Sarah died. I grieve every day, but I can't change it. No matter how many cabins I build or pieces of furniture I refinish—she's gone and I'm not."

"That's healthier than wallowing."

"I did enough of that. Anyway ... I better let you get to it."

"I'll call when the report is done and when I've got something on the Hansen case."

"Thanks!"

Ryan's Diner (and Pub), 1:40 PM

Marnie, Teddy, and Poppy were saying their goodbyes, standing on the sidewalk outside of the diner. The rain and sleet had subsided, and the sun was shining, but the wind was relentless, blowing leaves in its fury. The green and white awning above Ryan's Diner squeaked and squawked with every gust.

Teddy's phone dinged and she checked the screen. "Dang it! Casey canceled. I guess it's chili at yours, Marnie."

"So, Poppy. Do you have dinner plans tonight? I would love it if you could come out to the ranch and meet my business partner, Carl Parkins. Like Teddy said, we're having chili."

"I'd hate to intrude. Besides, talking shop over dinner is boring?"

Teddy squeezed Poppy's elbow. "Come for dinner."

"Please," said Marnie. "It's nothing fancy. Sam will be there too. You remember my brother, right?"

With a raised eyebrow and lower lip out, Poppy stepped back.

"Hmm ... Wasn't he in prison for murder?"

"He's been exonerated. None of the bad stuff you heard is true."

"Okay. Well. Sure. I'll come out for dinner. What time are you planning? I need to go to the inn and swap rooms before three. Mrs. Charles has a family coming into town and she needs the big bedroom."

"I thought you'd be staying with your folks. Sorry for assuming."

"No. Mother and Dad split about six months ago. They sold the house, and she's living in a one bedroom over the hardware store. He moved to Hudson. I'm pretty sure he's hiding a girlfriend."

"Ouch! Is your mother okay?" asked Teddy.

Poppy waggled her hand. "So-so. Staying with her was out of the question, though. All she does is snipe about Dad. He isn't perfect, but neither is she."

"Why don't you crash at the ranch for a few days until you can figure things out? I have heaps of room," offered Marnie.

"She really does. Two bedrooms downstairs. Four spare up. You'll love it!" Teddy clenched the woman's hand, excited to spend more time with her.

"And sleeper sofas in the living room and study," added the psychologist.

As if the sidewalk could divine an answer, she stared at the cement for a long moment before lifting her head.

"I think it would be nice to spend time with friends."

"Yay!" said Marnie. "My house is at 818 Hallowed Hills Road. It's right across from the Founder's Cemetery."

"You live in Spooky Hollow?" said Poppy with an eek and a gulp.

"Yeah. The old Billingsly ranch. Do you remember it?"

"I do. Did I read somewhere that Jonas is in jail for killing Lanie Howard?"

"Gawd! We have so much to catch up on!" said Teddy.

Marnie gave Poppy a quick hug.

"Dinner's at six-thirty. Come earlier if you want. We have to grab groceries, but we'll be back at the ranch in about ninety minutes."

"Cool! I'll see you in a few hours. Can I bring anything?"

"Your appetite! See you soon!"

With a wave, Poppy said, "See ya!"

Creekwood Police Station, 1:42 PM

With a fresh cup of coffee in hand, Danny entered the ground floor of the precinct. He wrinkled his nose and waved to Sergeant Lou Beaumont, who stood in his windowed cage eating his lunch.

"Gawd, Sarge! What's that smell?"

Lou held up a plastic container and finished chewing.

"My lunch. I've been trying to lose weight. Too many meals at the diner have caught up with me."

"Yeah, but *that* stinks!"

Lou shrugged, oblivious to the stench.

"Leftover liver and onions with a side of spinach. It's not bad if you don't leave it in the microwave too long."

"Better you than me," said Danny with a grunt.

"Cap's lookin' for you. Word is, Randy had a tantrum because you don't play nice or share."

"Randy can kiss my ass. Is Cap still around?"

"Yeah. He and the chief are upstairs."

Danny frowned at the prospect of getting yelled at by Captain Sterling with his father sitting there. He wasn't afraid of Mac Gregg. It was the disapproving looks that got him.

"Thanks for the heads up, Lou. Enjoy your lunch."

He took the steps two at a time and swung open the door to the squad room, trusting his bosses knew that Randolph Stuyvesant was a pain in the ass and a world-class whiner. Before they could summon him, he walked straight to the captain's office and knocked twice.

"In!" came the response from the other side of the door.

Danny turned the knob and entered without hesitation.

"I wanted to give you an update if you're free," he said.

Chief Gregg was the first to speak.

"How's Marnie? Pete filled me in."

"She's bruised and has had a fright, but she's doin' okay. You know how she is. Even if she wasn't, she'd say she's fine."

"Would you prefer dinner at the ranch tonight rather than leaving her alone?"

"She's whipping up a batch of chili. If that sounds good, I'll call her and tell her to set the table to include us."

Mac rubbed his chin, his blue eye sparkling with the possibilities of a home cooked meal.

"Chili, you say. The one with pepperoni, served on yellow beans? And those little oyster crackers, too?"

Danny nodded. "Yeah."

"I'm in if she has enough."

"Okay. Let me call and find out how big a batch she's making. I'll be right back."

Danny stepped out and called his girlfriend, who answered on the first ring.

"Hello, Detective. Miss me?"

"Always, Ms. Reilly. Hey. Have you got room for two more at dinner? The Chief is partial to your chili."

"Uh. Yeah. I'm at the grocery store now, picking up supplies."

"Pepperoni, yellow beans, and oyster crackers?"

"Amongst other ingredients."

"Great. Count us in."

"There's plenty for Captain Sterling, too."

"Mm ... It would be rude if I didn't invite him, huh?"

"If he's sitting right there, yeah."

"Okay. I'll let you know."

"Great. Dinner is at six-thirty."

"We won't be late."

The detective returned to the office with the happy news.

"It's the chili you like, so I told her we'd be there at half six."

"Perfect!" said Mac.

"She invited you too, Cap. Want to join us?"

Peter Sterling rubbed his bearpaw hands with their sausage fingers together.

"I was hoping you'd ask. Now, shut the door and tell us what the hell is going on with Stuyvesant."

Captain Sterling's Office, 1:50 PM

Danny settled into the seat next to his father, who sat beside the window with his legs stretched out and his size fifteen boots propped on the edge of a credenza. Pete sat behind his desk, reclining back in his executive chair with his fingers laced and resting on his barrel chest.

"Look. I'm not gonna beat around the bush. Stuyvesant is lazy, whiny, paranoid, and he's spending a lot of time with that reporter, Carrie Sutherland."

Sterling stretched his neck and steepled his fingers.

"She's tried to reach me several times. I haven't returned the call."

"The Creekwood rumor mill, if it can be trusted, is telling me that Sutherland is trying to dig up dirt on the Reilly family. She wants to write some sort of exposé. There's a lot for her to find, but nothing that will stick. Sam's been exonerated."

Mac Gregg cleared his throat and dropped his feet.

Holding out his hands, he said, "Why don't we *give* her a story? There's nothing there, so what will it hurt?"

"That's the point. There is a *there*. Marnie's clairvoyance. The dirt on Ken Wilder abusing her. Her and her business partner's involvement with The Collective, however brief, is still information she could create into something ominous. How people keep dying on her properties ... there are things she could massage into a great hit piece."

The chief sucked on his bottom lip, his steely gaze on the captain.

"He's got a point, Mac. Bad things do find that girl. Now, with Bob Humboldt's body being found and Marnie's near abduction, it could cause more harm than good. Plus, that young woman was taken near the four ways," said Sterling.

"Yeah, and Rick Price told me a female college student has disappeared."

The chief leaned back and glanced at his son.

"What's your gut say?" he asked.

"They're all connected."

Mac gave Danny's shoulder a firm pat.

"I agree. See what you can find out about the college girl."

"Yes, sir."

"And listen, we know Stuyvesant is a pain in the ass. Do what you can to cope, huh?"

Sterling added, "He'll either hang himself or he won't, but my bet is that the noose is tightening. He hasn't given me a report in days. I know yours will be on my desk by six, though, right?"

"It's nearly done."

"Great. I'll return Carrie Sutherland's call and see if I can thwart her activity. I'll make it clear that I know about her and Stuyvesant's palling around. The gals at the drugstore are chatty bunch, aren't they? Ha-ha!"

"Thanks, Cap. That may be enough to end that duo."

"Or drive them underground," said Mac, getting to his feet. "I need a coffee. C'mon, Pete. Let's go to the diner and harass Margaret. I haven't been insulted yet today."

Wild Creek Ranch, 3:30 PM

"What time is it?" Marnie asked, looking at the microwave clock.

"Three-thirty," replied Teddy.

"Do you mind if I go curl up on the couch for half an hour?"

"Are you okay?"

"Yeah. Today's been more active than in my last few months. I'm wiped out and my knee hurts."

"We walked a lot. And sometimes we were traversing icy paths. That alone can make you hurt—trying to catch yourself from taking a spill is hard work."

"Yeah, it is. I'll rest for a few minutes if you could keep an eye on the chili? Turn it to simmer in about fifteen and give it a stir every couple of minutes."

"Sure. I can cook, you know."

Marnie giggled and left with the knuckleheads following. She added two logs to the fire, snuggled up on the couch and pulled the quilt over herself. Tater curled up on the rug beside her, and Gus and Dickens huddled together on a cozy braided rug that blanketed the wide slate hearth. She dropped her hand to Tater's back, brushing his soft coat with her fingers before falling into a deep sleep.

Chapter Eighteen

Wild Creek Ranch, 5:20 PM

"Shh ... C'mon in. Marnie's having a snooze," said Teddy.

Poppy handed her a plastic bag with two bottles of wine wrapped in brown paper bags.

"Is she feeling okay?"

Teddy nodded. "Yeah. We had a busy day. She hasn't been out and about much since the explosion. You heard about that, right?"

"Mm-hmm ... My mother told me. She said it was awful! People around town were absolutely devastated."

"None more than Marnie. She beats herself up every day."

"I bet. She and Tom ... Wherever one was, the other wasn't far behind in school. College too. But you know that. You were his girlfriend."

"For a while, yeah. Anyway, have you got bags to bring in? We should grab them before it gets dark."

The knuckleheads wandered into the kitchen, yawning and stretching. When they caught sight of Poppy, their tails sprang to life, and the Border Collies trilled with excitement.

"Settle," said Teddy, holding her hand flat. "Don't wake your mom."

"Marnie always did love dogs. What are their names?" asked Poppy.

"This handsome boy is Tater," she said, giving his scruff a gentle ruffle. "Dickens is that little black and white terror right there, and the big boy is Gus. He's Tom's."

"Oh! I bet he misses his dad. Poor boy," Poppy said, patting the Labrador's head.

"Let's take them outside while we grab your bags. They haven't been out in a while. Is it raining again?"

"Not yet, but it looks like it could. The clouds are low and they look like they're full of snow."

Teddy threw back her head in disgust and reached for her jacket. "No! It's too early!"

Poppy opened the storm door, and the dogs raced outside. Tater and Dickens caught sight of the geese and darted off, herding them back to their pen. Gus trotted off to his favorite tree and lifted his leg before joining the Border Collies in the chase.

"I'd forgotten how beautiful it is here in the fall. I mean, it's spooky as hell, but the view is stunning," said Poppy as she walked to her car, popped the trunk, and heaved out a large hardback suitcase.

Teddy took a duffel from the trunk and slung it over her shoulder, then picked up a smaller case with wheels.

"Waking up here is a dream. I walk out my front door every morning, thankful Marnie took pity on me and gave me a place to live. I work here too—logistics and other administrative stuff. And Carl is nice, but the new nurse they hired is painful. She has a superiority complex."

"Does she? Or are you being sensitive?" As soon as the words came out, Poppy wanted to put them back in, and she clamped a hand over her mouth. "Oh! Gosh! Teddy! I am so sorry. Ignore me. I say the first thing that pops into my head sometimes."

"Ha-ha! Not a big deal. I've worked with Marnie long enough … She has foot in mouth disease too. Her filter is either broken or it never existed."

"Or she's comfortable in her own skin and doesn't care. Ha!" said Poppy.

"That could be. She's a good sort, though. Kind, generous, and really funny."

"She's always been odd in an excellent way."

Teddy peeked into the car. "Is that it? Do you have anything in the backseat?"

"That's everything for now. I have all my stuff stored in a pod in my father's garage."

"Alrighty, then. Let's get the knuckleheads and go back in where it's warm." Teddy looked up at the sky. "You might be right on that snow prediction. Look at those clouds."

A thick shelf of shadow blue clouds almost shimmered above them as the sun's rays did their best to creep through. The sound of gunfire from the wooded area behind the house to the east made both women's heads snap left.

"Must be a hunter," said Teddy. "Although I doubt anyone should be on Marnie's property."

"But that sounded awfully close. Is there still a game warden in the area?" asked Poppy.

"I think so. We can ask Danny when he gets home."

Creekwood Police Station, 5:28 PM

Reports finished and after another bad cup of department coffee drunk, Danny emailed his father and the captain his documents, locked Bob Humboldt's murder book and other case files in his desk drawer and pocketed the key.

Officer Cheryl Garcia entered when he was getting ready to leave. Her sour expression made the detective stop.

"What's up?" he asked.

"Your partner is a vile creature," she spat.

"Uh-oh! What did he do now?"

"It's what he hasn't done. He pawns off his work on everyone and goes off to the pub."

Eyes popping, Danny growled, "He's at a bar?"

"Yes! And I've been running around trying to dig up information for him about Bob Humboldt. I spoke with Marion Doyle, but she wouldn't spill anything. She feigned ignorance about the man. And by the way, that warrant you wanted came through. I didn't tell Randy."

"Oh! Great! I can check out Bob Humboldt's house. Want to come with me?"

"You going now?"

Cheeks burning with anger, Danny said, "Wait a minute! Did you say Marion Doyle?"

"Uh-huh."

"Where did he get that name?"

"That would be me. I told him they worked together at The Times," said the officer.

"Ah. Okay. And you say she wouldn't tell you anything?"

"Zilch." Garcia pulled a zipper across her lips.

"Marnie and Teddy told me about her. I may take a swing by tomorrow morning after I go to Bob's house. Where's the warrant?"

"In an envelope taped to the underside of your top drawer."

"Thank you! Did you discover anything useful in your digging?"

"No. People said he was nice, kind-hearted, et cetera. You know the spiel. Folks around here don't like to speak ill of the dead—unless you're asking about Lawrence Parish. Mr. Heslop at The Times said he was a nice guy and an ace investigative reporter, though."

"Hmm ... okay. Well, I'll check out his house in the morning," said Danny, retrieving the warrant from beneath his desk. "Thanks for hiding this. I don't want Detective Dipshit screwing up a crime scene, which I know he would."

Danny snagged his jacket from the back of his chair and headed for the door.

"What time should we meet to go to Mr. Homboldt's house?" asked Garcia.

"How's seven-thirty sound?"

"Early," she replied with a roll of her eyes.

"See you then!" He waved and left.

Wild Creek Ranch, 5:30 PM

Marnie woke with a start, rolling off the couch and onto the floor, her head clunking the coffee table. Teddy and Poppy ran into the living room—the dogs close on their heels.

"Are you okay?" asked Teddy.

Sitting awkwardly between the sofa and table, she rubbed the back of her head and yawned.

"What time is it?" she asked as she scooted across the floor on her backside to free herself from the confines of her furniture.

"Five-thirty," said Poppy, crossing the room to help her friend stand.

Tater nosed his mistress under the chin, and she wrapped him in a hug.

Still clinging to her dog, she said, "Gosh! I had a horrible dream. It's the most horrifying vision I've ever had. I was being chased through the forest by a man. He had an ice pick in his hand, and he was trying to stab me."

She released the dog and leaned against the couch, arms resting on her bent knees.

"That's awful," cried Teddy. "But it's no wonder after last night."

"It was so real. He had on a green jacket, a red scarf, and had the whitest hair." Marnie closed her eyes, trying to picture him again. "I can't see a face, but I could smell blood."

"Gawd! Smell blood! Jesus, Marnie!" Poppy pulled a face and shivered.

"I hope it wasn't a premonition," said Teddy.

Mouth agape, Poppy sunk into a chair.

"Why would you think that? That's crazy!"

"That's not my specialty. At least not when the danger relates to me," said the psychic.

She stood, wobbled a moment, then caught her balance and Teddy shooed her toward the stairs.

"Go wash up. Dinner will be ready when you come down and we'll set the table."

With a nod, Marnie disappeared upstairs. Tater trotted after her a second or two later.

"What the hell was that about?" asked Poppy, massaging Gus' ears, his tongue lolling out of his mouth.

"You know she's clairvoyant, right?"

"Well, yeah. But visions and premonitions? Is that new?"

"Nah. She's always been that way, but lately it's gotten worse. That's a poor choice of word. But after the accident, her gift expanded?"

"She's more sensitive?"

"Yeah."

"What happened last night?"

"A thug tried to kidnap her."

At the word *kidnap*, Dickens dove under the coffee table, only the shepherd's lantern of his tail visible.

Poppy's jaw dropped, and her eyes widened. "What? You say that so matter-of-factly. What the hell has been going on around here?"

Hallowed Hills Road, 5:45 PM

Window open, Danny drove the last few minutes to Marnie's house. He loved the smell of fall and the crispness of the air. The turnoff to the long driveway always came up fast—no matter how often he made the trip. He spotted his landmark—a rusted bathtub Mary standing in a sea of cattails and dead wildflowers at the side of the road. The detective wondered why anyone would bury part of a tub and think of placing the Madonna inside as a shrine. He questioned if it wasn't somewhat sacrilegious. Slowing down, he turned on his signal and made the sharp turn into the drive.

"That's gonna be a bitch in winter," he said aloud. "I'll pick up reflectors this weekend." He hit the brakes, and the Jeep jerked forward, stalling out. "Whoa! Who the fuck are you?"

A hunter with what looked like a doe slung over his shoulder darted across the driveway and into the thicket on the west side of the driveway. Danny turned the ignition and waited for the man to appear, but he didn't. Coming to a stop, he made a call to the local game warden, Hollister "Holly" Parmeter, and reported what he'd seen. There was no answer, so he left a message. He put the Jeep in gear and continued up the road.

Mumbling, he told himself it was wise not chasing someone into the woods without backup, and that he and Sam had to talk Marnie into a better security system. When he reached the house, he took his field glasses out of the glove compartment and checked the eyepieces for marker. He laughed and thought, *old habits die hard.* Tom Keller was a prankster who often ringed Danny's binoculars with black marker or soot. The detective laughed to himself as he held the glasses up and searched the west paddock but saw no one—only two deer dashing toward the creek.

Wild Creek Ranch, 5:56 PM

The knuckleheads surrounded the detective when he walked in the door. He kneeled, gave them pats, and let them all give his face one lick.

"Where's Marnie?" he asked Teddy and Poppy, who were setting the table.

"She's washing up," said the former, grabbing her handbag off the counter. "Danny, I need to talk to you. In private."

Fingers raking his hair, he replied, "This isn't good, is it?" He shrugged out of his jacket and tossed it over the back of the bench.

She shook her head slowly, pursing her lips—then pushed him toward the study, pulling the books out of her bag along the way.

"Marnie received these when all the packages were pouring in after the accident. They were wrapped in brown paper with no return addresses."

"But there's a menacing note on the flyleaf, right?"

Her mouth popped open, and she slammed it shut.

"How did you know?"

"I've seen this movie. Give me."

He held out his hand, and she passed him the books. Opening The Three Billy Goats Gruff, he sneered, but didn't say anything. When he flipped the cover of Hansel and Gretel, his face turned to stone and his jaw flexed. Teddy knew holy hell was about to break loose by the throbbing vein in his forehead.

"Did she see these?" he growled.

"Only the goat one."

"Okay. So, who found her and who's planning to kill her?"

"It sounds like they know her, doesn't it?"

"Yeah. But don't tell her about this. After last night..." He stroked his beard and thought about the situation. "Hmm ... that could be a mistake. If she knows what's coming, she might agree to a security upgrade."

"Use it to your advantage, Danny. She has to take it seriously."

He nodded tightly. "Yeah. I'll talk to Sam first, and then we'll tell her together."

"Excellent plan."

Wild Creek Ranch, The Living Room, 7:47 PM

Danny stared into the bottom of his whiskey glass, swearing under his breath, while Mac leaned on the mantle, swirling a glass of scotch.

"Daniel, it's a great opportunity for you. Pete and I believe you're the best person to speak at the academy this year. It's only two days, son. Who knows how many young people you will influence? We need recruits."

Pete Sterling sat opposite the detective in a comfy stuffed chair—one leg crossed atop his knee; an unlit cigar clenched between the fingers of one hand and a snifter of cognac in the other.

"It will help you politically, too, Danny. You want to move up and this will help. The exposure can only help your career. Besides, the superintendent and commissioner have both requested your presence. You don't want to disappoint them."

"Or your father," added the chief.

The detective eyed Marnie, who sat next to him on the sofa, her socked feet resting on the coffee table.

She shrugged and said, "I believe you should do what makes you happy. But I think if you don't ..." she paused, pointing a finger at Mac and the captain, "they will make your life miserable. Have I got that right, fellas?"

Mac stuck out his bottom lip and wagged his head.

"Yeah. Pretty much."

Pete frowned. "I wouldn't say miserable. Uncomfortable is reasonable, though."

The detective looked to Sam for support, but he held up his hands in surrender.

"Hey. What do I know? As a hired gun, I go where I am told."

Danny sat forward, set down his drink, and asked the dogs.

"Hey, knuckleheads, what do you reckon?"

A chorus of mumbles and grumbles didn't help.

"Okay. I'll go if Sam sticks around."

"My current contract says I go where Ransom goes. I will be here until the end of next month."

Marnie clapped her hands. "You'll be here for Thanksgiving! Yay!"

Her brother nodded. "And I expect all my childhood favorites to be on offer at the festive event."

"You've got it!" she said, hopping up from the couch and giving him a hug. "I'll leave you to it. The gals have been slaving away, cleaning up the kitchen. I better make them a toddy to say thanks."

As she made her exit, Danny stood, asking them to join him in the study where he and Teddy had hidden the books earlier in the evening.

Chapter Nineteen

Wild Creek Ranch, The Study, 8:30 PM

"Why does Marnie insist on calling this a safe?" asked Danny.

Sam turned the upper dial left, right, then left again, and twisted the lower dial in the opposite pattern. He spun the spindle and heaved open the heavy door.

"She thinks it sounds less pretentious than vault," he said, stepping aside to allow the detective inside.

The captain and chief took a peek, and Mac let out a low whistle.

"Does she have enough guns and ammo?" he asked.

Sam said, "No. You can never have enough. After what she has been through the last year, I await the day she puts cannons on the roof."

"Or a Gatling gun," added Danny with a snicker, before pulling the Radio Flyer filled with Bob Humboldt's belongings out of the vault. "I'll pour over this tomorrow evening. The warrant came through for his house, and I want to talk to Marion Doyle tomorrow, too. She used to work with him."

Mac pawed through the wagon, lifting out a notebook. "You don't want to get help from Stuyvesant?"

"No. I don't trust him. He'll share anything he finds with Carrie Sutherland."

Captain Sterling agreed. "Let's keep it safe here. I've been locking my office door nights since he came to Creekwood. I believe Danny is right not to let him in on this case."

The detective retreated and approached the bookcase behind the desk, retrieving the two books Teddy had given him.

"These are the reason we came into the study." He held up the books. "Marnie received these after the accident. They had no return addresses. She saw the message in The Three Billy Goats Gruff, but not Hansel and Gretel. Teddy intercepted them and gave the books to me. Look at the flyleaf in each."

He handed Sam the books first, who opened them and read each, before passing them to Mac and then Pete.

The captain gave them back to Danny, and said, "Thoughts on who would send these?"

Sam sat on the sofa and said, "Those fairy tales terrified her as a child. Of all her books, she would bury those at the bottom of her toy chest so the troll and the witch couldn't come out of the books and get her."

"Who would know that?" asked the detective.

"Well, me. Mom, Dad, Uncle Giles, and Aunt Janet, and any number of friends from childhood."

"Kate Parish?" asked Captain Sterling.

"Possibly, and I wouldn't know who she may have told when she was older. As a child, those books are scary, but as an adult, one might laugh at having feared the characters in a story."

They all turned at the knock on the door and exhaled a feeling of calm when Carl poked his head in. Sam explained what they were talking about.

"Did you know Marnie was afraid of these books as a child?"

"She never mentioned either to me, but she told me there was a figurine in your room that terrified her."

Sam thought about that for a moment, then grinned.

"Mm-hmm. I had a few action figures she believed watched her when she came into my room."

Danny laughed. "You told her that to keep her out, right?"

"Guilty!"

Carl picked up the books and leafed through them. When he read the notes, he closed the covers and set them on the desk.

"You have to tell her."

Danny nodded. "Yeah. That's what Teddy and I thought, too. And it might help in getting her to upgrade the security."

Sam pushed himself off the couch, continued to the desk, looking at the books again.

"Why don't you let me talk to her? That keeps you away from pressuring her. The security upgrade is long overdue. Let me be the bad guy. I have had practice at using her fear to get things done."

Danny agreed. "That's what brothers are for. Thanks."

Wild Creek Ranch, The Kitchen, 9:52 PM

"Thanks for dinner, Marnie. As always, the food and company were wonderful." Mac Gregg wrapped two big arms around the hostess and squeezed until she couldn't breathe.

Patting his back, she said, "You're most welcome. Next time, I'll bake a pie and not take a nap."

"Did you tell them about your dream?" asked Teddy.

"Gawd! No! Living it once was enough," replied Marnie, scowling at her friend in the hopes she would shut up—which she didn't.

"I guess nightmare was more like it. I really hope it wasn't a premonition, though."

Danny asked, "What was it about?"

So, she recounted the dream to the group, and said, "It's no biggy. After last night, I'm sure my imagination is working overtime."

The captain and chief exchanged a knowing glance, but it was Mac who spoke.

"Marnie, you should talk to Margaret about that dream."

She rolled her eyes. "Why? It's nothing."

Pete disagreed. "If it were anyone but you, I would agree. But it is you, and you just described The Poacher."

"Or The Taxidermist, as some called him," added Mac.

"What?"

"Urban legend, myth, whatever it is, part of it is true."

"Oh! Stop it! You're trying to scare me."

Mac shook his head. "I wouldn't do that."

Danny looked at his father and knew he was quite serious. "Marnie, I think you should listen. Captain Sterling and my father aren't the type to raise an alarm without good reason."

"Give me a break. It wasn't real, and this isn't Nightmare on Elm Street. He cannot hurt me in my dreams. Stop it!"

But then she looked past them and shivered. They all did, but didn't know why. Standing near the door, a form took shape. Marnie and Danny saw Bob Humboldt manifest before their eyes, then dissipate into a fine mist.

"You saw that, right?" the detective asked, out of the corner of his mouth.

"Uh-huh," replied the psychic.

The others turned to see what they were looking at but saw nothing—they only felt the slight chill Bob left behind.

Second Floor, 10:23 PM

At Danny's urging, Teddy spent the night in one of the upstairs bedrooms and they settled Poppy into another.

"If you need extra blankets, they're in the linen closet at the end of the hall," said Marnie before closing her bedroom door.

Danny sat on the bed, a sock in one hand—a dazed expression on his face.

"I saw him plain as day. Then he disappeared. What did he want?" he asked.

Marnie entered the bathroom and put toothpaste on her brush and came back out, shaking her head as she brushed.

"I dunno."

"Do you think he wanted to speak?"

She nodded. "Mm-hmm."

"Will he come back?"

"Yeah."

"So, he knows you saw him."

"Mm-hmm."

"What if he tries talking to me?"

She took her brush out of her mouth and said, "Listen."

"Are they all gonna be that easy to see from now on? Or was that an isolated incident?"

Pulling up her shoulders, she returned to the bathroom, spit in the basin, turned on the water, and spit again.

"I'm not sure. A few months ago, spirits were blurry to you. They were for me sometimes, too, but not recently. But I'm not going to let your dad and the captain scare me. The Poacher and The Taxidermist? C'mon. I have never heard about him—not even as a ghost story at a sleepover."

"They wouldn't do that. Try to scare you. They seemed genuinely spooked by your dream," he said, tossing his dirty clothes in the hamper.

"Pfft," she said, pulling back the covers and crawling into bed.

Right after Danny stepped into the bathroom, Tater hopped up onto the bed and settled down with his head on the detective's pillow. While Gus and Dickens snuggled together in a dog bed, too small to share.

"Have you heard about him?"

He appeared in the doorway, spotted Tater, and rolled his eyes.

"Nah. But I didn't grow up in Creekwood."

He retreated into the bathroom, closing the door. Marnie turned on her side and scratched Tater's head.

"What do you think, buddy? Should I call Gram?"

He nuzzled his nose into her neck before mumbling something incoherent. Gus and Dickens agreed, offering a grumble and a yipe, respectively.

Marnie's Bedroom, 3:08 AM

"Danny? Wake up." Marnie shook his shoulder, whispering in his ear.

"Yeah."

"That guy is over by the closet."

"What? What guy?" He grabbed his sidearm off the bedside table and sat up. "Where?"

"He's right there!" she hissed.

Tater hopped down and growled—his scruff standing on end, then planted himself between the closet and the bed. Gus raised his head before dozing off again, but Dickens bounded across the floor and snapped.

The detective squinted his eyes, trying to focus.

"I don't see anyone. Oh! Hang on! Does he have on a red scarf?"

"Yes!"

"What should we do?"

"Point your gun at him and tell him to get lost."

"What? Really?"

"Yes!"

Danny backed out of the bed and took aim.

"Get the fuck out of here!" he yelled.

They heard feet hit the floor in the other rooms, and Danny set the gun down and grabbed his sweatpants off the floor, struggling to get a leg into them.

Marnie burst into a giggle as Teddy and Poppy knocked once and raced into the room, as light from the hallway streamed into the bedroom. The detective dropped the pants and pulled the duvet around his waist.

"Are you okay?" said Teddy, sleepy but somehow wide awake.

Poppy stood with a hand on the other woman's shoulder.

"What happened?"

"We're fine. Everything's fine," said Danny. "Go back to bed."

"Ah. And Danny thought it would be fun to yell *get the fuck out* while completely naked?" asked Teddy with a snicker.

"Leave or I will drop the comforter," he threatened.

Teddy's face reddened, and she backed out the door, pulling Poppy with her, and shut it.

Marnie rolled across the bed, roaring with laughter. "You wouldn't have!"

"Yeah. I would," he said, dropping the duvet, and throwing himself on to the bed to kiss her.

Distracted by the prospect of otherworldly beings watching them, his face lined with worry, Danny paused mid-kiss and rested on his elbow.

"Are they watching us?"

"Who?"

"The ghosts."

"Who cares?"

"It's kind of creepy," he said, craning his neck to see.

Marnie scooted from under the covers, grabbed the salt cellar from the windowsill, and sprinkled a generous supply of flakes near the bottom of the door.

"Will that work?" he asked.

The psychic glanced between him and the door, dumped the lot and scurried to the warmth of her bed and the detective's waiting arms.

Chapter Twenty

October 13th

Wild Creek Ranch, The Kitchen, 5:03 AM

Dressed in flannel pajama bottoms and Danny's blue Creekwood PD hoodie, Marnie poured a cup of coffee and settled at the trestle table with her laptop. She typed 'The Poacher' into the browser and received a Brad Brownfield's song of the same name; a short film on YouTube about a poacher in Yellowstone National Park during the October 2013 government shutdown; and an IMDb and Wikipedia entry for a television series shot in India about elephant ivory poaching; a book by novelist H.E. Bates; and numerous posts and articles relating generically to the topic, including a surfboard. She then entered 'Creekwood, New York, The Poacher' and found nothing relevant to her query.

Her next search was 'The Taxidermist', which delivered a short film, a series, taxidermy methods, links to Facebook pages, and several listings for taxidermists in the local area and beyond.

Sucking her bottom lip, she glanced at the clock. Five-thirty wasn't too early to call Gram at the diner, was it? She tapped her fingers against her chin, deliberating her next move when Danny and the knuckleheads entered the room. He kissed her forehead as she stood to take the dogs outside for their morning run around the property.

"Sit and drink your coffee. I'll take them out. There was a guy in the driveway yesterday who sent off a vibe I didn't like," he said.

"A guy?"

"Yeah. A hunter. I put in a call to Holly and I'm waiting for a call back. There was something odd about him. He had a doe slung over his shoulder and he was running."

"He was hunting on my property?"

"Looks like it. He was coming from the east side of the house. That little patch of woods has a deer trail. He's probably a local who knows where to look."

"But we put up posted and no trespass signs up. They're everywhere."

Danny quirked up the corner of his mouth and gave her an "are you kidding me" look.

"And what have I told you..."

"I know! Locks and signs only keep out honest people. But c'mon! I can't possibly fence off every section of land."

"You don't have to," said Sam, holding the books in his hand.

Both turned to see him in the doorway.

"Squirt, we need to talk."

Copper Woods, 5:25 AM

Twelve marbles rolled across an old dining room table, marred with dimples, flaking varnish, and a wonky leg. The spinning glass orbs made a satisfying sound before skittering to a halt against the warped crease where additional leaves could be added for a big family dinner.

Two naked women watched in horror as their abductor picked up a marble and put it in his mouth, sucking it clean, then setting it on a bed of yellowed cotton batting. He repeated the motion for each, before inspecting them thoughtfully and choosing four from the dozen. Two bright blues with white swirls. The others, amber with golden swishes. He turned to his company and put a finger to his lips—a warning to be silent lest he keep his promise and cut out their tongues.

Secured by chains hooked through iron rings on the floor, they whimpered and held onto one another as if their life depended on it. But they knew they couldn't be saved as he picked up an ice pick and headed their way.

Wild Creek Ranch, The Kitchen, 5:30 AM

Sam poured himself a cup of coffee and sat across from his sister. Placing the books on the old oak table, he pushed them toward her.

"You received these with the get-well packages after the explosion, right?"

Her eyes teared, and she shook her head.

"No. Three Billy Goats Gruff arrived before that. Tom found it on the back porch, and I forgot about it. It ended up in the study with the other stuff."

"Have you read the inscriptions inside each?"

"No. Only the first one."

Keeping eye contact, he flipped open the covers one at a time and nudged them closer to her. She looked down, a tear dropping onto the table, which she wiped up with her sleeve.

Glancing between the books, she read: "I found you" and "I will kill you."

"What the hell?" she gasped.

"Who couldn't find you and why would they want to kill you?" he asked.

Palms to her face, she thought about people she had pissed off over the years.

"Hey. Tell me." He reached across the table and pulled away her hands, revealing tear-filled green eyes.

Getting up from the table, she disappeared into the bathroom, returning with a box of tissues and was wiping her nose when she took a seat, and blew out a shaky breath. Marnie looked her brother in the eyes, then up at the ceiling to stop her tears.

"Where do I start? Kate Parish springs to mind. Lawrence Parish. Kitty Parish. Grace Wilmot. Fringe-dwellers within The Collection. I mean, I helped close that whole drug operation, didn't I. Erin Matthews. Cy Barnes. Jethro Barnes. I'm a psychologist so any number of clients. People I've helped send to prison because they didn't cooperate with court-ordered therapy. You."

"Son of a bitch," he whispered.

Wild Creek Ranch, The Study, 6:15 AM

"Marnie has agreed. We can upgrade the security system. She said the sooner the better and handed me her debit card," said Sam, snapping the card down on the desk.

"Good stuff," said Danny.

"Should I call my guy, or do you have someone in mind?"

"No. Your guy is fine. As long as the job is done right, I don't care who does it. Besides, I assume your guy is better connected than anyone in my circle."

"Yeah. He's a specialist."

Danny gave him a long look, then waved his hands.

"I don't wanna know."

"You do not. Leave it with me and I will have a plan by close of business."

"That's fast."

"Did I mention my guy is a specialist?"

"Ha-ha! Yeah. I'll stay out of it. But you know, I'm leaving tonight for a couple of days, right?"

"Yes. I will email you the plan as soon as I have it. We can amend where we see holes. Then they can start installation. I want it done before you get back."

"I'd prefer it done yesterday. How did she react to the inscriptions?"

"We got our way. She looked terrified when she read the note in Hansel and Gretel."

"I bet."

"My little sister has pissed off a veritable cornucopia of psychos, clients, and average, everyday people over the years. She's got a smart mouth, hates injustice of any kind, and calls it as she sees it."

"Who's on the list?"

"Kate Parish. Lawrence Parish. Kitty Parish. Grace Wilmot. People who profited from The Collective's drug dealings. Alice Wells. Allen Schofield. Erin Matthews. Cy Barnes. Jethro Barnes. Clients she reported for violating court-ordered therapy. Me."

"Shit!" said the detective.

"Hmm. Obviously, she can't give us a list of clients, but can you dig into anyone else who is not a specter? And any family or associates who may want revenge. Let's see if we can locate them," said Sam.

"Sure. I'll do that before I head out today. They would have to know those books terrified her as a child too. That could narrow the list. What about Carl?"

"Hmm ... Kate, me, Tom, other family friends ... Carl would fit the people who know about the books and who she has pissed off, but I doubt he would do anything to threaten her."

"I agree. Kate would be my guess. She's found another patsy to work on her behalf," suggested Danny.

"Is that not too easy?" asked Sam.

"Yeah."

"I have a favor to ask, and it is big."

"What's that?"

"It would be wise for me to have backup. I would like Ransom to stay while you are away. I know there is history, but he would protect Marnie with his life. He is the right man for the job."

"I don't like it, but it's a solid plan."

"Okay. That is good news."

"You already called him, didn't you?"

"I did. I also asked Carl to be vigilant."

"And there's always Patrick if you need another set of eyes."

"He has already been briefed."

"Teddy should probably stay in the house until we have the security upgraded."

"Agreed. I will talk to her."

"You know Poppy. Marnie invited her to stay."

"Yes. They will all be well looked after."

"I wouldn't be leaving if I thought otherwise."

"The trip is cogent."

"Very."

Wild Creek Ranch, The Kitchen, 6:36 AM

"Hey, Marnie. Do you mind if I make breakfast? My stomach is growling," asked Teddy as she peered into the fridge.

"Yeah. Would you like French toast?"

"Oo! Yes, please? Poppy, want French toast?"

"Uh ... that would be nice, thanks."

"Good morning!" said Danny, walking into the kitchen with Sam and the knuckleheads, who settled beneath the table.

Sam took a seat at a bench—his demeanor drawing his sister's attention.

Marnie tipped her head, studying his mood.

"We're about to get a lecture, ladies. Pay attention," she said, her tone grave.

Her brother held up his hands. "Not at all. While Danny is away, he wants to be assured everyone is safe. So, we have a few rules until the new security system is installed."

Danny took over. "If you go anywhere on the property, go in pairs. Do not go alone—even during the day. Don't let the dogs out to run on their own. There is a poacher in the area who may mistake them for a small deer."

"Keep the doors and windows locked at all times, including the trapdoor in the study and the hidden door behind the bookcase. There are several entrances to the tunnel system we may not know about."

Poppy's eyes widened, and she slunk down in her seat. "Maybe I should find other accommodation. This sounds scary and dangerous."

Sam shook his head. "Not if we are vigilant."

The detective said, "Two women have been abducted in the last seventy-two hours. One was taken just beyond the four ways. The other from Twin Creeks University. The threat is not isolated to the ranch."

Teddy raised her hand. Danny couldn't help but smirk, and Sam dropped his head to hide his lopsided grin.

"What will be different about the security?"

"We have two friends coming to stay with us while we work through installation. Patrick Kowalski, who you and Marnie know," said Sam.

"And Ransom Elliott, a colleague of Sam's," added the detective.

"What?!" Marnie's eyes shot daggers into the men. "I will not be under house arrest with Ransom Elliott!"

"No one is under house arrest. We are simply taking precautions," said her brother.

"Oh. No! Carl is here all day. He will help. I'll ask him myself."

"Carl has other obligations after three every afternoon, Marnie. Evenings and overnights are out for him. You know, I wouldn't have asked Ransom if there was someone else. Danny put on his grownup pants. You need too as well."

She looked up at Danny, who stood behind her brother. He gave an encouraging nod while she shot him a death glare.

"Pfft! Whatever!" she said, crossing her arms and turning away.

Sam cleared his throat as a warning to his sister to stop being petulant, then addressed Teddy's query.

"We will have security staff added to the current roster. The system will be upgraded with new cameras and motion lights, and where possible, we will add electric fencing on the perimeter. And a gate will be installed at the front entrance. It is only a deterrent, but that is better than we currently have."

"We don't want blind spots where someone could slip through, even though they will. That's where the additional cameras will help. And they will all be backed up by generators. That means the Wi-Fi won't go out for long if the power goes off," explained the detective.

"We will also have a control room staffed twenty-four hours a day to monitor activity on the ranch."

"What about the wildlife trails? You can't fence them out of their home or their path to water? If the electric fences are only a deterrent, don't put them up. I don't want any of this to affect the animals," said Marnie.

The men looked at one another and shrugged. What Marnie didn't see was Sam winking at Danny.

"Valid point, Squirt. What do you think, Danny? Can we do away with that aspect of the upgrade?"

The detective rubbed his whiskers for effect. "Yeah. I think that's fair."

Marnie got up from the table to refill her coffee.

With her back turned, she said, "I know what you did there. Give her something she can change in the plan, and she'll accept the rest. I'm not stupid, you know."

Danny looked down at Sam with an "I told you so" glance and clapped his hands.

"Okay. Good chat! I've gotta get to the office, but I will stop here on my way out of town to pack. If you need me, call."

Chapter Twenty-One

Wild Creek Ranch, The Study, 7:13 AM

Flames crackled and popped in the fireplace next to Marnie's desk as she settled in her chair to review a stack of client files. She lit a sage and bayberry candle, fanning the scent toward the French doors before getting to work. Sam came in without knocking and she didn't look up.

"Where should we put Ransom and Patrick?" she asked.

He took a seat on the leather sofa and put his slippered feet on an ottoman.

"Upstairs. I want one in the room at the top and one opposite the laundry."

"Not one up and one down?"

"No. I'll be downstairs, and someone will be awake in the living room or kitchen overnight."

"Uh-huh. And how long will it be necessary?"

"Until Danny returns."

"Fine. But tell Ransom to stay out of my way."

"He knows."

"I'll have to go out for groceries soon. Should I take Teddy and Poppy?"

"Who do you want to go with you?"

"No one."

"Okay. I can see you want to be difficult, but you won't goad me into an argument, so you can storm out and go alone."

Eyes narrowed, she tightened her jaw.

"That bitch face thing you have going on won't work on me either, so knock it off. You might scare others, but not me." He dropped his feet on the floor and stood. "Take one of your friends—and your gun."

"And my stun gun, pepper spray, and carbon steel baton."

"Damn straight," he said, slapping the door on his way out.

Creekwood Police Station, 7:20 AM

Officer Cheryl Garcia swung through the doors to the squad room and before she could get to her desk, Danny flagged her down.

"Hey, Garcia. Are you ready to rock and roll?" he asked, takeaway coffee in hand.

She threw back her head, displaying an anguished expression. "You already got coffee? Ugh! I haven't had one yet."

"We'll stop and get you one. No big deal."

"Thank you!"

"C'mon! Let's go!" Danny strode out the door, letting it swing shut behind him.

Garcia snatched her notepad off her desk, then hunted for a pen before finding one under a desk.

"Why can't people keep their hands off my stuff?" she huffed, racing after the detective.

Creekwood Plaza, 7:35 AM

Creekwood Plaza was a small strip mall on the outskirts of town, a ten-minute drive from Town Square. Like the downtown area, the shops had green and white striped awnings and quaint frontages. The out-of-town landowner/developer of the shopping center was forced by the scrappy town council to blend the ugly architecture into the flavor of the town. Still, locals called it an eyesore but spent their money there begrudgingly because, for groceries, it was the best shopping for miles. With a butcher, a bakery, a gift store, grocery store, and liquor store, it was as close to a one-stop as you could get.

"Okay. I'll go to the butcher if you can get the shopping started." Marnie handed a list to Teddy. "You know the brands I buy, but grab anything else you want. That list only covers dinners and lunches. It's a start and we'll have more delivered if we need to. We'll stop at the farmer's market for fruit and veg before we head back."

"Can I buy Pop-Tarts?" asked Teddy.

"I don't care. For the record, I like brown sugar and cinnamon. Frosted."

"Oo! So do I," said Poppy, clapping her hands.

"What about munchies?" asked Teddy.

"Sure. Knock yourself out. I'll be in as soon as I'm done."

Walking through the plastic curtain door, she spotted Irving Klein—his fuzzy brown hair plastered to his head under a net.

"Marnie! How's tricks?" he asked with an exuberant wave.

"Great, Mr. Klein. How about you?"

"Fine, thanks. What can I get for you?"

"It's a big order today. Four roaster chickens with giblets, a five-pound and three-pound chuck roast, five pounds of chicken wings—drums and flats, two-pounds of ground pork and two of Italian sausage. Uh … the spicy one."

"Sounds like you've got company."

"Yes, sir."

"Bacon and breakfast sausage, too?"

"Oh! Yes, please, and three pounds of bratwurst. I nearly forgot!"

"I've got calves liver this week. Interested?"

"Ha-ha! You know I am, but there wouldn't be other takers."

"They don't know what they're missing." He paused and looked over the counter. "Thought you should know. That nosey reporter from the times was in here asking questions about your family. I think she's visiting proprietors who have been in town a long time. I informed her I didn't know you."

"Thanks, Mr. Klein. I appreciate it." Marnie stared at her boots, wondering about Carrie's vendetta against her.

"It's early still and I need to get things out of the cooler. If you don't mind, your order will be ready in fifteen minutes," said the butcher.

"See you in fifteen, then."

Eyeing the bakery, she considered a double-chocolate glazed doughnut but changed her mind.

"You don't need the calories, Reilly."

She reached to open the grocery store door, changed her mind, and reversed position.

"I do want doughnuts. Two of them."

Waving to Mrs. Trivilino, a tidy gray-haired woman with round glasses, she said, "Good morning! Could I please get a dozen mixed doughnuts?"

"You sure can. It's been ages since you've been in. Would you like the usual? Four jelly, four chocolate glaze, and four bear claws?"

Tears stung the back of her eyes, and she gave a tight jerk of her head to confirm. Bear claws. Tom's favorite.

"Have you seen Everett Channing to congratulate him?"

"No, ma'am, I haven't. But it's high time I call him. He's worked hard."

"To think he started out making the coffee. Now, he's editor-in-chief." She lowered her voice to a whisper. "That Carrie Sutherland is trouble. She was in here asking me questions about you last week. God forgive me, but didn't I lie? Told her I didn't know you. Irving did the same."

"Thanks for that. She has a bug up her bum. I don't even know her, and she despises me."

"Oh, that bug is because you stole Ken Wilder from her. Didn't you know?"

"What?"

"Oh, yes. He dropped her like a dead cat as soon as he met you."

"Wow! That's news to me."

Mrs. Trivilino placed the white box tied with red and white string on the counter, and Marnie handed her cash.

"Thanks for the information and the doughnuts. Have a great day!"

"Don't forget your change!"

"You keep it. Buy yourself a coffee on me."

Bob Humboldt's House, Reddick Lane, 7:55 AM

The street was lined with sugar and red maples and a sea of fallen leaves being tossed about by a gentle breeze. Danny stepped out of the Jeep, looking in windows to see what neighbors were home, watching them.

"How do we get in? We don't have a key," said Garcia.

"I got it," said the detective, pulling a leather case of lockpicks from his breast pocket as they walked onto the veranda of the craftsman-style bungalow.

He worked the doorknob quickly, but the deadbolt took longer and when he opened the door, they were met by a horrendous odor.

"Phwaw!" Danny stepped back, pulling his shirt over his nose.

"Oh! Gawd! What is that?" the officer gagged, slapping a hand over her nose and mouth.

"Death, Garcia. That's death."

Creekwood Public Library, 9:03 AM

Marnie put the car in park and left it running.

"I will be back in ten minutes. The research director is helping me out with a project, and I need to run in to give her some information."

She jogged up the wide steps and through the front door of the three-story Victorian mansion and bee-lined it to the research section on the third floor. Riley Leventas sat behind an antique banker's desk, surrounded by book stacks and file boxes. Her shoulder-length mahogany hair was pinned up with a number two pencil and her rimless glasses rode halfway down her nose.

"Hi, Riley. How are you?"

The researcher glanced over her glasses and put aside the document she was reading.

"Hi, Marnie. I received your email, but I haven't had a chance to start my search. I'm looking forward to it, though. It sounds intriguing."

"Hmm … It's strange that I've never heard of The Poacher or The Taxidermist. You would think a town steeped in rumors, someone would have mentioned it. Especially when we were kids. We loved that kind of thing around bonfires."

"It may have been buried for a reason. Are you sure you want to dig it up?"

"Yes. I had a weird dream and then something happened at the ranch and a few packages arrived that are … umm … threatening. Something in my gut tells me they're all connected."

"Shouldn't you let the police handle it?"

"Of course, but what would be the fun in that? I have been cooped up recuperating. I need to stretch my legs and my mind. Ha-ha!"

"Okay. I'll do my best, but the police have better resources than I do."

"Why do I think that's not entirely the case?" The psychic shot the researcher a cheeky grin.

With a blank stare, the woman said, "What makes you think that?"

"C'mon, Riley. You haven't always been a mild-mannered researcher. At some point in your mysterious history, you wore a cape—of sorts."

The researcher's eyes dropped to the papers on her desk, and without looking up, she said, "I've heard stories, but until right now, I wasn't sure they were true. Not that I believe in psychics, but I do believe in strong gut feelings and the gift of observation."

"Well, between you, me, and that bookcase, the stories *are* true. Believe in that stuff or not. It's entirely up to you. But when a ghost tells me something good about a person, I generally believe it."

Riley glanced over her shoulder and shivered.

"Shall I email you what I find?"

"That would be great. You'll have to come out to the ranch for dinner some night."

"So we can continue the conversation? Look, Marnie, I don't like people gossiping about me and ..."

"Riley, that is the last thing I would do. But remember, I'm a psychologist. Reading people isn't always about my gift. You need a confidante in town. Someone you can trust. Client-patient confidentiality is one of my superpowers."

"Gotcha! I'll email when I've got something."

"Thank you!" Marnie waved as she disappeared down the stairs.

Bob Humboldt's House, Reddick Lane, 9:05 AM

"Hey, man. Sorry it took so long to get here. I was on a conference call and couldn't get loose," said Rick Price.

"No worries," said Danny, leading the way to the source of the stench.

Rick stopped in front of the body and blinked.

"Red hair," he said.

"Yeah," replied the detective.

"Krista Hansen and Jess Alder have been described as auburn."

"What would you call Marnie?" the detective asked.

The doctor pictured Danny's girlfriend. Closing his eyes, he said, "Strawberry-blonde. And someone tried to grab her, too."

"How soon before you know if this is Jess or Krista."

Rick shook his head. "It's not. This woman is taller and older. She has a sprinkling of gray hair at her temples. If I were you, I'd be checking missing persons. Stick to mountain towns."

"Okay. Why's that?"

Rick bent and plucked a conical flower from the woman's hair.

"This is from a bearberry willow, and I've only seen those in Alpine regions of the Northeast. I'm just guessing, though."

"No, you're not. You never guess. I'll leave you to it. Let me know when you're done."

"Where are you going?"

"To make sure Garcia's okay."

"Did she chuck her breakfast?"

"Yeah, but I got her outside before she spewed."

Chapter Twenty-Two

Hallowed Hills Road, 9:15 AM

The radio blasted a local rock station, and between Bohemian Rhapsody and Gloria, Marnie noticed Poppy wasn't singing along.

"Poppy, you've been quiet. Is everything okay?"

"Shell-shocked is what I'm feeling. I came back to town hoping to ease back into life in Creekwood. That's not going to happen, is it?"

"Well, I can guarantee you won't be bored," said Marnie.

Teddy leaned back and patted Poppy's knee.

"Don't worry. It took me time to get used to hanging out with her, too. But we've had a lot of great times, haven't we?"

"There are moments when all is calm. It doesn't last long, but if you're looking for that, working on the ranch might not suit you. We have a clinic in town, and we can go there tomorrow. My assistant Andrea is there most days. After July, she doesn't like coming here."

"Would that work for you and Carl?"

"Sure. He and I can manage the load here, but we'll both be in town some days. If you'd feel safer in town, there are three small apartments above the office. You could use one short-term. We had them renovated in September. We like having a space for women to stay if they're in a dangerous situation."

The Founder's Cemetery came into view and Marnie turned on her signal light, slowed and turned into the long drive.

"Uh ... What are we doing here?" Poppy asked, peering out the window—goosebumps prickling her arms.

"If you want calm, it's here."

Marnie stopped the car in front of the mausoleum, retrieved a spotlight bulb from the console, and turned off the engine.

Opening the door, she motioned for them to join her.

"C'mon. It's peaceful here."

The woman followed, even as their skin crawled. They took in the still air and the ancient gravestones and monuments, creeping with moss and dust of the ages.

"Why isn't there a breeze here?" asked Poppy.

Teddy wrapped a hand through her arm.

"The wind is afraid to enter. I know I am."

"Me too."

Walking straight to the mausoleum, Marnie reached up, unscrewed the lightbulb above the entry and replaced it with the spotlight she brought with her.

"There! Now it won't be so gloomy here at night," she said, stepping back.

"Why would anyone come here at night?" asked Poppy, eyes wide and showing signs of tears.

"There's a system of tunnels running under Creekwood and one of them comes out here. It's nothing to worry about. But if we need to run, we'll see where the exit is."

"Mm ... That didn't make me feel better."

"Don't be so worried. There's joy on the way. I can feel it in my bones."

Poppy gave Teddy a sideways glance, and in return, she tightened her grip on her friend's arm.

"It's okay. That's the first reassuring thing she has said in a while. I'm taking it as a positive omen."

Two gray squirrels skittered up a hemlock tree behind them and the women jumped—except Marnie, who was next to her vehicle. She opened the trunk and removed a shovel and two white chrysanthemums she'd picked up at the market.

"Give me a few minutes, gals. I have family here and want to drop these around."

She disappeared around the corner of the mausoleum, and Teddy couldn't help herself and followed. Hand still crooked through her friend's arm, she dragged her along too.

"Where are we going?" hissed Poppy.

"Dunno. But I'll bet she's convening with spirits," she replied with a nervous giggle.

Stopping dead on the trail, Poppy shook her arm loose from Teddy's grip.

"You think this is funny?"

"No. But I think you need Marnie more than you know. People come into our lives when we need them and when I found her again, she helped me, and I helped her. And right now, lady, I believe you are in a sad, sorry place that requires strong women in your life who don't give two shits that your world has fallen apart."

The woman blinked back tears, shoulders drooping.

"You know?" she gulped.

"Of course. We both know and don't care. We're just glad you're home."

"But…"

"Zip it, chick. I don't want to hear about it until we're all snuggled up in front of a warm fire with a glass of wine."

They found Marnie kneeling before a large gravestone inscribed with the name Flannigan. As she patted the rich, dark earth around the plants, she chattered away, oblivious to her friends, who were behind her.

"I'm expecting you to behave yourself this year, Nolan. Please do your best not to scare the bejesus out of the gals at the museum or library. I don't want a call to come get you."

She opened her bag and removed a bottle, tipped it and poured a hefty portion on the grave, then put the cork back in.

"Irish whiskey to keep you warm, Grandpa. I'll be back in a week or so. Behave yourself."

Getting to her feet, she realized the women were standing on either side. Uncorking the bottle, she took a swig, then offered it to her friends. Both women took a slug and handed it back.

Poppy smacked her lips and wiped her mouth with the back of her hand.

"I can't believe how good that is."

"Let's go home and have some lunch. Once our stomachs are full, we'll have a glass by the fire. Sound okay?"

"Hell, yeah!" said Teddy.

Wild Creek Ranch Entrance, 10:25 AM

Two sawhorses were placed at either side of the driveway, with two six-by-six, eight-foot posts laying lengthwise on top, blocking passage. Marnie stopped the Jeep, got out, and called her brother.

"I'm home and some asshole has barricaded the driveway."

"There should be a guard there to move it."

"Yeah, well, there isn't."

She hung up in a huff, shoved her phone in her pocket and picked up the end of one post. A man appeared from the brush and had the nerve to yell at her.

"What the hell are you doing?" said a sturdy man with jet-black curls and bulging biceps.

"I'm trying to get home. Please move the beams."

"I'll need to see ID. No one goes in without identification."

Hands on her hips, she took a step forward. "Excuse me?"

"I'm following orders. The owner…"

"I am the owner. Move the damn posts!" she howled, green eyes flashing.

Ransom Elliot jogged down the drive, a radio in his hand.

"Let her in, Griff. That's Marnie Reilly."

The man looked at her and apologized. "I was following orders."

She turned on her heel, stomped to the car, and got in.

Griff and Ransom moved the posts, and with an exaggerated bow, the latter waved her through.

Marnie rewarded him with a scowl and a New York salute.

"That was harsh," said Teddy.

"Tough shit," Marnie replied, her face burning with anger.

"Would you rather have a lunatic running around threatening us?"

Poppy nudged Teddy's shoulder.

"Don't poke the bear, Theodora."

Chapter Twenty-Three

Wild Creek Ranch, 10:45 AM

Marnie huffed and puffed as she got out of the Jeep and stalked around the back to get out the groceries. Her brother appeared on the back porch and motioned for Teddy and Poppy to go inside.

"Ransom and Griff were following my orders. Please apologize to them after we have unpacked the groceries."

She didn't speak, continuing to walk bags from the trunk to the steps.

"The silent treatment does not work on me, Marnie. I know the situation is not ideal, but it is the best option." He stepped in front of her and placed a hand on each shoulder. "You were abducted a few nights ago; grabbed off your front porch with a cop and a highly trained agent within proximity. You have a clinic full of veterans on the property. And Teddy, Poppy, and staff. Securing the ranch is a priority."

"No shit!" she growled.

"Then why are you giving Ransom a hard time? He wants to help."

"Because all of it makes me feel like a victim, and I had enough of that when I was with Ken. All these people milling around my property, ensuring my safety. It's..."

"Necessary," he said, pulling her into a hug. "Let it go, Squirt. You are not a victim, and all of this will make sure you never are. The gates and lights. The guards and the cameras. These simple things put the power in your hands. And may God help anyone who thinks Marnie Reilly is a victim."

Marion Doyle's House, 71 White Pine Lane, 10:50 AM

Detective Gregg and Officer Garcia parked a cruiser in front of a tiny white pine cabin, sitting up on a hill with a long walkway lined with tufts of wild goldenrod.

"How are you feeling?" asked Danny, walking up the path to Marion Doyle's house.

"Mortified that I lost my breakfast at a crime scene."

"You're not the first cop to do that."

"Have you?"

"Well, no. But I'm a super cop."

"Ha. Ha."

"C'mon. Let's get this interview over with so I can take you home to brush your teeth. Your breath is killing me."

They'd reached the front door and Danny rang the doorbell, glancing down at Garcia, who was breathing into her hand and sniffing. She glared at him, and he winked. The door was answered by a tall, willowy woman in her sixties with stunning China-blue eyes and shoulder-length silver hair. She wore a sapphire sweater dress with black leggings beneath. Her toes were tucked into black suede lambswool slippers.

"Mrs. Doyle. This is Officer Garcia, you met her yesterday, and I am Detective Gregg. I called you earlier. May we come in and chat about Bob Humboldt?"

She stepped aside, welcoming them in. "Yes. Of course. Could I get you coffee or tea?"

"If you're having one, we'll join you. Otherwise, please don't go to the trouble," said Danny.

"I have a pot of coffee brewing. Join me in the kitchen. It was Bob's favorite room."

The scents of cinnamon and honey mingled with traces of clove and pine.

"I've been canning the last few days, but this year I won't be canning venison. Bob always brought me that from one of his hunting trips. Getting used to not having him around ... Well, he was a dear friend. We kept great company over glasses of wine and wonderful meals."

Keeping her back to them, she poured earthenware mugs of coffee from a stove-top percolator, then turned and set the cups on a square, red pine table next to the crackling woodstove. Her eyes, shiny with tears, met the detective's gaze.

"Yes, Detective, we were more than friends."

"I'm sorry for your loss, Mrs. Doyle," he replied.

"It's 'Miss', I'm afraid. Bob never made an honest woman of me, but I never expected he would. He was married to his work and so was I."

She took a seat at the table, where cream and sugar had been placed before her visitors arrived.

"Now, how can I help?"

Danny and Garcia took seats and took out their notebooks and pens, both conscious of how difficult talking about a deceased loved one could be.

"Miss Doyle? Did you know Mr. Humboldt was staying at the schoolhouse on Marnie Reilly's property? And if you did, do you know why?"

"I did. He thought he could protect her. Bob never forgave himself for Colin Reilly's death. It haunted him until the day he died. That poor girl. First her mother. And then she never got to say a proper goodbye to her father. His body was never found and his grave, I'm afraid, is vacant."

Wild Creek Ranch, The Kitchen, 11:45 AM

Sitting at the kitchen table eating egg, olive and chive sandwiches on sourdough bread, Sam set down a quarter with a bite out of it.

"Thank you for making this, Marnie. It is almost like Mom's."

She raised an eyebrow.

"Almost?"

"Yeah. She used that horrible bread that sticks to the roof of your mouth. This is much better."

"Ha! She didn't have time to go to a farmer's market when we were kids. She had a busy life."

"Did Creekwood even have those back then?" asked Poppy.

Teddy bit into a dill pickle and shrugged.

"I don't remember one."

Sam cleared his throat and broached a subject he had been struggling with for months.

"Do I have a grave at St. Michael's?"

Choking on her water, Marnie said, "What? That's a horrible topic for lunch."

"It is a valid question. Where was I interred?"

"Well, the fact that we are having a conversation makes it clear you weren't buried."

Sam laughed, and so did Teddy. Poppy stared at them as if they were all mad.

"We know that is not entirely true. You speak with the dead."

"You know what I meant. And yes, there is a grave at St. Michael's near our parents' plot."

"But it's empty, right?"

"We weren't given remains or personal effects. In fact, Tom and I got in a lot of trouble asking for proof of death and your belongings. It was a bad situation, Sam."

He ran his tongue around his bottom teeth and grunted.

"Huh. They didn't return anything?"

"Nope!"

"Okay. That is something I will discuss with Ransom. I had Papa Jack's service medals. I would like those back, wouldn't you?"

"Of course, if they haven't been incinerated."

"Let me look into it."

Marnie rolled her head, relaxing the muscles in her neck.

"It has always bothered me. I never got to say goodbye to you or Dad. Knowing that neither of you was laid to rest properly ... two plots ... two empty caskets."

"Hmm ... I want my gravestone removed. Do you think we could do that?"

His sister reached across the table and took his hand.

"I'll take care of it in the morning."

"Thanks, Squirt."

Marion Doyle's House, 71 White Pine Lane, 11:50 AM

Happy to listen to Marion Doyle reminisce about Bob Humboldt, his hobbies, work, and quirks, Danny was becoming impatient. They had been here for an hour and were no closer to finding out why he was on Marnie's property, other than the fact he felt responsible for her.

"Miss Doyle, what can you tell us about Bob's presence at the schoolhouse? Did he tell you anything that could be helpful to us in finding his killer?"

Putting an orange cloth napkin to her lips, she apologized.

"I'm so sorry. I was lost in the moment. Bob was there because he believed the same man responsible for Colin Reilly's death was after Marnie. He prattled on and on one night after too many sherries. He talked about someone named The Poacher. I honestly can't remember the whole story because I had too many tipples myself."

The detective's spine tingled, and his gut wrenched. That was the second time in as many days he had heard that name.

"Before I forget. Has anyone seen Marvel? Bob's crow. He usually took him wherever he went."

"Ah! One got into the house a few days back. I'll bet that was it."

"Did he poop on anyone? That's his signature move," she said, rolling her lip.

"Ha-ha! Yes. Sam Reilly took the brunt of that. If I see the bird, do you want him?"

"Goodness, no. But he is trained and talks when he feels like it, so he would make someone a nice pet."

"I'll tell Marnie. She has a collection of pets."

"You're Margaret Ryan's grandson?" she asked, searching his eyes.

"Yes, ma'am."

The woman patted his hand.

"Ask Maggie about it. She will remember, I'm sure."

"Did Bob talk to my grandmother about it?"

"I wouldn't know, dear. But in my experience, your grandmother knows everything that happens in Creekwood."

Chapter Twenty-Four

Creekwood Police Station, Forensics Lab, 12:10 PM

The detective and Garcia each carried takeaway coffees and a bag of hot apple cider doughnuts into the lab.

"Kelly Munson," said Rick, before they could speak.

Danny handed him a coffee and a white paper sack soiled with grease marks.

"The woman at Bob Humboldt's?"

Accepting the bag, the doctor looked inside and grinned.

"I love this season! Hot doughnuts and coffee are gifts from the gods. Which ones? I don't care. Thanks, and yes."

"She from around here?" asked Garcia before tasting the pastry.

"Look at you! Eating and everything!" Rick teased, wiping sugar from his mustache and nodding. "Yeah. She owns a chalet up on Wahta Mountain."

"I didn't know anyone lived up there," said the detective.

"Hmm ... there are few properties hidden in the trees."

"Next of kin?"

"Yeah. Tartetto called me with info and emailed this," said Rick, handing a sheet of paper over. "Said he was instructed to not leave things on your desk. That got to do with Stuyvesant?"

"Yeah. Don't tell him anything if you can help it."

"I shan't and I can."

"Thanks for this. Anything back on Krista Hansen? Or Bob's tech?"

"Negative. I'll chase the Hansen tests. I'm still waiting on Jess Alder, too. Giles' office has Munson's body, but it won't be today. He's at home with the flu."

"Hmm … I'm gone for the next couple of days. Sit on whatever you get or hand it off to the chief or captain."

"Downstate, right?"

"Yeah. Please call if you get anything."

"Will do. And, hey Garcia! I've got a gift for you." The doctor handed the officer a pretty pink bag dotted with daisies and yellow tissue paper fluffing out the top.

"Oh! Wow! Thank you! It's not my birthday."

She removed the tissue, looked inside, and gave him a dirty look. Thrusting the bag at the detective, she stomped off, calling Rick an expletive. Danny peeked in the bag and roared with laughter.

"Vomit bags and Vicks are great gifts. What's wrong with her?" said Rick, biting the doughnut, eyes sparkling with mischief.

Creekwood Police Station, Squad Room, 12:32 PM

"Without next of kin, who do we notify?" asked Garcia as they entered the squad room.

"Leave it with me. I'll give the details to the captain," said Danny.

"Okay. I'm going to grab lunch. Want anything?"

"Nah. I gotta go home and pack. I'm outta here shortly."

"See you soon, then. Thanks for letting me ride shotgun today."

"I trust you, Cheryl. You're going to make an ace detective."

"Thanks, Lieu. Have a safe trip."

When she'd left the squad room, Danny settled at his desk and wrote up his report to leave with the captain. It was an unusually quiet day, and he surveyed the room, wondering why no one was around. Then he heard a whoop from one of the interview rooms and his curiosity sent him to investigate.

"Happy birthday!" said Captain Sterling, setting a cake on the table in front of Officer Sam Jalnack, who was surrounded by colleagues.

Danny stuck his head in the door. "Nobody told me there's cake. Happy birthday, Sam!"

"Thanks, Lieu. Gonna stick around and have a slice?"

"Wish I could, but I gotta finish a report and get downstate."

"Oh! That's right. Well, you get back to it and thanks for the sentiment."

The detective backed out of the room and returned to his desk, turning on his monitor. Captain Sterling joined him with a piece of chocolate birthday cake on a paper plate and a plastic fork.

"Have you seen or heard from Stuyvesant today?"

"No, sir. He called in. Told Beau he's got a stomach flu."

"Think he does?"

"Nah. I call bullshit."

"Me too," said Sterling, licking frosting from the fork and going into his office and closing the door.

Wild Creek Ranch, The Clinic, Game Room, 2:21 PM

Marnie and Carl lounged with their feet up in two large leather recliners. Cups of coffee in hand, they chatted about the Halloween festival and how the clients could get involved. The comfortable room featured four seating areas with color televisions, recliners, and couches, as well as tables for playing cards, foosball, and pool.

"Who's that?" asked Marnie, her eyes following a tall man entering the game room.

Carl craned his neck and said, "Toby Munch."

"What's his story, and not to be rude, but what's up with his face?"

"He got a referral from the VA. His file is light and I'm hoping he'll warm to us. He's not a chatty fellow. Millicent said he had a chemical peel a day or two before intake. Looks painful, doesn't it? Want to meet him?"

"Sure. I've met everyone else."

The psychiatrist stood, crossing the room to the veteran. He said a few words and returned with the man.

"Toby, please meet Marnie Reilly, my partner in crime. She's a psychologist."

Getting to her feet and holding out her hand, Marnie said, "It's nice to meet you. How are you enjoying your stay?"

The veteran looked at her hand, but didn't take it, nor did he make eye contact.

"It's okay. I wasn't expecting to be in the middle of nowhere."

"You weren't told where you were going?"

"No. My family organized it. I was happy with my doctor in New York."

"You don't like the country?"

"For hunting, it's fine, but they won't let me do that here. I'm told I can't have a weapon on the property."

Marnie looked up at Carl, who said, "That's for safety."

The man rolled his eyes.

"Pfft! Yours or mine."

"Both," said Marnie, turning away and widening her eyes at the psychiatrist.

"Can I go now?" Toby asked.

Carl replied, "Sure. I'll see you at 4:00. We have an appointment."

"Whatever," said the man, skulking away.

Marnie punched Carl in the shoulder. "How long has he been here?"

"Not long. His parents brought him up from New York City a few weeks ago, and he jumped on a bus for home before they could check him in. They had to schlepp all the way back and get him. He is court-ordered to be here."

"So, he's dangerous?"

Carl quirked up his mouth. "More to himself than others."

"Does Danny know he's here?"

"Yes. I discussed it with him and Sam. They're aware."

"Oh, great!"

Wild Creek Ranch, The Kitchen, 3:38 PM

Tater put his front paws on the windowsill and woofed at the crunching tires of the vehicle in the driveway. Dickens, Gus, and Marnie all peered out too. Danny slowed to a stop and got out of the driver's side of the Jeep, and Ransom exited from the passenger side. Marnie wrinkled her nose and growled.

"What's wrong?" asked Teddy, who sat at the big trestle table, her laptop open.

"Danny's home and brought Ransom with him."

"I think he's cute," said Poppy, looking up from the paperwork she was filling out.

Teddy agreed, "I do too. And he smells amazing."

Nose wrinkled; Marnie opened the door to let in the detective.

"Honey! I'm home!" he said, his dimples putting on a show.

Marnie leaned up, meeting his lips halfway.

"Now, this guy, he's cute."

Danny frowned.

"I thought I was handsome."

"That too," she said, giggling. "I did most of the laundry, so you should be ready to pack. Everything is folded on the bed."

"You didn't need to do that, but thank you," he said, giving her a hug. "Want to come and visit while I pack?"

"I'll be up in a few minutes. Want a coffee?"

"One to go, please. By the way, do you know where my grandmother is? She's not at the diner and she's not answering her phone."

"Did you ask Dorie?"

"Yeah. She said Gram asked her to keep an eye on things and that's it."

"What about Hannah?"

"She doesn't know either. I need to ask her about some things. It's not like her to take off and not tell me where she's going."

"Where's Jack?"

"She must have taken him with her."

"Huh. That's curious. I'll call Ellie. Maybe Gram left him with her."

"Thanks."

Marnie picked up her phone and called Ellie Nikol, the knuckleheads' veterinarian.

"Hello, Ms. Reilly."

"Hello! Is Jack staying with you?"

"Way to jump right in there, Reilly. I'm fine. How are you?"

"Sorry! How are you?"

"Fine, thanks, and no, Jack isn't here. I'm assuming you're talking about the fuzzy-faced Jack Russell variety, right?"

"Yeah. Gram's missing, and now so is Jack."

"Are you being melodramatic?"

"A little, but it's unusual for her to not keep her grandchildren in the loop."

"I don't disagree, but she may have a boyfriend hidden somewhere."

"Ha! Wouldn't that be fun!"

"How are the kennels coming along?"

"I haven't checked lately, but I'm sure everything is fine. I would have heard if not."

"Would you mind if I drove out tomorrow afternoon?"

"Mind? I would love it! Come for dinner."

"I'll try. Business is busy! I've got one free patch between 2:00 and 4:00. After that, who knows? It will depend on appointments."

"That's what you get for being the best vet for sixty miles."

"Yes. Lucky me. See you tomorrow."

Marnie hung up, and tapping the phone to her chin, she said, "I wonder what Margaret Ryan is up to."

Wild Creek Ranch, Marnie's Bedroom, 4:03 PM

Marnie flopped onto the bed next to Danny's overnight bag and sighed.

"Jack is not with Ellie."

"They can't be too far. Gram wouldn't take off for any length of time without letting me know."

"Has she ever disappeared like this before?"

"You know. Now that I think about it, today is the anniversary of my grandfather's passing. I wouldn't be surprised if she and Jack weren't holed up in her apartment celebrating his life."

"With Irish whiskey," Marnie asked, grinning.

"Ha! It's probably the only time you might catch her drinking scotch. A really expensive one. That was my grandad's favorite. Especially when he drank it with my father."

She sat up, eyes twinkling. "I've never thought to ask. Do you have a kilt?"

He gave her an 'Oh, please' look and shoved a pair of sweatpants into the bag.

"But your father's family is from Scotland, right?"

"Yeah."

"So ... do you, or don't you?"

"I'm American. I wear pants, thanks."

"Ha-ha! Not always! Sometimes you wear the duvet."

Chapter Twenty-Five

Wild Creek Ranch, The Back Porch, 5:06 PM

The detective stood with his back against the door, holding his overnight bag and laptop satchel over his shoulder. Marnie leaned against him, arms around his waist, looking up into his face.

"I'll be back in two days. It's only tonight and tomorrow night. Will you be okay without me hogging the bed?" he asked, giving her a kiss.

"If I get lonely, I'll let Tater sleep in your spot."

"Ha! Don't start that. He won't give it up when I get home."

"I'll call you tonight before I go to sleep."

"I'd like that. You know what else I'd like?"

"There are so many things I can think of," she said.

Her cheeky grin and waggling eyebrows made him laugh.

"Can we have a big dinner when I get back? I'll help you cook."

"Sure. Roast chicken?"

"As long as it's a bird you haven't named."

"Ha-ha! Deal. I have four in the fridge from the butcher that will keep until you return."

"Sounds perfect! I'll be home early, and we can get dinner ready together, huh?"

"That's a plan, Dan."

He gave her a tight hug, two long kisses, and jogged down the steps.

"I'm taking my car, okay?"

"Yeah! I was going to ask you for mine back. My knee is feeling much better. Drive safely."

"I will."

"By the way, Detective."

"Yeah."

"I love you."

"Love you too, Ms. Reilly."

Sam trudged across the lawn, stopped at Danny's car, and had a chat as Marnie looked on from the porch. Carl joined them a few minutes later, as did Ransom. Finished with their discussion, the men stepped away from the Jeep, and the detective waved and tooted the horn before blowing a kiss to Marnie.

"Hey, Squirt, I need a few things at the hardware store. Did you have dinner plans?" asked Sam.

"I planned to pick up the pizzas I ordered half an hour ago. I'll cook tomorrow night."

"Let's go!"

"I'll get my keys."

Creekwood Town Center, Benedetti's Italian Restaurant, 5:40 PM

Marnie dropped off Sam and drove to the pizza place to pick up the pies. The restaurant's tiny parking lot was jammed full of cars, so she parked on the street and walked a block. Benedetti's bar area at the front of the building was packed to the gills with happy hour clients. Too many scents hit her nose, and she cringed when stale beer, musky body spray, and a sweet floral perfume hung in the surrounding air. She made her way to the takeout window, leaning an elbow on a wooden shelf. Her stomach stopped churning and growled as the aromas of pepperoni, Italian sausage, red sauce, and garlic tempted her appetite.

"Hey, Marnie!" said the chef. "How's tricks?"

"Pretty good, Mr. Benedetti. How about you?"

He threw pizza dough skyward, catching it in mid-air, and replied, "Ups and downs. You know the routine."

Even though they'd had this same conversation a million times, she laughed—not because it was funny. But because the proprietor's face was dusted with flour and pizza sauce dotted his cheeks.

"I'll have your order ready in two shakes."

"Thanks," she said, moving to the side so the next customer could check in.

Every table in the restaurant was occupied, and the décor hadn't been updated since Marnie was a kid: red and white checked table clothes, candles in the top of waxy Chianti bottles, a jukebox that flipped between Dean Martin, Frank Sinatra, Mario Lanza, and a few others she didn't know.

She spotted Randolph Stuyvesant and Carrie Sutherland huddled under a Peroni sign in a back corner with a bottle of wine and wished for bionic hearing.

Mr. Benedetti shouted, "Sutherland!" from the window as he slid a Hawaiian pizza onto the shelf. He looked at Marnie and rolled his eyes.

"These people. Ruining my food with their pineapple and ham."

Marnie snickered and slid further away near a plastic fig tree, where she hoped she would blend into the scenery. But Carrie saw her as she zig-zagged through tables.

"Are you spying on us?" Sutherland demanded.

Marnie thought she sounded like an angry mama cat protecting her young and pulled a face and held up her hands.

"Why would I be interested?"

Shoving a finger into the psychologist's face, the reporter backed her into a corner. "I have a right to eat dinner with a friend, so don't you go running back to your boyfriend, telling him you saw us here."

Marnie straightened her shoulders and took a step toward Carrie, who backed away.

"What are you? Twelve? I don't care who you spend time with, but I do care when you trespass on my property. Something you should think twice about in the future."

Looking the psychic psychologist straight in the eyes, the reporter lied, "I wasn't on your property."

"I've got pictures that say otherwise, which means the police have seen them, too. You and Randy have no right to lurk in the shadows near my house. Don't do it again! Next time, I will have you both charged with trespass."

"You better be careful who you're threatening," hissed Carrie.

"That wasn't a threat. You swan back into town and think everyone is going to give you the scoop. People talk. I know who you've been speaking to."

The reporter took a step back, surprised that people in Creekwood had ratted her out. Rather than back away, to fight another day, she attacked—saying the only thing that came to mind.

"No one believes you can speak to spirits, let alone see them. You're still the *ghost girl* everyone mocked in school."

Marnie chuckled. "Ah! You've been chatting with Kate Parish. Are you aware she's crazy? Not that it matters. I'm not bothered by your inability to believe in spirits, clairvoyants, or other paranormal possibilities. I guess I should be flattered that you've taken an interest when I have shown *none* in you. Although, I occasionally wonder why you're such a bitch. Did someone hurt your feelings? Is that it? Could something more sinister motivate you? Convincing you that destroying innocent people's lives is righteous? Or perhaps Ken Wilder dumping you for me was too much for that ginormous ego of yours?"

Carrie grabbed her pizza and side-stepped the psychologist, who stood in her path.

"Marnie Reilly, you are the most sanctimonious person I have ever met!"

"Well, we both know *that* isn't true. You're in cahoots with a self-righteous ass." She pulled her keys from her pocket and paused before picking up her order. "You know the gals down at Drake's share intel on you too, right? It's a small town. Tongues wag and word on the street is Randy's your source. Have a good night, Carrie. But a bit of advice—if you're coming for me, you better sharpen your claws. I won't fight fair."

The red-faced reporter marched to the back of the restaurant, dropped the pizza on the round table and stormed out the rear door, leaving Randy to toss bills down and run after her.

All eyes turned to Marnie, who had forgotten she was in a room full of townies.

"Show's over, folks. Enjoy your evening."

She winked at Mr. Benedetti as she grabbed her boxes, then exited via the front door to a flurry of small-town whispers.

Hackett's Hardware, Isabella Street, 6:03 PM

"You look like the cat that ate the canary," said Sam, stepping into the truck. "Who did you piss off?"

Marnie put the Jeep in gear and laughed as she pulled out of her parking.

"Carrie Sutherland. She was at Benedetti's with Randy."

"Really?" he said, his eyebrows up. "Did you tell her we saw them at the ranch?"

"Yeah. And that we have pictures."

"How did she react?"

"She threatened me, made fun of me, and then stomped off when I *slammed* her," she replied, smacking her hand on the steering wheel.

Sam stared at his sister in disbelief. "What? You hit her?"

"No! I wouldn't do that."

"Pfft! Who are you trying to kid?"

"Well, if provoked, I might. But no. I didn't. I insulted her, which may have felt like a slap."

Marnie's phone lit up with a text alert.

"Who's that from?"

Sam looked at the screen.

"You've got one from Teddy. Another from Alice. Oh! There's one from Ellie. And David Bennett. And Stew. Marnie, what did you do?"

Wild Creek Ranch, The Kitchen, 6:30 PM

"Oh my god, Marnie! That must have felt so good. You looked like you were going to pop her one!" said Teddy, passing paper plates around the table.

"Who filmed it?" asked Poppy, putting a roll of paper towels in the center of the table. "You're out of napkins, by the way."

Marnie looked at the video again and laughed.

"It had to be Mr. Benedetti. He was the only one who could have gotten that angle. Who posted that?"

Teddy checked and said, "This one was posted by Carol Chadwick. Irene Hazelton has it in her timeline, too. And the original came from Sue Benedetti Marco. Ha-ha! Maybe she filmed it. Was she there?"

"Apparently. Wait until Danny sees it. Gawd!" She placed her hand against her forehead, wondering how he would react to her outing Randolph's traitorous behavior to everyone in Creekwood. After all, if Carol Chadwick and Irene Hazelton were there, it was just a question of time before everyone in town knew.

Poppy's eyebrows drew together. "Will he be mad?"

Teddy and Marnie roared with laughter.

"No! Not at all."

Sam said, "I can hear him now. In that gravelly voice of his, he'll say, 'She's *back*!' and he will finish with that drawn-out baritone chuckle."

"It's more of a guffaw, isn't it?" said Marnie with a giggle, but her mood changed quickly, thinking of the toxic exchange with the reporter.

Ransom strutted into the kitchen carrying a bottle of wine. "Why the sour face, kid?"

"Yeah! You should be feeling great ..."

Marnie cut off Teddy. "Great? I embarrassed Carrie Sutherland for all Creekwood to see. Now that the adrenaline has worn off, I feel awful. I mean, she's a public presence in the community and I took her legs out from under her."

"You did that to The Collective. And that was on a stage before hundreds of people," said Sam.

"Yeah, but they deserved it. They were charlatans."

"Carrie is too in media circles. She twists the truth, bends rules, trespasses on the property of people she wants to expose." Her brother shrugged. "It is the same thing without the hoodoo voodoo, if you ask me."

She scrunched up her nose, thinking of the fallout. "What about Randolph?"

Sam laughed. "He is a dick. Stop worrying and eat pizza."

"And drink wine," added Ransom, pouring her a glass of red.

She scanned the room. "Where's Patrick?"

"He's running late. A lead came through about a guy he has been tracking. A carpenter reported seeing a man of the same description on the island," said Sam.

"*My* island?" she asked.

"Yes."

"*Your* island?" asked Poppy, eyes popping.

"Uh-huh. The one in Perch Pond. I bought it last spring," said Marnie.

"Why?"

"Long story."

"I've got time," she said.

6:40 PM

Between bites of pizza and drinks of wine, Marnie regaled the encounter that fateful summer's day.

"In a nutshell, when Sam, Tom and I were kids, we took the boat out to the island one day to swim with my brother's friends. When we arrived, I saw a ghost standing on the shoreline. He gave us a hard time and told us to leave because his murderer, the ghost's killer, was still around."

"So, the spirit was giving you a warning?" asked Poppy.

"Yeah. In life, he was Cy Barnes. Do you remember him?"

"No. He's not familiar, but the island is. We picked apples there once when I was probably three or four. I remember because my grandmother was with us, and she died when I was five. We collected pebbles from the beach, too."

Sam interjected, "There was a small orchard, but it's long gone now."

"Wasn't there a rickety old bridge? Didn't it collapse? I noticed when I got into town the old bridge had been repaired. Was that you?"

"Yeah. We're building an event venue and picnic grounds. It's a beautiful property."

"Okay, so what happened to the spook?" asked Poppy.

"We heard a scream across the island and before Sam ran off to investigate, he hid Tom and I in the shallows and weeds. I decided not to wait, so we picked pebbles and found sticks to hit the killer if he came after us. Anyway, the bad guy found us and dragged me off, kicking and screaming, to the house and locked me in a trunk in the cellar."

"Oh, my god! That's horrible!"

"Yeah. But Tom found me and got me out. But while I was in there, my grandfather gave me the lowdown on Barnes, who had killed his wife and buried her in an old ice shack beneath the bridge. Papa Jack also told me about a treasure Barnes had hidden in the coal chute. We found it but put it back with a plan to go back and get it someday because Sam arrived with his friends to rescue us.

"Did you?"

"That's a different story. But yeah. So, Sam had sent his friend Marcus to get Mom and Dad. Umm ... wait. You sent him for our folks before I was grabbed. Gosh, the story is jumbled." She looked at Sam, who nodded.

"Correct. Then our parents arrived and pulled their weapons. Detective *Mac* Gregg and Officers Beaumont and Sterling showed up a few minutes later and took him into custody, but not before Marnie punched him in the nose." Sam nudged his sister's hand across the table. "And by the way, Jethro Barnes is dead. I thought you should know that."

"Really?" she said. "Wow! That's a relief, but what about the books?"

"I bet Kate Parish had them sent. She knows the story from her father's files and my sessions."

"I hadn't thought of that. You're probably right. Did you tell Danny?"

"I did. I told him before he left."

"How did he die?"

"A fire at a factory where he was working as a janitor after he got out of prison."

"Hmm. What about others on the list?"

"We eliminated everyone on the spectral sphere first. Kitty Parish is in prison. Alice, Allen, and Carl are unlikely candidates. Your relationships with them are supportive and cordial. Kate is locked up, but that is not a deterrent. We are hamstrung regarding your clients because divulging details is unethical. Any other suggestions?"

She shook her head.

The mood getting heavy, Ransom asked, "Who's ready for another glass of wine?"

"No, thanks. I'm going to take the knuckleheads out, then soak in a bubble bath," said Marnie.

"I'll come with you," he replied, handing bottle duties over to Teddy, who batted her eyelashes at him and poured.

7:20 PM

"It's beautiful here, Kid. You must love hiking in those hills over there," said Ransom, pointing northwest beyond the creek.

"I haven't done much yet. My knee is better though. Maybe when Danny is back, we can take the dogs for a long walk."

"Do you still have pain?"

"Yeah. When I'm on my feet a lot. But it's better than last month and the month before."

"That's how it works. Most wounds heal with time."

"Mm-hmm."

"Marnie, what aren't you saying?"

She stopped and stared at him. "What do you mean?"

He ran a hand over his spiky blonde hair and looked over her head.

"I've known you a long time. You're hiding something."

She shivered and pulled her scarf around her neck. A tingle crawling across the top of her head told her something bad was going to happen. What that was, she didn't know.

"I'm not hiding anything. If I knew something, I would tell you."

"But you've got a gut feeling."

With a dismissive shake of her head, she said. "Nah. It's all in my head."

But she knew it wasn't.

One of the Border Collies yipped, and all three raced around the corner of the house, kicking up dirt in their wake. Their scruffs were at attention and Dickens' fluffy tail was between his legs.

"Marnie, get the dogs inside. Go!" said Ransom, pushing her with one hand, drawing his gun with the other. "Get Sam!"

Chapter Twenty-Six

Wild Creek Ranch, The Kitchen, 7:45 PM

"False alarm. It's another one of those morbid scarecrows propped up against the cottage out back," said Ransom.

Teddy's mouth popped open. "That's my house!"

Poppy, who was sitting next to her, put an arm around her shoulder. "It's okay. You're safe here with us. We can go out when the sun's up to check everything is alright."

"You called Danny?" Marnie asked Sam, pouring herself a glass of wine.

"Yes. He reached out to Rick, and he will be here soon with his team."

"I'll put on a pot of coffee, then."

Ransom paced back and forth, clenching and unclenching his fists.

"How could this happen? We have guards crawling every inch of this property. And cameras everywhere! The guy must be a ghost."

All eyes turned to Marnie, who grimaced and shrunk against the counter.

"Why are you all looking at me?"

"Could a ghost do that?" he asked.

She scowled over the top of her wineglass. "No! Are you crazy? Spirits don't carry around life-size objects. They might hide little things, like jewelry or keys, but not a scarecrow."

"Are you sure?"

Jogging her shoulders up and down, she stuck out her bottom lip before saying, "No."

9:23 PM

Marnie met Rick at the door with a mug of coffee.

"What's the prognosis, Doc?"

He took the coffee and sat on a bench, removing his glasses. Tater poked his head from under the table and gave Rick's arm a nose bump. He patted the seat next to him and the dog jumped up, resting his head on the doctor's shoulder.

"Same as the last. I'll run tests and keep you guys in the loop."

Ransom and Sam sat opposite, both wondering if the scientist was telling them everything.

"Is that it?" asked the former.

"For now. I'm waiting for Danny to call me back."

"Doesn't a Federal Marshal have any pull?" asked Ransom, stone-faced.

"You guys get involved in small time misdemeanors, do you?" Rick laughed and took a sip of coffee.

"That's what you think this is?" asked Sam.

Rick's phone rang, and he took it from his pocket. "Saved by the bell. Back in a sec."

As soon as he left the room, Ransom was on his feet again, peering into the front room.

"The cameras need to be checked tonight and if we need more, we get them."

A rap on the door made them all jump—except Sam, who had seen Patrick Kowalski through the window. Ransom swung the door open and welcomed him with a handshake. The canines crowded around him, offering licks and paw shakes.

"It's good to see you," said Marnie, crossing the room and wrapping him in a hug.

As usual, Patrick blushed as he embraced her, before stepping back to assess the room. His hazel eyes landed on Poppy, the only face he didn't recognize.

"Evening. Sorry I'm l-l-late."

They overheard the end of Rick's conversation as he returned to the kitchen.

"Yeah. No worries. I'll have her call you. See you tomorrow night."

"He's coming home early?" Marnie asked.

"Yes, ma'am. Give him a call before you turn in, huh?"

"Of course," she said, happy to hear Danny would be home early.

He turned to Sam, then nodded toward the door. "You guys wanna walk me to my car?"

"Right behind you!"

9:40 PM

"Okay, ladies. I am going up to bed. Are you coming up or waiting for the guys?" asked Marnie.

Teddy quirked up the corner of her mouth. "What are the chances they'll tell us what's going on?"

"Zero."

"Might as well go to bed. What do you say, Poppy?"

Stretching her arms over her head, she half yawned and smiled.

"I say there are a lot of fine-looking gentlemen running around this ranch."

Marnie laughed. "Patrick's cute, isn't he?"

"Patrick. Ransom. Sam. Even Carl has something about him."

"What about Danny?" she asked.

"Oh! He's gorgeous, but taken."

"Yes, he is. To both."

9:55 PM

Snuggled up in bed with Tater beside her, his head on Danny's pillow, Dickens on his back at the foot, and Gus sprawled at an angle in the middle, Marnie called the detective. He answered before the first ring was finished.

"Hi!"

"You're coming home early?"

"Yeah. I'll leave here around three. Home in time for dinner, if that's okay."

"Well, I wasn't expecting you so soon," she teased.

"Ha-ha! A sandwich would make me happy."

"I can clear everyone out. We can have a blanket picnic by the fire."

"Hmm … As much as that sounds delightful, I've got things to discuss with Sam and Ransom as soon as I get back. Sorry."

"That's no fun," she said, her bottom lip protruding.

"I know, but Rick told me the scarecrow was wearing similar clothing to what Jess Alder was wearing when she disappeared."

"Ugh! I had a feeling."

"Have you heard from Gram?"

"No. She hasn't returned my messages."

"Mine either."

"I can drive over and check on her tomorrow. I'll be in town anyway to pick up the Halloween decorations I ordered for the barn."

"If you wouldn't mind, but don't go alone. Take one of the guys, please."

"No worries."

"Are you in bed?"

"Yeah."

"Does Tater have his head on my pillow?"

"He might," she said, running a hand over the dog's silky coat.

"Ha-ha! Make sure he knows who the boss is, huh?

"He is very well aware it's me, Detective."

"You got me there. I kind of like it when you're bossy. It's sexy. And by the way, I saw the video."

"Ah! Geez!" she said, covering her face with a hand. "How did you get your hands on that?"

"I've got connections, Ms. Reilly."

"Grr! Anyway. It wasn't one of my finer moments. I'm sorry for outing Randy."

"Drop it. She provoked you. I already talked to Sal Benedetti. He was surprised you didn't clock her, and I am glad you didn't. I wouldn't want to arrest you."

"Ha! There's a whole handcuff spiel I could break into there but won't. I'm too tired."

"Alright, Sweetie. I'll see you tomorrow."

"Have a safe trip."

"I love you."

"Love you too."

Marnie set her phone on its charger and reached for the light, but hesitated. Getting out of bed, she gathered up chunks of raw amethyst from her nightstand, dresser, windowsill, and an end table next to a comfy chair. She lined them up outside her closet door and withdrew two steps. The dogs' heads popped up and followed her every move, before boredom set in and they dropped back down with a goodnight grumble.

"You all listen up. I've had enough of your nonsense. If you weren't a friend or family in life, you are not welcome. Piss off! And stay out of my dreams or I'll sic Gram on you! And I am quite certain you don't want any of what she'll throw your way."

She crawled back into bed, turned out the light, and snuggled up next to Tater.

Chapter Twenty-Seven

October 14th

Wild Creek Ranch, 4:28 AM

The man moved stiffly through a line of trees running parallel to the western paddock, the bundle on his back slipping to the dewy grass. With a grunt, he bent and hefted it over his shoulder, before trudging on to his destination. He stopped and stood motionless when a security vehicle shone spotlights into the woods. Knowing his camouflage clothing would hide his large form amongst the trees, he breathed through his nose so steam from his breath wouldn't alert them to his position. Satisfied with their security sweep, the guards moved along, and the man continued his trek. He had a body to dump on the doorstep of an enemy.

Wild Creek Ranch, The Kitchen, 5:12 AM

Bacon popped and squeaked in a cast-iron skillet while Sam scrambled a bowl of eggs, and Ransom made toast.

"Did you check the video?" asked the marshal.

"Yes, from my phone as soon as I woke up. The definition is grainy, but I think we had a visitor near the kennel construction this morning. We'll check it out first thing."

"Marnie mentioned last night that she needs to go into town today. Who's going with her?"

Without a thought, Sam said, "You."

"I'm not her favorite person."

"No, but you are my choice for keeping her safe."

"Not yourself?"

"Uh-uh. Too many people in town will be distracted. They still see me as a threat. If anything should happen, we want townies focused on reality, not what they have made up in their heads about me."

"But all that nonsense has been debunked. They know the Parish family is responsible."

Sam snorted and shook his head. "If people believed truth over fabrication, it would be ideal. But they prefer the scenario where I am the enemy, not part of an upstanding family who has lived here for years."

"So, we have to shift those beliefs."

"Good luck. My family and close friends are privy to my previous career. These people are not. They would never understand. How do you think the folks in Creekwood would feel about a retired assassin living in their backyard?"

"Retired? That's news to me." Ransom laughed and buttered two pieces of toast, tossing them on a plate.

Sam smirked and poured eggs into a pan.

Creekwood Town Square, 8:30 AM

"I still don't understand why you wanted me to drive. All you've done is bitch at me," said Marnie, backing her truck into a parking space and shoving the gear into first. She turned off the engine and pulled on the parking brake.

"You drive like the devil is on your tail," said Ransom, taking off his seatbelt.

"I didn't break the speed limit once."

"You got stopped by a cop, kid."

She rolled her eyes. "For going through a yellow light. I didn't get a ticket, did I?"

"No, but that's only because you're sleeping with Danny."

She gasped. "That is not true. There was so much green left in that yellow. If I had braked, I would have been back ended by a tractor trailer."

"Okay. Fair point."

Marnie took a breath and calmed herself by searching through her tote bag for a notebook.

"You okay?" he asked.

"Honestly, no. My nerves are shot. Nearly twelve months of ... of ..."

Ransom squeezed her knee. "I know. A lot has happened. Now. To answer your question. I asked you to drive so my hands are free." He pulled his gun from an inner pocket and smiled. "And I know you're a good driver, but you and I spar. It's what we've always done, and it's probably why we didn't work."

"Danny and I were like that when we first met. We disagreed constantly."

"Yeah. But Danny's a grownup and has more patience."

"Hmm. That's true."

"Are we gonna sit here all day, Reilly, or are we going shopping?" he said, stepping out of the vehicle into a soft mist of mountain rain.

Ryan's Diner, 10:30 AM

With the shopping done and the Halloween decorations collected, the last stop was the diner to check on Gram. The morning rush was over, but a throng of customers entered the building as they sat in the Jeep waiting for the rain to ease.

"Let's grab a coffee and a cinnamon roll before heading back," suggested Marnie.

"I can't believe you don't have an umbrella in your glove compartment. You have everything else in here," said Ransom, removing a box cutter, napkins, a folded map, and a flashlight.

"There used to be one, but it could be in Danny's car. We haven't completely swapped back."

"Okay. Let's make a run for it. I'll hold my coat over your head."

"That's okay. I don't mind getting rained on."

He rolled his eyes, unlatched his door, and ran around to the driver's side, pulling his arms out of his sleeves as he went. When she opened her door, he held the jacket over her head, protecting her from the big drops.

"Chivalry isn't dead if Ransom Elliot is allowing his perfectly spiked hair to get wet with rain."

"Shut up and get inside," he said, laughing.

"Whoa!" cried Marnie, tripping over the threshold and falling through the door.

Ransom toppled after her, both landing with a thud on the wet welcome mat.

"Damnit!" said Marnie, getting up on her knees before standing to see the diners staring at her and the marshal.

Ransom scrambled to his feet and brushed mud from his jeans, waved, smiled, and took a bow, which delivered a few whistles and applause from Gram's customers.

"Gawd! I hope no one filmed that sad display." Marnie pasted on a sheepish grin and scooted to the booth at the back that was always reserved for Danny.

"Ha-ha! Let it go, Kid. No one is looking at us," said Ransom, slipping into the seat opposite.

Waitress Dorie Haber appeared at their table with glasses of water and menus.

"Are you okay? That was quite the tumble."

"Yeah. Bruised egos never killed anyone," he said.

"Fine, thanks, Dorie. Could we get coffees and cinnamon rolls, please?" said Marnie.

"Sure. We just took a batch out of the oven."

"Is Gram here? I wanted to invite her to dinner tonight."

"She sure is. Came out of her cave this morning. You know she always gets like this on the anniversary of her husband's death."

"I wasn't around this time last year, but Danny mentioned it."

"Gee, Marnie. It seems like you and the detective have been an item for forever." Dorie gave the marshal a dirty look, then turned back. "I'll tell Maggie you're here."

"Thanks!"

Ransom watched her walk away. "What the heck was that?"

"She thinks you're up to no good, apparently," she said, giggling.

Gram appeared from the kitchen with two cups of coffee in one hand and two plates of cinnamon rolls in the other.

"Hello, Lass! Ransom." She set down the dishes and stepped back. "Dorie mentioned a dinner invitation."

"Danny will be home tonight. I'm roasting a few chickens. Can you come?"

"Roast chicken? Isn't his favorite pot roast?"

"Yeah, but we can have that another night."

The older woman gave her a disapproving glance. "You know I never involve myself in your relationship, but I think Daniel would prefer pot roast tonight."

Marnie frowned, not used to the tone. "Okay. I can change the menu, no problem."

"I'll see you at six," said Gram and she scurried off to the kitchen without another word.

Leaning across the table, she whispered, "Was that weird?"

Ransom shrugged. "I've always found her odd, anyway."

"Mm. Fair point."

Wild Creek Ranch, 12:30 PM

The dogs lounged peacefully on the hearth in the cozy study as a pattering of rain showered outside. Leaves flew past the windows in a flurry of fall colors, a few sticking to the French door panes, giving the illusion of stained glass.

"This should go in the 'I'll consider it' pile," said Marnie, handing a piece of ivory stationery to Teddy, who frowned.

"You can't give money to everyone who asks!"

"I didn't say to send them anything, but we can consider it, can't we?"

"No! Don't you read my emails? I sent you background information on at least twenty charities who reached out to you that are shonky and this is one of them."

Marnie dropped her chin to her chest and sighed. "Okay. Okay!" Lifting her head, she pushed a stack of correspondence across her oak desk. "You weed out everything you think is dodgy and give me back the rest. Happy?"

Bottom lip protruding, Teddy scooped up the papers and tapped the edges on the desktop to neaten the pile.

"You need a proper business manager to take care of this stuff. Things are falling between the cracks. I still have stock to order for the clinic and reports to file for Carl. Andrea is swamped. Carl doesn't have a free moment, and you're still ... Face it. We need help!"

"I'm still what?" Face red, Marnie pushed back her chair and shot to her feet, grabbing the desk to balance herself.

Teddy pursed her lips. "I saw that. That little thing you do every time you stand up fast. Your balance is still off. Admit it, Reilly! You are not invincible!"

"Never said I was," she replied, dropping back into her chair. "But I am resilient! My balance will come back. It's only a lingering effect. At least I'm eating."

"Have you been doing your exercises? Mental and physical?"

"Yes, *Mom*! I've been following doctor's orders. Think you could get off my back?"

"I can. But if you are hiring Poppy and are heading back to work, that's going to create more paperwork. We need help."

Marnie blew out a breath and looked up at the ceiling. "Okay. Put an ad in the local paper or do whatever it is that you do to find what we need."

Clapping her hands, Teddy grabbed her laptop and got to work.

"Anyway! I better get the roast in the oven. I should make a pie, too."

Teddy's face lit up. "Raspberry?"

"Uh-uh. Can't bring myself to it."

"Whatever you bake will be delicious. You want help with dinner?"

"No, thanks."

"Okay. I'll run down to the clinic, but I'll be back by five-thirty to set the table."

"Deal."

Marnie's phone dinged, and she glanced down at the screen.

"Oh! Ellie canceled. She doesn't fancy wandering the paddocks in the rain. Can't say as I blame her."

Tater's head popped up—ears at attention, and he tipped it to the side, staring at the floor.

"What's with him?" asked Teddy, standing up from her side chair.

"Mice?" she said with a laugh as a thundering knock from the floorboards boomed through the study.

With a quick side-eye at one another, they turned their attention to the trapdoor in the center of the room.

Hand to her heart, Teddy backed closer to Marnie when an echoing bang followed. Her hand moved quickly to her mouth.

"Don't vomit. It's probably the guys." Marnie crossed to the table and pushed it with her foot. Bending, she moved the area rug and reached for the latch.

"What are you doing? You can't open that. You don't know who's down there."

So Marnie knocked back and waited for a response and a voice shouted from the other side.

"Open the damn door. It's me! Ransom!"

His blonde spiky hair poked out of the opening, and he brushed a cobweb from his nose as he moved up a step.

"What were you doing down there? Where did you go into the tunnel?" asked Marnie, offering him a hand.

"The cemetery. I saw a big dude run in and I followed, but I lost him."

"Oh! Great! Now we have to worry even more!" said Teddy.

"Worry about what?" said Poppy, coming into the room.

Ransom stepped up, brushing dust and silvery strands of webbing from his clothes.

"Nothing, Poppy. Everything's fine," he said, dropping the hatch and latching it. "We need a two-way system to open that. If we need to get in, there should be a key or a combination."

"We've tried a few, but we haven't found one that works. Even the locksmith didn't have anything Danny would approve."

"Leave it with me. I know a guy." Ransom stalked off, leaving the gals alone with the dogs.

Marnie glanced at the floor, then up at her friends, eyebrows knitted together.

"What was he doing in the cemetery? He's supposed to be keeping an eye out."

The Living Room, 4:33 PM

With pot roast in the oven, veggies prepped, and a cranberry pie cooling on the counter, Marnie indulged in the coziness of her home on a chilly, rainy day. Curled up on the couch with a book of poetry, and the dogs at her feet, she sipped tea with her favorite poet, Robert Frost. She imagined her father's voice in her head as she recited *Nothing Gold Can Stay.*

> Nature's first green is gold,
> Her hardest hue to hold.
> Her early leaf's a flower;
> But only so an hour.
> Then leaf subsides to leaf.
> So Eden sank to grief,
> So dawn goes down to day.
> Nothing gold can stay.

She closed the book's cover and sat quietly enjoying the fire. Then a thought occurred to her, and she slammed down the book on the end table and snatched up her phone. The call she placed rang once.

"Damnit, Ransom! You chased the big dude from the ranch into the cemetery, didn't you?"

The Study, 5:13 PM

Gathered in the study, the women sat together on the couch, arms crossed and casting cold, judgmental eyes on Ransom and Sam. If not for the flames crackling in the fireplace, the men would have frozen to death from the chill. Carl leaned against the doorway, uncertain why he had been summoned to the meeting.

"Full disclosure, right? That's how you do things around here?" said Ransom, holding out his hands in surrender.

Between clenched teeth, Marnie said, "Yes, and you knew that. Don't pretend you thought it was okay to not tell us you chased someone from the property and into the tunnels. Danny talked to you about the *big dude* because of what happened to me a few nights ago. That's why you're here."

"I know. And Sam has already given me hell for not telling you. I'm sorry. The three of you had a right to know, but I didn't want to scare you."

"Pfft! Scare me?" Marnie frowned and let out a disgusted breath.

Poppy said, "Well, I appreciated it. Not knowing…"

"Could have gotten one of us killed!" said Teddy, getting to her feet. "How dare you?"

Sam patted Teddy's shoulder, trying to calm her, but she slapped away his comfort.

"Don't think you can make it all better by patting my shoulder. I'm not a dog!" she snapped.

Tater, Dickens, and Gus took offense at her remark and grumbled protests from the hearth.

Sam threw up his hands and side-eyed Carl, knowing his presence might get them out of the proverbial doghouse.

"Okay. I'm going to throw in my two cents," said the psychiatrist. "First, Ransom acted without malice. He was trying to do the right thing. Second, now we know the … uh … big dude knows about the tunnels, so that means he must be a native of Creekwood. It's a clue to follow, right?"

Stone-faced, Sam agreed. "Excellent point, Carl." But before he could go on, the dogs clamored to their feet, yipped, and raced out of the office.

"Danny must be home," said Marnie, hearing the back door open.

She stood to go greet him, but her heart stopped the next moment when she heard a familiar phrase and the excited barks and trilling of the canines.

"I'm starving!"

The room gasped and with tears in her eyes, she yelled, "Tom?!"

She pushed her way past the others, skidded on the rug in the hallway, and raced into the kitchen to see her best friend kneeling, surrounded by the knuckleheads. He hugged Gus, burying his head in the dog's neck to hide the tears in his violet eyes.

The Kitchen, 5:28 PM

"I can't believe you're here! Your parents said it would be another month," said Marnie, flinging her arms around his neck, her face wet with joy.

Tom wrapped his arms around her waist, hugging her tight and swinging her around.

"I know, but the doc said I was good to go. I'm not fit for work, but I'm here," he said, setting her down and squeezing her shoulders. "You're thin."

"And you've got gray hair and a beard. Look at all those silver strands," she said, messing up his curls.

He laughed. "I need a haircut. Haven't had one since June."

Hands over her mouth, she burst into tears, and he drew closer, allowing her to collapse against him.

"It's okay, Marn. I'm home," he whispered, caressing her back.

"I missed you so much. Why wouldn't you let me visit you?" she pushed away and wiped her eyes on her sleeve.

"Because I couldn't walk, and it was frustrating. And I was angry. I knew you'd want to take care of me, and you couldn't. You had healing to do too. But I'm walking now and everything's fine."

"Really? Is your hearing okay?"

"Yeah. Still a bit of ringing *and* nausea if I stand up too fast, but it's getting better every day."

Danny came in the door with his overnight bag and a suitcase, setting them on the floor. Marnie crossed the room, gave him a kiss, then scolded him.

"Why didn't you tell me you were bringing him home?"

With a sheepish grin, he said, "I told Sam and Ransom. They got the other downstairs bedroom ready because I didn't want you tied in knots and running around trying to make everything perfect."

As the three stood at the door, together once again, and the dogs paced with excitement, the others stood at the kitchen door, waiting to come in. They didn't want to intrude on the joyous reunion.

"This calls for a celebration," said Teddy, waltzing into the room, clapping her hands. "Ransom? Could you walk me over to my place? I've got four bottles of champagne in my fridge I've been saving for a special occasion."

As she passed Tom on the way out the door, she hugged him.

"It's great to have you back."

"It really is, isn't it?" he said, chuckling and shaking Ransom's hand.

Sam put out his hand as he approached, and Tom grabbed it, but rather than shake, he pulled him forward and embraced the assassin.

"Thanks for staying in touch. Your notes helped keep my spirits up."

"Of course. I know how hard it can be to be away from family and friends," he said, patting him on the back.

Poppy watched from the doorway, unsure what to do, so she waved and smiled when she caught Tom's eye.

"Do my eyes deceive me? Poppy Chomsky? Wow! It's been a lifetime," said Tom, walking the short distance.

She stuck out her hand, but he ignored it and offered a hug instead.

"Ah! Geez!" Marnie erupted. "If I'd known you'd be here for dinner, I would have made raspberry pie."

"But you made pot roast, right?" said Tom.

The psychologist eyed Danny. "Hmm … Yes. At Gram's insistence."

The detective held up his hands. "I did not tell her. Scout's honor!"

"Mm. You were never a boy scout."

"No, but my grandmother knows stuff none of us can explain."

"True," she agreed with a grin.

Carl stuck his head in the room. "Has everyone greeted the invalid?"

"Doctor Parkins! Give me a kiss!" yelled Tom, making his way to the psychiatrist.

"No. I don't think I will, but a bear hug isn't out of the question."

Chapter Twenty-Eight

Wild Creek Ranch, The Dining Room, 6:28 PM

The low light and candles in the dining room made for a cozy dinner, even for a table of eleven—though set for twelve. Patrick Kowalski was absent, opting to keep watch from the loft of the red barn. He knew a plate would be saved and he could eat while the others slept. Whoever the big dude in black was, he didn't stand a chance against the veteran and his sniper rifle.

"Are you cleared for desk duty?" asked Danny, fork halfway to his mouth.

"Mm-hmm," Tom replied, chewing his food. Wiping a napkin across his mouth, he swallowed and took a drink. "Yeah. But I'm not ready for the station. Give me a day or two to get my bearings, huh? The day I go back will be crazy."

"No problem, but the sooner we can get rid of Randy, the better. I've been watching the reports online for the last twenty-four hours, and he hasn't added one note or update to the current cases. Garcia and Tartetto have done well, staying on top of things. Still no lead on Krista Hansen—other than what we assume to be her clothes on the scarecrow."

"Rick hasn't gotten the tests back?"

"Mm-mm. I hope he has them tomorrow. Speaking of, can you go through Bob Humboldt's stuff? It's in the study."

"Yeah. I can do that in the morning if Marnie will make me a pot of her cinnamon coffee."

"I will make you anything you like."

"Raspberry pie?"

"Yep."

"Cornflake chicken?"

"Done!"

"Waffles and bacon for breakfast?"

"Ha-ha! Don't push it!"

"Where's my truck?"

Danny said, "It's in the gray barn in the east paddock. We started it a couple times a week, and I took it for a drive two days ago. The registration is up to date, too. Your folks sent me the paperwork. So, you're set to go."

"I would love to see ya at the diner soon," said Gram, grasping his hand from her seat beside him.

Bringing her hand to his lips, he kissed the back. "Then I'll come in for a burger and fries this week."

"I'd be in for lunch. Maybe we should make a plan, Tom," said Carl, grabbing a vegetable bowl and scooping broccoli onto his plate.

"You wanna make sure my mind is healthy?" asked Tom with a hint of anger.

"No. Not at all. But I would be interested in picking your brain about the mental wellness treatment they provided downstate. We have an interesting group of blast clients I'm sure could benefit."

"Yeah. Sure. I get that," he said in a more even tone.

Ransom and Sam excused themselves when Patrick's voice came over their radios.

"Back in a few," said Sam, squeezing Marnie's arm as he passed.

Concern creasing her forehead, she watched them leave and looked down the table to Danny.

"Did you hear what Patrick said?"

"No." He wiped his mouth on his napkin and left the table, a sense of urgency in his stride.

Tom stood, balancing himself on the edge of the table. "I'm going with them. Being left out is boring me to tears."

Teddy stood to protest, but Marnie kicked her shin—not hard, but enough to get her attention.

"Let him go. He needs to acclimate himself."

"Yeah, but he wobbled."

"I do it every day. He's fine."

The Pinecrest Restaurant, Creekwood Town Square, 7:15 PM

"This is interesting, Randolph. Each woman has red hair," said Carrie Sutherland, playing with a strand of her honey-blonde mane. "And you said a man tried to abduct Marnie Reilly at the ranch, too. I'd say her long locks are what, strawberry-blonde?"

"Yes," he said, shielding the report with his hands.

"From a bottle, no doubt, but that doesn't matter. We can break this story and the case. You'll put Danny Gregg in his place, and I won't have to stoop and pretend I need Marnie's help."

"What do you mean?" he asked, sipping a very expensive glass of Pinot Noir.

She batted her lashes and twisted a golden strand. "How do you think I would look as a redhead?"

"Beautiful, but it's a terrible idea."

"Look, Randolph, I have taken enough personal defense courses that I can take care of myself. You only have to follow the breadcrumbs, arrest the bad guy, and save me."

He closed his eyes and tried to reason with her. "And what if I don't get there in time wherever *there* is?"

"Have faith! Now, let's make a plan. You have access to tracking devices, don't you?"

Randolph opened his satchel, prepared to put away the report, but Carrie snatched it from him.

"What are you doing? I'm not done reading."

"I took this from Captain Sterling's desk and have to return it before morning."

"Pfft! Why didn't you make a copy?"

"You have got to be kidding. Do you know how much trouble I will be in if anyone finds out I took it? If I made a copy and gave it to you, it would be worse."

"But it's a public record."

He sighed. "Not yet, it isn't. The investigations are ongoing. You know they would never release this to the press at this stage."

"No, but you did. Take it to the station, make a copy, and put the original on the old geezer's desk. I'll order our dinner, and it will be here when you return. Steak? Medium well, right?"

"Well. With a baked potato. Nothing on my salad," he said, putting on his coat and tightening the belt. "You had better keep your end of the deal, Carrie."

She muddled over his warning when he was gone. The sternness and edge of malice in his voice had her reconsidering her opinion of Randolph. Perhaps he wasn't as much of a pushover as she presumed. When the waiter placed a basket of sourdough rolls on the blood-red tablecloth, she arranged for another bottle of wine. Helping herself to the warm bread, she set it on the side plate and took out her notebook. They could order dinner when the detective returned.

Wild Creek Ranch, Western Paddock, Red Barn, 7:23 PM

The detectives, Sam, and Ransom entered the barn, where Patrick sat on a hay bale chewing a piece of straw waiting for them. Halloween decorating had begun, with cornstalks tied to the columns, and black, orange, and purple buntings tacked to the beams over the doors at each end. Brooms piloted by witches with black cats perched on brooms soared overhead.

"Ha! Marn's goin' all out!" said Tom, smiling with approval.

Patrick jumped up and stuck out his hand.

"Tom! It's g-g-great to see you."

"You too," he said. "You're keeping watch while we have dinner. That doesn't seem fair."

"I volunteered. The big d-d-dude they've described s-s-sounds like a dealer I've been chasing for months."

"Really? The one at the Ridge?"

"You remember?"

"Yeah. I've thought about a lot." Tom turned to Ransom. "Have you still got that video? The one you showed us in July?"

"It's on my laptop."

"Okay. We'll look at it later."

Danny and Sam pulled bales up next to Patrick's, and they all took a seat.

"What have you got?" asked the detective lieutenant.

"There's a lot of traffic on the ranch, but m-m-most of it's w-w-wildlife and farm critters. I've heard a few owls, red-w-w-winged b-b-blackbirds, and there's a b-b-big crow who sweeps past, carrying stuff. It looks like he's c-c-camping on the third floor of M-M-Marnie's house."

Danny and Sam glanced at one another.

"That's how he got in. I'll bet there's a window open in the attic," said the former.

Patrick frowned. "That's not like a crow. They usually roost in pine trees."

"Unless he's a pet," said Sam.

"Marion Doyle told me that Bob Humboldt had a crow named Marvel. I think we met him a few days ago in Marnie's living room."

Sam laughed, pretending to brush something from his shoulder. "We did."

"We'll check when he's out digging up worms. I'm not keen to scare him and have wings and a beak in my face," said Danny.

"So, why'd you call us out here?" asked Ransom.

Patrick nodded toward the clinic. "There's a client at the clinic who's g-g-giving m-me the willies. All dark and sulky. He's tall, b-b-but not what I would refer to as a big g-guy, unless he were to put on a hoodie over a couple of sweaters."

Danny nodded. "Yeah. That's Toby Munch."

"Carl knows very little about him. He told us his file is light, which usually means he worked in special ops and any injuries sustained happened in a confidential operation," added Sam.

"Like your injuries?" asked Patrick.

"Some of them. Yes."

"Okay. If C-C-Carl h-h-has it under control, I won't worry yet, but he was poking around the kennel construction earlier."

Ransom stood. "I'll check it out. Sam, you wanna come with? I think it's best we team up when patrolling the property. Agreed?"

Everyone nodded.

Danny clapped Patrick on the shoulder.

"Why don't you pack up and come eat? The security guards can keep watch."

"Yes! My stomach's growling. How was the pot roast?"

"Best thing I've eaten since July fourth," said Tom.

Nothing untoward was found at the kennel, and Sam and Ransom ran to catch up with the others.

"It's a chilly night," said Tom with a shiver. "Any idea where my clothes are? This is the warmest I've got, and I am freezing my ass off." He looked down at his cargo pants, long-sleeved T-shirt and sneakers, which were now wet.

"Why didn't you say something earlier? Your mother and father brought all your clothes and other personal effects to the ranch. You've got suitcases stored in your favorite bedroom upstairs. The rest of your stuff is stored in an outbuilding. Which one, I haven't a clue," said Danny.

"Excellent," he said, rubbing his hands together. "It would be nice to wear something other than shorts and a T-shirt. The rehab center was so damn hot all the time. And we couldn't open our windows."

"Why not?" asked Ransom.

Tom gave him a long grave look, and Ransom smacked himself in the forehead.

"Sorry. I wasn't thinking."

Patrick asked, "Does Hannah know you're home? I d-d-don't want to say something if she doesn't."

Danny said, "I haven't told her, and I doubt Gram has. She knows all, but she doesn't tell everything."

"I haven't spoken to her," said Tom.

The Kitchen, 8:20 PM

Warmth surrounded the men when they walked into the kitchen and hung their coats on the pegs inside the door—except Tom, of course, whose coat was still packed away. The aroma of coffee teased their noses and the sight of two cranberry pies taunting them from the table made their mouths water, even though they'd eaten more tonight than necessary.

Marnie limped into the room and handed Tom a ratty old sweatshirt.

"I hope you don't mind, but I dug through your suitcases and pulled this out. I know it's your favorite."

He cocked an eyebrow and looked under the kitchen table where the dogs were snoring.

"No. That's my favorite under there."

"Oops! Ha-ha! I'll wash it in the morning. They have you back. I doubt they need it anymore."

"Thanks. Hey, what kind of pie is that?"

"Cranberry and orange."

"Have I ever had that?"

"Uh-uh. It's a new recipe."

"Well, what are we waiting for? Slice it up! And throw a dollop of whipped cream on top!"

"Go get settled in the front room or the dining room and I'll bring it in."

"I'll be on the couch."

"Patrick, there's a plate in the oven for you, but if you want more, help yourself. You know where everything is."

"Thanks, Marnie," he said, grabbing an oven mitt and opening the door. "Mind if I sit here where it's quiet?"

"Knock yourself out."

"By the way … where's Carl?"

"He had to leave. Something about a friend in town."

"Squirt, should I cut the pie and plate it up?" asked Sam.

"Yes, thanks. Ransom, could you please get the whipped cream out of the fridge? It's on the top shelf in a glass bowl with a red lid."

"Sure."

Danny caught her hand while she poured coffee.

"Are you okay? You're limping."

"Yeah. I twisted my knee at the diner today and again coming down the stairs in my sock feet. I didn't realize how slippery the steps are. We better get those skid thingies, huh?"

"Tomorrow," he said, kissing her cheek. "Let me get the coffee. You sit and visit."

"I want to ask Gram about The Poacher. Do you think she's game to tell us a story?"

He grinned. "Hmm ... Let me think. Would my grandmother be happy to share Creekwood lore?"

"Ha-ha! Okay! It was a stupid question."

"Go. Sit. We'll bring in pie and coffee."

The Living Room, 8:34 PM

Gathered before a popping fire, the group stretched and groaned from consuming too much food. The dogs rested on the hearth, having eaten their share of the top edge of pie crust from everyone who wasn't a fan of that thicker bit of pastry. As a note, Tom, Sam, and Danny gobbled up theirs and Marnie told the dogs the threesome didn't love them as much as she did, having saved hers for them.

"Hey, Marn, did you see any sweatpants in that luggage upstairs?" asked Tom, unbuttoning the top of his cargos.

"I can confirm," she said, sitting on the floor and stretching long legs under the coffee table and leaning her back against the foot of the couch.

Danny, who sat on the sofa above, ruffled her hair. "Gram, Marnie was hoping you might be up for sharing some Creekwood history."

Sitting in a comfy chair with a blanket over her legs and her feet on a hassock, his grandmother nodded.

"I'd be willin' to share my tales for a glass of Irish whiskey." Her twinkling blue eyes traveled across the room, landing on a console sitting in the corner.

"I am happy to pay that price. Daniel, would you please get that lady a drink?" said Marnie, patting his foot.

Patrick joined them, taking a seat next to Ransom in one of the club chairs. Sam leaned on the mantle, chewing a toothpick, while Teddy and Poppy sat on the loveseat, feet tucked under, and sharing the quilt.

Handing his grandmother her drink, Danny switched off the table lamp as Marnie sat up and lit eight church candles at the heart of the coffee table.

"If we're going to hear a ghost story, we better set the scene. Mwahaha!" she said, her evil laugh sending Teddy and Poppy closer together.

Gram cocked an eyebrow. "Ghost story?"

Her face lit by candles, the psychologist leaned forward, resting her elbows on the table.

"What can you tell us about The Poacher?"

"Jesus, Mary, and Joseph! Why would ya be askin' about that?" she said, drinking down her whiskey and holding out the glass for a refill.

Danny obliged, retrieving the bottle and filling her glass, but when she pointed at the table, he raised his eyebrows, and put it down. It wasn't easy to rattle Gram, but Marnie had just done it.

"I had a dream and told Mac and Pete Sterling about it. They said to ask you."

Gram shifted in her chair, pulling the blanket tighter.

"I'll tell ya this, love. If you're dreamin' about that demon, God help us all."

"What can you tell us?" pushed Marnie.

"Are ya sure ya wouldn't prefer a good old-fashioned ghost story? I've got plenty about your great-great-grandfather or how about the

Ghost of Pulpit Rock? Or the hauntings of Fort Ticonderoga? There's a spooky one."

"Is the story really that bad, Gram?" asked Danny, returning to his seat.

"Oh, darlin', it isn't a story, and it doesn't get much worse."

"So, it's not an urban legend?" asked Teddy, clinging to Poppy.

Gram shook her head tightly. "No. And every time someone dreams of him, the murders start again. It's been years—maybe thirty or more, and that was my fault. I had the dreams of him chasin' me with an ice pick."

Marnie tensed, and whispered, "That's the dream I had, and he was in my room two nights ago."

"Well then. I better tell ya about him so you can stop him this time."

Ransom laughed. "C'mon. A ghost can't kill people."

"Maybe not. But he can damn well inhabit a life-force who can."

"You mean a possession?" asked Sam.

"Or kin with the same blood thirst, hearkened on by an evil spirit."

"Ah! Geez! You couldn't have talked about this before I got home?" Tom pulled his feet up off the floor and crooked his knees. "If I'd known this shit was goin' on, I would've stayed in rehab."

Marnie reached out and rubbed his shin. "Don't worry. We'll figure it out."

"Before one of us gets hurt?" he asked.

"I hope so."

The Pinecrest Restaurant, Creekwood Town Square, 8:34 PM

"I don't agree with your tactics, but I wouldn't think of ruining your story," said Randolph, throwing his napkin down and draining his glass of wine.

"How about a brandy before we leave? Would you join me?" asked Carrie, taunting him with a smug expression.

"No. And don't think for a moment that I approve of you putting yourself in danger."

"We have been over this, Randolph. You'll have a tracker on me the whole time. I'll be safe unless you fuck up. Do you do that often?"

His ego getting the better of him, he said, "No. I do not."

"Well, then. We have a plan."

Wild Creek Ranch, Upstairs and The Living Room, 8:57 PM

Having decided it would be better to hear Gram's story in comfy clothing, Teddy and Poppy ran upstairs and changed into their flannel pajamas and sweatshirts. When they returned looking cozy, Marnie announced she would do the same and limped off, followed a moment later by Tom.

As the psychic psychologist stepped out into the hallway in leggings and Danny's sweatshirt, Tom called out and she followed his voice.

"Do you know which suitcase has my warm clothes?" he asked.

"Yeah. That big blue one and those cartons on the dresser."

He hefted the suitcase onto the bed and unlocked it, before pawing through to find a pair of gray sweatpants and a navy-blue Creekwood PD hoodie.

"What's on your mind?" she asked.

"I really wanted to talk to you and Danny alone tonight. I've got some stuff goin' on."

"*Stuff?* What sort?"

"Spooky. Ever since I died on that operating table, I've been seeing things and my doctor said it's the aftereffects of the accident."

"But you don't think so."

"If I didn't know you, I would."

"Ah! You could have talked to Danny on the drive home."

"Nah. We talked about the open cases and Randolph Stuyvesant. Is he really as bad as Danny says?"

"Worse!" she said.

"Damn. Well, I can't do anything about that yet."

"Let's get downstairs and see if we can move things along. Otherwise, we can talk over breakfast, huh? Waffles and bacon?"

He nodded, and she turned to leave so he could change.

"Marn?"

"Yeah?"

"Can you wait in the hall for me?"

"I'd planned to," she said, closing the door.

Danny added another log to the fire while Ransom and Sam prepared drinks for the crew, and Patrick retrieved beers from the kitchen.

Handing Poppy and Teddy rocks glasses filled with cider and Fireball, Ransom asked, "Can I squeeze in here between you two?"

"Sure," said Poppy, squishing closer to the arm.

Teddy didn't slide over, but welcomed him to join them, patting the cushion and batting her eyelashes.

"Marnie, pick your poison," said the detective when came down the stairs.

"Uh. I'll have whiskey with Gram."

"Tom?"

"Beer! I want a beer!" he said.

Poppy frowned. "Are you allowed to drink? What medications are you taking?"

"I'm not on any meds. Pain or otherwise, but I do have it handy if I need it."

Patrick handed Tom a beer and held his bottle up to clink.

"Glad you're home."

"Cheers!" said Tom, tapping his long-neck ale on Patrick's before dropping onto the couch.

Marnie got comfy on the floor again and leaned against the couch.

"Gram? Tell us about The Poacher," she said, a shiver running up her spine.

Taking a healthy sip from her Glencairn glass, she set it within easy reach on the side table. Her face grew weary, as if the story was draining her energy, but she began.

"His name was Walter Platt, and he worked at the lumbermill. He and his family lived in a stone cottage not far from here. I think you may own the land his property was on," she said, looking at Marnie.

"Was it the Belmont's lumbermill back then?" the psychologist asked.

"Yes, dear. They've owned it for generations. Now Walter had a large family. Five boys and four girls, if you can believe, and he struggled to feed all of them mouths and he often poached wildlife to keep food in their tummies."

Ransom laughed. "Didn't anyone tell him abstinence makes the heart grow fonder? Nine kids? Who in their right mind would have that many?"

Gram shrugged. "It was a different time. On eighty or ninety years ago and up here in the mountains, they were isolated—especially in winter. The Platt family wasn't known for being social and the children were homeschooled. They didn't even own a car. Lots of folks got around on horseback or wagon back then. As the story was told to me, Platt flew into a rage when he lost his job at the mill and went on a bender. When he'd had his fill of whiskey the next day, he walked home, killed his wife, all five sons, and three of his daughters. The littlest got away, and no one knows what became of her. She was all of three and I don't recall her name."

"Oh! How horrible!" gasped Poppy as she wrapped her arm through Ransom's, who didn't seem to mind.

"Well, when Mrs. Platt, and I believe her name was Molly, didn't bring eggs into town to sell, folks started worryin'. So, the police made a trip to the house to check and make sure they were alright. But when they arrived, they found the family dead. They'd been chopped to pieces with an ax. And there was nearly a dozen animals strung up in the trees, bleedin' out. That's how Copper Woods got its name. The metallic scent of the blood-soaked ground and color of the dirt beneath the bodies."

Marnie slapped a hand over her mouth. "Gawd! Copper Woods is part of my property. I saw it on the deed, but I didn't know there was a house."

"We haven't hiked or explored every acre. We should get a drone and do a flyover," said Sam, glancing at Ransom.

"I've got one in the back of my vehicle. We could."

"If that's all there is to the story, I'm off to bed. I'm not used to staying up beyond nine these days. Rehab rules," said Tom, yawning, with his arms stretched above his head.

"Keep your seat a while longer. I've got more to tell ya," said Gram. She took another swallow of her whiskey and refilled her glass. "Marnie, dear, I may need one of your couches tonight."

"Of course. But I have a pseudo bedroom with a double in the bow window alcove upstairs. It would be more comfortable than the couch."

"It will do fine. Where was I? That's right. When the police arrived, Walter was hysterical. Saying he came home to find his family slaughtered, and the cops bought it. They weren't clever like our boys. Anyway, he confessed to killin' the animals to feed his family, so the cops looked elsewhere for those responsible for the grisly deaths of his wife and kids. In the end, a group of travelers was blamed. They settled here for the summer and stayed through the harvest. Many didn't believe it because the gypsies had been helpful to farmers and even worked at carnivals, telling fortunes and such. They weren't angels by any means. Some of the men had been hauled in for petty larceny and drunken shenanigans, but none had been violent."

"That's because our ancestors weren't on the force. Isn't that right, Tommy?" said Danny, reaching out and shaking his friend awake.

Tom sat up, blinking his eyes, and reached for his beer. "Yeah. Right."

"Go on, Gram," encouraged Sam.

"Not long after he killed his family, Walter Platt became a hermit. He continued to poach and people in town would hear the cries of the beasts he would kill. They say he would trap a moose or a deer, string it up in a tree, stab it repeatedly and leave it to bleed out. No mercy. There was nothin' humane or sportsmanlike about that!"

"Why didn't someone do something?" asked Marnie, green eyes wide.

"Folks were scared of him and with good reason, because ten or so years later, women and children in the area started goin' missin'. An eyewitness to one abduction swore up and down it was Walter Platt. They saw him drug the woman with a hanky and drag her off into the woods."

"How many women and children, Gram?" asked Danny, sitting forward, his hand on Marnie's shoulder.

"One woman, five boys, and four girls. All redheads like his wife and children."

"Did they find them?" asked Teddy.

"Not in time, I'm afraid. Walter killed them. He punctured their femoral arteries with an ice pick, let them bleed out, and he stuffed them. That's how he got his other nickname, The Taxidermist."

Poppy squirmed. "This is the most horrifying story I've ever heard!"

"It gets worse," said Gram.

"How could it?" cried Teddy.

"I know you're wonderin' if it's fact or fiction." The older woman's eyes shimmered before confirming their fears. "It's true, and the legend says that he would knock out his victims with ether and scoop out their eyes so they couldn't watch him work on the others. He put 'em in their mouths and sewed their lips together with the daintiest of stitches. Then he would put Shooter or Bowler marbles in their sockets, so they had eyes and not black gaping holes."

"I feel ill," said Teddy, rolling her head on the back cushions of the loveseat.

"Not that I want there to be more, but is there?" asked Marnie.

"When a three-year-old girl disappeared, the authorities finally decided to do something. They gathered a group of men from town and came out to confront Platt. What they found haunted them for the rest of their lives. The men hiked in to see a family of stuffed corpses sitting around a campfire, but no father. He was discovered by hunters days later, hanging from a tree. His femoral artery had been punctured, and he'd bled out on the forest floor. The murder weapon was never found, but many believe the daughter who got away came back seeking revenge."

Finished with the gruesome story, Gram picked up her glass and sipped. As she set it down, she noticed Marnie rocking gently and staring into the candles—her eyes as brilliant as aquamarines. She waved to get Danny's attention, and she pointed to his girlfriend. Ransom, Teddy, and Poppy leaned forward, while Sam and Patrick observed from the fireplace.

The curtains fluttered as a cool breeze swirled around the group, who tensed and shivered, and with watchful eyes, scanned the room for the source of the wind. But their attention was drawn to the psychic psychologist.

"When the candles burn out, and darkness falls, he will come. Be still, now. It won't be long," she whispered, in a voice that was not her own.

"What does that mean?" said Tom, bending to peer into her face.

Gazing into his eyes, she laid her palm on his cheek.

"You're safe. For now," she said, before shutting her eyes and opening them again with a jerk.

Heart racing and eyes popping, Tom hoisted his feet up onto the couch.

"What the fuck was that? What just happened?"

"Who was that?" said Teddy, snuggling up to Ransom.

"Huh. I haven't seen her do that in ages," said Sam, entranced by his sister's abilities.

Danny eyed him, mouth agog. "What? She's done this before?"

Gram flapped her hand for everyone to be quiet.

"Marnie, love, are you a medium?" she asked.

Pressing a palm to her forehead, she said, "Never on purpose."

"Did you hear the end of the story?"

Eyes glassy, she said, "I didn't need to. I saw it. All of it."

Chapter Twenty-Nine

October 15th

Marnie's Bedroom, 3:03 AM

A candle flickered on the windowsill, casting shadows of dancing ghouls on the walls. Danny rolled onto his back and stared at the ceiling, but wouldn't allow himself to look at the closed closet door. Marnie lit the candle, hoping it would keep away The Poacher and Lawrence Parish so they could sleep. It hadn't helped. The detective had tossed and turned and now lay wide awake after tonight's creepfest. Gram's story was horrifying, but when his girlfriend channeled a spirit, it unhinged everyone—excluding his grandmother and Sam.

Turning to his side, he explored her features in the candlelight. The near perfect nose, strawberry-blonde lashes and brows, her kissable bow mouth, and her defined cheekbones. He ran a finger across the back of her delicate hand resting on her pillow. When Marnie Reilly slept, she was an angel. Even on the nights she snored and kept him awake. He laughed to himself, knowing how indignant she could be when he brought it up.

Her eyebrows knitted together, and her jaw tightened. The rapid motion of her eyes beneath their lids and clenched fists told him she was dreaming or having a nightmare. Her once peaceful features turned terrified, and she kicked, hitting Tater in the snout. He yipped and sat up, one ear cocked and his nose twitching. Danny knew he shouldn't wake her, but when she clipped him on the chin, he'd had enough.

"Marnie. Wake up!" he said, blocking her punches with his forearm.

He grabbed her wrist on the next swing and held it.

"Marnie! You're having a nightmare. Wake up!"

Her eyes snapped open, and she struggled to free herself from his grasp. When she realized her boyfriend had hold of her arm, she relaxed against her pillow.

"Hot cocoa?" he said, bending to kiss her forehead.

"Dose it," she replied, which, of course, meant add a healthy shot of peppermint schnapps.

The Kitchen, 3:18 AM

Gram was stirring a pot on the stove, whistling a familiar tune, and glanced at them when they entered the kitchen. Working with only the light over the stove, the large country kitchen remained in the shadows.

With a tight smile, she said, "No sleep for the seers of wicked?"

"It's nightmare central upstairs," said Marnie, pulling out a bench and sliding in to sit.

"It was a doozy. She clocked me." Danny pointed to the spot on his chin where her fist had connected.

Mouth agape, the psychic stared up at the bruise and then down at the red knuckles of her right hand.

"I am so sorry!" she said, before leaning her forehead into her hand.

He caressed her back. "I've been hit harder. Besides, you didn't escape unscathed. Your knuckles took a hit from my beard."

Gram snickered. "Add a razor burned fist to that list of injuries."

"You couldn't sleep either, huh?" asked Marnie.

"No. I tossed around like a rag doll and counted sheep, before decidin' warm milk and whiskey might do the trick.

"Hmm ... That sounds nice too, but Danny suggested hot chocolate with peppermint schnapps."

"No. I said cocoa. You said schnapps. Speaking of ... Is it in the console or out here?" he asked.

Marnie pointed to the pantry. "Should be in there."

He looked inside and produced the bottle, a bag of mini marshmallows, and a tin of cocoa.

"Oo! Old school hot cocoa!" She clapped her hands and slid from the bench, retrieving a cannister of sugar, milk from the fridge, and a pot from the cupboard.

Danny patted her shoulder. "Sit. I'll make it."

"Not gonna get an argument from me," she said, taking a seat again. "Gram, you mentioned you had dreams about The Poacher once, too."

"Thrice, dear. Once about thirty years ago, eight years after that, and then again last year."

Danny thought about Paige Reynolds and Cissy Miller. Both women fit the victim profile.

"Are you having them now?"

"No. I'm afraid he's chosen you this time. Maybe you can stop him. People like that are beggin' to be caught, aren't they, Danny?"

"Yeah. But Walter Platt is dead. We don't know who we're looking for."

"Might be someone he knew or kin. Maybe even him reincarnated."

Marnie raised her eyebrows. "Hang on! You're Catholic. I didn't think you believe in reincarnation?"

"I've seen too many things in my life not to believe. Did you know Danny's grandfather was Protestant? Imagine that. An Irish Catholic marrying a Protestant. Oh, the ruckus!" She tittered as she poured warm milk over Irish whiskey into a pottery mug. "Don't bring religion into it, love. We can't be fully defined by that, now, can we?"

"I guess not."

Gram settled at the table across from her. "So, Marnie, how are you going to get him?"

She inhaled, leaned against the back of the bench, and pursed her lips. "I have no idea."

Forehead wrinkled; the older woman shook her head. "I didn't know back then, and nothin' is comin' to me now. But I'll stew on it."

"Thanks. I will too."

Danny set two mugs of cocoa on the table and asked Gram if she wanted one.

"No, thanks. I'm headin' up. I'll reacquaint myself with that old Agatha Christie Marnie has on the bookcase next to the bed."

"Goodnight!" said the psychic.

"Night, Gram," said her grandson, giving her a peck on the cheek.

"Okay, Detective Gregg. Any ideas how we catch this guy?"

"Phantom or not, we're gonna get him."

"How can you be so sure?"

"My partner's back. The three of us can do anything."

"With a little help from our friends."

"Goes without saying."

"Cheers!" she said, holding up her hot chocolate.

He tapped her cup with his, then jerked his head toward the door.

They heard the tapping of claws coming down the stairs, and the knuckleheads bolted into the room. Tater put his paws on the sill and growled. But Dickens and Gus scooted under the table, poking out their noses and grumbling.

Danny picked up the radio from the counter and checked in with security while Marnie moved to the window and peered out into pitch blackness. The house lights flickered, and the security lights blinked as the generator kicked in. Marnie jumped away from the glass, having caught sight of a dark figure army crawling away from the house.

"Danny! There's a guy out there creeping across the lawn!"

He spoke into the radio. "We've got movement at the house. The boss saw someone crawling near the back porch. I'm unarmed, but I'm going upstairs to get my gun."

Stretching and yawning, Tom loped past Danny and stopped short—surprised to see others were awake.

"What are you doing up?"

"Couldn't sleep. You okay?" she asked.

"Is there somethin' goin' on?"

"Yeah. The security guys are on it."

"Did I hear Danny say he was getting his gun?"

"Yup."

"Well, that doesn't sound good. How much are you paying them to guard your property?"

"Too much," said Danny, patting his arm as he returned with Ransom and Patrick.

"I'll get Sam," said the marshal.

"Right here," said the assassin, standing in the doorway, dressed and ready to go. "I heard a blip before the power was cut."

"How the hell did you guys get dressed so fast?" asked Marnie.

"Never undressed. Jobs like this, I sleep in my clothes," said her brother.

"Me too," said Patrick.

"We're hardcore, kid," said Ransom, clapping her on the back, making her spill her hot chocolate.

"Freaks!" she said, mopping up the cocoa with a paper towel.

"Tom, get a gun from the safe and stay here with Marnie. There's a radio on the counter if you guys need anything," said Danny, opening the door.

Tom gave him a look. "You'll hear me scream through the walls if something happens. Don't worry about that!" he yelled after them.

Marnie stirred the hot cocoa in time with the tick of the clock's second-hand, which hung over the coat pegs at the backdoor. The silence between her and Tom was uncomfortable, something she had never experienced before.

"Marshmallows?" she asked, shaking the bag.

"Nah," he said, fiddling with the hen and rooster salt and pepper shakers he was sure her mother had on her table when they were kids.

"Are you going to look at me, or is this the new us?"

"You really freaked me out, Marn. You didn't see what I saw in your eyes. It was the eeriest thing I've ever seen."

She took Tom's favorite mug from the cupboard, placed it right before him, and poured in the cocoa.

"Not that it's a competition, but I watched The Poacher kill that woman and the children, and there was nothing I could do to snap out of it."

"Who do you think it was? The voice I mean, because it sure as shit wasn't you."

She slid the cup across the table and sat opposite him.

"I have no idea, but here we are again, getting divine guidance from someone on the other side of the veil. You know I didn't go looking for her, right?"

He bobbed his head. "I know. You have your rules."

"Sorry about all this crap happening on your first night home."

"Not your fault." He turned and glanced at the door. "What do you think's goin' on out there?"

"Ask Tater. He hasn't moved from that window."

But they didn't have to wait for the dog to tell them. The detective, marshal, agent, and assassin trooped into the house a minute later, grim expressions all around.

"Are you gonna share?" asked Tom, testier than usual.

Danny said, "Rick's on his way."

"Another scarecrow?" asked Marnie.

"Yeah."

The Study, 6:08 AM

Rather than going back to bed, Marnie had gone upstairs, showered, and dressed while they waited for Rick and his team to do their forensic thing. She was in the study at her desk with a fire, keeping the chill off. It wasn't cold in the house. But a chilly breeze kept following her.

Feeling helpless, Tom had gone back to bed but couldn't sleep, so he followed suit. He was now lounging on the couch in the study, reading Bob Humboldt's notebooks.

Danny had been in and out over the last hour, and returned, extending his phone.

"I've gotta get to the station, but can you look at these pictures and tell me what you see?"

Stoic, she took the phone and slid through images.

"Do the clothes belong to another missing person?" she asked, studying the pants and T-shirt.

"Blow up the image of the T-shirt."

She did, and her jaw dropped when she read it.

"That's mine! I've been looking for that and a few other things."

"I thought so since I don't see many people wearing a Thousand Islands shirt around here."

Tom got up and circled around the desk to look over Marnie's shoulder.

"My parents got you that shirt, didn't they?"

"Yeah! And it's one of my favorites."

"What about the cargo pants?" asked Danny.

She flipped to another image and enlarged it.

"Also, mine. See that black dot? A Sharpie broke in my pocket. And there's a little tear in the thigh where I got stuck on the barbed wire when we were fixing the eastern fence, remember?"

"How would someone get your clothes?"

"Easy. I hang them on the line."

"Wait a minute! Somebody put Marnie's clothes on a scarecrow? What for?" asked Tom.

Danny explained about the previous effigies they'd found on the property, and his old partner flipped out.

"No! This is not happening again. I'm goin' down to the station to get my badge and gun, and I'm gonna find this piece of shit and kill him myself."

"Tommy! You can't!"

"Why the hell not?"

"Because I need you here, not on the roster. After last night's shenanigans, the security guys quit. Ransom and Sam went off on them and I did, too. They kept telling us someone cut the electricity, but that wasn't true. A transformer blew a couple miles up the road. If they were professionals, they would have known because when those blow, it's a helluva noise."

"Why didn't we hear it?"

"You've got the best windows in town and the way you've got this house insulated, it's damn near soundproof. We don't even hear cars driving by at night or into the driveway when the windows are closed. We hear when we're downstairs during the day because you open them when you cook."

"I open them any day it's above fifty."

"There you go."

"What's the plan, then?" asked Tom, returning to the couch and sitting down.

"We have a theory that the guy is traveling through the tunnels, but we don't know all the entrances."

"I might be able to help with that. There's something in Bob's notebooks about a map. Hang on! Let me find it." Tom flipped through the pages of a red leather-bound book, scanning for the reference. "Here! He says that the only map he is aware of was in Colin Reilly's workshop and that he kept it folded in a book of fairy tales."

Marnie gulped. "I know that book. He took it to work because it scared me. It's probably in the attic."

Danny asked, "Can you guys look? In the meantime, Patrick has friends coming out to assess the security. When he mentioned them to your brother, he and Ransom were enthusiastic about their special abilities. I didn't ask questions. All I know is the other guys failed miserably, and from what Sam tells me, they're greedy."

"Okay. We'll schlep to the third floor and find the map. What else can I do?" asked Tom.

"I'll call you from the station. Rick left files with Captain Sterling that might answer your question."

"Did Gram leave?"

"She was out the door at five. I'm surprised you didn't see her," said Marnie.

"I was too busy punching a security guy in the face."

"There was a fight?" asked Tom.

"Don't ask—but Sam, Ransom, Patrick, and I escaped without a scratch."

"My heroes!" said Marnie, kissing the detective on the cheek.

Chapter Thirty

Shear Genius, Creekwood Town Square, 7:03 AM

"Thanks so much for getting me in early, Chantelle," said Carrie Sutherland, taking a seat in a hot pink salon chair.

"No problem. When my gal wants a new look, she gets it! What are we doin' today?" said the twenty-something stylist with her electric blue pixie cut.

"The style is perfect, but I would like to change the color."

"Again?"

"Yes. I've never been a redhead."

"I'm happy to do anything you want, but I have to tell you, red won't complement with your skin tone."

"Well, Marnie Reilly is your client, right? She and I have similar coloring, don't we? What color is hers?"

"Au naturel. She doesn't color her hair."

"You're kidding!"

"No, ma'am, but if you want something similar, I can try."

"Get it as close as you can."

"Yes, ma'am," said Chantelle, curling her lip and mimicking the reporter as she turned her back to get a cape.

🎃

Creekwood Police Station, 7:18 AM

Sergeants Lou Beaumont and Bill Halpin stood at the desk, jelly doughnuts in hand, and waved to Danny when he came through the door.

"Hey guys! All quiet on the western front?"

"So far," said Lou, wiping sugar from his lips with his hand.

"Overnight was another story. We got five bozos in the drunk tank. Stinks to high heaven in there," added Bill. "When are these guys gonna learn that scarin' people ain't funny?"

Danny laughed. "You mean that literally. Five guys dressed up as clowns?"

"Yeah. Dumbass fraternity prank. Had girls screamin' their tits off all over campus."

Lou held a box of doughnuts and waggled the box. "Raspberry jelly. Your favorite."

"No, thanks. I had a piece of cranberry pie for breakfast. I couldn't resist."

"Not if your grandmother or Marnie made it. Those gals can cook," said Bill.

"Is the captain in?" asked Danny.

"Nah. But your father is up there blustering at Stuyvesant. That guy is useless," said Lou.

"Tell me about it. I'll go up and join the bluster. Thanks!"

He took the stairs two at a time and heard his father's bellow before he hit the top step, and ducked his head so they wouldn't see his shadow through the pebbled glass.

"You've dropped the ball, Randolph. Not one report in over four days. Where have you been? What have you been doing to close cases?

I want reports on Captain Sterling's desk within the hour. And I want a copy of your notebook entries, too."

"Chief Gregg, it is clear to me that you favor your son. Perhaps I should take this matter up with the Superintendent."

"Ha! Go ahead. Call Cafferty. You know what he'll tell you?"

"Follow the chain of command," said Danny, pushing through the door.

Chief Gregg looked at his son and pointed at him. "That's right. You gotta gripe, take it up with your lieutenant. He'll pass it up the proper channels."

"Nepotism creates distrust within the ranks," said Randy, nose in the air.

"Ha! The chief has never made allowances. In fact, he expects more of me than any other officer in this department. I get my ass chewed by him and Captain Sterling. You should try having Chief Mac Gregg as a father."

Nostrils flaring, Danny stalked to his desk and pulled out his chair, but before he sat down, he added, "Get the damn reports done, Randy. And the next time you speak to the chief that way, I'll suspend your whiny ass for insubordination. Are we clear?"

"Daniel. A moment, please."

The chief unlocked the captain's door and flung it open.

"Yeah. I'll be right there."

Coffee in hand, the detective followed his father into the office, closing the door behind him.

"Did I go overboard with that suspension warning?" he said with an uncomfortable grin.

"No. You said exactly what I was about to say. I wanted a briefing on last night."

"Oh. I came in early to write that up, but yeah ... Another scarecrow. This time dressed in Marnie's clothes, so we're taking that as a serious threat. The security crew we hired didn't work out. They quit this morning after we blasted them for incompetence, but I think we may have been unfair, because now we believe the guy is getting onto the ranch under the property."

Mac considered this as he looked out the window into a morning dark as night.

"The tunnels. He knows where they lead."

"That's what we're thinking, yeah. Anyway. Tom found a note in one of Bob Humboldt's notebooks about Colin Reilly having a map. So, he and Marnie are searching Reilly's books this morning."

"And the security crew?"

"We're replacing them. Patrick knows some guys."

"Who is vetting them?"

"Sam and Ransom."

"Didn't they vet the last group?"

"Both admitted not as thoroughly as they should have. One or the other worked with them previously, but people change."

"They sure do. How's Tom?"

"Glad to be home and pissed off we're dealing with another threat."

"Huh. When's his fitness exam?"

"Two weeks. He says he's ready to come back."

"But you don't think he is?"

"He's edgy. I say we give him the two weeks."

"Hmm ... Edgy may be just what we need."

"Yeah. And I don't want him on the roster yet."

"You want him with Marnie."

"Don't you?"

The chief gave a curt nod. "Other than you, no one is better suited to look out for her than a pissed off Tom Keller."

Wild Creek Ranch, The Attic, 8:08 AM

"You know. I bought a whole box of doughnuts the other day and gave them to Elk and Arnie to share with the hands. I couldn't bring myself to eat one without you. Let's go into town later and get some, huh?" said Marnie.

"Sounds like a plan. I haven't had a bear claw in months!"

The psychic shivered. "Do you feel a draft?"

Tom stood still and glanced around the wide-open space. "Yeah. You've got a broken window over there. We can get some glass and putty in town, and I'll fix it."

She crossed the room to examine the broken pane.

"Eww! There's bird poop everywhere. This must be where the crow got in. Look! That big old maple tree out there. Its branches are hitting the house."

"That's how it got broken, then. One swift wind would do it. Danny and I can cut those branches back before we fix the window."

"There's a nest over here too. Uh ... Tom. Check this out."

"Whatcha got?" he said, walking to the window.

She leaned over, inspecting.

"A couple of big marbles, bits of cotton, twigs, tufts of red hair, and ... Ah! Geez!"

Tom stood next to her, peering into the nest.

"That's an eyeball," he said, turning away.

"It is, isn't it?"

"We better call Danny."

Creekwood Police Station, 8:30 AM

The detective's phone dinged and as he looked at the sender, he knew it wasn't good news. He closed the folder he was reading and shoved it into his briefcase before sticking his head into the captain's office.

"I gotta run out to the ranch. Marnie and Tom found an eyeball in the attic."

Captain Sterling didn't look up, but waved his hand.

"Yeah. I won't ask. I've read your report about the scarecrow." The captain paused, took a breath, and peered over the top of his readers. "You ever wonder why trouble finds that woman?"

"Every day."

"Go away and take Stuyvesant with you."

"What? Why?"

"If you keep him under your thumb, Lieutenant, he would be less inclined to break into my office and copy files."

"Are you kidding me?" Danny shouted, entering the room and closing the door.

"I am not." The captain removed his glasses and set them on the desk. "Your father rigged up two cameras that connect to my phone. I watched Randy jimmy the door, take the case folders you're working on and leave. He came back an hour later, copied the contents, broke into my office again, and put them back. I don't know what he's up to, but I have Sam Jalnack trailing him everywhere he goes."

"Carrie Sutherland is where the trail leads."

"Yes. I'm afraid you're right."

"Okay. He's with me."

"Go away and shut the door."

Which Danny did, and stepping back into the squad room, he called out to his partner.

"Randy! You're with me. Let's go!"

The Creekwood Times Editorial Office, 9:23 AM

"Sutherland, you're late!" said Everett Channing, a handsome man in his forties with thick, dark brown hair and rimless glasses. He leaned against a tall olive-green file cabinet, reading pinned story updates from a wall of corkboard.

"I was working," she said, setting her satchel on her desk in the reporters' bullpen.

"Looks like you were getting your hair done—again. What's with that color?"

"Don't you like it?"

"Not on you, no. Look, you haven't filed a substantive story all week. Where are you up to on Bob Humboldt's murder?"

"The police aren't cooperating. They keep saying they won't comment on an ongoing investigation."

"I thought you had an informant?"

"I do, but I still think the broader story is the Reilly family. Why do people keep getting killed and injured on her property?" She flipped her hair and opened her laptop in a disgusted huff. "Let me work *that* story, and I know we'll have a winner."

"That's where I've seen that color before! You trying to steal Marnie's identity? It won't work. Your hair is too short. You're not tall enough. And you don't have her eyes. Or husky voice."

"Why don't you just marry her, Ev? Gawd! What is it with you men?"

He laughed, knowing he was pushing Carrie's buttons.

"Well, she has that detective now, doesn't she? Besides, we're friends. She's a nice lady if you take the time to know her."

"No, thank you! I'd rather put her in her place."

"The last time somebody tried to do that, they ended up in prison."

"You're talking about Grace Wilmot? I hear she's up for parole. Compassionate release, they say."

"Wouldn't surprise me. She plays a good game. Do a story about how a convicted killer and drug trafficker scammed the system."

"Boring! Let's knock Marnie Reilly off her high horse. That's much more interesting."

"What's your beef with her?"

"I don't have one, but I know she's hiding something."

"Get me a story, Sutherland. Human interest stories are great, but the town wants to know what happened to Bob. Can you do that for me? We've got enough stories about prize-winning pumpkins and fraternity pranks."

"I have a plan, and I need to go under the radar to finish it."

"Is Stuyvesant helping you?"

Pulling a face, Carrie put a recorder and a can of mace into her bag.

Everett blew out a disgusted breath.

"The whole undercover thing doesn't work well in a town like Creekwood. Everybody sees and hears what's happening. You think people don't give me scoops? Watch your back and don't do anything stupid. And leave the Reillys alone. They've been through enough."

Wild Creek Ranch, The Attic, 9:35 AM

"Yeah. That's an eyeball," said Rick Price, holding it up in his gloved hand. "I'll get it to the lab and see if we can find the owner. Pun intended."

"What about the other stuff?" asked Danny.

"We'll bag the nest."

"Is that human hair?"

"Looks like it."

"What aren't you telling me?"

"I don't *know* anything yet, Danny." The doctor took off his glasses and put them in his pocket. "Have you read Kelly Munson's autopsy yet? Or my report on the first two scarecrows?"

"I've skimmed them."

"Read them. Then call me."

"Does the blood match Hansen or Alder?" asked Danny.

"No. It's deer blood, same as the one we found last night. Read the Munson autopsy. Giles said you and your father will find a similarity," said the doctor.

Danny's stomach knotted, and he ran his fingers through his hair.

"Cissy Miller," said Danny.

"Yeah," said Rick.

"The Poacher," whispered the detective.

"What?"

"Nothin'."

Randolph Stuyvesant had been standing in the doorway, not keen to see an eyeball, but he overheard what Danny said and scratched it in his notebook. He would share it with Carrie as soon as he could get away from the detective.

Chapter Thirty-One

Wild Creek Ranch, The Kennels, 9:40 AM

"Who was that? He's not very friendly" asked Ellie Nikol, frowning at the man's back as he walked away without returning her 'good morning' greeting.

"He's a client at the clinic," said Marnie.

"What the fuck is wrong with his face?" asked Tom. walking backward across the field, inspecting the man.

"C'mon! You both know I can't talk about a client," said the psychologist.

"Sorry!" said Ellie.

Tater, Dickens, and Gus raced around them, sniffing the ground and rolling on their backs in the wet grass.

"There it is, Doc! What do you think?" asked Marnie, arms out with pride.

"Well done! This is perfect!" said Ellie, clapping her hands together. "I can't get over how big it is!"

"You said you wanted room to grow, so we gave it to you."

"The runs are wonderful. Thank you so much, Marnie!"

"You gave us the plans. We built it. No need for thanks."

"Except for the lumber, fencing, stainless-steel benches ... Gosh, Marnie! This is more than I was hoping for. My rescues are going to love it here."

"All tax deductions, baby! It was mostly out of love, but hey, a business gal has to be smart. Now all you need is a large animal clinic and you'll be set."

"Let's wait a couple of years on that. I need more staff to tackle a project of that magnitude."

"You've got several volunteers over at the clinic ready and waiting for dogs and cats. Let us know when you'll be ready to bring them out, and we'll introduce you to the veterans."

"Let's plan for the first of the month. That gives us time to sort out the supplies we've been stockpiling. Julie will be happy to have the spare bedroom back."

Tom wasn't listening. He was looking past them with a smile on his face.

"That is the most awesome hay maze I have ever seen in my entire life!" he said.

"Go check it out," said Marnie, giving him a nudge. "After that, I've got another project I want to show you."

"Okay," he said, eyebrows raised.

When he was gone, Ellie said, "Is there much work left on that project?"

"Nope. They've been held up because of rain, but they'll be back tomorrow."

"Excellent! Hey. I better go. I've got a new tech to interview in forty minutes. Thanks again, Marnie."

"Pleasure, my friend. See you soon."

Wild Creek Ranch, The Construction Site 10:02 AM

"What have you got goin' on down here?" asked Tom.

"You'll see in a minute," said Marnie with a smirk.

As they drew closer to the construction site, Tom's eyes lit up, and he did a double take.

"You didn't!" he said, looking at his friend in disbelief.

"Yup!"

"Are those the stones from that old orphanage?"

"Yes, sir!"

"Danny was telling me you bought the stones and reclaimed wood, but he didn't say what you planned to do with it. This is fantastic!"

They stood admiring a two-story colonial home built from stone. Its white trim, red shutters and matching front door, covered by a tin-roofed portico, gleamed beneath a big blue sky.

"C'mon, Tom. You have to see the creek-side," she said, grabbing his hand and pulling him along.

The creek bubbled and splashed as they walked around the side of the house.

"A millstone and a covered porch? That is brilliant!" he said.

"The guys are hooking it up so it's a power source part of the year."

"Can it be lifted in winter? The creek does freeze when we get a week of negative forty."

"Yes, but I don't know how. You'll have to ask Hugh Barber. He's managing the construction."

"Cool! Can we go inside?"

"Sure," she said, handing him a key.

He took it, stopped, and read the fob, which read "Welcome Home."

"Are you serious?"

"I told you I'd build you a house where you could fish off your back porch, didn't I?"

"Marn, this is too much."

"No, it isn't. You're my best friend, and if you love the house, it's yours. If you don't, I'll use it as a guesthouse. But I'd prefer that you stay."

"What am I gonna do with the money from the sale of my house? Besides paying medical bills."

"Buy an investment property. I don't know, but let's look inside and see if this feels like home first."

"Okay."

Tom unlocked the door and stepped in, moving aside for Marnie to enter. Mouth agape, he took in the natural wood-beamed ceilings, red oak flooring, and white-washed walls. The repurposed French doors on the back wall allowed natural light into the space, and the double stone fireplace dividing the living and dining rooms, gave the house a cozy feel.

"I didn't want them to do too much painting in case you didn't like the colors. All you have to do is tell them what you want, and they'll do it. There are paint samples on the kitchen counter," said Marnie.

"It's perfect as is," he said.

"There are three bedrooms and two full baths upstairs, a powder room off the mudroom, and a bedroom and ensuite bathroom down here. Oh! There's a small study upstairs. with bookcases and a window overlooking the creek."

"Where's my furniture? I'll move in tomorrow."

"Ha-ha! In an outbuilding in a container. We didn't want it to get dusty."

He crossed the room and unlatched the doors and strolled out into the cool fall day. The creek below raced by, and he could see himself sitting out there with his fishing pole and a bottle of beer. Walking the length of the porch took him to the kitchen. He put the key in the lock and peered inside to see a cozy kitchen, with a small dining area, and stainless-steel appliances. He knew he didn't need to see what was upstairs. This was home.

"Marn! You've got yourself a neighbor!"

Creekwood Police Station, 1:20 PM

With a tuna and celery sandwich unwrapped on his desk, Danny read Kelly Munson's autopsy, shocked to read the parallels between hers and Cissy Miller's. He pushed the papers aside and picked up his lunch, looked at it, then put it down. Eyeballs in the woman's stomach wasn't an image he could get rid of and so his lunch would go uneaten.

"Daniel, I'm heading home," said Mac Gregg.

"Oh. You're not staying at the cabin tonight?"

"No. I'm looking forward to sitting in a recliner that has my ass imprinted on its cushion."

"Ha! I get that."

"I'll be back next week, but email anything new on your cases."

"Yeah. Sure. I'll keep you posted. Hey. Did you see Kelly Munson's autopsy?"

"No. I haven't.

The detective handed him the folder and waited for his reaction. The chief pinched his bottom lip as he read, then froze, and looked over the folder at his son.

"Yeah. You see it too," said Danny.

"It's that Miller girl all over again," he said, eyes back on the report.

"What are you thinking?"

"Keep it between us for now. We've got ourselves a serial killer. We don't need the feds crawling all over town."

"The captain?"

"I'll tell Pete. But no one else. I want twenty-four hours to think."

"Yes, sir."

"I'll go home for the night and be back late tomorrow. We'll talk then."

"Safe trip."

The chief waved and walked out the door with the report in his hand.

Pine Ridge Sanitarium, 2:00 PM

"Thanks for getting me in to see Dalton. I really appreciate it," said Danny, walking down a long sterile hallway with Carl Parkins.

"Him killing Paige Reynolds never felt right to me. When you talk to him, I think you'll agree."

"Why did he confess?"

"Shock is only a hypothesis. He hasn't actually said anything about it. But there were witnesses to what he did at the ranch. Everyone saw him launch the fireworks at Marnie and Tom. Perhaps he believed that if he could do that, he probably did the other. I don't know. I'm still working with him. There's a lot to unpack."

"It's okay that you're talking to me about him?"

"I only gave you a hypothetical. Now, should I stay with you while you speak with him?"

"If you think it's best for him, yeah."

"Let's play it by ear. I need him to trust me, so if you press him too hard…"

"That's not my intention. There's something fragile about Dalton Hooley that makes me feel protective of him. Even after what he did to Marnie and Tom. I know he was a victim, too."

"Okay. I'll be close by if you need me, but I doubt you will."

They approached a door and Carl nodded to a guard, who opened it and let the detective pass through. The psychiatrist situated himself in a mirrored room next door so he could analyze the exchange.

Dalton sat handcuffed to a metal table at the center of the room. The chair on which he sat was two sizes too small for his seven-foot frame. Danny took the seat opposite and nodded.

"I'm Detective Danny Gregg from Creekwood PD. Do you remember me?"

"Yes, sir. You knocked me down on July fourth."

"That's right. I wanted to ask you a few follow-up questions if that's okay."

"If I can help, I will."

"Thank you."

"How is Ms. Reilly?"

"Fine, Dalton. Thank you for asking. Should I send her your regards?"

"Yes, please. And tell her I'd like to apologize to her personally someday."

"I will. Now, what can you tell me about Paige Reynolds? What happened the day she died?"

"Can I tell you the truth about that?"

"That's why I'm here."

"Detective, I did not kill her. I've never even been on that island. If someone says I was, it's possible they had a grudge. But I swear on my momma's grave. I did not murder Ms. Reynolds."

"What about the modified stun gun you said you had?"

"That was nothing. I was scared. Cops were all around me. Ms. Reilly and Mr. Keller were in the hospital, and I even heard that he had died. I figured I had nothing to lose. I was goin' to prison anyway."

"Mr. Keller did die on the operating table, but they got him back and he survived."

"I'm glad to hear that."

"Dalton, I want you to know that I hope you get past what Lawrence Parish did to you. What Kate did to you. I may be a cop, but I know you were a victim. Marnie and Tom know it too. Thanks for talking to me."

"You're welcome. Thanks for treating me like a human being. And please send my regards to Mr. Keller, too."

Carl met Danny in the hallway.

"Do you believe him?" he asked.

"Yeah. I do. We'll figure out who killed Paige and maybe get his sentence reduced. I feel bad for him. Is he being abused?" asked Danny.

"You'd think a guy that size could take care of himself, but he's really just a big teddy bear. If we could get him moved, it would help."

"I'll do what I can," said the detective.

"I'll walk you out. There's something I would like to discuss."

"Ha! You're finally going to confess to dating my sister? It's about time. I'm not stupid, you know."

Carl halted, and his jaw dropped. "You knew about me and Hannah?"

Danny stopped and turned around, a grin on his face. "I know everything. Be kind to her and don't put up with too much of her shit. That's all I have to say."

"Okay."

"See ya later."

Mac Gregg's House, Saratoga Woods, 3:47 PM

Chief Gregg pulled up outside his house, got a duffel, groceries, and his briefcase from his backseat, and walked up the stone walkway to his bungalow in the woods. A fox scurried from the porch when he slammed the car door. He stumbled on the bottom step, dropped the duffel, and a stream of expletives followed. Bending to pick it up, he came face to half-chewed face with the corpse of Krista Hansen, and it looked like she'd been there a few days.

Hallowed Hills Road, 4:53 PM

Danny was on the phone with Marnie, telling her he would be home soon, when a call came through from his father.

"Dad's trying to call. I'll see you in a few," he said, swapping over the call.

"Hi, Dad. Did you get home okay?"

"Krista Hansen's body is on my front porch. Can you get Rick here as soon as possible? I don't want anyone else touching her, but he needs to hurry. The wildlife has already been after her."

"Jesus! Yeah. I'll call him now. Should I drive up?"

"No. I'll take care of the policing and send you a report. But I can tell you she wasn't killed here."

"Dad?"

"Yeah."

"Is it like Kelly and Cissy?"

"Looks like it."

"Fuck!"

Chapter Thirty-Two

October 16th

Wild Creek Ranch, 10:30 AM

Hands cupped, Marnie yelled to Danny and Tom, who were cutting branches from the maple at the front of the house.

"Don't you two hurt yourselves. I'm heading into town with Teddy and Poppy to pick up supplies for the Halloween party."

"Will you bring back lunch?" asked Tom.

"What do you want?"

"Philly cheesesteak from Gram's."

"Make that two," said Danny.

"You got it. Love you!" she said, blowing a kiss to Danny.

"Love you too," the detectives called back.

"Ha-ha! Tom! It's good to have you home!" she said, getting into her truck.

"Can we stop and get a coffee?" asked Poppy.

"Yeah. What's your preference?"

"How about that new place in Town Square? Full of Beans?" said Teddy.

"Well, that sounds about right for the three of us."

The drive into town was uneventful except for a moose who stared them down before ambling off into a stand of pines.

"Wow! I've lived here all my life, and I have never had a moose encounter. That was so cool!" said Teddy, drumming her hands on the dash.

"That's my first sighting too," said Poppy. "What about you, Marnie?"

"I've seen them around Danny's cabin when we've been hiking. I try to steer clear. They're nasty when they feel threatened."

"Kinda like you, huh, Marnie?" said Teddy.

"Ha-ha!"

Town Square, 10:45 AM

"Oo! Marnie! Look! A Halloween store?" said Teddy, pointing out the window.

"I was here yesterday. I didn't see that."

"Let's go there first! I've heard they do pop-up stores to get rid of stuff they've overstocked. We might get a deal."

"Okay. We'll do coffee after," said Marnie, braking and backing into a free spot.

A brilliant blue sky and warmer weather had the townies out in hordes. Food carts dotted the square with vendors serving coffee, cinnamon rolls, hot cider, doughnuts, and breakfast sandwiches.

Teddy pulled Marnie's sleeve. "Hey. Isn't that Carrie Sutherland over there?"

The psychologist scowled. "Yeah, and she's dyed her hair my color."

Poppy tugged one of Marnie's long locks. "Yours is better. It's real, longer, and comes with a prettier face *and* personality.

"Unless I feel threatened," she replied, gritting her teeth. "C'mon. Let's get our Halloween stuff."

The store had everything they needed from their list, and they filled two carts with decorations, candy, treat bags, and pumpkin and skull flashlights. They even found cute luminary bags and votive candles for the hay maze.

Loaded with paper sacks, they walked to the truck and deposited their parcels in the cargo.

"Let's get a coffee and I'll call Gram to order sandwiches for the guys while we sit and drink," said Marnie. "Do either of you want a Philly cheesesteak? Or anything else from Gram's?"

"I could split one if anyone wants the other half," said Teddy.

"I'm in," said Poppy. Then she apologized. "I'm sorry. Unless you want the other half, Marnie?"

"Ha! Half? My appetite is back. A whole one will suit me fine. Besides, I always pick out bits of the steak for the knuckleheads."

Full of Beans thrummed with chatter as they entered and spotted Carrie Sutherland again. This time, she was with her editor-in-chief, Everett Channing. The psychic herded her friends to the counter, averting her eyes from the press.

Coffees sorted, they gathered at a table away from the reporter, and called Gram to place her order. As she hung up, Teddy nudged her under the table.

"Incoming," whispered Poppy.

And before she could pretend she was on the phone, she felt a hand on her shoulder.

"Marnie, how have you been?" said Everett, giving her shoulder a warm squeeze.

She craned her neck and saw him standing alone. Her look of relief made the newspaperman laugh.

"She's gone. You're safe," he said, waving to the other two women.

"Thank Christ for that!" she replied, getting up to give him a hug.

"How are you settling at the ranch?" he asked.

"Good, thanks. You should come out for the Halloween festivities. It won't be a big deal this year, but I'm planning to make it an annual event."

"I would love that? I hear Tom's home," he said.

"He is and doing quite well."

"Great to hear. Is he going back to work soon?"

"I hope so. Danny misses him a lot," she said.

"I bet. Stuyvesant is a wet blanket. I've never met a more boring person."

"Ha-ha! You said it."

"You saw Carrie's hair, huh?" he asked.

Marnie scoffed. "You know what they always say about imitation."

"Hmm … I think she's hiding something. That hair has something to do with a story she's working."

"What makes you think that?" asked Marnie, beginning to worry Carrie might know about the women and the red hair connection.

He shrugged.

"I've got a nose for that kind of stuff. She's definitely plotting something. Anyway, I've got a paper to put to bed. Send me the details about your party. I'd love to come."

Everett kissed her cheek, waved to the gals again, and left. Slumping into her chair, she got the sick feeling Stuyvesant had shared too much detail with the reporter.

"You okay, Marnie?" asked Teddy.

"Let's go pick up lunch. I've got to get home to talk to the guys."

Wild Creek Ranch, The Study, 12:48 PM

Danny sat at Marnie's desk reading Krista Hansen's autopsy report, with Tom reading over his shoulder. Even with the fireplace lit and the flames dancing, both men felt a chill run through them.

"I kinda wish Rick hadn't dropped this by," said Tom.

"Yeah, but he did help us with that last branch. We couldn't have done it without him."

"Who knew he could climb a tree like a monkey?"

Danny chuckled.

"I was surprised he's that agile."

"Hmm ... Danny, we've got two women dead and one missing. One more death and we've got a serial killer."

"Again. But the chief and I think we already do. Kelly Munson and Krista Hansen may not be the only deaths. Like I said to you and Rick earlier, Dalton Hooley never seemed right for Paige Reynolds. I think she and Cissy Miller fit this killer's profile. I believe he was interrupted by you and Marnie with Paige."

"Who's Cissy Miller?"

"My childhood crush," he said, leaning back and looking up at his partner.

"No kidding?" said Tom, moving around the desk to sit in a side chair.

"Yeah. It's the first case I ever worked with my father."

"And you never found the suspect."

"Nope. But I sure would like to tell the Millers we got him."

"So it looks like the missing eyeball is Krista's. Pardon the pun."

"Seems to be. Only one was found in her stomach contents," said Danny.

"Where are Ransom and Sam?"

"I don't know. They took off late last night. Patrick's gone home too now that we have a new crew."

"Well, to be honest, I felt it was overkill. And it's a lot of work for Marnie," said Tom.

"Yeah. But I think Teddy and Poppy should stay."

"I do too. Teddy makes her laugh."

"And Poppy is helping Carl with clients, which gives her extra time to heal," said Danny.

"She's doing okay, though," said Tom.

"But the Halloween party is coming up and you know her."

"Yup. She'll run herself ragged getting it done."

Tater, Dickens, and Gus loped in and sat beside him. The former put his paw on Danny's leg and gave him a nudge with his nose.

"You guys wanna go out?" he asked.

Before he could say 'out' and stand up, the dogs were at the door, scratching.

Western Paddock, 1:20 PM

"C'mon, Tater, let's go home. Your mother will be here soon!" hollered Danny to the ringleader, having received a call from Marnie saying they were five minutes away.

"What do you think of the house?" asked Tom.

"It's perfect. I can see the two of us sitting on that back porch sipping beers and fishing."

"So, you're okay with it?"

Danny pulled a face. "Of course. It's great you'll be a ten-minute walk away. But I still think we need four-wheelers to get back and forth. Marnie and I have been looking for a model that fits the dogs in the back."

"How do you think Gus will cope living away from Tater and Dickens?"

"He'll adjust. It's not like they won't see each other every day."

"That's true."

"I gotta tell you something. Uh ... My sister and Carl are seeing each other. They haven't made an official announcement, but I don't want you blindsided."

"Carl called me this morning. I'm fine with it. Hannah and I weren't a good fit, anyway."

Danny agreed. "No, you weren't. I love my sister, but she wanted to change you."

"Tchah! Tell me about it!" said Tom. "Marnie doesn't do that to you?"

"Not yet and speaking of, there she is with our lunch."

The Study, 2:40 PM

"What's goin' on, Marnie. You look worried," said Tom, glancing back as he looked through the bookcase.

Danny sat on the sofa with his sock feet on the coffee table while Marnie stood next to the fire, trying to chase away a chill.

"I think Carrie Sutherland is about to do something stupid," she said, rocking on her toes.

Tom screwed up his face. "She's back? Gawd. I thought we'd gotten rid of her forever."

Danny dropped his feet and sat forward.

"What makes you say that?"

"Could she have gotten hold of your reports regarding the Poacher and the women with red hair?" asked Marnie.

"Yeah. It's possible. Stuyvesant broke into Captain Sterling's office, took a file, and copied it, then left the office with it in his hand," said Danny.

"Get. Out!" said Tom, spinning around.

"Cap's trying to give him enough rope to hang himself."

"He's not popular with the brass either?" asked Tom.

"Nope. Cap has Jalnack tailing him."

"Someone should tail Carrie Sutherland, too. She's dyed her hair strawberry-blonde, and Everett Channing thinks she's up to something," said the psychic.

Danny ran a hand down his face.

"Son of a bitch. If she and Randy are working together, we're going to have to get him to spill the beans."

"What's missing from your reports?" asked Tom with a knowing glance.

Danny smirked. "Only a few minor details. That the Poacher smells worse than a skunk, may chloroform his victims, and that the women's eyeballs were found in their stomachs."

He shivered, thinking about the autopsy photos.

"So Carrie wouldn't see or smell him coming and she'd get knocked out," said Marnie.

"She'd be defenseless even if she'd planned to take him down with mace or pepper spray," added Tom.

"That's what I'm thinkin'," said the detective lieutenant.

Danny got up and paced in front of the bookcases with his hands behind his back.

"I better call the captain. Randy needs to know that he's given Carrie bad information. It could get her killed."

The Living Room, 8:40 PM

"Thanks for dinner, Marn. I'd forgotten how much I love cabbage rolls," said Tom, sitting on the couch eating his second piece of raspberry pie.

"It's funny how they're a favorite, but I only make them once a year," she said, sprawling near the fire with the dogs.

Danny fluffed a pillow on the back of an overstuffed chair and stretched his back before taking a seat.

"Teddy and Poppy took off in a hurry when you said you were making them," he said.

"They made plans while we were out, so I'm not convinced it was the menu. A few people we were in school with heard Poppy's back and called when we were driving back. They're going to The Howl for dinner and drinks."

"Who's going?" asked Tom.

"Shelby Hamilton, Leslie Tilman, and that crowd."

"Why didn't they invite the two of you?" asked Danny

"They did. I didn't want to go."

"Okay. What about Tom?"

"I'm not in the mood for twenty questions," he replied. "They would've been asking about the accident and, to be honest, I didn't like them much, anyway."

Marnie tapped Danny's toe.

"What did Randy say?"

"He lied. Said he took the files because I'd shut him out of the case."

"Did you?" asked Tom.

"Of course, I did. He was supposed to secure the schoolhouse and get forensics in to investigate and didn't. He's been seen having secret squirrel meetings with Carrie Sutherland in back alleys and out of the way coffee shops, and his car has been parked at her home. Then he took her to the schoolhouse and berated one of Rick's guys."

"That's not good. I wouldn't share information with him either. Does he know how to get into your desk?"

"Not that I can see, but I've put everything important in Cap's office or I bring it home. Garcia and Tartetto are keeping an eye on him, too."

"I'll get back onto the Humboldt notebooks and effects tomorrow," said Tom, putting down his plate and stretching out.

"Yeah. I'll hunker down in the attic and find that map. It has to be somewhere. Oh! I forgot. I did some research on crows. Did you know they seek revenge on their enemies? What if it is Bob's bird, and he's stealing from the guy who killed his dad?" said Marnie.

"We might not know. He can't get back into the attic, but he knows the schoolhouse," said Danny.

"Want us to check tomorrow when you're at the station?" asked Tom.

"No. Go through Bob's stuff first. There might be a clue."

"Before I forget to ask … Marn, can I get a gun?"

"Yeah. Don't you have your own?" she asked.

"I do, but my parents locked them in the safe at their place along with all of my important paperwork, my wallet, and my license and only their thumbprints will open it."

"Sucks to be you, Keller. When are they back?"

"Two weeks."

"So, you can't drive until they return?"

"I can—just can't get stopped."

"Ha-ha! Wouldn't it suck even more if I put a BOLO out on your truck so you get pulled over?" said Danny.

"I'd tell your grandmother on you."

"She'd laugh, you know that, right?"

"I do. By the way, Marn, I was wondering about the treasure when I fell asleep last night. Have you opened it?"

She sat up quick—eyes wide with excitement.

"I haven't. Let's get it! And we can get you a gun while we're at it."

"Okay. It's in the study?"

"Locked up and we won't need a thumbprint."

The Study, 9:20 PM

Marnie ushered Tom and Danny into the office and the dogs trotted along behind. She switched on the lamp on her desk and cleared a space to place the treasure.

"I can't believe you didn't open it," said Tom, rubbing his hands together with excitement.

Eyebrows raised, Marnie said, "I would never open it without you."

Danny pulled back a section of hinged bookcases, revealing a bank-style vault, and began turning the dial to unlock it. When he heard the final *clunk*, he turned the wheel and pulled open the heavy door.

Tom stepped around him and inspected a shelf of firearms before choosing a Smith & Wesson M&P9.

"Can I take this one?" he asked, holding it up.

"Take whichever you want," said Marnie, squeezing by him to a section of drawers, where she retrieved an oilskin roll.

He grabbed two clips and a polymer holster and exited the vault.

"Have you been to the range much, Marn?" asked Tom.

"Not the one in town, no. But Danny, Sam, and Carl set up one in the old milking shed above the north pasture fence-line."

Danny shrugged. "Sort of. It's not the best, but it works for target practice. We can lock out the dogs at least."

"Let's go over tomorrow. I'm gonna have to qualify before I can go back on duty."

Marnie sat in her chair, and hefted the roll onto the desk, and pushed it toward Tom.

"You do the honors," she said.

Eyes on the prize, he said, "Nah. You go ahead. It was your idea to get it."

It took her a moment to untie the roll, the cotton cords brittle with age. Tom and Danny hovered in front of her desk—both praying they wouldn't be disappointed by the contents. The knuckleheads gathered beside her, hoping the parcel contained treats.

As she unrolled it, she stopped halfway, clenching her fists with excitement. She looked up at Tom and he gave an encouraging nod to keep going.

"We've waited so long to see what's inside. I'm nervous," she squeaked.

"Just open the dang thing," said Danny, chuckling.

Once unfurled, a flap of oilskin covered the treasure, and when she threw it back, it revealed several pocketed sections, each with bumps and bulges in varying shapes and sizes.

Marnie chose the middle chamber first, easing a cross from the tight fabric. She set it on the blotter and the guys leaned forward to inspect the intricately carved, rose gold artifact. The word "Air" appeared at the head of the cross and depicted a tree reaching to the sky. The foot read Earth, and tree roots were carved into the point. "Water" was engraved into the left arm with flowing water reaching to the center. "Fire" adorned the right arm with flames pointing east. The cross was bejeweled at the center, where the four points merged with a smooth, round, smoky quartz.

"Wow!" said Danny, picking it up. "It's heavy. You know, I think Gram has one of these."

"Really?" asked Marnie. "That would be great because I don't know what it is—other than beautiful."

Tom accepted it from Danny, who held it out to him.

"Air, Water, Fire, and Earth. Aren't those the elements?" he asked.

"Yeah. I wish it wasn't too late to call Gram. Anyway, we have more pockets to open. I'm sure we'll have more questions," she said.

When they had finished emptying all but one section, they stood admiring two silver and one gold bar; three unset emeralds that Marnie said must be a couple carats each; two red stones she believed to be rubies; a satchel of diamonds in assorted sizes; a heavy rose gold bracelet; six engagement rings with matching wedding bands; and a yellow gold tiger pin with emerald eyes—which made Danny gasp, of course, because of the tiny statue he'd given his mother.

"That's quite the haul!" said Tom, violet eyes gleaming in the light from the desk lamp.

"I'm gobsmacked. I never expected there to be so many … uh … treasures in that one little satchel," said Marnie, admiring the stash.

Danny scratched his beard and tapped the remaining pocket.

"One left," he said.

"Tom, you open the last one. I feel selfish," she said, pointing to the object that remained a mystery.

"Any guesses?" he asked.

"Open it. I'm tired," said Danny, throwing back his head.

And so, he did, but it wasn't what they expected—at all!

"Eww! No! No! No! Gawd! Is that blood?" said Marnie, rolling her chair away from the desk.

Tom dropped the offending item on the roll and stepped back, wiping his palms on his jeans.

"Is that an icepick?" he asked.

"I think so," said Danny, pulling the lamp closer to examine it.

"Marn, touch it. See if you can get spooky vibes off it," said her best friend.

"I will not!" she yelled, jumping out of her chair. "Danny, wrap that up and put it somewhere."

The detective lieutenant tilted his head and quirked his mouth. "I hate to say it, but I agree with Tom. Maybe it's a harmless icepick.

Then again, it could be a murder weapon because that does look like dried blood," he said.

"Used by the Poacher!" she shouted, her face red. "If I touch that and it was his, he might come back."

The men stood staring at her, but when Tater put a paw on her leg and smiled up with an encouraging nudge, she sat back down and weighed up the pros and cons.

"C'mon, Marn. It won't bite," urged Tom.

Green eyes flashing, she said, "Says you. How do we know what's connected to that … that … thing!"

Danny walked up behind her and kneaded her shoulders. "If it's anything bad, we'll call Gram."

She craned her neck and scowled. "You touch it, then! And I can call her if it's something bad."

He kissed her nose, and said, "But I don't have your gift."

"Geez! Fine!" she said, digging in her heels and dragging herself back to her desk.

With a deep breath in, she steadied her nerves and let her hands hover over the icepick.

"If anything happens to me, you're both to blame."

The lamp on the desk flickered as she shut her eyes and touched the object. At first, nothing happened. Then she shuddered. Her shoulders tensed, and her body drooped before her head fell forward, inches from the desk.

The detectives exchanged a worried glance. They stooped and peered into her face as she bolted upright, and her eyes flew open.

"Boo!" she cried, and both men jumped back—one falling backward into a side chair and the other crashing into the bookcase. The dogs barked, racing in circles around the desk.

"Jesus!" said Tom, trying to sit up straight. "You scared me half to death."

"I can't believe you did that," said Danny, catching a book before it fell on his head.

"Ha-ha! You should have seen your faces," she said, picking up the icepick and waggling it at them.

But before she could set it down, a tingle spidered across her scalp and a chill ran up her spine.

"Uh-oh," she murmured, falling against the back of her chair, sliding to the timbers, and banging her head on a caster while still holding the weapon.

Tater pushed past the detective lieutenant and stared into his mistress' face, licking her chin and then her nose. He put a paw on her chest and looked up at the men, his eyes intense.

"She's not playin' around this time," said her best friend as he grabbed the dog's collar and gently walked him back. "It's okay, buddy. We'll take care of her."

"We need to get that thing away from her," said Danny, kneeling beside her, trying to pry her fingers from the icepick—but she would not let go. He looked up at his partner. "Help me get her to the couch."

Each took an arm and a leg, and they carried her over and lay her down. Danny put a pillow under her head, and Tom covered her with a blanket.

"I'm calling my grandmother. I have no idea what to do."

Both men dropped on their knees beside her when she sucked in a breath, rolled off the couch and untangled herself from the blanket in her attempt to drop the icepick on the floor.

"Argh! Don't ever ask me to do that again!" she said, trembling. "Oh, my god! The Poacher used that to kill his family, the animals, the woman, and children. Please get it away from me!"

The psychic dragged her hands down her face, gagged and struggled to get to her feet. Danny grabbed her elbow and helped her up, but she glared at him and shook away his hand before racing to the bathroom, a hand covering her mouth.

"I guess you're sleeping on the couch tonight," said Tom, picking up the blanket and tossing it onto the sofa with an awkward grin.

Chapter Thirty-Three

October 17th

Wild Creek Ranch, The Red Barn, Western Paddock, 8:07 AM

A drizzling rain turned into a downpour as Marnie, Teddy, Poppy, and the knuckleheads arrived at the barn. The temperature had dropped overnight, and they were all bundled up in jeans, warm socks, boots, and heavy sweaters with skivvies beneath. Poppy had opted for a wool toque with a furry pompom on top, Marnie a baseball cap, and Teddy an unadorned pink beanie.

"I'll hop out and open the doors, then drive in. It's better than all of us getting soaked," said Marnie.

"Hang on," said Teddy from the passenger side. "There's Elk. He'll open the door."

A mug of coffee in hand, Elk loped through the rain, pulling his black leather gambler hat down to keep the raindrops off his nose. He pointed to the doors, and continued on, pulled them open and bowed, welcoming them inside with a cheeky grin.

Poppy opened her door, and the dogs rushed out, running happy circles around the farmer.

"Mornin', ladies," he said, tipping his hat. "Need help? Milking's done, beasts have been watered and fed, eggs are collected, and the fence-line checked. I'm at your service until three, cause I ain't working outside in this shit today."

"Ha-ha! I don't blame you," said Marnie, giving Tater a pat and turning to her Jeep. "We've got a ton of decorations in the back, if you want to help us unload them."

"Arnie will be comin' along in a minute. I sent the others home until milkin' time. There's no sense in any of us catching our death of foolishness. If the sun returns, so will they, but I don't see it joinin' us anytime soon. That rain has settled in for the duration."

"Feels like it," said Marnie, pulling a tarp off the bed of her vehicle.

The Kitchen, 8:21 AM

"That guilty conscience will kill you," said Tom, pouring himself a cup of coffee and taking a whiff. "God! I missed this."

Danny looked up at his friend and nodded. "She does make a fine cup of Joe. And everything else, huh? I can't tell if she's still mad. She took off to the barn with the gals and the knuckleheads a few minutes ago to decorate the barn."

"Did she make you breakfast?" asked Tom.

"Nope. They were putting cereal bowls in the dishwasher when I came down."

"Then she's still pissed."

"That's what I was thinking."

"You off today?"

"Yeah, unless I get called in," said Danny.

"Let's go help them. It might put us back in her good graces," said Tom, dropping four slices of bread in the toaster. "But first, toast and peanut butter for energy."

Ryan's Diner, 9:10 AM

Randolph Stuyvesant dumped four packets of sugar into his coffee and stirred as Carrie Sutherland looked on in disgust.

"It's no wonder you're out of shape."

"My health isn't your concern, but I am worried about yours," he said, dropping the spoon on a napkin.

"There's nothing to worry about. We've got it all planned. There's a full moon tonight. I'll park near the four ways as if I'm having car trouble. You'll be hiding near that old shack and rescue me when, or if, someone tries to grab me. Easy peasy."

"And what if he kills you before I get there? One knife blade across your throat, and that's it. You don't stand a chance. Emergency services would never get to you in time," said Randy.

"The autopsies say nothing of that. He takes the women to another location and kills them there. The blood at the dump sites is nil."

"That may be true, but killers can change their methods. It's not unheard of."

She scoffed. "I've read enough about these things to know that it's rare."

"Carrie, these are crimes of opportunity. He couldn't have known that Krista Hansen's truck would break down where it did. She didn't have a pattern of traveling on Hallowed Hills Road. She only traveled that way because she had an interview and Miller's Pond was closed for construction."

"Then why is he only taking redheaded women?"

Randy gave up, throwing his hands in the air. "I don't know, but perhaps he isn't. There is a possibility others have been abducted that we don't know about."

"Or he sees a woman with red hair, stalks her, and then takes her. He has been spotted wandering around Wild Creek Ranch numerous times and allegedly had an argument with Bob Humboldt near the four ways."

He narrowed his eyes. "And how do know that?"

"Teddy Jones has a big mouth. She was telling a table full of people about it at The Howl last night and I overheard," said Carrie with a smug smile and a flip of her hair.

"She's that girl who lives behind Marnie's house, right? Short? Perky?"

"You forgot annoying. But I don't know where she lives. All I care is that she is a source of reliable information," she said.

The twosome stopped talking when Gram delivered their breakfasts—waffles and bacon for the detective and muesli and yogurt for the reporter.

"Enjoy your meals," said Gram, sweet as honey, but added, "I hope you choke on it," when she was out of earshot.

Wild Creek Ranch, The Red Barn, 9:23 AM

"What a gloomy day," said Tom, as they drove across the field in Danny's Jeep.

"Look how low those clouds are. You can't even see the tops of mountains. Does the drop in temperature make you ache?"

"Yeah. I've got to get back to my fitness regimen, or the physical therapists will have a conniption. My gym membership lapsed while I was in rehab."

"Ask if you can use the one at the clinic. I've used it and it's better than either of the centers in town."

Tom frowned. "I've missed a lot. What else does the clinic have that I don't know about?"

"Have Carl give you a tour. He loves showing off what they've created," said Danny.

"I'll do that. I was rude to him the other day and I feel bad about it."

"He might understand, considering what you've been through. The arguments he and Marnie had were epic. It's rare for him to lose his patience with her, but he didn't put up with her feeling sorry for herself. They had decisions to make about the construction and she wasn't engaged, so he came over, told her to get dressed because they had a meeting with Hugh Barber. Anyway, he fixed himself a coffee and told her he'd wait while she got ready," said Danny.

"And did she?"

"Of course. She knows tough love when she sees it."

"You know, he and Sam sent me notes almost weekly. I answered some, but I didn't always feel up to it," said Tom.

"Yeah. Marnie mentioned you didn't answer any of hers, so she stopped writing."

"I didn't know how to apologize. If we'd figured it out, none of it would have happened. That was our job, and we didn't get it done," said Tom.

"Tell me about it. But she told me she saw me tackle Dalton and that you pushed her through the door, wrapped yourself around her, and protected her. She didn't blame either of us. Lawrence Parish and his family got all her wrath. I think it's why she wants to see Kate."

"It could do us both some good to vent."

"Yeah. If that's what you want, Carl can arrange it," said Danny.

"Let me talk to Marn. I'm only goin' if she does," said Tom.

"Chicken," replied his friend with a chuckle.

"You know it!"

Elk and Arnie stood in a misting rain outside the barn when the detectives drove up and got out of the truck. Both were looking up at a crow sitting on top of the ridgepole.

"What's goin' on?" asked Danny, slamming his door.

"That crow keeps flying through while we're tryin' to hang decorations. We're afraid he's gonna knock one of us off a ladder," said Arnie, hands in his pockets.

"Can't you shut the door?" asked Tom.

"It doesn't work. He keeps findin' a way in," said Elk.

"What if we throw some food out there for him?" suggested the detective lieutenant.

The farmers rolled their eyes.

"We'll leave it with you, then, and go help the womenfolk," said Danny with a laugh.

Strutting through the door, Tom yelled out, "I hear you pretty ladies are looking for strong, handsome men to help you!"

Marnie glanced up from the ghoul she was fashioning from an old sheet, and said, "Oh! It's you. I thought you brought Patrick and Carl."

With a grimace, Tom picked up a pinecone and tossed it at her. "Hey! That was mean."

She turned around, pointing to a string of raven lights hanging from a beam. "You could hang those. We stopped because the crow kept dive-bombing us."

Danny joined them, head tipped back. "What's up there that he's protecting?"

"Dunno. But I'm not looking. It might be more eyeballs."

"What?!" screeched Poppy, mouth open in horror.

"Kidding! Halloween humor," she replied, wincing and looking away.

"Help me with the ladder, Tommy. I'll go have a look."

The detectives carried it closer to the beam, and Danny climbed up.

"He's got another nest up here. I can't see what's inside it, though. Have you got a taller ladder?"

"No. What about the cherry-picker? I can ask the guys to get it."

"Hmm ... I'll see if I can reach it," he said, stretching up on his toes and leaning right.

"Be careful!" shouted Teddy.

The nest in his grasp, Danny stretched further, lost his balance, and wrapped his arms around the beam.

Poppy and Teddy screamed, the dogs barked, and Marnie and Tom raced to the ladder, with Elk and Arnie not far behind.

"Damnit!" he yelled, as his feet found the rungs and he righted himself. "I'm okay! The cherry-picker would be appreciated," he said, catching his breath—heart pounding in his ears.

"Get down here before you kill yourself!" scolded the psychologist.

"I'll get the lift," said Elk, walking away as the crow flew in, squawking and making a beeline for the detective.

"Look out!" screeched Poppy—but not in time.

The bird swooped, and the detective crashed eight feet to the floor, the ladder toppling sideways into the wall.

"Danny!" screamed Marnie, racing to him and kneeling in the hay, the dogs already on top of him, sniffing his ears.

"Yeah. Yeah. Don't touch me. Give me a minute," he grunted, trying to roll over in the loose bed of hay.

Tom had his phone out calling nine-one-one before his partner had landed.

"Ambulance is on the way," he said, rushing to Danny's side. Crouching, he checked his partner's head for lacerations and bumps while Marnie inspected his legs and arms.

"I'm okay. I landed in the hay. It's not so bad," he said, trying to sit up.

"You're probably concussed," said Teddy, looking into his eyes. "I'm calling Carl."

"Danny, stop trying to get up. You could have broken ribs," said Poppy, fluffing up hay to make him a pillow. "Lay back down and wait for the ambulance."

He held out his hands and said, "Okay. Everybody stop it! I'm fine."

Getting to his knees, he put a hand on Marnie's shoulder and stood up, wobbled, and Tom caught him before he could fall again.

"C'mon. Take a seat. The EMTs know it's you, so they'll get here as fast as they can."

"You didn't tell them an officer was down, did you?"

Tom shrugged. "I said Detective Lieutenant Daniel Gregg fell eight feet and needed assistance."

"Geez! That's gonna make the news."

"No. I asked them to keep it quiet and not to broadcast names and addresses out. They were so happy to hear I'm home, they didn't argue."

Carl ran into the barn, a medical bag in his hand.

"What happened?"

"Danny fell from the beam," said Marnie, pointing up.

"Are you nauseated? Dizzy?" said the psychiatrist, taking a flashlight from his bag.

"No, and no."

"Bullshit!" said Tom. "You would've fallen on your ass if I hadn't caught you a second ago."

"Zip it, Keller!" growled Danny.

Wild Creek Ranch, The Kitchen, 4:03 PM

"Where's Danny?" asked Teddy, meeting Marnie and Tom at the door.

"They're keeping him for observation, whatever that means. His father and Hannah are with him now, and Gram's on the way," said Marnie, kicking off her boots.

"The nurses were getting testy, so we said we'd go back later," added Tom.

"How bad is it?" asked Poppy, putting the kettle on to boil.

Tater put a paw on his mistress' leg and whimpered. She bent and scratched his ears and kissed the top of his head.

"Don't worry, pal. He'll be home soon."

"Three cracked ribs, a chipped bone in his left elbow, but no concussion," said Tom, giving Gus a pat on his rump.

Dickens ambled over to Marnie and leaned against her leg, tongue out and tail thumping. She tugged on his ears, ruffled his white shawl and gave him a hug.

"He's going to be okay," she whispered, brushing his head with a kiss.

Teddy rubbed the psychic's shoulder. "Sit, and we'll make you a cup of tea."

Marnie looked at the clock. "Have you two eaten?"

Poppy said, "We did. How about you?"

"I'm starving," said Tom, opening the fridge door. "Were you planning anything for dinner?"

"I hadn't thought about it. Does bangers and mash sound good?"

"Sure. I'll peel the potatoes. Do you want these beans snapped, too?" he asked.

"Yeah. We better eat early so we can get back to the hospital."

"What can we do to help?" asked Teddy.

"Nothing, thanks. Tom and I can get dinner sorted if you have other things to do."

"Well, we're finished with the decorations we had. Elk and Arnie gave us a hand, and so did Carl. It looks great."

Dropping her shoulders, Marnie said, "Thank you. You didn't need to do that, but I really appreciate it. Do we need more, or are we okay?"

"A few more pumpkins wouldn't hurt," said Poppy.

"I'm all out. I've gotta go into town tomorrow to see Everett Channing. He said he'll put a piece in the paper about the hay maze and the party."

"People know, though, don't they?" asked Teddy.

"Yeah. But positive press about the ranch would be nice after all the crap that's out there."

"True. That would help, wouldn't it? Anyway, I might go over to my place for a while and get some clean clothes, then throw in a load of laundry." She turned to the other woman. "Want to come?"

"Sure!"

"Dinner will be about an hour," said Marnie as they walked out the door. Turning to Tom, she said. "Now that we're alone, tell me about the spookiness in your world."

"I thought you'd forgotten," he said, rinsing potatoes in the sink.

"Never! It's been at the back of my mind since you told me, but crazy shit happened, and we haven't had time. I'm sorry."

"Meh. Don't worry about it. I've seen Annie a few times, and I'm pretty sure your parents have paid me a visit."

"Your sister and my folks. That's so cool!" she said, snapping a bean.

Hugging himself with his hands in his armpits, he shuddered. "Uh. No. It's not."

"I've read cases where people have had a near-death experience and saw spirits after the event. You know, I saw you in my hospital room when you were in surgery. You were standing in the doorway."

"Yeah. Danny told me. He said you tried to get out of bed, and he and Sam had to hold you down while Giles left to see what was happening."

"Yes. It was ... I don't know what it was, but I never want to experience it again. When Danny fell today ..." She sighed, her eyes tearing up. "I am so tired of bad things happening to people I love. It's exhausting!"

"Ever think you're jinxed?" he asked.

Wrinkling her forehead, she threw a bean at him. "No! Not until now. Geez, Tom!"

"Crows are vengeful critters, right? I was thinkin' it went after Danny because we boarded up that window. Maybe it didn't see me," he said with a shrug.

"Hmm ... That's possible. There! I'm not jinxed!"

He eyed her, mischief in his violet eyes. "It *is* your barn."

"Zip it, Keller," she said.

"Changing the subject ... Danny and I were talkin' about Kate earlier and how it might help us if we go see her to vent. Tell her how we feel about what she and her family did to us."

"Bring Sam along?" she asked.

His eyebrows shot up. "You think he'd go?"

"We could ask."

Marnie's phone rang, and they both looked at the screen.

"It's the hospital," she said, answering the call and hitting the speaker.

"Hello. This is Marnie Reilly."

"Hey. It's me. They won't spring me. I have to spend the night, and the doctor says I can't have any more visitors today. He practically pushed my family out the door."

"Can't I even bring you your pajamas?" she said.

"Ha-ha! Do I even have a pair?"

"That's more information than I needed," teased Tom.

"You didn't say I was on speaker."

"It's just us. Teddy and Poppy are over at the cottage. And yes, you do have PJs. I don't think you have any here, though."

"I'll call you in the morning and let you know when you can come get me."

"Okay. I'll bring your toiletries bag."

"I'd appreciate that. Have a good night."

"You too."

"I love you. You too, Tommy!"

"I love you too," said the friends with a giggle and a laugh.

Hopp's Gate Inn, 9:30 PM

Carrie Sutherland took the last sip of her wine and set the glass on the white tablecloth. She wiped a linen napkin across her lips and signaled the waiter for her bill, who nodded and scurried off to get it. He returned without haste, knowing how particular this customer could be.

"I hope you enjoyed your meal, Ms. Sutherland. I can take this up for you when you're ready," said the young man, handing her a leather wallet.

"You can take it now. I wouldn't have called you over if I wasn't ready," she snapped, handing over her card.

"Of course, ma'am," he said, taking the card and retreating to the back.

Her phone vibrated in the front pocket of her bag, and she pulled it out to see who was calling. She pursed her lips and put it back.

"I'll call you back, Randy," she said to herself.

When the waiter returned with the receipt, she scrawled her signature, gathered her coat and left without leaving a tip. The food and service were wonderful, as always. But Carrie Sutherland didn't tip anyone. She didn't feel the need. She was a celebrity, after all, and having her in their establishment was an endorsement of sorts. That was enough.

Once outside, she called Randy back, waiting four rings before he answered.

"Hello, Carrie, look, tonight isn't good. I've been sick since breakfast."

"It's no wonder with all that sugar you consumed. Suck it up, Detective. You have work to do. I'll be at the four ways by eleven-thirty. Don't call me. I don't want our phones lighting up and giving us away. You may need to park around the corner and walk to the shack, so get there early and hide. Dress warm. It's colder than a witch's you-know-what out there."

"Did you hear me? I'm really sick," he said.

"Stop whining, Randolph. I'll see you at … well, I'll see you when you come to my rescue. Make sure you have ammo in your gun."

She hung up and tucked away her phone and clicked off down the sidewalk in her high heels.

Wild Creek Ranch, The Living Room, 11:03 PM

The flickering television was the only light in the room when Tom announced he was going to bed.

"I can't watch anymore of this sap," he said, setting his feet on the floor and standing. "You gals enjoy the rest of it and don't bother telling me how it ends. I already know. There will be a misunderstanding. The two star-crossed lovers who once loathed one another will part ways only to come together again as the credits roll." He put his finger in his mouth and gagged.

"Ha-ha! I'm heading up. I can't keep my eyes open," said Marnie, throwing off her blanket.

"Do the knuckleheads need to go out again?" asked Tom.

"Nah. We took them for a wander forty minutes ago. They'll be fine until morning."

"Gus, are you coming with me?" he asked his Labrador, who stared up at him, then looked at Marnie.

"Go with your dad, boy."

"Will you two be quiet? We're missing the movie," said Teddy, pausing the television.

And Poppy confirmed her irritation with a pout and sideways glance.

Marnie and Tom laughed as they herded their respective canines to their bedrooms.

"Goodnight!" she said.

"See you in the morning!" he said.

Teddy threw a cushion at Marnie, and Poppy tossed another at Tom—both missing, but their point was made.

606 Black Bear Boulevard (2A), Randy Stuyvesant's Home, 11: 07 PM

"Nine-one-one, what's your emergency?"

"I think I'm having a heart attack."

Hallowed Hills Road, The Four Ways, 11:29 PM

Carrie Sutherland parked her car as close to the ditch as possible and sat in her car, scoping the scene. She shivered and checked her dashboard for the temperature—thirty-eight degrees.

"Brr!" she said to herself, pulling up her coat's zipper and putting on her gloves.

The Hunter's Moon played peekaboo, as heavy clouds drifted across the sky, blocking its brilliance. A *clump-clump* behind her made her jump, and she laughed when she saw two deer meandering across the road and into the brush on the other side. Chancing a look behind her, she searched for signs of Randy—but saw none.

She smirked and said, "Good boy."

While she checked her car doors were unlocked, headlights crept up and a police cruiser rolled by, pulling over ahead of her.

"Give me a break," she said, fuming about the interruption, but she rolled down her window and made nice with the officer.

The policemen shined his flashlight into her vehicle and leaned down, looking into her face.

"Ms. Sutherland, is everything okay?"

"Yes, it is, thanks. I need to make a call, and my phone won't connect to my car speaker."

"This isn't a great place to stop, ma'am. A young woman disappeared from here a few days ago," he said, placing a hand on the car door.

"I know! How dreadful! My paper has been trying to do a story, but your captain won't share any details with us," she said, eyes wide with feigned innocence.

"You know how it goes. They won't comment on an open investigation."

She smiled and patted his hand, leaving hers on top of his.

"Would you know anything about the case?"

"No, ma'am. That is way above my pay grade. You should call Detective Lieutenant Gregg. He knows everything."

"I'm sure he does," she said, averting her eyes and rolling them.

"Well, if you're not having car trouble, I'll be on my way. Don't sit here too long, though. I'm the last patrol car coming through here tonight, now that Ms. Reilly has a security team."

"Oh! Did you make special trips out here for her?" she asked.

"No, ma'am. Her team is helping us out. We used to cruise this road every hour or so because kids like to vandalize the cemetery. But she offered to put in security cameras and, of course, the captain said yes."

"Oh, isn't she wonderful!" said Carrie, wanting to vomit.

"Yes, ma'am. You have a safe night, now," he said as he walked to his car.

"You, too, officer! Now get the fuck out of here. You're ruining my story," she hissed.

The policeman drove away, taking a left onto Algonquin Road, which merged into Station Street by the railroad station and the silos. When she saw the last of his taillights, she pushed the window control to put up the window, but it didn't close.

"Damnit! I charged you yesterday," she said, stomping her feet, as she tried the window again. This time, it closed. With a sigh of relief, she settled her back against the seat.

"Where are you, Mr. Big Dude? You must be out there somewhere! Maybe I should get out and open the hood to draw you into my trap."

She unbuckled her seatbelt, but before she could open her door, a black mass appeared at her window and yanked it open. Carrie screamed and grabbed for her pepper spray, but two enormous arms reached in and dragged her out of the car. Kicking and flailing, she screamed, only to be silenced by a chloroform-soaked rag in the hand of her captor covering her mouth.

Carrie Sutherland got what she wanted—the attention of a serial killer who now carried her off into the trees under the full Hunter's moon.

Wild Creek Ranch, Marnie's Bedroom, 11:38 PM

Toasty and cozy under her big duvet, fleece blanket, and flannel sheets, Marnie rolled to her side and laughed at Tater. His left ear and hind feet twitched as his head rested on Danny's pillow. She had opened the window a squeak before crawling into bed, loving to snuggle beneath the weight of the blankets. She looked to the foot of the bed to find Dickens on his stomach, head tilted and ears perked. In the distance Marnie thought she heard the scream of a barn owl, but it only screeched once and then silence. After giving Tater and Dickens goodnight pats, she burrowed under the covers and fell asleep.

Chapter Thirty-Four

*October 18*th

Wild Creek Ranch, The Attic, 4:33 AM

With a travel mug of coffee in hand, Marnie trudged up the steps to her attic. The knuckleheads followed and settled on a braided rug near the gabled window. She pulled a box from a top shelf and set it on a vintage bureau filled with old photos. A Daddy Longlegs clung to the lid of the carton, and she shooed it away to live another day.

Peeking inside, she saw an assortment of carpentry books and did a little hop and clapped her hands. One by one, she removed the books, flipping the pages in search of a map. So far, she'd not found it but had discovered two-hundred dollars of her father's stash in twenty-dollar bills.

At the bottom of the box was the large and dreaded fairy tale book. She poked it with an index finger, making sure it wouldn't bite, before picking it up. Holding it over her head, she fanned the pages and was rewarded with one-hundred dollars and a folded parchment document.

With a whoop, she snatched up the money and the map and bounded down the stairs, straight to Tom's room.

Creekwood Medical Center, Room 333, 4:58 AM

Danny woke with a headache, painful ribs, and a throbbing left arm. The effects of last night's pain meds were long gone. He grabbed the metal bed rail and pulled himself up, wincing in pain. Before he could put his feet on the floor, a nurse was at the door, ready to assist.

"Mr. Gregg, let me help you," he said, pulling back the covers from the detective's left foot.

"Thanks. I've got it," he said, holding up a hand. "But if I could get some Tylenol for my headache, I would appreciate it. And please find out when I can get out of here."

"I'll get your doctor," said the nurse, backing out of the room.

Wild Creek Ranch, Hall Outside Tom's Room, 5:03 AM

Marnie knocked on Tom's door, hopping back and forth with excitement.

"Tom! Wake up! I found the map!"

He growled from the other side. "Go back to bed! What the hell are you doing up so early?"

"Get up! Get up! Get up! C'mon! This is exciting. Come look at the map with me."

He yanked open the door, his eyes bleary with sleep.

"It's five o'clock. What is wrong with you?" he said, his voice early morning husky.

She waved the map in front of his face.

"I'll make you breakfast!" she sang.

Tater and Dickens scooted around them and dove onto the bed with Gus, tails wagging and smiles on their faces.

He turned around and looked at them merrily messing up his covers and sighed.

"Give me a minute. Let me wash up and I'll be right there," he said, shutting the door.

It creaked open a moment later, and the dogs ran out and he shouted, "There better be bacon, eggs, and waffles!"

Copper Woods, 5:13 AM

Carrie Sutherland lay naked and trembling on an old plank floor and stared into the darkness. She searched for a blanket to cover herself, but when she reached out, she felt nothing but more timber and a gritty substance she assumed was sand. Not wanting to get the attention of the beast who grabbed her out on the road, she moved cautiously toward the sound of sniffling, holding out a hand to sense warmth if any existed. A slender hand clasped hers and squeezed it tight.

"He's not here," the woman whispered. "But he'll be back. It's my turn to die, now that he has you."

"Shh. Shh. What's your name?" asked Carrie.

Through a sob, the woman said, "Jess Alder."

"I'm Carrie Sutherland from The Times. Don't worry. A policeman is coming to save us."

Wild Creek Ranch, The Kitchen, 5:30 AM

Tom walked into the kitchen to find Marnie hunched over the table, studying a large map.

"Anything interesting?" he asked, looking over her shoulder.

"Yeah. The tunnels are way more complex than I knew. Look here. This tunnel comes out right next to Nolan Flannigan's grave."

"Aren't there tombstones on either side of his?"

Marnie nodded and followed another tunnel with her finger.

"Check this out! That's Ryan's Diner right there, and another tunnel opens close by."

He looked at where she was pointing and moved closer.

"I bet it opens in that big old cellar where she stores the beer she shouldn't have."

Perplexed by the comment, she glanced at him.

"I thought she had a license?"

"Ha! She says she has one, but I've never seen it."

"Well, isn't she the rule breaker? Ha-ha!"

"Hey, Marn. Where's your deed?"

"It's in the vault. Why?"

"This parcel of land, here," he said, pointing to a trapezoid shaped outline. "Is that Copper Woods?"

Creekwood Medical Center, 6:00 AM

Restless and angry, Danny marched to the cupboard and took out his clothes.

"Screw this. I'm getting out of here."

He winced, bending to put a leg in his jeans and held his breath while putting in the other. Removing the gown, he favored his left arm and struggled to pull on his Henley shirt with several expletives muttered while arranging it over his body.

Head pounding, he searched through his jacket pockets for his phone. When he found it and turned it on, he had three missed calls from Randolph Stuyvesant.

"I'll call you later, Randy. I don't have time for you right now," he muttered.

And as he pressed Marnie's number to plan his escape, the doctor came in with a clipboard.

"Mr. Gregg, good morning. Didn't the nurse tell you I was on the way?"

"An hour ago," he growled, growing angrier because this doctor wasn't his physician. "Where's Doctor Ellingham?

"Unwell, I'm afraid. I've been seeing his patients and my own. I'm Doctor Taylor."

"Uh-huh. Look, I'm leaving. When a guy asks for a Tylenol, and it takes an hour to get one ... Well, I could've driven home, taken some, and the headache would've been gone by now. *And* I would've had my breakfast. My girlfriend is on the way, so thanks, but I gotta go."

"Mr. Gregg ..."

"It's Detective Lieutenant Gregg," said Danny through gritted teeth, his steely blue eyes boring holes in the doctor's skull.

Wild Creek Ranch, The Kitchen, 6:06 AM

"Gosh! I thought the deed was in there," said Marnie, slumping down onto a bench.

Tom looked over his mug of coffee and suggested, "Is it in your safe deposit box at the bank?"

"Could be. Danny, Teddy, and Carl took control after the accident and handed a lot of stuff over to David Bennett. I'll call him at nine and see if he knows where it is," she said.

"So, you'll wake me up, but not him?" He cocked his head and gave her a look.

Laughing, she got up to check the oven.

"You're easy access," she said.

"How much longer on that bacon?"

"If you want it crispy, it'll be a few more minutes," she said, returning her attention to the map.

With her finger, she traced a line from her house to Copper Woods.

"It looks like there's an entrance on that property, too. Look here. But this one has a cross on it. I wonder if this is one that's been walled up."

"Well, if The Poacher stories are true, it would make sense. Who the heck wants that freak roaming the tunnels?"

"Or winding up there by accident."

"What's your plan for the day, Marn?"

"I've got client notes to review and two sessions down at the clinic, but I'll be free by noon. Want to have lunch? And I have to stop by the paper, too."

"Yeah. I'll go over to the house this morning and check out those paint colors. I like what you've done, but I haven't looked upstairs. And one of us has to pick up Danny. Have you heard from him?"

Creekwood Medical Center, 6:10 AM

"We apologize for the error, but if we could run more x-rays, we can confirm our original prognoses were accurate," said the doctor.

Danny scratched his head and sighed. "Yeah. I guess it's better to be safe."

"Exactly! Our radiologist feels horrible, but equipment failure happens occasionally."

"Can I get a Tylenol, please?"

"I'll be right back," said the doctor, leaving the room.

Wild Creek Ranch, The Kitchen. 6:33 AM

"You're spoiling us, Marnie. I never have breakfast like this unless I go to the diner," said Poppy, pouring maple syrup on her second waffle.

"Seriously, the smell of bacon wafting up the stairs woke me up," said Teddy, plucking a slice from the platter.

Tom munched on a sausage link, then licked his fingers.

"She made it for me. You know that, right? Neither of you would have this feast if I weren't here."

"Ha! I make breakfast for Danny and before the detective and Dickens, Tater and I enjoyed Sunday morning brunch often. I love breakfast," said Marnie, breaking up a waffle and handing the pieces to the knuckleheads.

"Any idea when Danny will be home?" asked Poppy.

"Nope. Tom and I haven't heard from him. I tried his phone, but it went right to voicemail."

"It's still early. But if you need me to pick him up while you're in appointments, I can," said Teddy.

Marnie nodded. "Between the four of us, we've got him covered. Okay. I need to get myself ready for clients."

"Going back to your stuffy suits?" teased Tom.

"I tried on a few things yesterday and I swim in everything. Cargo pants and a sweatshirt will have to do. It's okay if they look big," she said.

"Thanksgiving is coming!" said Teddy. "You'll be back in your suits in no time."

Everyone giggled and looked at their waistlines.

"I can't wait for the holidays," said Poppy.

"Spending them with your mother or father?" asked Marnie.

"Hmm ... There's a pickle. They'll both want me. Gawd! Now I'm not looking forward to the festive season," she said, covering her face with her hands.

Teddy rubbed her shoulder and said, "You can hang out with me. We'll have our own little party."

Tom looked up at Marnie and said, "Or ..."

"We'll have two turkeys, and everyone can celebrate here," she said, giving her best friend a look that told him he would be peeling a lot of potatoes.

He held up his juice glass and said, "May this year's holiday season be a damn sight better than the last."

Eyes wide, Poppy said, "Why? What happened last year?"

"Murder and mayhem," said the psychic.

Creekwood Medical Center, 9:23 AM

"Wearing the sling will help with pain and keep your arm stable," said Doctor Taylor. "Are you left or right-handed?"

"Right. Do I have to keep it on all the time?" Danny asked, already feeling constricted.

"I recommend it. Of course, you can take it off to shower and dress, but don't go prolonged periods without it. We want that elbow to heel."

"Okay. I'll wear the sling. Can I go now?"

"I cannot stress enough that you take it easy while your ribs heel. As you can see, there are no fractures, but bruising is significant. Ice, rest, and ibuprofen are what I prescribe. If you can go home and put your feet up for a few days, that would be best."

"Ha! I'm a cop with two homicides to solve. Taking it easy is not on the cards."

"You mentioned that before. Perhaps you can assist us. We're looking for an emergency contact for a gentleman who came in last night. He called nine-one-one, so we have his address, but when they got to the address, he was passed out on the sidewalk. If I take you to his room, you might identify him."

"Sure. Let's go."

The doctor and detective discussed the storm the weatherman predicted in the coming days and how water and food shelves were emptying at record pace, and that stores were out of generators.

"You'd think folks up here in the mountains would be well-stocked and have a generator ready to go as soon as October first hits," said Danny. "But not everyone has the luxury of buying groceries in bulk or can afford a generator."

"I agree. We have two generators and full cupboards and freezers, and my wife and I donate to the food bank every week, but we can because we're both doctors."

"But the food bank only works for those who can get to it. I'll have a word with my captain to see if Creekwood PD could help."

"We can all do more. And speaking of ...," said the doctor, stopping outside room two-fourteen. "This is the patient's room. Peek in and see if you recognize him."

Danny pulled on the door and looked at the man laying the bed with tubes coming out of his nose and arms, and monitors beeping around him.

Closing the door, he said, "That's Detective Randolph Stuyvesant. I work with him. What's he in here for?"

"He had a heart attack last night."

Wild Creek Ranch, Tom's House, 10:03 AM

Overwhelmed by Marnie's thoughtfulness, Tom sat on the oak floor of his new master bedroom, admiring the mountains and trees through a wall of windows overlooking the creek. Mid-ponder, his concentration was broken by the ringing in his pocket.

He brought out his phone and answered a call from the medical center.

"Are you free?" asked Tom.

"Yeah. I tried to call Marnie, but got her voicemail.," said Danny.

"She's with clients this morning. Want me to come get you?"

"If you're not busy."

"I'm sitting in my new house looking out at the mountains. I'll tear myself away and be there shortly," said Tom.

"You'll have to take Marnie's truck. Your battery is disconnected."

"Oh. Okay. I'll stop at the clinic on my way to the house."

"Hang on. Wasn't she planning to come into town this afternoon?"

"Yeah. She has to go to the newspaper, and we were going to go to lunch at noon."

Danny clicked his tongue on the roof of his mouth, then said, "You know what? Pick me up at the station at noon. I'll walk there and take care of a few things."

"Are you sure?"

"Yup. Randolph Stuyvesant is in the hospital. He had a heart attack last night, and he tried to call me, but my phone was off and now the battery is dead. I've got a charger at the station."

"See you in a few."

"Thanks."

Copper Woods, 10:30 AM

Curled into a ball to stay warm, Carrie Sutherland refused to cry. She knew Randy would save her. Why waste energy thinking otherwise? Even if he had lost them in the woods, he would ping the tracking device and be here soon.

Jess lay next to her, but hadn't made a peep in what seemed like hours. The reporter put a hand on her mottled and cold back to comfort her, but she didn't respond, so she shook her.

"Are you awake?"

The girl mumbled something incoherent.

"We need to move around to get our blood pumping," said the reporter, getting to her knees and swinging her arms.

The girl rolled to face her, and Carrie grimaced at her hallow cheeks, sunken eyes, and gray complexion.

"What for? He's going to kill us, anyway. Dig out our eyes with a spoon, stab us with an icepick and leave us to bleed out. He did it to Krista and that other lady. He'll do it to us, too."

"I won't let that happen. My friend will be here."

"Not in time," said Jess, turning away.

Carrie got to her feet and paced as far as her chained ankle would allow.

"Where are you, Randy? You can't let us die at the hands of this psycho."

And then she saw it. The tracking device. Smashed to pieces on the marred table beside a wooden bowl filled with marbles.

The Creekwood Times Editorial Office, 11:18 AM

The clatter of keyboards and ringing phones met Marnie and Tom when they opened the door to the newsroom. Everett Channing stood at a tall desk, a hand on his hip, with a phone pressed to his ear.

"Yeah. Listen. I'll have to call you back. Some people who could help just walked in," he said, dropping his phone on the desk.

"Hey, Everett, you look harassed," said Tom.

Raking back his hair with his fingers, the editor said, "You have no idea. Carrie has disappeared. Her car was found at the four ways this morning, but I can't reach her."

"We can track her phone," said Tom, taking charge.

"Danny already tried that. It's off."

"What was she doing on Hallowed Hills Road?" asked Marnie, her gut twisting in knots.

"A story, I guess. She thinks you're trouble, and she's been pressing me to let her write an exposé. I won't let her, of course. But ..."

Marnie scowled. "Oh! She has a bug up her ass about Ken Wilder choosing me over her. If she knew what he was really like, she would not be so quick to swap places. Anyway, we need to find her."

"You'd be surprised what she'd do. She'd swap because it's all about the Benjamins for her."

"Well, as pathetic as that is, Carrie put herself in danger, considering Krista Hansen," said Marnie, walking to Carrie's desk. "This is her desk, right?"

"It is. Why?" asked the editor.

"Can we go through it to see if she left any clues?"

"Yeah. Go for it. I'm going to call her mother and let her know there's no news. No pun intended."

Marnie pulled open a drawer and rifled through a mass of lipsticks, nail polish, and eyeshadows.

"Who needs this many cosmetics?" she asked, slamming the drawer and opening the one beneath. "Holy crap! Foundation, blush, moisturizer, eyelash curler, ad nauseam. I've got nothing on this side."

Tom pulled out a digital recorder and pressed play. The contents were Carrie ranting about Marnie Reilly and her brother getting away with murder.

"Wow! That's acerbic," said Everett, coming up behind them. "Don't worry. I'll set her straight."

"How'd her mother take the news?" asked Tom.

"She told me where to find a key to her daughter's apartment and asked if I could check on her. Of course, I said yes. Can you open the top middle drawer, please?"

Tom moved the chair and slid out the drawer, where they found pens, pencils, highlighters and two steno pads. Under the notepads was a package of GPS trackers with one missing.

The detective whistled. "I really hope she wasn't counting on Randolph to track her."

928 Seneca Avenue, Carrie Sutherland's House, 11:45 AM

Marnie picked up Danny at the station, and they met Everett and Tom at Carrie's home. The house was in the older part of town, where money and influence meant everything to neighborhood newcomers. The homes were spacious, elegant, and the lawns manicured. Nine-twenty-eight was a gingerbread Victorian, painted a velvety midnight-blue with deep beige trim work.

Standing outside, Marnie balked about entering the reporter's inner sanctum uninvited.

"I feel funny going in. It would bother me if she wandered around my house without me there."

"You can wait here. We'll run inside, check, and leave," said Danny.

"Unless ..." Tom paused and, running a hand over his beard, dared himself to ask for her help. "You could come inside and see if you pick up any vibes, if you know what I mean."

Eyes narrowed, she said, "At this precise moment in time, I dislike you. Very much."

"But you still love me, and you would never want something bad to happen to a person if you could stop it, right?"

Eyebrows squished together, Everett said, "So all that stuff is true?"

She glared at Tom and said, "Yes. I'm a freak. Let's get this over with."

The swollen front door took Tom's shoulder to open it, and when he fell into the foyer, he was pleased not to be met by the stench of death. The others trooped in after him, taking in the grand entryway.

On the left was a sparsely furnished parlor with pieces that didn't do the grandeur of the house justice. To the right was a library with ample shelving but not one book, nor a chair, desk, or any other furnishings.

"Carrie! It's Ev! Are you here?" shouted the editor.

An echo came back in response.

"Should we check upstairs?" asked Danny.

"Yes. If she's fallen and hit her head, she might not hear us."

Tom said, "Okay. Danny and Marn go up. That way, if she stumbled in the shower, Marn can cover her."

Everett agreed. "Great. You and I will cover the downstairs and also check the cellar stairs."

Upstairs was like down. Barely any furniture with a sterile feel, but they found her bedroom, and it was nicely appointed, but with modern furniture. The bathroom stood empty, as did the remaining four bedrooms and the attic.

"Are you up for touching something of hers?" asked Danny.

Marnie shivered and hugged herself. "Not really, but I will. Let's go to her bedroom. There should be something in there."

She scanned the top of Carrie's vanity, picked up a hairbrush, and closed her eyes. But she couldn't focus. A house with history also has spirits, and they knew she could see them and speak to them.

"This won't work. They're all talking at me."

"I can only see one," said the detective, squinting his eyes.

"Lucky you. I count eleven and they won't shut up."

Everett and Tom walked into the room and the latter backed out into the hall—his face pale and his Adam's apple bobbing for air.

"Find anything?" asked the former.

"No. But I'll take this and a few more things with me. I read objects better at home," she said, selecting a gold ring, a hair tie, and a lipstick. "I'll bring them to you tomorrow and you can return them."

"Is there something wrong? I mean, why can't you read anything here? Is the energy bad?"

"It's complicated, but with old houses there are always interfering factors," she said, squirming uncomfortably.

"You mean ghosts, don't you?" said Everett.

"Yeah."

"Okay. Let's get out of here then and leave them in peace."

"Excellent plan," said Tom, skipping down the stairs.

Hallowed Hills Road, 2:33 PM

"I love your truck, Marn, but it wasn't built for tall passengers," said Tom, his long frame stretched across the backseat. "And could there be more dog hair?" he added, pulling a strand of fur out of his mouth.

"Zip it, Keller!" she said, grinning at him in the rearview mirror.

"What happened back there?" asked Danny, turning in his seat, eyebrows arched. "You looked like you'd seen a ghost."

Tom pushed into the driver's seat with his knee. "You didn't tell him?"

"When have I had time?" she replied.

"What's going on?" asked the detective lieutenant.

"Ever since we went boom, Tom has been seeing ghosts."

Danny twisted around, winced, and said, "What? Really?"

"Yeah. Madam Séance said that it happens sometimes to people who have a near-death experience," he said.

"So, all three of us are spooky? Huh. Didn't see that coming," he said, turning back to watch the road ahead.

"Yeah. Well, I'm hoping it goes away soon. It's freakin' me out," said Tom, rearranging his long legs.

"Oh! There's Mary!" she announced, flipping on her signal light at the sight of the bathtub idol.

Danny laughed. "You use her too?"

"Yup!" she said as a figure dressed in black leaped out of the woods and hurled a scarecrow onto the hood of Marnie's truck.

Tires screeching, the vehicle swerved onto the shoulder and came to a stop before it could roll into the ditch.

"Didn't see that coming, either. What the hell was that?" asked Tom, rubbing his knee, having struck it on the console. "Are you two okay?"

Rubbing the back of his neck, Danny checked on Marnie, who sat staring out the windshield.

"If those are Carrie Sutherland's clothes, I'm going to vomit," she said, peering into the button eyes of a scarecrow, snagged on a windshield wiper, wearing a bloody Ralph Lauren suit.

Wild Creek Ranch, Marnie's Bedroom, 5:38 PM

"Are you sure you don't want to go back to the hospital?" asked Marnie, putting on a pair of red flannel pajama bottoms and a gray New York Mets T-shirt.

"I'll be okay," he said with a grunt, as he eased a foot into a pair of sweatpants.

"Want some help?"

"Nope. Yup, please," he said, standing up with a hand on a dresser for support.

"Here. Put your other foot in and then I'll get you a hoodie with a zipper. I wouldn't think lifting your arm over your head would be a painless effort."

"The sling can come off. I want to change out of this shirt, anyway. It's the one I had on yesterday."

"Do you want help to shower?"

"As lovely as that sounds, I took one at the hospital and brushed my teeth at the station. That emergency toiletries bag you got me for my desk gets a workout."

"How about socks? Your feet will get cold."

"Yeah. I don't have slippers here, do I?"

Clicking her tongue, Marnie left the bedroom, coming back with a carton.

"These were going to be for Christmas, but you need them now," she said, opening a box containing sheepskin-lined driving moccasins.

"Oo! I like!" he said, taking them out of the box and admiring the chocolate brown suede shoes.

"I thought you'd like them. Let's get them on your feet."

She helped him put on the slippers, change his shirt, and even found him a sweatshirt with a zip.

"You better put something warm over that T-shirt. It's chilly downstairs," he said.

"Yeah. I'll grab a hoodie. Do you want to rest up here?" she asked, selecting a sweatshirt from a pile on her bureau.

"Nope. The couch is fine while we wait for Rick to finish, but I wouldn't say no to a coffee."

"Poppy is making coffee and tea, and Teddy is making grilled cheese sandwiches and tomato soup."

"Where's Tom?"

"In the study with Bob's notebooks," she said, pulling on her hoodie.

Danny pointed with his toe at a packet of black jellybeans on the floor. "Did that fall out of your pocket?"

Her mouth falling open, she bent and picked up the satchel, holding it out like a prize.

"Bob Humboldt left these for me with a note under the floorboards at the schoolhouse."

She dug in her pocket and pulled out the slip of paper that she'd forgotten about and unfolded it.

With a wrinkle between her eyebrows, she showed it to Danny.

"Jed Rawlins. CB. IB. WP. Left of NF. Any idea what that means?" he asked.

"Not a clue. But Ransom is still searching for Jed Rawlins. He chased him back here."

"How long ago?"

She lifted a shoulder and stuck out her bottom lip. "Dunno."

Chapter Thirty-Five

October 19th

Wild Creek Ranch, The Study, 5:03 AM

"Yeah, Cap. I'm okay. Thanks for the update on Randy. See you in a couple of hours," said Danny, hanging up his phone.

Marnie tossed another pinecone on the sputtering fire and replaced the screen.

"The wood on the patio is wet. I should have covered it with a tarp," she said.

"Ask Tom to bring up a load from the woodshed and stack it inside. We're in for a wet few days from the looks of it," he said, taking a bite out of a drippy fried egg and ketchup sandwich on sourdough toast as the dogs drooled on his feet.

"Let's see if he's feeling as whiplashed as we do before I ask him. My neck and back are killing me!"

"I hear ya. I'm living on Tylenol. And by the way, thanks for the sandwich. It's just what the doctor ordered."

"Ha! If he saw how much butter I put on that toast, he might not have ordered it," she said, moving the screen and poking the fire. "Why won't this light?"

"You need lighter fuel," said Tom, coming into the room. "Step aside! Let a pro tackle it."

She handed him the poker and stepped back. "It's all yours, Hephaestus."

"Who?" said the detectives.

"The Greek god of fire."

"Whatever, smarty pants," said Tom, crumpling up newspaper and tucking it under the kindling.

"You want breakfast?" she asked.

He glanced at Danny's empty plate and asked, "What was that?"

"A fried egg sandwich."

"Oo! Yeah. Haven't had one of those in a while. Will you put ketchup on it?"

"If I have to," she said, leaving the room.

The Kitchen, 5:17 AM

"Geez!" said Marnie, grabbing her chest. "I didn't think anyone else was up?"

"Sorry," said Teddy, pouring coffee into her mug. "I didn't sleep well last night."

"What's up?" she asked, taking a bowl of eggs from the fridge.

Teddy itched her nose on her arm and sighed. "Toby Munch is a creep. He skulks around and leers. I don't like him, trust him, or want him anywhere near me."

Face stony, Marnie asked, "Has he done something? Has he touched you?"

Throwing her head back to keep tears from spilling from her eyes, she said, "No. But I'm afraid he will."

"Has he threatened you?"

"Not really. He just makes me uncomfortable."

"What do you mean, *not really*? "

"I was in my office yesterday and he came to the door … argh! It's the way he looks at me! He makes comments about what he'd like to do to me without actually saying what that is. It's his gestures and … Gawd! I don't know!"

"I'll speak with him," said Marnie, cracking an egg as if it were Munch's head. "You can work up here until I do, okay?"

"Thanks. Sorry to be dramatic," said Teddy.

"You're not. I think he's creepy, too. Would a fried egg sandwich on toast make you feel better?"

"Yes, thank you."

Marnie cracked three more eggs into the frying pan, set the spatula aside, and walked over to Teddy.

"I don't know about you, but I could use a bear hug."

"Don't you get those from Danny all the time?"

Marnie wrapped her arms around her friend and rested her chin on top of her head.

"Yeah. But his don't come with a chin rest."

Teddy cracked a smile and hugged the psychologist tighter.

"Smart ass."

The Study, 5:31 AM

The fire in the study crackled and hissed as Tom added a cinnamon pinecone to the flames.

"I'll spend the rest of my day reading through the notebooks and let you know if I find anything interesting," he said to Danny, who was stretched out on the sofa.

"Nothing useful, yet?"

"A lot of shorthand. I'm sure his scribbles meant something to him, but I'm not having much luck. Some notes are quite clear, but those are earlier entries, like the one about the map of the tunnels. Did Marnie tell you she'd found it?"

Danny sat up and cocked his head. "Why didn't she tell me?"

"You were in the hospital when she discovered it in a box in the attic."

"You've seen it?"

"Yeah. It's an elaborate system. We should all have copies and get down there to mark doors and passages. A code that only we understand."

"You could do that while you're waiting to go back to work."

"Hmm ... I'll take the knuckleheads down with me to keep me company."

Three heads popped up and the Border Collies' ears twitched. Gus grumbled and lay back down, but Tater and Dickens ran out of the room, coming back with their leads, and the Labrador's too.

"Not right now, guys. Maybe later," said Tom, taking their leashes and putting them in a chair. "Hey. Have you heard from Sam and Ransom?"

"Not a peep."

"Before I forget. We also found a letter to Bob from Colin Reilly, asking him to look after Marnie should something happen to him. He wrote it a year before the boating accident."

"Hmm ... Is that ominous, or am I just getting cynical in my old age?"

"I'll go with a bit of both."

"Are you starving?" asked Marnie, coming into the room with a plated sandwich dripping with yolk and ketchup and a mug of coffee, handing it to Tom.

"Thank you! I was telling Danny that you found the map," he said, taking the food and beverage.

"Wait until you see it! There's a passageway that goes to the diner," she said, walking around to the bookcase behind her desk and picking up the book of fairy tales.

"Where does it come out? Her beer cooler?"

"She's licensed, isn't she?"

"Yeah. I've made sure of it. It wouldn't look good if my grandmother were arrested."

"No," she said, handing him the book. "It's inside the front cover. And David Bennett told me where to find the deed in the vault, so we can compare notes as soon as I dig it out."

"Marn? Where'd you put Carrie's stuff?" asked Tom.

She curled her lip and opened a drawer, removing each item and placing them on the blotter.

"I abhor this! On my list of gifts I would like, psychometry doesn't appear."

"But it could help us find her and Jess Alder too," said Danny.

"I know! It's the only reason I'll do it."

"Want us to leave?" asked Tom.

"No," she said, pouting and flopping into the chair.

She picked up the hairbrush and shut her eyes, concentrating on the energy within the item.

"There's nothing on this," she said, moving along to the gold ring.

"That won't work. It was her grandmother's."

Next, she selected the lipstick and shuddered.

The men observed her quaking hand and stiff shoulders and sensed a breeze swirl around the room.

"Someone's here," said Danny, nudging Tom with an elbow.

"Where?" he asked, eyes dancing around the study.

"By the desk. I think it's Bob Humboldt."

"I don't see him," he said out of the side of his mouth.

"Never mind. He's gone."

"No, he's not," said Marnie, opening her eyes. "Walter Platt won't let him speak."

"Are you okay?" asked Danny, coming to her and caressing her shoulders.

"Hmm ... Carrie and Jess are with Walter Platt's grandson."

"But his grandson would be ancient," said Tom.

"I don't think so. The energy I picked up is late forties or early fifties."

Danny did the math in his head and agreed. "That's possible, I suppose, from the tale Gram told."

"I've got Riley Leventas working on it for me. She's never heard of The Poacher, but she's drilling down into the town records. And I called her back with Walter Platt's name too."

"Who's she?" asked Tom.

"The research director at the library. You'd like her mysterious ways. She intrigues me."

"Did the mystery woman say when she'd get back to you?" asked Danny.

She lifted her hands. "When she's got something, I guess."

Danny's phone rang, and he cursed. "It's about fucking time he called me back," he griped, answering the call.

"Holly, where have you been?" he said, leaving the room to speak with the game warden.

"Are you working today?" Tom asked.

"I'm taking two group sessions for Carl. One's at nine and the other's at ten-thirty. Why?"

"Let's get out and stretch our legs."

Suspicion rising, she replied, "Okay."

"Copper Woods doesn't look that far."

"We can take one of the old four-wheelers as far as we can, then hike."

"Yeah."

Danny returned and sensed a conspiracy by the looks on the friends' faces. "What are you two up to?"

"Nothing," they said.

The Clinic, 7:40 AM

Marnie strolled into Carl's office as he packed his briefcase.

"There's a lot going on, huh?" he said.

"You heard about the scarecrow flying out of the woods?" she asked, pulling on the ties of her hoodie.

"I did. Rick and Danny were on the road when I left last night. Any news whether the clothes belong to that missing reporter?"

"Nope. But Everett Channing put in a missing person's report last night."

"Fingers crossed she doesn't meet the same fate as Krista Hansen."

"I know. That poor girl," he said, snapping closed the case. "I'll be in town if anything comes up. I had to drop in and grab some files, and Poppy is coming with me to meet Andrea."

"That's great. I think she fits right in."

"Moreso than Millicent Stroud."

"Uh-oh! She's pissing you off, too?" asked Marnie, wrinkling her nose.

"She's a royal pain in the ass!" he said.

"I'll get Teddy on to finding someone else. She's already searching for help."

"Perfect! She's doing great, by the way. Organized. Intuitive. Funny."

"I think so too. She keeps things ticking along."

"Before I ride off into the rising sun, did you need me for something?"

"Toby Munch," she said, closing the door.

"My turn to uh-oh! What did he do?"

"He makes Teddy very uncomfortable."

"He is a lurker and awkward."

"More information, please," she said.

"I have the guards watching him. He wanders off and explores. I caught him grooming horses late yesterday."

"Well, that's not a bad thing. If he's kind to animals ..."

Carl wagged a finger. "The word *caught* should have given it away."

"What?" Her green eyes flashed with anger and her hands rolled into fists.

"I took care of it. The guys know he isn't to go into the stables again. "

"You told Elk and Arnie?"

"And the rest. Don't worry. Do you want me to speak with him about Teddy?"

"Nah. I'll handle him."

Carl laughed. "I know you will. Just don't hit him. Our insurance doesn't cover that."

Creekwood Police Station, Forensics Lab, 7:56 AM

"I come bearing coffee," said Danny, handing a cup to Rick. "How goes it on those clothes?"

"They belong to Carrie Sutherland. I found tags sewn into the side seams confirming it," said the doctor, taking the lid off his coffee.

"Damn. I was hoping they didn't. October has shaped up to be a sinister month, hasn't it?"

Rick wagged his head, then held up a hand and began counting off.

"Let's take a trip down memory lane. By that I mean, let's review the last twelve months. Thanksgiving, how many murders?"

"Three," said the detective. "Ken Wilder. Officer David Webb. Officer Andy Weaver."

"That's right. How about Christmas?"

Danny glanced at the ceiling. "Four. William Billy Williams. Justin Chambers. Reuben Wilmot. Erin Matthews. But that last one wasn't murder. It was a righteous shot."

"I agree. Now, we did have a lull between January and May, but June kicked up a storm and so did July."

"Paige Reynolds. Lanie Howard-Billingsly. Lawrence Parish doesn't count. He did that to himself. And Marnie and Tom were close calls."

"That big boom on the fourth of July was a doozy!"

"So, what are you trying to say?" asked the detective, cocking his head, mouth tight.

"I can see the tourist posters now. 'Welcome to Creekwood. Where the holidays are murder!'"

"Call that into the Chamber of Commerce. I'm sure they'll jump right on it."

"Well, here we are with Halloween looming, and we've got a collection of effigies and corpses."

"I hear what you're saying."

"It's funny though. When Marnie was away those few months, it was quiet around town. Nary a murder," said Rick, picking up his coffee.

"Don't think I haven't thought about that," said Danny, resting his shoulder against the wall. "Both parents died tragically. Her ex-boyfriend was garroted. Two childhood friends killed last summer. Tom nearly."

"I'm a man of science, but I've gotta wonder if that lady is cursed."

"Hmm ... Can we keep that between us?" said Danny, rubbing his temples with a thumb and middle fingertip.

"We can. But you could ask your grandmother to work her druid magic and cleanse that girl's aura."

"Ha! I'll have a word with her," said the detective, his dimples making an appearance. "Hey. I spoke with Holly this morning. He's had multiple complaints of poaching in the area. Have you had problems over your way?"

"No, but I wouldn't expect it. My land isn't worth the bother. Even the wildlife doesn't like it, except for amphibians, Red-winged blackbirds, ducks, and Canadian geese. Too wet."

"Valid point," he said. Pausing, he added, "Any luck on Bob Humboldt's tech?"

"Not yet."

"Try iterations of Marvel."

"Like the comics?"

"Yeah. Bob had a crow of the same name."

"Could work. I'll tell the guys."

"Thanks. Anyway ... I better make my way to the hospital to check on Stuyvesant."

"Good luck."

"I'll need it, right?"

"Hope not!"

Wild Creek Ranch, The Clinic, 8:10 AM

Marnie found Toby Munch in the gym, walking on a treadmill and drinking something out of a paper cup. She saw another man lifting weights and a woman riding a stationary bicycle—both focused on their own routine.

As she drew closer, she tried keeping it casual, and said, "Hey, Toby. Drinks and food aren't allowed on the equipment. If you could please step off with the cup, it would be appreciated."

She strolled toward him and his dismissive glance in her direction told her the situation would escalate if she wasn't careful.

A guard appeared in her periphery, no doubt tailing her at Carl's request.

"Toby, please finish your beverage in the breakroom or lounge."

He pushed a few buttons and steepened the incline and speed of the machine.

"Mr. Munch! Ms. Reilly asked you to get off the treadmill. Do it now and I won't submit a report to the authorities."

The guard sidled up next to the psychologist and crossed his arms across his broad chest. Marnie checked out his physique in a mirror opposite, comforted by his bulging biceps and resting bitch face.

Munch turned and looked at them, held out the cup, and dropped it on the floor, spilling an orange liquid on the rubber mat beneath the machine.

"Okay. You've chosen poorly," said the guard, walking over and pulling the plug, causing Toby to stumble, but not fall. "You've got two minutes to walk over to the baskets, get a towel, and clean up that mess. In one-hundred-and twenty-one seconds, I'm calling the cops and having you removed from the premises."

"On what grounds?" Munch stepped down and moved on to a rowing machine.

"Aggravated nuisance."

The client rolled his eyes, grabbed a towel, wiped up the juice, and chucked the towel in a laundry bin.

"Thank you, Mr. Munch," said the guard, before turning to Marnie. "Anything I can help you with, ma'am?"

She said, "Stick around for a moment, please? But could you wait by the door?"

"You got it," he said, retreating into the background.

"Toby, I want to speak to you about boundaries."

He scoffed. "Let me guess. Theodora and Millicent have complained."

"It doesn't matter who discussed your behavior with me. What I care about are people who feel uncomfortable because of your suggestive language and gestures. You have no need to enter the administrative offices unless invited. Carl is aware of the situation and if it continues, we will have no other choice but to remove you from the facility. And if you are behaving in this manner to manipulate your removal, I will ensure the next facility is one you loathe even more."

"Pfft! You don't have the power to do that," he said, eyes scanning the room but never looking at her.

"Continue on your current path, and you'll find out," she said, her eyes never leaving his face.

"You can't threaten me. I pay to be here."

"You are court-ordered to be here or a similar facility. We are trying to support you, Toby. Please don't sabotage your best chance at a better future."

He took a step toward her, right arm raised, but Marnie caught him by the wrist as he pulled back his left to knock her in the head. But before he could connect, she released him, ducked, and swiped his legs from underneath him with her own.

Heart thumping, she stood up, jumped away from his grasp and said, "I don't recommend you try that again. The guy behind me won't hesitate to subdue you."

"Mr. Munch, I'll escort you to your room," said the guard, offering Toby his hand to help him up.

Toby slapped away the guard's hand and got to his feet. "I know the way," he said, stalking out of the gym.

Marnie stuck out her hand. "I'm Marnie, but I guess you know that."

"I'm Briggs, ma'am. Doctor Parkins pointed you out this morning and asked me to monitor your discussion with Mr. Munch."

"Thanks for having my back."

"You're welcome, but the doctor told me you could hold your own. I didn't want to interfere if it wasn't necessary."

"It was a comfort having you here. It could have gone either way."

"You've taken martial arts training."

"Years ago, but I think it's time I take a refresher course."

"If you want help with that, let me know. I was an instructor in the Army."

"Thank you. A self-defense program would be great for my girlfriends too—if they're interested."

"We can make that happen."

An idea popped into her head, and she asked, "What about kick boxing?"

"Yeah. Sure."

"Let me ask my friends and I'll get back to you. But for now, I have to get ready for group. Thanks again, Briggs."

"You're welcome."

Creekwood Medical Center, 8:28 AM

Danny rapped on the door of two-fourteen and entered an empty room. He opened the cupboard but found no sign of Stuyvesant, so he schlepped back to reception and flashed his badge at a nurse sitting in front of a monitor, typing on a keyboard.

"Hi. I'm Detective Lieutenant Danny Gregg. What can you tell me about the guy in two-fourteen? Randolph Stuyvesant. He's not in his room."

The doe-eyed nurse looked up and sighed. "Against our advisement, he left this morning."

"Is that right? What time was that?"

"Around ten past eight. You just missed him," she said.

Shoulders dropping, Danny said, "Of course I did. Did he say where he was going?"

"He did not. Doctor Taylor had a devil of a time with him. But he just kept saying it was a matter of life and death. Which we tried to tell him that him choosing to stay, or leave, was also ... well, you know."

The detective scratched the back of his head and said, "What are the chances he'll have another attack?"

"I can't answer that, Detective."

"Is the doc around?"

"No. I'm sorry. He went home right after Mr. Stuyvesant left."

Danny took out a card and handed it to the nurse. "If Stuyvesant checks back in, let me know. He's got information that could help me locate a missing person."

"I will," she said, taking the card.

Out on the street, Danny got in his vehicle, started the engine and sat watching passersby on their way to work or scurrying to appointments. Many with their heads down, staring at phones. A man in the greenway across the street caught his attention, and he sat up, seeing an uncanny resemblance to Marnie. Not taking his eyes off him, the detective got out of his Jeep and crossed the street, dodging traffic along the way. Reaching the sidewalk, he jogged, eyes scanning the park, certain Colin Reilly was ahead of him. He stopped with a hand on his painful ribs and searched the playground and ball field—his eyes not finding the man, but landing on a dedication plaque that read, "Colin Reilly Baseball and Softball Field." He had no idea this park was named for his girlfriend's father. She'd never mentioned it, nor had her brother.

Shaking his head, he pulled out his phone and snapped a picture of the bronze sign before turning around and heading back to his vehicle. As he stepped off the curb, a tractor trailer took the corner too tight and rammed into the driver's side of his car, shoving it up onto the sidewalk. Mouth hanging open, the detective pivoted to the plaque and saw the man he'd been chasing several yards away. With a nod of his strawberry-blonde head, he disappeared into the crowd of people who had gathered to check out the crash.

"There is no way that wasn't Marnie's father," he said to himself.

The detective leaned his back against a sugar maple shedding its leaves and added the near -miss to his list of threes. Not because he had been hurt, but because he loved his Jeep and knew the insurance company would consider it totaled—leaving the current tally at two.

"Two more," he whispered, shaking off a chill.

Wild Creek Ranch, The Kitchen, 11:43 AM

Marnie pushed through the back door and dropped her satchel on the table. Happy to see the dogs trotting in to greet her, she was worried about a message from the detective.

"Tom!"

"Yeah! Hang on!" he said, coming around the corner from the study and through the dining room. "Chill out. Danny's fine. His car is another story, though. He's at the station. Garcia is ferrying him around today and he's got a rental ready to pick up."

"What happened? I got a cryptic message from him when I turned on my phone a few minutes ago," she said, a hint of panic in her voice.

"A semi took a wonky turn."

"He said he saw my father. Did he say anything to you about that?" she asked, shoulders relaxing.

"Yeah. Apparently, he was sitting at the curb, saw a man who looked like your dad, so he got out and followed him."

"That's kind of weird, isn't it?" she said, tilting her head.

"Ha! No. It's par for the course around here, don't you think?"

"Hmm ... good point." She took a deep breath before continuing. "I tried to call him, but it went to voicemail."

"Possible he left to meet with Holly Parmeter. The service is shit at the barracks."

"Game warden, right?"

"Yeah. You want to stick around the house, or are you up for an adventure?"

"As long as Danny's okay, I'm fine to go after I change. The weather is obnoxious today. I recommend layers," she said. "I'll be back down in a minute."

Wild Creek Ranch, Northwest Boundary, 12:23 PM

The four-wheeler came to a stop at a thicket of trees—scraggly pines, white birch, and tall grass tangled together, creating a natural fence.

Tom tapped Marnie's knee. "Hop off. I've got to stand up and stretch. My back is killing me."

"I was thinking the same—except it's not my back. There is no padding left in the seat. Let's take a less bumpy path back, huh," she said, scooting off the back and rubbing her backside.

The knuckleheads lay down in the grass and rolled, collecting leaves on their coats—their tongues out, panting. Marnie opened her backpack and took out a jug of water and three collapsible bowls, filling each for the dogs, who lapped the refreshment with gusto.

"I love this place," he said, reaching his arms over his head and twisting his shoulders. "Everywhere I look, it's trees and mountains."

"I can't wait to go snowmobiling and cross-country skiing," she said, capping the water and putting it away.

"The dogs are going to have a ball come winter, but I wish there was a big hill for sledding," he said, bending and touching his toes.

"There is. Don't you remember sliding here when we were kids? I bet Sam will remember."

"We went somewhere, but I didn't know it was here," he said, giving Gus a pat.

"We'll never get through that mass of trees," she said, pointing to the thicket. "Let's ride down further and see if there's a break."

"I concur. Hey. Danny told me about Dickens chasing tires. He's been well behaved on this outing. How'd you break him of that habit?"

"One hour of recall and reward training on a long leash. Elk and Arnie helped. He's a smart boy, and wants my praise, so it wasn't all that hard."

She bent to give Dickens a hug, and after guzzling water, he burped in her face.

Tom burst into laughter and patted his knee, calling the dog over. "Ha-ha! You little stinker. You know that isn't polite, right?" He scratched the pup's ears and stood, ready to leave.

"How much further do you think?" asked Marnie.

"It can't be any more than a couple of miles," he said, climbing on the vehicle and starting it.

Marnie hopped on behind and whistled for the dogs. "Let's go!"

Creekwood Police Station, 1:15 PM

"Hey, Cap," said Danny, leaning into the office. "Garcia and I are going out to see if we can find Randolph. We'll check his house and favorite haunts."

The captain looked up from a file, wrinkling his forehead. "He has haunts? Jalnack doesn't have eyes on him."

"Jalnack was off last night and lost him at the hospital this morning. And he does have haunts, but he hasn't turned up at any. I've got patrols out looking for Carrie Sutherland."

"Yeah. I don't have a good feeling. Jess Alder still hasn't turned up, though, so maybe they're both still alive," said Sterling.

"I sure hope so. Anyway, I'll call if I find anything."

"Be careful. Tell Jalnack to get back on Randy once you locate him. And I think it's time Keller gets his ass back to work. We need him."

"Yes, sir!"

Wild Creek Ranch, Northwest Boundary, 1:25 PM

Tom parked the four-wheeler in a clearing and pulled from his jacket a photocopy of the tunnel map. He had photocopied the original in sections and taped together eight, eight-and-half by eleven sheets.

Studying the map and then their surroundings, he estimated their location.

"Let's leave the bike here and walk the rest of the way. I don't think it's far." He pointed to a dilapidated building to their right, then to a spot on the chart. "See that? I think this tunnel led over there. We could check or just cut through the woods and see if I'm right."

"I'm for walking. My ass is asleep," she said, sliding off the back.

"Should we leash them?" he asked, nodding at the dogs.

"Yeah. Better safe and all that," she agreed.

They clipped on the leads, put their packs over their shoulders and hiked into the trees.

"It's quiet," said Marnie after they'd gone a few hundred feet.

"Too quiet," said Tom, peering into the treetops.

"There's not even a squirrel," she said, and all the dogs' heads twitched, searching for a furry critter.

"The Poacher probably killed them. We're gonna see the poor little fellas hanging by their bushy tails from trees," said Tom, face scrunched up and wary.

"Oh! Don't say that!" said Marnie, tipping her head back, checking the branches above.

The crack of a twig caused them to jerk their heads left, and the dogs stopped and stared into the foliage. Scruffs up and tails in a low and slow wag, Tater and Dickens crouched, ready to launch. But Gus sat at his master's side and let out a high-pitched bark, to which the Border Collies added a long ah-roo!

"Who's there? Who's out there?" asked a man, struggling to free himself from branches and high grass.

Marnie glanced at Tom and frowned.

"That sounds like Randy," she said, as he struggled out of the woods and dropped to his knees.

"What are you doing out here?" he asked, trying to catch his breath. "If you're interfering in an investigation..."

"Oh! Shut up!" said Marnie, cutting him off. "You're on my land, so we'll ask the questions. By the way, meet Detective Tom Keller. I'll leave the interrogation to him."

"What are you doing out here, Stuyvesant? Shouldn't you be recovering in the hospital?" he asked.

"I've got to find Carrie Sutherland," said Randy, wiping his forehead with a handkerchief.

"You think she's roaming the woods?"

"No. I think she's been kidnapped by the man who killed Krista Hansen and Kelly Munson."

"Why's that?" asked Tom.

"Because she had a crazy plan that she would park on Hallowed Hills Road and pretend to be stranded so that I could save her when the kidnapper made an appearance."

Chewing the inside of his cheek so not to throttle the man, Tom said, "But you went and had a heart attack and abandoned her."

With eyebrows gathered and downcast eyes, Randy scrubbed a hand over his face. "No. I told her not to go forward with her irrational and dangerous scheme. That I couldn't make it because I wasn't feeling well. She didn't believe me and came, anyway. I tried to call Danny, but he didn't answer his phone. I tried!"

"So, you attempted to find her with that GPS tracker she had and couldn't. Is that right?"

"Yes! These woods are the last location it pinged."

Marnie took a bottle of water from her bag and handed it to him. He muttered a thanks, took it, unscrewed the cap and drank.

"The two of you thought you could one-up Danny. You showed her the case files, didn't you? You knew she would put her life in danger for a story," said the psychic, her fists in balls and fuming with anger.

"Yes. Yes, I did."

"Wow! Are you stupid!" she shouted and turned away. "Of all the idiotic … Argh! You better hope she's still alive."

She marched off and disappeared into the trees, her dogs trailing after her.

"C'mon. Stand up," said Tom, offering his hand.

"What are we going to do?" asked Randy, accepting help.

"We're going to find Carrie," he said, walking away with his dog.

Copper Woods, 2:24 PM

Nestled in the trees, about ten yards away and shrouded by overgrown bushes and grass, stood a stone cottage with a rotting porch and mossy roof. Marnie and Tom faced the structure and Randy leaned on a tree, mopping his forehead and catching his breath—again.

"He doesn't look so good," said the psychic.

"Nah. We better make a call and see if we can get some help to get him out of here," said the detective.

"Are we going in?" she asked.

"Yeah," he said, moving into the clearing. "Someone has been here. These tracks are fresh and that's blood over there on that stump."

Randy came up behind them and asked, "Is she in there?"

Both shrugged and took another step forward, then glanced at each other. Marnie set down her bag, retrieving two pistols and handed one to Tom, as he grabbed Gus' and Dickens' leads and gave them to Tater to hold.

"You be our lookout, buddy," he said to the fluffy boy.

"Okay, Marn. Let's get this over with."

"Do you want me to go with you?" asked Randy.

"No!" they growled in unison.

Creekwood Police Station, 2:33 PM

Danny and Garcia returned to the station, deflated and hungry.

"Where to next?" she asked him.

"I'm out of ideas. Have you got any Tylenol?"

"Sure, I do, but you haven't eaten," she said.

"Hmm ... Let me fill in Cap and then we'll get out of here. I have to pick up a rental."

"Okay. It's nearly quitting time for me, anyway."

"Can you give me a lift to get the car?"

"Yeah. I'll wait."

Before seeing the captain, he packed his briefcase with his laptop, the murder books, and open case files.

Garcia tossed a wad of paper at him. "You need to get Keller back to work."

"Yeah," he said, knocking on the captain's door, before walking in.

Copper Woods, 2:38 PM

The cottage was empty of people, but remnants remained. They took pictures of the chains screwed into the timber floorboards, the smashed tracker on the table, and two pink glass marbles sitting in the table's crease.

"He was here," said Marnie, her face wrinkled with disgust as the man's odor assaulted her nostrils. "That smell is something I will never forget."

She bent and picked up a manacle, wrapping her hand around the metal band.

"Carrie's alive," she said, setting it down, taking a breath, and picking up the other, feeling a shudder of despair, fear, and exhaustion.

Tom edged closer, a comforting hand on her shoulder. "Marn? Is that Jess Alder's?"

Eyes brimming with tears, she dropped it, creating a cloud of hundred-year-old dust.

"She's giving up. We have to find them!"

With a curt nod, he said, "Okay. Let's go back to the four-wheeler, call Danny on the way, get Rick out here, and find Randy a lift to the hospital."

"Yes. And then we'll find Carrie and Jess."

"Before it's too late," added her sidekick.

Chapter Thirty-Six

Wild Creek Ranch, The Study, 5:38 PM

Gathered in their favorite meeting spot with a platter of fruit and cheese to feed their grumbling stomachs, the psychologist and detectives milled about the room, too wound up to sit.

"I want to know where my brother and Ransom are," said Marnie, eating a section of a juicy clementine that puckered her cheeks.

"Sam usually checks in, but I haven't heard a word from him in days," said Danny, popping two pieces of the fruit into his mouth and pulling a face.

"These are tart," said Tom, savoring the seasonal citrus. "That's a fun word to say. Tart."

Marnie and Danny gave him a look and grinned.

"Well, I sent an SOS half an hour ago, so one of them better call. What did your father and the captain say about calling in the feds?" she asked.

"They were fine as long as it was your brother."

Tom frowned. "Is Sam a fed? I mean, did he go back to the FBI?"

Marnie picked up a piece of cheese and lifted her shoulders. "I dunno. My best guess is he's still a hired gun, but I don't ask. Not that he would tell me. But what if the chief and captain know something we don't?"

Danny said, "No. They wouldn't hide anything from us."

"Where are Poppy and Teddy?" asked Tom.

"Over at the cottage, celebrating happy hour. I think they needed a break from the nonsense and then they are going into town to have dinner with friends. And before you say anything about drinking and driving, they will be driven in by Arnie. He has a 4-H fundraising thing, and he said he would bring them home after."

"You believe both Jess and Carrie are alive?" asked the detective lieutenant.

"That's what I felt and saw," she said.

Tom scratched his forehead, wondering aloud, "But that was a few hours ago. What about now?"

Face grim, she said, "I don't know. Bob has been trying to tell me something all day, and he's being blocked. If it isn't The Poacher, it's Lawrence Parish and I haven't been able to push them away long enough."

"Not for nothing, but I think you should call Gram and get advice. That cross you found in the treasure keeps calling out to me, and I reckon it could help you," said Danny.

Her eyebrows shot up, and she pursed her lips, moving to her desk to get her phone. "You know. That might work. I've had enough of those bullies. This is my home, and they will not dictate who can speak to me."

"Did you hear that?" asked Tom.

"Thunder," said Danny.

On her way to the desk, Marnie opened the French doors and peeked out. "Wow! It's black as pitch over the west paddock," she said, as a bolt of lightning raced across the sky and the clouds opened in a downpour. "Here comes the storm!" she said, punching Gram's number and stalking out of the room.

The detectives exchanged a glance, amused and bolstered by her determination.

"Look out, Larry and Wal! Marnie Reilly *is* the storm, and you are so screwed!" said Tom with a snicker.

The Tunnels, 5:53 PM

"He went that way!" whispered Ransom, adjusting his night vision goggles and pointing left.

Sam darted forward and ran into a wall.

"No, he didn't," he growled.

"Your cat-like vision and reflexes are failing you, man," said the marshal, feeling the solid stone where he believed an opening existed. "That's not right. I saw him go this way."

The assassin wiped his arm across his sweaty forehead. "Maybe he's a ghost, then. Walked right through solid granite."

"Don't get shitty with me. Maybe there's a secret passage or something."

"He left his putrid scent behind, so he can't be far," said Sam, pushing on the blocks of stone.

"Do we even know where we are?" asked Ransom.

"Yeah. I have some idea. Creek Road should be above us."

"Is that significant?"

"Could be," said Sam, clenching his jaw.

Wild Creek Ranch, The Kitchen, 6:28 PM

"You better have an exceptional excuse for making us cancel our plans," whined Teddy.

Poppy, bottom lip out, agreed. "This is above and beyond the call of duty," she said, flicking a crumb across the table. "We were going to Benedetti's."

Harried, Marnie slid a glass of wine in front of Teddy and poured another for her whinging partner. "We'll all go out for dinner when this is over, but I need your help."

Gram and Hannah burst through the door, the older woman dragging her granddaughter by the hand.

"That's only five," she said, counting heads. "We need one more and that cross from the treasure."

"I can get the guys. They're around," said the psychic.

"No. But if we're going to cast away those ghouls forever, we need all the power we can muster. Could you call Alice Wells?"

"What the heck is going on?" said Poppy, stone-faced and sliding away her glass.

Gram patted her arm and said, "Nothin' to worry about, dear one. We're getting' ourselves ready to banish evil spirits."

"Cool!" she responded, clapping her hands. "All of them?"

"Yep. The ones hanging around my house, anyway," said Marnie. "Including that fellow clinging to you."

Her mouth dropped open, and her eyes darted around the room. "You can see him?"

"Unfortunately, yes," the psychic replied.

Unknown Location, 6:36 PM

Carrie struggled to sit up and shivered against the cold cement floor. Every joint in her body ached, and her mouth felt like sandpaper. While their captor had given them water, her thirst wasn't quenched. She didn't know how long Jess had gone without food, but she guessed she hadn't eaten in at least two days. They had been carried into this room either last night or early morning. It was hard to know because the days were blending together. But she was certain it had been dark outside.

The man had been gone a long time, and while she wished he were dead, the reporter hoped he wasn't because no one would ever find them. She didn't even know how far they had traveled to this new location because he had knocked them both out for the journey. All she remembered was waking up and being carried into this dark, frigid room.

Jess lay feet away, her hair covering her face. She no longer responded to questions—not a grunt or a groan. Carrie called out to her often, if only to let her know she wasn't alone.

Wild Creek Ranch, The Kitchen, 7:08 PM

Alice Wells bustled into the house, bringing a brisk wind and a wet umbrella with her.

"Can you believe this weather?" she said, pulling off her purple jacket and handing it to Marnie to hang.

"It's crazy, isn't it?" she said, shaking out the coat. "I'll put this and that umbrella in near the fire, Alice."

"Thank you. Where are the pups? I brought treats," she said, digging a bag of biscuits from her purse.

"In the study with Danny and Tom. They can come out when we're through."

Once upon a time, Marnie and Alice had been adversaries, loathing one another for years. But a mutual enemy brought them together. Poor Alice had existed between light and dark because of a woman named Grace Wilmot who tortured her emotionally, physically, and financially. When Alice finally told Marnie the truth of what had transpired, a friendship was formed, and they worked together to send Grace to prison.

"Alice, you've met everyone but Poppy, that plucky pocket rocket over there," said Marnie.

"It's lovely to meet you. Have Marnie tell you the story of our once-strained relationship. We were archenemies. Ha-Ha! It's quite funny now."

"Oo! That sounds ominously delicious."

"Oh, it is," said Alice, tittering and turning to the psychic. "I had only four black candles at home, but that should be fine."

Marnie agreed. "Okay, gals. Let's get this show on the road. Teddy, can you please put the white candles around us—on the counter, the stove, and the windowsills? We want to be surrounded in white light. The black candles go on the table, and I say we place them in a cross for north, south, east, and west, or air, fire, earth, and water. How does that sound, Gram?"

"Perfect. The elemental cross you found should go in the middle. It will give the magic added oomph! Have ya written your intent?"

"Yes, but I'd like you to check it, please. I'm terrible with rhymes. Ha-ha!" she said, handing the older woman a slip of paper.

"I'm sure it's fine, love. Let me have a look," she said, putting on her glasses.

The Tunnels, 7: 28 PM

"We've lost him," said Sam, bending at the waist to catch his breath.

"Let's go back to the hotel and regroup. Have you been memorizing the layout? We can start again tomorrow," said Ransom.

"Yes. I will map it out when we get back, but I need a large sheet of paper."

"We'll stop at a stationery store and get supplies. And one of us should call Marnie or Danny," said the marshal.

The assassin ran a hand across his mouth and said, "Danny. If this is what I think it is, I want Marnie as far away from it as possible."

"Okay. Are you gonna tell the detective everything?" asked Ransom.

Sam gave him a look.

"I didn't think so," said the marshal.

The Study, 7:32 PM

"She needs a TV in here," said Tom, tossing another of Bob Humboldt's books on the floor. "I can't look at any more of this."

"I'm with you. He's too cryptic for me. I've been looking at this note he left for Marnie, and I can't make head or tails of it," said Danny.

"What are you chasing tomorrow?" asked Tom.

"I don't know, but I sure wish I had my partner back," he said, testing the water.

"Let me get time in at the gun range."

"Go early so you can be back on the job tomorrow afternoon."

"Can Beau still qualify?"

"Yeah. Halpin too."

"Okay," said Tom. "Not to change the subject ... Did Randy go back to the hospital?"

"He did. How did you and Marnie get the television station's helicopter to pick him up? That was nice of them."

"Ha! When I called and asked for help, they said no. I mean, they were right there—hovering over the four ways. Anyway, Marnie took my phone and said she'd pay them to pick up Randolph. That's when they zipped around and landed in the paddock."

"They were over the four ways?" Danny asked, sitting up, mouth tight. "Son of a bitch! We've got a leak."

Looking at one another, they both said, "Teddy."

The Kitchen, 7:43 PM

"You've done well, Marnie. I couldn't have written it better myself," said Gram. "Now, could you make a copy for each of us?"

Face beaming, the psychic said, "Really? Wow! I felt so much pressure writing that. And I worried I would forget something."

"Go on. Make the copies and we can be done with it," said the older woman.

"Back in five," she said, half skipping out of the room.

"Should we light the candles?" asked Hannah, holding up a lighter.

"Yes, dear. You know what to say, right?"

"I think so. Umm … Thank you for lighting the way. May it be for the highest good of all. Is that right?"

"Yes," said Gram, clasping her hands together, pleased her skeptical granddaughter remembered.

"Do you want help?" asked Poppy, picking up a box of matches from the back of the stove.

Hannah nodded. "Yes, thanks."

Teddy joined in and the candles were flickering by the time Marnie returned and had passed out copies of the intention.

"Are the guys up to mischief?" asked Hannah, winking.

"No. They're trying to solve the world's problems while drinking whiskey."

"Hmm … don't they know women are better at that?" said Teddy.

"Drinkin' whiskey or solvin' problems?" asked Gram with a chuckle.

"Both," said Hannah.

"Okay. Everyone, please stand, put your notes in front of you, and we'll hold hands in a circle. We'll say the intent together, then I'll blow out the candles. Ready?"

A chorus of 'yes' went around the table, and they read their intent as the wicks sizzled and the flames danced.

By the roots of Earth, so strong and deep,
We call upon the soil to keep,
Only those who bring harm and dread,
Banish the evil, the cursed, the dead.

By the breath of Air, so light and clear,
We call upon the winds to hear,
Guide the wicked far from sight,
Banish the evil into the night.

By the blaze of Fire, fierce and bright,
We call upon the cleansing light,
Burn away the darkened soul,
Banish the evil, make us whole.

By the tides of Water, vast and free,
We call upon the endless sea,
Wash away the hate and spite,
Banish the evil from our sight.

By Earth, Air, Fire, and Sea,
Only evil shall now flee.
Good may stay, but dark must go,
This home is safe, let it be so.

"There," said Marnie, gathering up her hair and bending to blow out the candles. "Olly, Olly, oxen free. Friendly spirits who need to speak with me can come out now?"

They all stayed in place to see what would happen, but nothing did.

"We've said our peace. Now, we wait. It could take a few hours for Bob and the others to come through, but they will," said Gram.

"Does the house feel lighter?" asked Alice.

"I think so," said Poppy.

Teddy agreed. "Me, too."

Loud thumping echoed through the dining room and Danny, Tom, and the knuckleheads rushed into the kitchen.

"What the hell did you do out here?" asked Danny as the dogs dove under the table.

White as a sheet, Tom crooked his thumb toward the study. "You better get in there. The doors won't stop slamming!"

Eyes wide, Gram and Marnie looked at one another and said, "We forgot to open a window!"

The Study, 8:03 PM

"Well, I think they're out. We gave them a nudge, and the universe opened the door and shoved them through," said Marnie, shutting the French doors.

"I'll get a towel and mop up that rain," said Hannah, backing out the door and heading to the kitchen.

"Are they really gone?" asked Danny.

The psychic took three steps away from Poppy and focused on the space over her shoulder. The man who had followed her around for days was absent.

"Looks like it," she said, reaching out and squeezing her friend's shoulders.

"Yay! That's a burden lifted."

"Marnie, go check the master bedroom and see if they're gone," said Alice.

"Oh! That's right. Back in a tick!" she said, dashing out the door, nearly colliding with Hannah, who had returned to wipe up the rain.

"Who was haunting you, Poppy?" asked Tom.

She dropped her chin to her chest, gathering her thoughts. When she picked up her head and opened her mouth to speak, her emotions got the better of her and she choked on tears.

Danny filled in where she couldn't. "You knew you couldn't come back to Creekwood without the whole town knowing your business, right? That's rhetorical. Of course, you did." Putting a hand on her shoulder, he continued, "Poppy here worked as a child psychologist at a private school for a time. A teacher formed an unhealthy attachment, stalked her, and one night, after reporting the man to the police and filing a restraining order, he came after her and she defended herself."

"So, you whacked him," said Tom with a compassionate grin.

"With a baseball bat," she said.

"That was at that snooty school in Hudson, right?" asked Hannah.

"Right outside, yes. I'll never forget the sound. Not if I live to be a hundred."

"I remember that. The guy was on our radar. He was dealing opioids to parents and kids. Good riddance, I say. I should probably mention I'm a special agent with the DEA."

"Ah! That makes sense. In a nutshell, it was ugly for a time, but things worked out for me."

"The spooks are gone!" sang Marnie, dancing into the room.

"Woo! Hoo!" said Danny, picking her up and swinging her around. "We can sleep without being watched."

Gram snickered and waggled her eyebrows. "Is that all they're watchin'?"

Shocked, her grandson blushed. "I can't believe you said that!"

"Pshaw! I'm not dead yet, Danny Boy."

The group burst into laughter, and Tom suggested they all have drinks, everyone agreeing one was warranted.

"Where are the knuckleheads?" asked Marnie, searching the room.

Danny whistled, and they came running, tails still between their legs.

Chapter Thirty-Seven

October 20th

The Study, 5:08 AM

"I don't know what you're trying to tell me," said Marnie, rubbing her temples and doing her best to focus.

She'd come downstairs early to talk to Bob Humboldt, but he was new to the spirit world and his communication was as sketchy as his shorthand.

"Dad? Are you there? Danny said he saw you in town yesterday. Thanks for getting him out of harm's way. Can you please explain what Bob is trying to tell me?"

While she waited for divine guidance, she got busy lighting a fire to warm her icy toes. The storm the previous night pushed in a cold front and a north wind was rattling the windows.

"Morning!" said Tom, coming through the door with a coffee and a handful of papers, which he deposited on the corner of her desk.

"You scared the hell out of me!" she said, palms to her chest. "I'm gonna put a bell on all of you."

He cocked his head and grinned. "That could be fun. Where do you plan to attach said bell?"

"Jackass!" she said, rolling her eyes. "Could you please get this fire going? My toes are like ice cubes."

"Yeah. Sure. Have you gotten through to Bob?" he asked, moving around her desk and putting his coffee on the mantle.

"Not for a lack of trying. But I'll give it another whirl later. If I could get some help from my father, that would be fantastic, but he's not around. He probably used up a lot of energy helping Danny yesterday."

"What about your mother or your grandfather?" he asked.

"Hmm ... I'll try them later."

"Tater and Dickens are upstairs, I presume? Gus ran up before I could take him out."

"Yup. They're snuggling with Danny, who will be awake soon once the knuckleheads start their morning brawl."

"Are you working today?" he asked, lighting a match and holding it to wadded up newspaper.

"No. It's a quiet day. I thought we could go to Pine Ridge and bury a demon. What do you think?" she asked.

"I'm all in. Let's get that monkey off our backs once and for all. It's been bothering me, you know, what I want to say to her. What she did to us. How her family affected our lives for so long," he said, dropping dried pinecones into the flames.

"Can you imagine how Sam feels? Gawd! I'd hate to be her if he ever unleashes his thoughts about all that."

"No kidding. But before we castigate Kate, can we go to the gun range? My presence has been requested at the precinct. They miss me," he said with a satisfied smirk.

"How quickly can you get qualified?" she asked.

"If I'm lucky, I'll have my badge and firearm by the end of the day."

"Woo! Hoo!"

Pine Ridge Sanitarium, 11:23 AM

Pine Ridge loomed before them, a place where past and present were in deep contrast. The imposing Federal-style design spoke of an era when the building was a high-end hotel, hosting the rich and famous in lavish suites. Current day found the original brick and limestone structure interrupted by stark, utilitarian additions of glass and steel, housing a growing population of the disturbed and dangerous.

Marnie slid her vehicle into the slot closest to the sanitarium and she and Tom got out, zipping their jackets and pulling up collars. Both dreaded this visit, but knew they would feel better at the end.

"Why can't they have a visitor's parking lot closer to the building?" asked Tom. "I mean, you're already anxious about the visit, and then they give you this never-ending sidewalk to obsess about it."

"Ha-ha! I know what you mean. By the way, Carl told me Kate was moved out of a cell and into a private room. One without bells and whistles. But somehow, she got a room upgrade two days ago. He doesn't believe Preston Belmont footed the bill."

"Someone with deep pockets. That's for sure. Who could be the evil princess' benefactor?" said Tom.

"Mm ... It makes be woozy to think she might have tricked someone into believing her sob stories."

"From what my folks say, the Parish money is gone, and that there never was much in reality. The house must have been worth something, unless it was mortgaged to the hilt. But you know what always bugged me about that house?" said Tom.

"What's that?"

"Did you know they had a bedroom filled with Kate's childhood clothes and toys? It creeped me out. Why would you keep all that stuff?"

"I wouldn't, but I'm not them. They had unhealthy relationships. You could liken it to the mad scientist, the lab assistant, and the monster. Codependency and enmeshment in the extreme."

He laughed. "Yeah. But some would say you and I have a codependent relationship."

"We're not toxic, though. I don't think our friendship is one-sided, do you? One of us doesn't rely on the other for validation or emotional support without giving back. We have several people in our world, and welcome others into our inner circle. And how many times have we called bullshit on the other? Besides, we don't run around killing people like the Parish family."

"Yikes! There's the door. You go first," he said with a hand on the middle of her back.

Pine Ridge Sanitarium, Kate Parish's Private Suite, 11:31 AM

"Are you sure you want to go in there alone?" asked the beefy corrections officer, who escorted them to Kate's room.

"We'll be okay," said Tom, not quite certain it was true.

"She throws things, so be on guard."

"You don't have to tell us. We grew up with her and she's tried to kill us at least twice," said Marnie, her eyes meeting Tom's.

"I'm gonna stand outside while you're in there. Any trouble, just knock," he said, turning the knob and opening the door.

Peering inside, Marnie summoned her courage and stepped over the threshold, grabbing Tom's hand and pulling him along. Neither had seen Kate Parish since June, and at the time, they didn't know her family would try to blow them to smithereens.

Marnie spotted her on the far side of the room, trying to hide from them behind a wardrobe. "Hmm ... you have your own room again. Who arranged that? Satan?" she asked.

Kate Parish stepped away from the cupboard and faced them. "Ha. Ha. Your sense of humor is hilarious."

Marnie assessed the suite, taking in the lavish furnishings, cashmere throws, and fluffy pillows. A waxy leafed philodendron crept from the chiffonier to a curtain rod, and African violets of pink, purple, and white dotted the coffee table, end table, and desk.

She shrugged, running fingers through her long locks. "It's nice you have so many potted plants. At least you're doing your bit to replace the oxygen you waste."

Tom nudged her. "Are you trying to get us killed?" he whispered.

"Hello, Tom. Nice to see you're still breathing. But I can't say the same about you, Marnie. I would rather have you dead and buried in a pine box."

"I've wished the same about you every day for almost a year now. You're evil, Kate, and it shows in your face."

The detective observed the exchange and thought it silly to waste time on Kate. She didn't matter.

"You know what, Marn. I don't need to say anything. I don't care about her." He turned away from Kate and took his friend's hand. "We came here because we needed to get things off our chests, but it isn't important. She's not important. What is, is that you and I are very much alive and free. We have amazing friends, brilliant dogs, successful careers, and beautiful homes. What are we doin' here but opening old wounds that have mostly healed?"

"When you put it that way, yeah. Let's get out of here and have fun. Let's pick up Danny and have lunch at the diner," she said.

Kate lurched forward and grabbed Marnie's hair, but Tom caught her by the wrist, and squeezed until she cried out and let go. She raised her left arm to scratch him, and he latched on to that arm too, driving her backward away from the psychic.

Marnie knocked on the door to get the guard, and he opened it and stepped inside.

"Everything alright?" he asked.

She put up a hand and said, "Wait."

"If you ever come after Marnie, me, or anyone we love again, I won't hesitate to hurt you," he growled. "You're not dealing with little Tommy Keller, Kate. You tried to kill me twice. There will not be a third." He shoved her back onto her bed and when she bounded to her feet, he held up a finger and warned, "Do not even think about it."

Jaw clenched, he rolled his head until his neck popped, then backed away, turned and walked out the door with Marnie.

"Holy crap! I've never seen you that mad," she said, hanging onto his arm to keep up.

"I was so close to wringing her neck," he said, teeth grinding.

"Are you sorry we came?"

"No. It's exactly what I needed."

"Well, you took your power back, that's for sure."

"I took yours back too," he said, holding out his hand. "Better put that in your pocket because if she ever breaks out of here, we're gonna need it."

"You had to say that, didn't you? Geez!"

Wild Creek Ranch, The Study, 3:42 PM

"How does it feel to have your badge back?" Marnie asked Tom as she put down a box of sandwiches and cups of lemonade.

"Excellent!" he said. "Now I have to get my blood pressure down so they'll let me back out on the streets."

"Yeah, but you explained that. Kate Parish would have that effect on anyone. C'mon! It will be back to normal tomorrow. We'll go down to the clinic in an hour to check it."

"Why are we having our lunch in here?" he asked, bending to pat Dicken's head, who sat on the couch with Gus and Tater. "C'mon, knuckleheads, get off the couch. That's for humans."

One by one, they slunk to the floor and pranced out of the room, toenails clicking all the way to the kitchen.

"Because Danny is home and we'll eat lunch while he updates you," she said, digging into the box and taking out their drinks and food. "By the way, did you or your parents send me a necklace with two Border Collie charms?"

"Not that I know of. Did you get another mystery package?"

"Yeah," she said, setting the box on the corner of the desk. "It arrived while we were in the hospital. Teddy tucked it away and gave it to me two weeks ago."

"Danny didn't send it?"

"No."

The detective lieutenant came into the room and flopped on the couch.

"I am beat! We have no leads, and I don't know what to do next," he said, sitting forward with his elbows on his knees.

Tom went to the desk and got a sandwich for Danny and one for himself.

"You've been there before and somehow, something turns up. Marn's been trying to talk with Bob, and she'll try again." He handed him a sandwich and sat in a chair near the French doors.

"My focus will be on Bob as soon as we've eaten, okay?" she said.

He gave a weary nod. "Sorry. I don't want to dump this on you."

"You're not. Enjoy your lunch and relax."

He opened the wrapper and smiled. "Is this pastrami? Oh! Yes, it is!" he said, devouring a quarter in one bite. But before he could take another, his phone rang, and it was Garcia.

"Yeah," he said, mouth full of bread.

"We got a call about a body being thrown off a silo on Station Street. Cap asked me to meet you there."

"I'm at the ranch. Eating lunch."

"It didn't sound like a request, Lieu."

"Okay. On my way."

He wrapped up his sandwich and got up, grabbing a drink as he stopped to kiss Marnie goodbye.

"Gotta go. A body got thrown off the silos. I'll keep you posted," he said, stalking out the door.

"See you soon!" she yelled after him.

Tom started to say something, but she held up her hand.

"Shh!" she said. "There is someone finally speaking. Where's that note from Bob?" She moved papers around until she uncovered it.

"What?" said Tom.

"Look! This is easy!" she said, pointing at the note. "Jed Rawlins is that guy who escaped with Sam in June. Remember, they thought he was dead, but he wasn't. Okay. CB. Cy Barnes. Who else could it be? And that means IB is Ida Barnes."

"I'm following. What's WP?"

"Walter Platt. The Poacher!"

"Hmm ... That's a reach. What's the connection? And what about Left of NF?"

"I don't know that yet. I've got to make a call."

The Study, 5:13 PM

Marnie dove for her phone when it rang, and fist punched the air when she saw who was calling.

"Riley! What have you got? Detective Tom Keller is with me, and we have you on speaker."

"Check your email. But that little clue you gave me panned out. Cy Barnes was Ida Barnes' second husband. She had a child with her first husband and Cy adopted him. I'm looking at their marriage license and the adoption papers now."

"Holy shit!"

"That's what I thought. Now, Left of NF is stumping me. But based on CB and IB, I think we are looking at initials. Does NF mean anything to you?"

Tom slapped her shoulder. "Nolan. It has to be him."

"Who?"

"Yeah. My great-great-grandfather, Nolan Flannigan."

"Does that make sense? Would he have a connection to the Barnes family?"

"No. But does Walter Platt?"

"He does. After you told me Margaret's story, I did more digging. The child who ran away was three-year-old Ida Platt. She was found and placed at Saint Luke's Orphanage. I'm surprised I found records that far back, but lucky for us, the files were added by two interns last year."

"They didn't return her to her father?"

"No. He was considered unfit."

"Okay. I will check my email and try to figure out Nolan's connection. Thanks, Riley. We'll have dinner some night so we can discuss that grant you need."

"Oh, Marnie, I was only kidding. I've already submitted paperwork and should have the funding soon. Let me know how the story ends, huh?"

"Yeah. But I'm buying you dinner and drinks to say thanks."

"Okay. I've always wanted to try Hobb's Gate."

"It's a date."

Marnie opened her laptop, and her best friend stood over her shoulder as they read Riley's report.

"No freaking way!" said Tom. "I can't believe it."

"I knew it! They told me he was dead! I felt it in my bones!" she said, leaping up from the desk, knocking the green jewelry box on the floor.

Tom picked it up and shook it. "Is this the necklace?"

"Yeah. But it's on my dresser. What rattled?"

He took off the lid, revealing a velvety cushion, and when he lifted it, there sat a key. An ancient key.

"I know what that's for," she said. "But we can't get distracted. Call Danny. Tell him to meet us."

"Where is he meeting us?"

"The Island."

404 Creek Road, 4:58 PM

Patrick met Marnie and Tom on the front porch when they arrived at her childhood home. He handed them a key and asked if they wanted him to go with them.

"If you could drive across the bridge and park, then walk in, I would appreciate it," said Marnie. She handed him a map of the island with an X marking their final destination and a key to the entry gate with instructions to leave it open for Danny.

"We'll take the skiff and meet you there," said Tom.

"W-Won't the motor g-g-give you away?" asked Patrick.

"No. We'll run most of the way with the outboard, then use the trolling motor to get to the dock. It barely makes a sound," said the detective.

"Okay. How f-f-far away is D-Danny?"

"That depends on when he listens to his messages. I left one for him, and Tom left another with Captain Sterling," said the psychic.

"Are you armed?"

They nodded their heads.

"What are you bringing?" asked Tom.

"The usual," said Patrick, a rifle case over his shoulder and a 9mm on his belt.

"Ready, Marn?" asked Tom.

"Yup. Just have to get Tater and my pack out of the truck."

Perch Pond, 5:14 PM

"Why are we taking the skiff?" asked Tom with a shiver.

"We missed summer. And besides, we both survived the last few times when we went over by water. Let's not jinx ourselves."

He agreed.

Tater stood on the bow, his nose twitching, and his fur ruffling in the chilly breeze. Marnie sat in the middle, trying Danny's phone again, and Tom piloted the boat.

"I'm surprised no one's fishing. It's a beautiful night," said the psychic.

"Most people are getting out of work at this hour. I spoke to the captain today. He said Jalnack and Garcia are up for promotions."

"That's nice to hear. You and my overworked boyfriend might get days off if they keep them around."

"They'll float between Creekwood and Hudson Hollow. It's not ideal, but it's better than what we've got now."

"What about Randy?" she asked.

He stared straight ahead, the island coming into view, and shrugged. "Your guess is as good as mine. There it is. I'm switching motors."

Creekwood Police Station, 5:23 PM

"Can you believe those kids, Garcia? I would never have spoken to an adult like that," said Danny, throwing a pen and pad on his desk.

She pulled a face. "When I was that age, you would've scared the crap out of me. They need a lesson in respect."

The detective pulled his phone from his pocket and saw two messages from Marnie. He held it up and grinned, showing off his dimples. "Look at this, Garcia! She misses me. Two missed calls."

"You're a lucky man. In reality, though, she probably needs you to pick up something on your way home," she teased.

"Let's find out."

He played the first message and grabbed his jacket without playing the second.

"Cheryl, I need a lift. Lights on."

"Where are we goin'?"

"The island."

The Island, 5:27 PM

Tom handed Marnie her pack and stepped up onto the dock.

"How do we do this, Keller?"

"I think we make sure Carrie and Jess are here. Is there any voodoo magic you can do before we get too close?"

"Nope. I'm going on gut feeling and I feel they're here. What about you?"

"I'd say it's a decent bet. What do you think, Tater?" He tugged the dog's right ear and ran a hand over his shawl.

The Border Collie nudged him with his nose and flashed a bright smile.

"Okay. The Tot says we should get moving," said Tom.

"What if they're not there? Or worse. Dead?"

"Let's not think that way, Marn. Remember, I've got your back."

"And I've got yours."

The trek from the shore through the woods was easier than their previous trip to the island. The dead trees had been chopped down and cut into firewood and the overgrown shrubs and bushes pruned. They passed by the granite boulder where they'd found Paige last June and paused for a moment before hiking on. The old Barnes house appeared in front of them, and they exchanged a glance. A single light burned at the back of the house, but they saw no movement inside.

Staying low, they crept around the side of the house. Marnie clutched Tom's sleeve and pulled him down and pointed to the cellar window. Taking her small Maglite out of her bag, she handed it to him while she peered through the kitchen window and quickly ducked down.

"He's in there!" she hissed.

"Hang on a minute. I think the women are in the cellar. Look!"

She crouched down and followed the beam and grabbed Tom's leg when a woman's face was illuminated.

"It's Carrie Sutherland! She's down there."

"Okay. Calm down. We have to deal with the big dude first. Let me get a look at him," he said.

Tom stood and peeked through the glass, his eyes following the man's movements through the room. The detective spied a bowl of marbles on the table, with four set aside on a paper towel with a silver tablespoon.

He squatted down and said, "We gotta get in there. He's got four shooters set aside with a spoon. I think he's gonna take their eyes out tonight."

Marnie tensed and sat with her back against the foundation, pulling Tater close and hugging him. The telltale head tingle had returned, and she scanned the area for the culprit.

"What's wrong?" asked Tom.

"If Mr. Barnes is still hanging around, he could be a problem."

The detective squirmed and dropped his backside to the ground. "Geez! Why'd you have to bring him up? The second worst day of my childhood flashed before my eyes. That geezer was in my dreams for years. I even had one about him when I was in the hospital."

"We're all haunted by something; ghosts, our pasts; failed relationships; a teacher who picked on us. It's when they come after us in our weakest moment that it sucks. But I'm not weak and neither are you. Damaged, yes. But I say we take down this asshole. He tormented our dreams for too many years, and he is right here where all of Sam's problems started. You and me, Keller."

Tom scratched his neck, twisted it left, then right until it cracked.

"Yeah. Let's do what we were too small to do thirty years ago."

He held out his pinky, and she wrapped hers around it.

"Got your gun?" she asked.

He stared straight ahead—face tight. "I'm not gonna need it. He's not so big."

The Bridge Parking Lot, 5:43 PM

Patrick Kowalski drove into the small, paved parking lot and backed his pickup into a spot. He wondered if he should wait for Danny, but the flashing red and white lights heading his way told him he had arrived.

The detective lieutenant threw off his seatbelt and opened his door before Garcia could jam the cruiser into park.

"Where are they?" he asked, raking fingers through his mussed hair.

Patrick thought about timing and how long it would have taken them to get across the pond, dock the skiff, and walk to the house.

"They should be at the old Barnes place by now." He held out the map and pointed to X.

Danny glanced at the sky, wondering how much daylight they had on their side, and said, "Okay. Garcia, come with me and we'll let Patrick do what he does."

"What's that?" she asked.

"He's the invisible man until he's not," he replied, clapping the man on the back. "I hope we don't need you, but thanks for joining the party."

"No problem. I was just s-s-sitting around cleaning my g-guns," said Patrick with a wink.

"We'll see you when we see you. C'mon, let's check on my partner and Madam Séance."

"Who?"

"Never mind."

The Old Barnes House, 5:48 PM

"I think we should bust a window. I'll lower you in, and we get them out first," said Tom.

"Won't the breaking glass alert him we're here?" asked Marnie.

"It might, but what's the difference? We're gonna have to deal with him, anyway."

"Okay. Break away!" she said.

The detective pulled on a glove and punched the window, but it didn't break.

"Is this double-pane?" he asked.

"Triple," she said with a sheepish grin. Searching through her bag, she dug out a hammer. "Here. Try this."

"What else do you have in there?" he asked, giving her a look.

"Never mind. Just smash it."

And he did, the glass falling into the cellar and scattering on the tarp-covered workbench below.

Pleased no ruckus ensued, Tom said, "Luck was on our side. The painter's cloth absorbed the sound. Are you ready?"

"Yeah." She placed her pistol on her belt, pulled bolt cutters from her bag and hugged Tater. "Be a good boy, for Uncle Tom."

As she backed into the window, the detective held her arms, then lowered her to the bench.

Hopping to the floor, she turned to the women, placing a finger to her lips to shush them.

"Is that Jess Alder?" Marnie asked.

"Yes. She's not doing well," said Carrie.

The psychic returned to the broken window and asked Tom to get bolt cutters, blankets, and a bottle of water out of her bag.

"You've got bolt cutters and blankets in here? Geez. Hang on."

He handed her the water first, then found three packs of emergency blankets, and a medium-sized bolt cutter, and passed those down too.

Marnie stripped out of her jacket and handed it and the water to the reporter, who, with little haste, put on the coat and drank from the bottle.

"I'm going to cut the chains and then we'll get you out of here."

"Let me help you with Jess. She's going to be difficult to get through that window," said Carrie.

The psychic glanced back and agreed. "Yeah. Okay, but I'll cut your chains first. When was he last down here?"

"I don't know. I've lost track of time."

It took all of Marnie's strength to cut the reporter free. Then she went to Jess and struggled to break the links, but they finally snapped, and Carrie helped her wrap the prisoner in a blanket and they carried her to the workbench. Tom stretched through the window and wrapped his hands around Jess' lifeless arms and pulled her through with the help of the women below.

"Okay, Carrie. Up you go."

But the reporter froze at the clunk of footsteps above and clung to Marnie, who shook herself free and pushed the woman to the workbench.

"Go! Get out! I'll take care of him. Go!"

She helped the reporter onto the table as Tom reached out and took her hands, pulling her up. Marnie supported her feet with her palms until she was out of reach, and spun around, facing the man who haunted her childhood.

"Jethro Barnes," she said, reaching back for her gun—but it wasn't there.

"Where's Marnie?" asked Danny, eyes darting.

"She's in the cellar with Jethro Barnes. We'll go in through the front and down the stairs. Don't worry. She's armed." Tom grabbed Danny's elbow and nudged him to the front of the house, while Garcia called an ambulance and comforted Carrie and Jess, who was sipping water.

"It's gonna be okay, ladies. The detectives will get Marnie out of there," she said and turned away, muttering, "Or die trying."

Barnes laughed and took a menacing step toward Marnie. "You'll do, little one. Do you know how many years I've waited to get you?"

"I'm not afraid of you. To be honest, I never was. You're a bully and killer and you stink! You're the same piece of shit now as thirty years ago."

"This was always meant to be your end. I knew you'd come here."

"Pfft! Bullshit. You got out of Copper Woods because you knew we'd find you. How long did you think it would take us to figure out you were Walter Platt's grandson? Oo! The Poacher. Sick, sick bastards. Both of you. Do not take another step."

"Push the door!" said Danny, shoving Tom out of the way.

"It opens in, and he's locked it from the other side. Why the hell did Marnie put a security door in this old house? We'll have to get in through the cellar windows."

"Shoot the lock," said the detective lieutenant.

"Yeah, and chance the bullet flying back and hitting one of us. I don't think so."

"Jesus! Okay. We'll go through the cellar windows," said Danny.

"You won't fit, big guy. Those shoulders of yours would never get through."

"If he has a gun, he will shoot, you know."

"Well, let's hope my cat-like reflexes come with nine lives," said Tom, turning to run out the back door behind Danny.

The detective lieutenant kicked through a window at the front of the house to distract, as Tom scrambled through the broken cellar window at the back, landing on the workbench with a thunk, before rolling to the floor and springing up on his knees, gun trained on Barnes.

"Let her go!"

"You won't shoot. I've got your little girlfriend, and you might hit her."

Tom and Marnie stared at one another. By the look in her eyes, he knew she planned to stomp on Jethro's foot, but with an icepick

399

resting on her carotid, he gave a tight jerk of his head, warning her not to do it.

Sam Reilly and Ransom Elliott arrived in a lather.

"Where's Marnie?" asked the assassin.

"In the cellar. Tom has a gun on Barnes, but he's holding onto Marnie with an icepick to her neck. And I can't get a bead on him. He's between two support columns."

"I've got an idea," said Sam. "If Marnie hasn't changed the original design, we've got a way in."

The trickle of blood oozing from Marnie's neck made Tom fight back wooziness. He breathed through his nose and out his mouth, trying to fight a wave of nausea and a muscle spasm screaming in his lower back. *Hold it together, Keller.*

In a chaotic cacophony of muffled echoes and thumps, Sam flew into the room, exiting the coal chute with a thud, cracking his head on the cement floor. With Barnes distracted, Marnie smashed her head into his jaw. But it didn't have the desired effect and while he dropped the icepick, he tightened his arm around her neck and lifted her off her feet.

"You bitch!" he yelled, bringing a protective hand to his face.

So, the psychic did the only thing she could. She squiggled and squirmed and drove a fist backward into his crotch. Doubling over in a stream of swear words, he dropped her. Marnie scurried to her brother and eyed her weapon that must have dropped from her belt when she struggled with the bolt cutters.

"Don't move," shouted Tom, his gun pointed at Barnes.

"Tom! Look out!" she screeched, as the spirit of Cy Barnes headed his way.

"Shit! Marn, I need some help here! Get Danny to throw down cuffs."

"On it! Keep your eye on Jethro. I'll deal with the old man."

She raced to the window and called up. "Handcuffs, please!"

Danny tossed her his, and Marnie handed them to Tom, who wrenched back Jethro's left arm and wrestled with the other, but finally restrained him.

"Mr. Barnes, get out of my house!" she said, and took a slip of paper from her pocket. "I wrote this especially for you! Cy Barnes, your time is done. By moon and stars and setting sun. From this place, you must depart. Leave no trace, no evil heart! Let it be so!" she said.

The spirit of the old man disappeared, and Tom shoved the younger Barnes to his knees as Marnie ran up the steps to unlock the cellar door.

Danny, Tater, Ransom, and Patrick rushed down, and the dog trotted over, snarling into the bad man's face.

"Get away from him, pal. He's probably got rabies," said Tom, taking his collar and leading him away.

"Or d-distemper," said Patrick, covering his nose. "Phwaw! What's that st-stench?"

Ransom helped Sam to his feet, checking the back of his head.

"Look at that! Your melon is hard as a rock. Not a scratch," said the marshal.

"No. But did he crack the floor?" said Tom with a smirk.

Danny wrapped his arms around Marnie. "Next time, wait for me."

She hugged him and said, "I am so happy you didn't crawl through that window. It would have been like Pooh in the beehive."

"Are you saying I'm fat?" he asked, checking his waistline.

"No, Detective Gregg. You are perfect. Can we get out of here and take my brother to a doctor? I think he's concussed."

"No, Squirt. I'm fine. Just don't anyone say her name for a while in case that bump to my head caused a relapse," he said, pointing to his sister.

"Gawd! Don't say that!" said Tom.

"C'mon, Barnes. Get movin'," said Danny, pulling the killer to his feet.

"Tater. Let's go, buddy," said Marnie.

The dog made a wide berth around the killer, but not big enough. Before anyone could react, Barnes kicked the Border Collie, sending him across the concrete floor with a pained yip. Danny jerked the man's cuffs and drove him to his knees as Marnie and Tom rushed to Tater and kneeled beside him.

"He's okay, Marn. His tail's wagging," said Tom.

She put her head next to the dog's, and he licked her cheek and nose-bumped her chin.

"Good boy," she whispered, holding his face between her hands. "I'll be right back, little man."

Then she pushed herself up, stomped over to Barnes, and punched him square in the nose, just as she did thirty years ago.

Chapter Thirty-Eight

October 21 ***st***

The Study, 5:33 AM

Marnie held the elemental cross in her hand and recited a blessing she had written for her home.

Peace and calm now fill this space,
Safety wraps a warm embrace.
May love and light forever stay,
Bless this home both night and day.

"Let it be so! Short and simple. What do you reckon, guys? Will it work?" she asked the dogs, who were curled together on the hearth. Tater lifted his head and smiled, then nosed the bright blue cast Doctor Ellie Nikol had put on him late last night.

"How's the Tot?" asked Tom, carrying a steaming mug of coffee into the room.

"He's okay. Ellie said it's a hairline fracture and should heal in no time with the cast. You and Danny came in late."

"Mm ... Jethro didn't wanna play nice. But tissue samples from under Kelly Munson's nails where she clawed his face, the statement from Carrie and hopefully one from Jess Alder is all we'll need to put him away for the rest of his life. He's goin' back anyway, considering he's an escaped convict."

"So, who's the guy who died in the factory fire? Sam said Jethro was working as a janitor."

"Your brother and Ransom are looking into it, and they also took Barnes into custody. The marshals have been chasing him since the beginning of the year. But at least we got to question him."

Marnie touched the mark on her neck where Barnes broke the skin.

"That could have been worse," said Tom.

"We say that a lot!"

"Yeah, we do. Oh! That key we found yesterday. What's it for?"

"When everyone wakes up, I'll show you," she said with a twinkle in her green eyes.

The Tunnels, 8:28 AM

Map in her hand, Marnie led the way through the passages, ending the morning jaunt at an oak door.

"If I'm right, and I know I am, the key we found yesterday will fit the lock. WD-40, please," she said, holding out her hand.

Danny pulled it out of his sling and passed it to Tom, who presented it like a fine bottle of wine.

"Thank you, garçon!"

She sprayed the lock, waited a moment, then inserted the key and twisted. When it clicked, she did a dance before opening the door. Tom took out his phone and pressed the flashlight and shone it into a twelve-by-twelve room. It revealed stacked wooden crates filled with bottles, a chair, and a mahogany tambour desk.

Danny stepped inside and checked out the bottles first. Taking one from a crate, he laughed and held it up.

"Look at the label! Flannigan's Irish Whiskey."

"You are kidding!" said Marnie, moving closer to see. "That is hilarious! Is it still good?"

"Should be as long as it isn't open," he said.

"Hey, Marn, open the desk," said Tom, making his way across the room.

"Go ahead," she said, joining him at the antique.

The nooks and crannies revealed an assortment of yellowed paperwork, ledgers, a recipe book, a ring full of keys, and a note.

God willing and even if he doesn't, it's my last wish that a Flannigan descendent finds my stash.

If you are kin, keep the recipe flowing, please. You now have the keys to my kingdom.

Respectfully,
Nolan Flannigan

P.S. If you are not family, bugger off and lock up behind you.

The three laughed and reread the note, wondering if the old man knew his great-great-granddaughter found his stash. The psychic said probably but couldn't sense him in the room and neither could the detectives.

"I want to know how Bob Humboldt knew about this room and the empty grave next to Nolan. I mean, this room sits right under that plot," said the psychic.

Danny shrugged. "From what I hear, he was the best investigative reporter around. Like Gram, he probably knew where a lot of Creekwood's skeletons are buried. And from what Rick told me, they got into his laptop and phone and checked that SD card. Bob had already started writing a story, and it's a whopper."

"You should pass it along to Everett Channing. Give Bob one last byline—even if it is posthumously," said Marnie.

"Brilliant idea," said Tom. "What was the password on the tech?"

"Marvel or variations of. He did what many do. He used his pet's name."

"What's going to happen to Randy and Carrie?" asked the psychic.

"The chief and captain are discussing it, but for the moment, Randy is suspended," said Danny.

"I'm hoping they demote his sorry ass," she said.

"Marn, who sent you that necklace and the key?" asked Tom.

"I don't know."

Danny chewed his bottom lip, asking, "Did you ask the jeweler?"

"Yeah. They haven't used that box in over thirty years."

"Great! Another mystery to solve," said her best friend.

Marnie held up a hand. "Wait. I've got one you guys might solve."

"What's that?" asked the detectives.

"How the heck did Jethro Barnes get to Mac's house and the island?"

"We found Bob's Range Rover in an outbuilding on the island."

"Of course! He would have stolen his keys when he killed him to get into his house to dump Kelly Munson."

"That's right," said Danny.

"So, was he using the tunnels? Is that who Sam and Ransom were chasing the night we caught Barnes on the island?" asked the psychic.

"Also correct, and Abel Jackson identified him as the man who accosted him and terrorized the Zonta gals," said Tom.

"Alright, then. Let's take a bottle with us, grab the keys, and lock up. We'll come back and explore on November first," she said.

"What?" said the detectives.

"We have a Halloween party to get sorted. C'mon!"

Chapter Thirty-Nine

October 31st

At the Edge of a Forest, The Writing Room, 12:03 PM

Under a beautiful cerulean sky, families came together at Wild Creek Ranch for the first annual Halloween party. Thanks to a story written by Carrie Sutherland, people flocked to the farm without reservation. The reporter had cleared up any rumors about the Reilly family and the strange goings on at Marnie's home. It was a follow-up piece to one written by Everett Channing that headlined on October twenty-first, titled, *Homegrown Heroine Saves Reporter.*

Marnie clarified the original piece on October twenty-second with a radio interview at the local station. She gave most of the credit to Danny, Tom, Cheryl, and federal officers without naming names because anonymity is important to assassins and agents.

Everett asked to interview the killer, and the detectives got Ransom to agree. And when given the opportunity to become even more infamous than he already was, the convict said yes. Before sharing his story, the felon told the tale of his mother seeking revenge on her father in the heart of Copper Woods so many years ago. She had hidden the icepick in a bundle with jewelry and baubles she stole from her second husband's store. Her plan was to sell them and escape the abusive relationship, but Cy Barnes put an end to her before she could flee with her son.

The killer also had to set the record straight about his name. He never liked being called Jethro. It's what his stepfather who used that name because he thought him stupid. He likened him to a character of the same name from a sixties television show. Regardless of the moniker, he was back in prison with murder charges pending answering to Rawlins62.

Mac and Danny cleared Cissy Miller's murder, along with the killings of Paige Reynolds, Kelly Munson, and Krista Hansen, and were able to close three cold cases in Hudson Hollow, Oswegatchie Mill, Albany, and Saranac Lake. Jethro Barnes was responsible for each. And yes, all the women had reddish hair. While Walter Platt's motive was his family, Jethro's was different. A five-year-old Marnie Reilly with strawberry-blonde hair was the reason he went to prison, and Mac Gregg helped put him there. So, Jethro killed women with hair of similar coloring to the psychic psychologist during the rare times he was out on parole, or in this case, escaped.

And if you're wondering how Barnes knew about Marnie's fear of fairy tales, her big brother confessed in a text message to telling a group of inmates about her while incarcerated at Bayside, not knowing his prison mate was the man who started their nightmare. He felt terrible, but in his defense, he hated his sister at the time, thanks to Lawrence Parish. The psychic psychologist will deal with him when he's home for Thanksgiving.

The ethereal voice speaking to Marnie about the man with three faces is still a mystery, but they were right. Jed Rawlins, Jed Barnes, and Jethro Barnes were one and the same. She hears the spirit often but hasn't got a clue who it could be.

Bob Humboldt had dirt on Barnes going back years. Another of his notebooks was found in the schoolhouse under the slate hearth of the potbelly stove. He'd found his ghost voice and directed Marnie straight to it. Marion Doyle was able to decipher some of his scribbles, but not enough to use the book as evidence. He had believed the big dude was responsible for Colin Reilly's boating accident, but a lack of evidence couldn't confirm it. When questioned, the convict sneered but wouldn't confess.

Everett and Carrie finished the story Bob Humboldt started and were proud to share the byline with the ace investigative reporter.

Of course, the story of The Poacher was in the Halloween issue of The Times, together with several other Creekwood urban legends. Everett convinced Gram and Riley Leventas to help him create the spooky and sensational twelve-page insert. Rumor has it, there's a book in the works.

Danny, Mac, and retired Detective Gavin Anderson drove out to the Miller farm to tell her parents that Cissy's killer was behind bars. But when they arrived, the house was no longer there—a convenience store now stood in its place. So they grabbed a coffee at Stewart's Shop and headed home. The detective said he would find them and pass along the news.

Wild Creek Ranch, Western Paddock, 12:05 PM

"Did you hear Grace Wilmot was released on compassionate parole?" asked Everett Channing, swirling a mug of hot cider spiked with Fireball.

Marnie wrinkled her nose and said, "Yeah. We heard while we were having breakfast. Is she ill? They didn't go into much detail."

"I'm surprised they didn't contact you, considering the threats she made," said the editor.

"Maybe she's not a threat anymore," said Tom.

Danny picked up a log and tossed it into the bonfire. "I'll look into it," he said and grabbed Marnie's arm, ducking behind her to shield himself from an incoming gaggle. "How did those damn geese get out of their pen?"

"Ha-ha! Poor Tater has been bored out of his mind. He must have figured out how to open the gate."

"He's not supposed to herd anything until his leg heals."

"Dickens and Gus are doing most of the work. The Tot's supervising. Look at that smile on his face," said Tom.

"That d-d-dog is always so happy," said Patrick, his eyes on the gals walking their way.

Poppy arrived with a mug of hot mulled cider in hand.

"I have found the perfect apartment above Mrs. Backus' bookstore. I'll be out of your hair soon, Marnie."

"I've loved having you here. But I will be happy for things to go back to some sort of normal. Whatever that is? Tom is moving into his house soon, too," said the psychic.

"Hey, it's been rosy spending time with you and all, but I think a calm place in town would be better. Besides, Theodora needs a place to crash when we go out on the prowl," said Poppy with a snicker.

"Yay!" said Teddy. Her choice of beverage was red and served in a test tube.

"What's in that?" asked Tom.

"Rick handed it to me, so I said thank you and took it. It's quite tasty."

Marnie nudged Everett with her elbow and wagged her chin toward a man with black hair wearing dark sunglasses, tailored gray trousers, black leather moccasins, and a midnight-blue sweater.

"Hey, Ev. Who's that man over there, eyeing the candied apples?"

"Oh. *Him*," said the editor. "That's Ezra Toth. He's a new lawyer in town. I hear he is friends with Kate Parish."

Marnie eyed Tom, and he knew what she was thinking.

"Is he wealthy?" asked the psychic.

"Old money and a lot of it. His parents live in the Catskills, and I understand he and Kate went to law school together. Rumor has it he has visited her several times in the last couple of weeks."

"Would he have the kind of cash to get the princess moved into a private suite at Bayview?" asked Tom.

"And then some."

Duck-lipped, Marnie nodded and shot a knowing glance at her best friend, who mimicked her action.

"Mystery solved," said Tom.

"Hmm ..." said the psychic. "Would he have the legal nous to get her out?"

Everett said, "Yes. He has a reputation for winning the unwinnable."

"Shit," said Marnie.

Carl, Hannah, and Gram arrived, each with white skull glasses.

"What have you got?" asked Marnie.

Irish eyes sparkling, Gram grinned. "Private stock, I believe. Flannigan's Irish Whiskey."

Carl scanned the crowd. "I haven't seen Sam or Ransom. Are they joining us?"

"No. They're off somewhere doing something they can't talk about," said Marnie, rolling her eyes. "But my brother sent good news my way. Ransom has all of his belongings, so our grandfather's medals are safe and sound. I don't know how the marshal pilfered items out of a *secure* federal evidence locker, but I have learned not to ask questions."

Gram sidled up to the psychologist and gave her a hug. "You're wearin' the necklace! I thought maybe ya didn't like it, since I knew you found the other trinket." She held up her glass of whiskey, waggling her eyebrows.

"This is from you?"

"Of course, dear. Didn't you read the note?"

"What note?" asked Marnie.

"There was a card."

"It must be in the study somewhere. Where did you get the key?"

"Do you think you're the only one to have late night visitors?" asked Gram.

"But ... Bob Humboldt mentioned NF in his note."

"He'd been searchin' for Nolan's reserve for years. He was workin' on three stories when he died. Flannigan's legendary stash. Your father's accident. And the Barnes family's ties to The Poacher. Albeit I only knew about the first until the article. Bob was a talker when persuaded."

"With Irish whiskey, I'm guessing," said Marnie, quirking up the side of her mouth.

The group had a giggle at the ace reporter's expense and wondered how many skeletons Margaret Ryan was keeping hidden for others when Riley Leventas strolled over with a beaker full of fluorescent green liquid with dots of red.

"Having the mad scientist mix cocktails was a brilliant idea. I love how he even dressed the part."

"Thanks so much for coming, Riley. This is Tom Keller, and you know everyone else, don't you?" said Marnie, shoving Riley closer to her best friend.

"Ah ... yes, you introduced us over at the hay maze. Hi, Tom. It's lovely to meet you. I understand that labyrinth was built for you."

"That's what I'm told. Have you walked through yet?" he asked.

"No. But I'd love to."

"Let's go," he said, turning and winking at the psychic.

Marnie put an arm through Danny's and led him away from the fire. "You've been unusually quiet the last few days. Penny for your thoughts, Detective Gregg."

"Two," he replied, running a hand through his sandy brown muss of hair.

A crow flew over, swooped the partygoers, then soared away on a chilly north wind.

-The End-

Acknowledgements

Harper, as always, thanks for being my guinea pig. First chapters always go to you. I greatly appreciate your expert guidance on the topics of mental health, veterans, and dog noises. And thanks for keeping the Pawsome Foursome somewhat quiet and for serenading me with your acoustic guitar. I still love you more than pizza.

Big cuddles and ear scratches to my lovely distractions: Dougal, Callee, Midget, and Mags. You fill my world with unconditional love and make certain I am never late for dinner. Where would I be without my furry schedulers?

Frances, you are one in a million. Your guidance, support, silly DMs, and friendship make this journey possible and worthwhile. I owe you a bear hug and a cocktail or two or three or four.

Nicole Ballingal, the cover is awesome! Thank you so much for wrapping my words in the most beautiful packaging. Love your talent—and you too, of course.

A huge thank you and loads of love to my beta readers, Jane Hackett Backus, Wendy Flood, and Laurie Lashomb.

Jane Hackett Backus, you will find your bookish namesakes in Chapters 15, 21, and 39. Many thanks for coming out of English teacher retirement once again to catch my typos and correct my grammar. Can you believe we've put four books out into the world? Hugs to you!

Wendy, I hope the Riley Leventas character arc is one you will love—now and into the future. She's going to stick around for a while, unless volcanoes exist in the Adirondacks—which they don't. I checked. Then again, my books are fiction. I could create one just for you … er … for her. Thank you for being a wonderful supporter of my writing and my favorite eldest sister.

Laurie Lashomb, thanks, soul sister, for diving into the story during Hurricane Milton. As always, I greatly appreciate your support and feedback. Your ability to pick up hometown references and lingo makes the editing process a treat. I share your love for the word toque. Are you sipping lolly water while reading this?

Karen, did you enjoy your brief stint at Drake's? While I didn't need your assistance in ways to murder people this time around, you can be sure I will call on you in the future. Thank you!

Rosie, Vacant Grave is just the start of Poppy Chomsky's Creekwood adventure. She fits right in with my crazy crew, don't you think? Oh, how I miss seeing your smiling face and mischievous eyes. See ya in Book 5.

Chronicles of Crime, your quote for my back cover makes my entire year. From the depths of my black heart, thank you X a million.

Tracy Brown, thanks so much for being a great supporter of me and the indie author community. Thanks heaps for your kind words on the back cover.

I am grateful for the Instagram Writing Community—a supportive village where my weirdness and dark humor are welcome—and encouraged.

As always, landmarks, other places, and references from my hometown of Ogdensburg, NY are mentioned throughout this story. The first Burger who finds them all in Vacant Grave will receive a signed copy of the series.

Mom and Dad, thanks for the divine guidance. I know you're there.

To all the dogs I've loved before, Tater and Dickens are for you.

Resources

Sources used in the writing of this fiction book include:

- Robert Frost, *Nothing Gold Can Stay*
- The Three Billy Goats Gruff, original story by Peter Christen Asbjørnsen and Jørgen Moe
- Hansel and Gretel, The Brothers Grimm
- Adirondack Park Agency of New York State
- New York State Department of Environmental Conservation
- Medscape website, https://emedicine.medscape.com/article/913575-overview
- The Mayo Clinic, https://www.mayoclinic.org/diseases-conditions/antisocial-personality-disorder/symptoms-causes/syc-20353928
- Priory, https://www.priorygroup.com/mental-health-druginduced-psychosis
- https://www.timeanddate.com/sun/@5106772
- https://www.flintrehab.com/blast-induced-traumatic-brain-injury/#:~:text=Even%20though%20the%20symptoms%20of,at%20making%20a%20functional%20recovery
- https://www.sciencedirect.com/topics/medicine-and-dentistry/blast-injury#:~:text=Blast%20injury%20is%20usually%20classified,ear%20structures%2C%20are%20most%20susceptible
- Doctor Peter Gray, MD

About the Author

Shari T. Mitchell is the author of the Marnie Reilly Mysteries thriller series, which includes Divine Guidance, Torn Veil, Fatal Vow, and Vacant Grave

Raised in Northern New York State, Shari's hometown and surrounds are the inspiration for her series' fictional town of Creekwood, New York—which is located somewhere in the Adirondack Mountains.

While Shari loves developing multidimensional characters with whom her readers can relate, her passion is plotting the twists and turns of a mystery. It feeds her analytical and creative mind.

She lives in North Carolina and shares her home with her partner in crime, Harper, and their crazy rescue dogs, Dougal, Callee, Midget, and Mags.

A thirty-plus year marketer, Shari loves spending time with her family, cooking, hiking, traveling, gardening, and reading. She is often heard chatting with her characters because they natter at her constantly!

Mystery is her favorite genre, having cut her teeth on Nancy Drew, The Hardy Boys, and Trixie Belden. Her favorite authors include Robert Frost, Agatha Christie, Mary Higgins Clark, Ruth Rendell, Michael Connelly, Jonathan Kellerman, Sue Grafton, David Baldacci, Louise Penny, Stuart MacBride, and Michael Koryta.

For Readers

Thank you for reading *Fatal Vow*. I hope you enjoyed the story. Please consider leaving a review on Goodreads, Amazon, or wherever you purchased the book.

Marnie Reilly Mysteries continues with Book 5. It's in the works!

Website

Visit ShariTMitchell.com for short stories, recipes, and to learn more about her books. Sign-up for her newsletter for updates from Creekwood.

Social Media

Instagram: @sharitmitchell
Goodreads: www.goodreads.com/sharitmitchell
Facebook: www.facebook.com/ShariTMitchellAuthor